D0949755

A GOOD
FAMILY

A GOOD FAMILY

ERIK FASSNACHT

ST. MARTIN'S PRESS ☙ NEW YORK

A GOOD FAMILY. Copyright © 2015 by Erik Fassnacht. All rights reserved. Printed in the United States of America. For information, address St. Martin's Press, 175 Fifth Avenue, New York, N.Y. 10010.

www.stmartins.com

Designed by Anna Gorovoy

The Library of Congress Cataloging-in-Publication Data is available upon request.

ISBN 978-1-250-05928-4 (hardcover)
ISBN 978-1-4668-7825-9 (e-book)

St. Martin's Press books may be purchased for educational, business, or promotional use. For information on bulk purchases, please contact the Macmillan Corporate and Premium Sales Department at 1-800-221-7945, extension 5442, or write to specialmarkets@macmillan.com.

First Edition: August 2015

10 9 8 7 6 5 4 3 2 1

For my father, Fredrick J. Fassnacht, 1949–2012

I am moved by fancies that are curled
Around these images, and cling:
The notion of some infinitely gentle
Infinitely suffering thing.

—T. S. ELIOT, "PRELUDES"

I

HANDFUL OF MARBLES

VINTAGE FAULKNER AND CIGARETTES

Barkley Brunson held a blue plastic folder over his head while he walked from Milwaukee to Damen, the rain coming down hard. Fat droplets thudded atop his shield against the elements, ran off edges and spilled inside openings, turned the papers inside to soup. The rain bent the edges of the folder and sent cold water down the back of his neck, which made him walk faster, as if he were chased.

Past the Bongo Room he went. It was a Friday, and pale-faced patrons with maroon umbrellas approached the delights of the brunch within— an extravagant grease bomb that Barkley knew he had to avoid. Through the window he caught sight of the Oreo and banana pancakes, buried under an arctic shelf of white frosting. Danger, he thought, gripping his potbelly. His socks were soaked. He should really get new shoes.

Two blocks more and finally, the sign for Myopic Books beckoned like a weathered hand. Barkley made his way to the entrance, navigating around the frothy water that spilled from the streets, bubbling over cars and curbs and snaking toward his feet. He swung open the door and shook off the rain. The door closed behind him and the city faded to a distant thrum. Dim lights and dust descended. Inside: labyrinthine pathways, creaky landings, and stale air, pleasant like a lived-in attic.

"Barkley? You made it."

"Huh? Oh, hey, Mr. Doring." Barkley looked behind the bookstore's cash register to find his graduate creative writing professor at DePaul—well, not quite a professor yet, but almost. The fifty-year-old PhD candidate had four piercings in his right ear, white hair, and a craggy face lined with smile and frown creases.

"You're late," Doring said.

"The bus. I mean, I had to transfer buses. Timed it wrong. Bus tracker—need to get an iPhone."

"You can't be late to these, Barkley. Understand? The summer classes put us all on a tighter schedule, and this is your *rescheduled* appointment. I'm doing you a favor, meeting you here."

"Right. I was also printing my story. Ink problems. I've got a new draft for you." Barkley waved the sopping blue folder in Doring's general direction.

"Is that readable?"

"I hope so. The rain—"

"Right, right. Well, I can't really read a new version of the story right now, can I?"

"It's only eight pages," Barkley said, wiping his forehead. "And I wanted to show you my new ending."

Doring scratched his chin, which was laced with dust-colored grizzle. "Let's just talk about the draft you gave me last week. Let me go grab my notes. Ginny, can you handle the register?"

A stumpy redhead approached the front, and Barkley immediately checked her off as too big-boned to seriously flirt with. Then he saw that she had a bit of a chest—in fact, the swell of it against her teal sweater was impossible not to notice. Her breasts were probably pale and freckled and even a little bottom heavy, but impressive. And her face was . . . interesting. Unusual, even. He watched her at the register for a moment longer, feeling the familiar jelly-legged sensation that arrived whenever he breached the perimeter of an attractive female. He concentrated, used the old Zen strategy, tried to look at her without *looking* at her—peripheral ogling, that's what they called it. Her skin was a smooth white—he would have called it milky if the description hadn't seemed archaic, like something from those Jane Austen novels his mother used to love. At the register, she seemed reserved, hesitant, content to peruse crumpled receipts. She still hadn't noticed him. This, he thought, was an opportunity.

He'd heard a theory on positive thinking from his older brother, who provided unsolicited wisdom whenever applicable (which his brother believed was all the time). This particular nugget: if he, Barkley, simply replaced his typically insecure thoughts with confident thoughts—alpha male thoughts—he'd actually start to behave like one of them. Those countless conversations where every word came out twenty IQ points lower than his capability, each syllable feeling like a wooden child's block between his teeth? Gone! Out the window. Think confident thoughts, Charlie had coolly advised him, before canning a jump shot from the corner of the driveway.

And yet, out in the field, with a pretty girl lurking on the horizon (he'd decided that she was pretty now), it wasn't so easy. Sure, he could *try* to do it, even if for him it seemed absurd. Instead of being afraid of this cashier girl—Ginny—he should be thinking something macho, chest puffed out like a matador. Like, for example, that he'd be getting laid tonight. Yes. That was the tactic. He would be the classic, modern-day conqueror—all machismo, zero cuddling. Out by morning, leave without a note. Sure, there was a misogynistic aftertaste to that, but he had to do it, had to pretend he was someone else if he wanted any chance of success. So say it again: he, Barkley Brunson, brother of the legendary Charlie Brunson, son of the even bigger, more legendary stud Henry Brunson, was getting laid tonight. *That* was his character arc, his sacred trajectory.

But Ginny still hadn't noticed him. She remained anchored at the register, solemnly reading a book by Tom-somebody—he couldn't see the rest of the name. He continued observing from a distance, and then Doring walked by and tapped him on the shoulder with his grading folder.

"Ready to review? This way, Barkley."

Doring opened a scarred black door and they entered his cluttered office, fortified with an abnormal number of fantasy magazines and orange highlighters. There was a square cedar desk in front of them.

"Sit," Doring said.

Barkley adjusted himself on the metal folding chair. He was twenty-three and without a full-time job; this class was either a step to something greater or yet another hopeless distraction. He put the blue folder on the desk, opened it up. The font of his new draft appeared to be bleeding mascara.

"Let's talk about the story you gave me last week, Barkley."

"Okay. What did you think?"

"Well, let's start with the beginning."

"Okay," Barkley said again. He felt apprehension, as he always did when hearing his work reviewed. But he was also mindful that Doring was no professor, at least not yet.

"The beginning works well."

Barkley nodded, waiting for the anvil to fall.

"It's about a twenty-something coming of age as a womanizer, right? And the catch, of course, is that it's all happening in the middle of a Chicago zombie apocalypse. This is a nice touch, Barkley. Really. You've got a knack for taking literary elements, or at least character-based ones, and using tried-and-true genre tropes as a backdrop. Now, finding the mundane within the fantastic isn't *necessarily* a new thing, but it's interesting enough, and you write with an exuberance that's hard to dislike. No one else in the class is doing it quite like that."

"Well, thanks," Barkley said. Was that a backhanded compliment?

Doring turned the page and moved his finger down a few paragraphs. "The main character—he's not confident in the beginning. That scene with the hairdresser shows that well. I like how he steals that Vavoom hair cream from the derelict salon to impress her. He's goofy that way. But lovable. And by the time they're on the run from the zombie horde, we actually care about the character."

"But," Barkley said, watching for the flicker in Doring's eyes. There was always an aggressive flicker—like the look from an assassin before plunging in a knife—that preceded an instructor's jump into rampant criticism. It convinced him, above all other evidence (like desert warfare or road rage), that human beings were essentially animals. Even in the ivory towers of intellectualism, even in those elevated attempts at literature and high art and reflection on life, all anyone wanted to do was kill each other. And the predatory flicker proved it. His brother knew about that, too, of course—but in a different way.

"Okay," Doring said. "Fine. Here's my 'but.' The problem really isn't the writing. You start with a lovable character who steals hair products to impress a salon worker, but then he has that near-fatal car accident, and when he wakes up, he's a new man. Just like that."

"That kind of thing happens, Mr. Doring. It's an awakening."

"Right. Right. Sure it does. But first of all, his evolution isn't earned. Secondly, his epiphany only influences his sexual magnetism and propensity for violence. It allows him to smooth talk the hairdresser, sleep with her, and then murder a roomful of zombies with a giant pistol. Anything of substance is left to the imagination."

Barkley leaned forward. "It was a .44 Magnum revolver. An ode to *Dirty Harry*. And he had to get it all out of his system, the sex especially. He was repressed!"

Doring uncapped an orange highlighter, held it aloft, then abruptly recapped it with a sharp snap. "The goofy character we love in the beginning is gone. He has a near-death experience that allows him to bed the aloof girl and become an apocalyptic action hero, but what could be charming or transcendent ends up being . . . honestly, a little uncomfortable. I understand you want him to mature, but I think you have to be mindful of your audience. What are you trying to say, exactly? Does your new ending change any of that?"

"Well," Barkley said, looking from the stains on the ceiling to the smeared font of his new draft, "I don't think you're going to like the revised ending at all."

Doring offered a conciliatory smile. "You'll have another conference in August, Barkley. We'll see what you've got on tap then."

On the way out, Barkley stopped short of the door and rummaged through a stack of novels atop the window display. It was unbelievable. He just couldn't win. Doring hadn't even mentioned his spectacular use of figurative language in the .44 Magnum scene, when zombie heads were exploding like overripe Michigan pumpkins, their pulpy guts making abstract paintings on the white wall behind them. The white wall served as a metaphor for the blank slate the newly created badass had emerged from, and Doring hadn't even caught *that* particular angle.

And here he was, hanging his head again—Charlie Brown after another missed kick. Didn't anyone still root for the little guy? Yet on the other hand, there was the nagging suspicion that all of his recent misadventures, from the dubious science fiction streak to the sad sack loner routine—all of them—were simply an attempt to distract himself from what was really going on. Big-picture shit, starring the whole Brunson family. Barkley sighed and tried to shake free of the buzzing neurosis, that ever-present cloud of gnats that hovered, as if he were doused in vinegar. On the other side of the bookstore, Ginny was still at the register, bent over a book by . . . there it was—Tom Robbins. He perked up, recalibrated, and chanced another glance at her face. Better than he had thought. Round but not fat. He took in her breasts again. From this distance—juggernauts. Swollen prisoners held captive in that straitjacket of a green sweater. His pants stirred. He raised his gaze and saw that she was staring at him. She smiled. He turned away.

Barkley yanked two paperback titles off the display without reading their names. He thumbed through them and cursed himself. Did she catch him ogling her? Probably not; otherwise, she wouldn't have smiled. Of course, she could have smiled because she liked being checked out, but that didn't sound right to him either. Ginny gave off the vibe of a shy, chaste, Puritan book maid. He looked back at her again. A long wave of dark red hair hung over her face. Reading again. At least she had a brain. And Tom Robbins—she liked absurdist literature. Good. He could do absurdist humor. Girls that liked books were easy game for him. True, his brother was the real master with girls, attracting almost biblical swarms of them in those years before his enlistment, but if the time was right, Barkley could hold his own as well. Sure he could. In fact, the real reason he hadn't had sex in eight months had more to do with—

"Need help with anything?"

It was Ginny. Shit—the guy was supposed to talk first. Barkley turned slowly, plotting out an intellectually pious sentence, something about the vintage, Parisian construct of the place. Yes, that sounded good, use the word *Parisian*, all girls liked Western Europeans.

But he was already talking—"Nope. Not needing any help, here . . . miss. Just looking. Yes. Um, looking for . . . looking for Faulkner, here."

"Oh great," she said. "That's in the fiction section. Through that little cubbyhole in the back."

"Right," he said. "The cubbyhole."

She smiled again and pointed to the back. "Faulkner will be right around the corner there."

"Tha-ank you," he said, drawing out his words. He walked stiffly toward the back. Faulkner? What was he thinking? He wondered if her eyes were on him. They probably were. He was a good-looking guy, minus the stomach. His hair got a lot of compliments, and that girl in his freshman Intro to Statistics class had told him once that his eyes looked "deep." Ginny was definitely watching him. He chanced a glance back and saw that her head was down, perusing the Tom Robbins novel. She had probably just looked down. For sure.

Inside the stooped cubbyhole was the beginning of the fiction section, and Barkley was faced with a second problem: he had mentioned Faulkner. Not only did he not read Faulkner, but he also knew only *The Sound and the Fury*, which he had quit at fifty pages. Which, if he picked it up now, would allow Ginny to tag him with the much feared "doesn't-read-Faulkner" bull's-eye. So he had to find a rarity, a Faulkner B-side, something to hint at his vast knowledge as a literature aficionado. He found the *F* section. An old hardcover of *The Sound and the Fury*? Check. What else?

As I Lay Dying? No. That had a certain familiar ring to it. Maybe he'd seen a movie version. He looked on. Here. What was this? *Go Down, Moses*? He pulled the book out. Seemed random enough. He hadn't heard of it. *Go Down, Moses* it was.

Barkley strode out of the cubbyhole, holding the Faulkner novel out like a vintage wine bottle. It would be suave to just unveil it at the counter in front of her. A conversation piece. Yes. She would love it—be impressed with him immediately. Pepper in some deft conversation and jokes (as well as Charlie's Jedi mind tricks), and he was probably getting laid tonight.

"What have you got there?" a man's voice called. Barkley looked up to see Mr. Doring standing behind the cash register. Damn.

"It's a Faulkner," Barkley said. "Something about Moses. He's just great, isn't he? Not Moses. Faulkner, I mean."

Doring nodded. "He is."

Barkley looked around the room. No Ginny. It figured, he thought. Bad luck was what he had—what his whole family had. But he didn't want to think about that.

"Did you want to buy that?"

Doring again. "No," Barkley said, and placed the book down on the counter. "Have a good day."

"I'll just reshelve that for you," his professor intoned behind him.

Barkley opened the door and saw that the rain was slowing. Vast sheets of drizzle waved across the streets in silver curtains, but the flooding of the sewers had subsided. He closed the door behind him, felt the stormy July wind on his cheeks. Tomorrow—that's when his luck would change.

"Did you get the Faulkner?"

Barkley jumped. It was Ginny. She was standing under the overhanging bay window from Myopic's second floor, taking a cigarette break, watching him without expression. He breathed in her scent—pineapple gum and book dust and nicotine.

"So that's where you went," Barkley said. "Smoke break?"

"Yeah. It's one of those college habits. All the hot guys used to play guitar and smoke in front of the dorms, and of course the girls would follow. And here I am, in front of a bookstore years later, still smoking."

"I can play guitar for you," Barkley lied.

"Ha."

He struggled to find another avenue of conversation. The rain trickled and popped around their perimeter of shelter.

"Well," she said. "How do you know my uncle? You're his student, right?"

"Who, Mr. Doring? You guys are related? No shit. Yeah, he's my writing teacher. It's a master's class."

"A bit of a hard-ass, he tells me."

"Well, he doesn't like my writing, that's for sure."

Ginny nodded and blew out smoke. "Growing up, he never liked the pictures I drew. We used to workshop my Big Bird sketches."

"You're kidding, right?"

"Yes."

Barkley reminded himself not to look at her battle cruiser–size chest. "So," he said.

"So," she echoed. She took another drag.

"What's your uncle really like? Is he like the cool hipster uncle or something? Some kind of old-school Chicago beatnik? Does he drink a lot of PBR?"

"Well, not really. He touches me sometimes. Down there."

Barkley coughed. "Sorry? What? He touches you?"

"You know, down there." She looked at him and brushed away what could have been a tear. "In my no-no spot."

"Your no-no spot? You're joking, right?"

She stared at him, unblinking.

"You know what, Ginny? I, uh, actually think I have to go. The bus. Taking the bus out of here. Or maybe the Blue Line."

Ginny laughed and punched him in the ribs. "Totally fucking with you."

"Jesus. You serious?"

"That's right." She took another drag. "Your professor does not fondle his niece. Are you relieved?"

"Wow," Barkley said. He sighed and scratched his head. "You had me going there." Chaste Ginny, Barkley thought. Looks like you don't exist.

"Now you're clamming up," she said.

"No. Actually, that was pretty convincing. I was sold."

"I'm glad. I tried to be an actress once. In high school. Got all the best roles. I played Pippi Longstocking in tenth grade. Didn't even need a wig."

"And now?"

"Well, some bad stuff happened senior year, during *Fiddler on the Roof*."

Barkley stared at her lips. "And?"

"My drama teacher, he was a guy. He kind of, you know."

"What?"

"He touched me. Down there."

"Shut up," Barkley said. "You can't play the abuse card twice."

Ginny cackled. "Come to think of it, know what you can't do?" she said. "From henceforth, you can't ogle girls when they're helplessly trapped behind a cash register. Am I right? You just can't do it."

"Ah," Barkley said. "Crap."

"Thought you got away with it, huh?"

"I think I should go," Barkley said.

"Just relax, kid. I'm joking around."

A beige SUV sped down Milwaukee, sending a wave of rainwater over the curb and onto his sneakers. Cold dampness soaked his socks, they both looked down, and Barkley saw how ratty his gray old tennis shoes really looked, and how they must look to Ginny. The formerly blue toes worn down and colorless, the heel practically detached. Damn it, he thought. This had actually felt like a semisuccessful conversation, no bullshit, and now his stupid shoes—

"So, this whole uncle-teacher thing makes us not really strangers," Ginny said.

"Right," Barkley said. "I hear you." He felt a vague sense of urgency but watched the rain instead.

Her green eyes bored into him. "Damn, son. That was your opening. I just gave you the biggest opening ever."

"Opening," Barkley echoed.

"Look," she said. "I've got a concert tonight. You should come and bring friends."

"Concert?"

"I'm in a band."

"Really? A band? What do you play?"

"What do you think I play?"

Barkley thought of her behind the register, then onstage. "The drums? You play the drums?"

She wrinkled her nose. "Drums? Why do you say that? You think I'm too top-heavy to stand up? Bastard."

He laughed, despite himself. "That's it. No, I don't know. Bass guitar, maybe?"

"Let me tell you something. Fuck bass guitar. Everyone thinks the chick has to play bass guitar and wear moody eye makeup. I'm lead electric, bitch!" And she threw her head back and howled.

"Well," Barkley said, "I'll go to the concert. But we haven't even been introduced."

"You need me to get my uncle out here and hold your hand? I'm Ginny."

"Barkley." They shook hands.

Ginny raised an eyebrow. "Well, if you can make it to the concert, do so. It's at the Empty Bottle."

"I will!" Barkley said, feeling like he'd just swallowed a balloon. "I'll see you there, Ginny. And—"

"Gotta go," she said, flicking down her cigarette and slipping back inside the bookstore.

CASUALTIES

At five thousand feet, Charlie pressed his face against the acrylic window and saw Chicago in miniature. The gray quills of the glowing skyline, the tangled intestines of the highways and exit ramps, the jutting bend of the light-flickered coast. Behind it all, the sun sank into its fishbowl, and Lake Michigan turned into a wide plain of slate. Charlie shook his gin and tonic—only ice remained. He tossed it in his mouth anyway, crunching, hoping something strong had been absorbed. At four thousand feet, the plane descended toward O'Hare, heading west, and all the skyscrapers began to light up—the Sears Tower's spires glowed bright ivory, while the rim around the Hancock flashed red and blue, supporting the middling efforts of Cubs baseball. At three thousand feet, the dying sun bloomed ink into the starless sky, and the lake retracted into blackness. Then the city was out of sight, and it was the low-hanging spread of the suburbs—Oak Park and Des Plaines and Elmhurst and Addison. The arterial flickers of headlights crisscrossed each other in the thousands. Charlie closed his eyes and waited for the *whump* of wheels touching runway, the rush that was actually time slowing down, brakes turning on, ears crackling and popping, everything far away becoming close.

It hadn't been long ago that the same plane had taken him away from this city—same plane, different person, anyway. Into the mountains. God, he remembered how panicked he had been, freaked out by his own apathy. He wasn't too young, like a lot of the enlisted. Not in trouble with the law, not too slow for college, not patriotic, not violent, not anything but bored with having everything his way, all the time. That constant, nagging thought, *this is all there is,* stinging his mind like sewing needles. Burning him as he went from bar to bar, girl to girl, training program to corporate job. And that first experience, that first contact with something beyond the fuzz he'd felt his entire life—that's where the change had begun. And even as he thought it, the plane swinging low, the ice crunching against his molars and sending pulses of tinnitus into his ears, the memory was clear.

Halfway through basic training, Charlie felt the baby fat—whatever remained, anyway—falling off him the way butter slides off a pancake. His cheekbones were pointed and visible, his pectorals taut and molded, instead of just *there,* as they'd been before. And while he'd always been skinny, now when he lifted up his shirt, he imagined a chiseled lifeguard emerging from the surf. His abs looked like rolling pins. He found himself enjoying the brutal early mornings and the smell of cut grass, the inhibition of the showers, the steady drills, and the ever-present white noise of boot soles: thudding and marching and scuffing and skidding. Barkley, his younger brother, couldn't have handled the regimen. Even Dad, who was an athlete in his time, would have had issues. Dad gave orders—didn't take them. And he wouldn't have understood the purpose or style of the drill sergeants. But Charlie liked it all. He liked the yelling and the assholes in charge and knew not to take it personally. What people didn't understand was that they weren't actually yelling at you, they were yelling at their idea of you, the image of the soldier. They were yelling at the idea of green recruits who didn't know shit and had to be told, sometimes very loudly, sometimes until flecks of spit were on their cheeks, what the score was. And Charlie let it all slide off, let it slide until he was cut and muscled and well trained and even dangerous, as easy as butter down the side of a pancake.

He'd turned twenty-six during that March—2010, then. Incredible. The fifteen months since had chugged by like a decade. And what had spurred him to enlist? To leave a management position with Lucent Technologies? To leave behind his degree in finance at Augustana, his on-again, off-again girlfriend, Karen, his fucked-up but tolerable family, and his Wicker Park condo overlooking the Chicago skyline? It all came down to a feeling. Charlie had woken up one day and the feeling was there. Urgent. Necessary. And the specifics of it—the tightness in his chest, the icy worm that seemed lodged inside his intestines, the dreams of needing to *do something good*—none of it went away until he signed up.

His family didn't understand. Not really. He gave speeches, sure—speeches about being an American and the need to serve and the idea of duty. But in truth it all came down to a feeling. And the army was a surrogate family for him, a family that stayed together. He knew part of his love for the drill sergeants was that his own father was not a yeller, and enduring the screams of his superiors was like being a tourist in a childhood he had never been privy to. Being pushed, disciplined, shouted at—there were benefits, sure. But it was also quaint and ironic, a part of the world Charlie had thought didn't exist anymore.

In the airplane, the lights of the runway burned ahead, and Charlie remembered meeting up with his old high school buddy during his first month overseas. He remembered how he'd sat with Eddie Campo and the rest of the company one July afternoon in 2010, outside another god-forsaken mountain village that smelled like dirt and shit. Hell, all of Afghanistan smelled like dirt. There was no other way to explain it. Iraq, Campo said, had smelled like burning garbage. But Afghanistan rarely had that scent, only once in a long while. Most of the time it was dirt. Mountains and ramshackle villages and bearded, sandal-wearing hajjis and the constant, unending smell of dirt.

Charlie had sat with Campo on the side of the road while the bomb squad checked the mottled outpost across the bridge. This town, like all the others, was filled with flat, squat, hollowed-out homes the color of earthy clay. No electricity for most. And the mountains were all around them, towering, snowcapped, beautiful, even—if it wasn't for the Taliban. The mountainous border of Afghanistan and Pakistan could have been the best ski resort in the world, Charlie thought, under different circumstances. They were at seven thousand feet already, but higher up, farther outside the wire and around the COPs, at altitudes of nine thousand feet, those fuckers were waiting, planning, living in dirt and mud, praying for the death and destruction of the Army and the United States.

Campo, fair-haired and a little chunky, lit a cigarette. "Another day in paradise, my friend."

Charlie grunted. "Reminds me of Cabo. No. Puerto Vallarta. Pool bar around the corner, right?"

"Nice try. And hey—it'll be your first full month over here tomorrow, won't it? Thirty days in the Stan?"

"Yeah."

"Any questions?"

Charlie hated asking questions, because over here, it was like poking a beehive. Once you asked one, a hundred more buzzed forth, and all the answers stung.

"Yo, Brunson."

"No questions, no questions—" and then, hearing movement, he pointed to a group of casually jogging Afghanis carrying AK-47s and wearing ragged blue uniforms. "Actually, yeah. Who the hell are those guys again? Recruits?"

"Christ," Campo said. "Afghan Local Police. What a waste of space."

"Who pays for them? Government?"

Campo shook his head. "NATO. Another one of their bright ideas. Guess how many times they've failed?"

"Fuck if I know," Charlie said. He watched them line up against a half-collapsing stone wall littered with white rocks. A commanding officer was yelling something in another language.

"Five times. Five motherfucking times. These are hajjis with big guns and big egos and no backbone—always unpredictable."

"Invertebrate fucking hajjis."

"It's serious, man. I was here in '08, and they weren't the Afghan Local Police, they were the Afghan National Auxiliary Police. They got disbanded that year for constantly fucking up."

"Horrible in battle?"

"Not even. Part of it's NATO's fault. They give local hajjis guns and power but only pay them seventy dollars a month. Seventy bucks. So of course they're going to be loyal, right? Who wouldn't be loyal for seventy bucks a month?"

Charlie raised his hand.

"Exactly," Campo said. "So some of these fuckers start squeezing Afghan civilians for extra cash. Leaning on them like goddamn Chicago mobsters. Others start cozying up to the bad guys. Now, I'm not saying they wouldn't have done it anyway, but if NATO didn't pay them like sweatshop day laborers, maybe they'd show some loyalty."

"Maybe."

"And then you get reports that they're not even loyal to the Afghan government, period. Some are helping out local warlords, passing along information, and again, taking extra cash under the table. Selling sensitive information to the Taliban, for Christ's sake."

Charlie watched the blue-uniformed men reorganize into two lines and, led by their commanding officer, march over the bridge and into town. "Jesus," he said, "they look like heavily armed Cub Scouts."

"But," Campo said, raising a dirt-caked finger, "it's important to note that this time it's supposed to be 'different.' They've got a new plan this time. The sixth edition will be a winner."

"A winner," Charlie repeated, lowering his sunglasses as the clouds parted and the Afghan sun opened up on them, turning all the sand and dirt and rocks a shade of white.

"This time the Local Police were initiated by the Afghan government and not NATO. So this time, NATO trains them and pays them for a while, and then the local government kicks in and takes over."

"Doesn't sound like you're buying it."

"I'll believe it when I see it." Campo put out his cigarette.

"Not to change the subject, but I really need to find myself some strange ass."

"Truth."

"Humping it wouldn't be so bad if we got a hold of some college students. Any good-size colleges around here?"

"You're fucking nuts, man."

"Although," Charlie said, "Girls Gone Wild Kabul would just be hajjis flashing their faces and then covering them back up. Seeing an exposed eyebrow isn't as titillating as I'd hoped."

"Yeah. Fucking noses and chins."

The sound of bells filled the air, and Charlie turned, half expecting to see a slew of shaggy Clydesdales towing a Budweiser sleigh. But instead it was yet another jingle truck. This one was medium-size, bouncing up the dirt road with tassels and chimes swinging like hippie beads from the bumpers, banging together and making an enormous racket. On the sides of the truck were colorful murals—the only color Afghanistan seemed to have—with painted depictions of inland lakes and rolling hills and white-pillared buildings, and, in the blur of its passing, Charlie saw the aqua blue of fresh water and the emerald green of sloping countryside and the bold lemon of a faraway sun. And then, just as quickly and loudly as it had appeared, the jingle truck was gone, the color faded, only dirt clouds and the desolate, rock-strewn village around them.

"Did you see those eyes on the back of that truck?" Campo asked.

"Eyes?"

"Painted, gypsy-looking eyes. They're on all the jingle trucks. I've been trying to figure out what they mean."

Charlie stared into the distance, at the back of the truck as it faded around the bend. It did look like there might be a pair of eyes painted on the back.

"You think it's some voodoo shit?" Charlie asked.

"Don't know. All these guys are nut jobs, anyway. I mean, have you smelled them?"

"Yeah," Charlie said. "What the fuck? Not to be a dick about it, but damn. They all smell bad."

Campo pulled out his second cigarette, flicked on his lighter, cupped his hands, and lit it. "No running water in half these villages, man. Well water. And no need to be coy—they smell like pigs. It's a fact. There's a reason for it, but it's also a fact."

Charlie looked into the distance at the steel-colored mountains and a swath of migrating birds, opened his mouth to respond, but then there was a hot wind on his face and he felt his body lift up in the air and move backward. There was no thought as he lifted, only scenery, blue sky and mountain tips and the white stone wall and, as he spun, a plume of ashen smoke. But then his body wheeled and the dirt road came forward like a jagged fist, and instantly he felt his nose break against the tiny white rocks and felt the heat of fire and the warmth of blood coming down the sides of his cheek, gurgling into his ear. There was no sound. There was only a reverberation—a wavering, inverted cymbal being smacked, and the dull scrape of dirt against his forehead. Was that really blood? It could be water. Had to be water because there was so much of it. The ringing became louder, and behind the ringing was muffled yelling, muffled from all around, as if he were inside a phone booth. He heard Campo groaning and murmuring *fuck, fuck, fuck* and then realized that some of the *fucks* were coming from him, maybe all of them, and then he rolled over and one eye opened and he saw blue sky and a shaking, dirty, blistered hand in front of that sky that had to be his own.

And then, as quickly as the other sounds had disappeared, as tremendously prevalent as that inverted, buzzing, perpetual cymbal crash had been, rearing up and taking him over, it disappeared and the shouting of men and the blowing of wind and the crackling burning of fire was all around him. He heard the trucks moving, could tell by the sound of the engines that one of them was an MRAP, one of those big, khaki-colored juggernauts, built to withstand mines and deflect the blasts—

"Jesus Christ, get these guys back," somebody yelled. "Back!" He felt himself being lifted up.

Charlie groaned. Heard himself groan. All of it was still very far away, although he could hear better now and was aware of the fire on *his* side of the bridge, the side that was supposed to be safe.

"You okay, pal?" a voice asked. "You okay? You need a stretcher? Give the word, Brunson. Can you talk?"

"Campo," Charlie said. "Where's Campo?"

The voice shouted something Charlie couldn't understand, he was getting only bits and pieces now, garbled words snaking in and out of his eardrums, drowned out by the thundering of automatic weapons and the passing of a Chinook helicopter, and then, then—"Assholes used a decoy to conceal the real IED. Brunson, hold tight—we're getting you out of here."

Charlie lifted a hand but felt it drop back down, and then time disappeared and consciousness wavered like he was half in half out of a pond, and through a dream he felt himself lifted again, and he worried that he was distracting the men, needing to be carried like this, that he was a hindrance, that he needed to walk, that he was being a pussy, but Charlie felt so tired and so far deep into that rippling pond that he couldn't help it, no amount of fighting could stop it, so he sank into the pond and the feeling of the hot flames vanished and everything became cool darkness, everything cold black silk, shadows, gone.

The plane shuddered, thumped, and screeched, and Charlie started, leaned forward, gasping. He must have said something out loud, or made some kind of awkward moan, judging by the way the flight attendant was looking at him. God, he thought, it was right out of a movie, the former soldier haunted by his daydreams. *Platoon, The Deer Hunter, Saving Private Ryan,* he'd seen them all, even written a movie blog in that other life within Chicago. But he wasn't haunted. It wasn't even possible to be haunted anymore, not when every human emotion was televised and twice-cliché, when every scrap of nuance was meta, steeped in a self-awareness that came with its own sound track. The brakes in the plane powered up, and everyone lurched forward. Charlie saw that he had dropped his cup. The last bit of ice rolled away from his feet. As the plane slowed, he felt the absurd urge to pick the ice up, to conserve it. He laughed at himself.

He and Campo had both survived the IED blast, recovered quickly enough, and Charlie's expectations had been turned on their head yet again. Instead of being sent home as a mangled mess or in a body bag, he'd been handed back his M4 with months of tour ahead, and been told to play the game again. And the IED had merely been his formal introduction—his opening ceremony for the storm of shit that was to come.

They were taxiing. The illuminated FASTEN SEAT BELT sign blinked off, and a collective unbuckling rippled through the cabin. Outside, Charlie saw the illumination of other runways, of O'Hare's many darkened gates, and the fluorescent lights within. He thought about the cube of ice, melting out of sight. Under someone else's seat. He bent down to reach for it.

"Ladies and gentlemen," the lead flight attendant said—and without looking up, Charlie could sense her beaming—"I want to be the first to welcome you . . ."

He kept reaching under his seat. It was only one ice cube. His fingertips grazed the rough fabric of the airplane carpeting, the steel strut supporting the chair in front of him, the wrapper of a discarded snack. *Fucking ice cube*, he thought, gritting his teeth.

"Well, I'll just say it," the flight attendant said. "Welcome home to the United States of America!"

Charlie punched himself in the leg, then leaned back hard in his seat. Some people in the cabin were cheering. He looked through the window, at the gate that extended into a bridge, connecting with the cabin. His mother was out there, waiting to take him home. There was more applause, more shouting, *America! Fuck yeah! Get it! Portillo's, bitch, Italian beef in twenty minutes!* Charlie wondered, feeling the tears on his cheeks, if any part of this was found in a movie.

INGREDIENTS

In the living room, they used to sit with little gaps between them, air pockets, afraid to touch. All three rigid, backs up against the brown leather cushions, knees apart yet not relaxed, and, for all their years together, for all their memories of past holidays and Christmases and towering Fraser firs that Henry lined with *Nutcracker* ornaments and glistening presents, her husband and sons always had at least one foot of space between them, all watching the television screen in silence. This was not what Julie had in mind when Charlie and Barkley were children, when they ran through the house as a pack, Henry leading. And all she wants is to remove these empty spaces; she's done everything she can to create an atmosphere conducive to a happy upbringing, to a welcoming home, to a place that children would desire to return to. But the thought that haunts her, though she doesn't want to use the word *haunt*, that hovers above her world like a burning sun, is the knowledge that for all her efforts, they are not happy, not one of them.

Zoloft is a funny thing. She doesn't feel it at first. The pills taste plastic, and so she washes them down with Country Time Pink Lemonade, a drink with enough sweet and sour bite to dispel the passage of that slippery egg, of that chemical snow globe of transplanted joy, that somehow tastes devious going down. She takes a 100-milligram pill early, when her 8:45 A.M. alarm goes off, then zaps the rectangular black snooze button on the bedside digital clock, which allows her to return to a partial state of slumber, her dreams nothing but lightly flapping curtains, before she arises in the warm embrace of her artificial friend. When she wakes up for good, around 9:00 A.M., the Zoloft has kicked in and she feels fuzzy, as if warm cotton balls have cushioned her brain and belly, as if, rain or shine or sleet, Henry or no Henry, as long as those cotton balls persist the world will be right.

She finds herself in the cockpit of her metallic blue 2010 Honda Odyssey Touring Elite, driving past strip malls and not hearing the radio. Something in Libya. Doesn't matter. Her stomach swells. More warmth. Henry—what he's done—it slides off, melts away, pain is an ice cube in summer; she'll drive today. She'll drive far. Maybe take the Eisenhower to Woodfield Mall, up in Schaumburg. Be gone all day. Shop. Shop for her sons, for herself. Bath and Body Works has that new lotion, Country Chic, as well as the new Lilac Blossom candle. Three of each, she'll get, giving a couple away to Laura and Kath when they meet for Wednesday lunch at Panera. They'll like that. The cotton balls swell. Life can be good. And she always thought the key was to focus, to zero in on the good things and use tunnel vision to remove the bad—to ignore what Henry has become down in the Gold Coast, to ignore her sons' refusals to stick together, to become what she wants. But the key, the crux of it, what Zoloft has taught her, is that happiness doesn't come from zeroing in, it comes from letting go, letting slack the hold on all those cosmic ropes, of *losing* focus, of allowing the fuzziness to be reality, like a snowy television screen that shows a picture through interference, through white noise, through loose reception.

And she feels good in her Odyssey, her hands resting on the leather wheel like bird legs, though she has forgotten what day it is—no she hasn't, it's Thursday, and she feels good and the road is an endless asphalt promise that life can be good, can endure, despite its breaking the promises it made when she was young and foolish and happy, when Henry was hers, when he lifted her and held her to him and whispered in her ear during the long nights when neither of them had money, his rough stubble against her cheek, strong arms around her shoulders. God, she can't believe how much she loved him and loves him still. And he's out there, out in the Gold Coast, in his penthouse doing God-knows-what, although she does know what but feels the reality of his affairs slide away and off the cotton balls; it's all right, he still loves her, she imagines him a child who needs to rebel for a bit, to steal fruit snacks from the corner store, to spray paint the neighbors' fences, to fool around under the bleachers. The Zoloft helps her forget that he's done it for two years now, because she knows he will come back, has to, because they are soul mates, she thinks of all the things they said to each other, she remembers when they were seniors in college and Henry had pressed his face against her neck and his big blue eyes were watering and he said that he couldn't imagine himself with anyone else, not for the rest of his life, and he cried, and she held him in that tangle of red sheets, her French posters of martinis on the wall, she held him and promised they'd be together, and two years later they were married, and he'd written her that *note* that was really a poem, a poem that she still kept in the bedside table under the Bible she didn't read, and she knew he was coming back because a love like that couldn't break, soul mates didn't just forget each other, he was going through a phase. The Zoloft let her know that it would be okay, she wasn't walking a plank but a long, wide, moss-covered bridge, and there were vistas on each side, there was babbling water and smooth, white rocks and graceful deer with flat fur and gentle eyes that urged her on, that told her she was going to be all right, they all would, the cotton balls promised this, life could be good, life could be, could be, could be.

The Odyssey comes back to the driveway and the radio is still going and she hasn't heard it though she knows it's NPR. It is not Thursday but Friday. She had forgotten, though it doesn't matter, because Charlie's plane will land today, because Barkley looks at her with not sadness, not anger, but love—love and some other emotion she can't identify, which the cotton balls prevent her from identifying. She exits the minivan and reaches into her purse and takes another 100-milligram tablet of Zoloft and washes it down with the Diet Pepsi Wild Cherry, the ingredients of which are carbonated water, caramel color, phosphoric acid, aspartame, potassium benzoate (preserves freshness), gum arabic, natural flavors, and caffeine.

Ingredients are fascinating to her now, she likes learning about them, about how they build temples of sensation inside the human body, their particles like tiny buzzing worker bees, everything she eats or drinks has tiny ingredients, and they all do something, and this is why Zoloft is not a cheat, because it's the same as everything else, just a series of ordered ingredients used to produce a feeling, a reaction, and why not have the reaction she wants? And last week when she called Henry and he yelled at her it was so hard to smile but smile she did even though she was at the end of a dose the cotton balls were still there and helped her get through the labor of cleaning up her uneaten meal and the feeling that all of the family had dispersed; it's like she needs glue or even cement to keep them together though togetherness is all she wants. But it was a good day of driving and shopping and she tries to remember the stores she went to; one of them was Coach and another was Pandora and another was Michael Kors and even though she didn't buy anything it was still nice to feel warm and feel the attention of the well-dressed and tanned young men who assumed she had a family; how could they not *assume* that she had a family and with this came a husband, came Henry.

What she couldn't think about was what it was like to be fifty-seven and surprised by her reflection every time. What were these bags under her eyes and these fault lines in her cheeks and these gray streaks in her hair that stuck out like the quills of a foreign, less elegant bird? But then when she stayed in front of the mirror she could see the places in which her face was still elegant; she saw the taut roundness of her face and what Henry called her "button" nose and her lips, which still looked young— he had to admit her lips hadn't changed one iota. Her short haircut was the one thing she'd altered since he'd left, and it showed more of her neck and she knew that was also a positive. But the negatives were these fault lines and these bags and the way her eyes seemed hollowed out, and the fact that she might be too skinny and even though her chest had never been big it now seemed shrunken and her breastbone showed but she was almost sixty; what did anyone want or expect?

But the Zoloft, the Zoloft, kicking in now, warmth, hot embers in a furnace growing to a roaring fireplace in the log cabin by her moss-covered bridge. She was going to be all right. And it was pleasant how these doses helped to make time stop and jump and pass, how it smoothed out the corn maze of each day, smoothed it out and took her above it all, and she was vaguely aware of having gotten emotional regarding Henry but now the cotton balls were back and Charlie's plane was landing and it was okay, it was okay, she still remembered what her living room looked like with her sons and her husband inside it, sitting with a space between them, little gaps, air pockets, afraid to touch.

A DAY IN THE LIFE OF A
WORLD CONQUEROR

Henry squinted into the sunlight. "Say again?"

"I said the horse is a beautiful animal," Glenn drawled, leaning his head back and staring into the distance. Three bay stallions, their coats the color of Brazilian cherry, were running together some hundred feet away, moving fluidly through the silver grasses. To the south was the repainted, split-level ranch house, and to the north, the fields, the twin ponds, and the horses on the horizon.

Henry put a boot on the wood rail fence and watched them move. "Almost like fish," he said. "The way they change directions." A breeze picked up and blew ripples across the water and reeds of the pond.

"See how the middle one, Tallack, turns his head?" Glenn asked. "The other two follow. It's like a biker making a turn signal."

The three stallions abruptly galloped toward the fence, their hooves tribal, purposeful, and Henry watched the sinuous muscles contort and flex, watched their manes move as they bore into the wind. The bays ran past the fences as one, Tallack leading, dirt kicking up and cascading with the rhythm of their gallop.

Glenn pointed at them as they left. "You see those dark hairs mixing with the rest of the coats? They're called the black points. It's what makes them bays."

"You sure are pretty knowledgeable, Glenn. Aren't girls supposed to like horses?"

"Those are ponies."

"Ha! There it is. Rationalization. Mankind's defense against the universe."

"Which you seem to be using quite a bit."

Henry took his boot off the fence and gave him a hard look. "Don't start."

"What?" Glenn said, raising his palms skyward.

"Quit it."

Glenn sighed and ran a hand through thinning silver hair. Hair that matched the wispy grasses all over the horse ranch. "Look," he said. "She calls sometimes. Talks like you're coming back. Called yesterday, even."

"That's proof right there," Henry said. "Mental instability. Anyone with an IQ of forty-five would see I've got no reason to go back."

"And you're still going stag? Living the single life at almost sixty? You're serious about this?"

"It's been two years. Everyone else can see that I'm serious."

"Uh-huh."

"It's over, Glenn."

"Uh-huh."

Henry turned away and watched the horses again.

"You know," Glenn said. "Pretty soon you're going to realize you're old. Can't run from it. Can't hide. Can't work out or tan or get plastic surgery enough to stop it. It's a mudslide. I realized this myself a couple years back."

"Nobody's running."

"And what do you call this Gold Coast penthouse deal you've made with yourself?"

"Let me ask you something," Henry said. "You see these horses? You see how Tallack runs? Beautiful animal, right? You appreciate him. You appreciate him as long as you can. But what happens when Tallack gets sick? I mean really sick. Or what happens when Tallack gets hurt? Breaks two of his legs? Nothing works then, right? He's not the same horse. Sure, you'll always appreciate the way the young and healthy Tallack used to move out here in the grasses, but old and injured Tallack is not the same. And what do you do? You put Tallack out of his misery. You shoot the poor bastard. There's nothing different between that and what I'm doing now, except in my case, no one is even harmed."

Glenn pointed to a small red stable where an older horse stood, watching the others. "See that mare, there? Her name's Rune. She's a sorrel. Twenty years old, recovered from a lot of injuries, including a broken leg. Won't breed, won't ride, makes no money for me anymore. But she's still beautiful, right? And I'll be damned if I ever shoot her."

They watched her lift a leg up and bring it back down. "It's not a bad analogy," Henry said. "But you don't have to sleep with Rune, and Rune sure as shit doesn't give you a list of her neurotic problems, and Rune doesn't care if you go out and ride any other goddamn horses. You follow me, now, you old coot?"

"But why not send Julie the divorce papers? Give the girl some closure, Henry."

He waved his hand and pulled his phone from his pocket.

"And Henry?"

"What, dammit?"

"It's not just Julie I called you up here about. It's business, too."

Henry sighed. Tallack had finally stopped running and was now bending over the shallows of the pond, quenching his thirst. It was raining in Chicago, he remembered. Hopefully it would be gone when he got back. He felt Glenn's hand on his shoulder.

"I'm your friend first, Henry, and we do business second. But I've got some bad news."

"Jesus. Here we go."

"It's a dying business, even if you're at the top of it."

"Aw, hell," Henry said. He felt the soreness in his chest and triceps and deltoids, soreness from lifting weights, from swimming laps, soreness he had begun to love. But lately, no amount of protein supplements or Swedish massages or postworkout stretching was making it go away. The aches would last for days, or sometimes, like when he had tried to max out on the incline press, even a week. The soreness he loved had begun to seem like something else entirely—as if his tendons were old ropes beginning to fray at the edges, his muscles ancient hills eroding against the wind. He pushed the thoughts away. Fuck it. He was in better shape now than he was ten years ago. Fifteen, even.

"Now, I can't control everything," Glenn said. "The board voted on it. The fact is, we just don't need the account. Shit, we laid off fifteen percent of our workforce last year. CFO thinks we can do without a glorified printing company."

"This isn't the 1980s, Glenn. You know full well we do more than financial printing. My guys briefed you on our new projects. Come on: technology integration, document composition, digital delivery—"

"Digital delivery? The CFO doesn't even know what that means. And the world's been going digital since the 1990s. It's too late. Hell, you guys have performed admirably."

"We're not static, Glenn. We're transitioning. Didn't my guys give you the multimedia presentation? All the bells and whistles about Trend-Star's evolving digital services? Document management means more than it did in the printing days. I mean, some of the technology we're developing—"

Glenn put his hand on Henry's shoulder again. "If it was up to me, I'd call you over, we'd light our cigars, look out at the Chicago River, and sign a twenty-year contract. But it's not up to me, it's up to the board. And you can't smoke indoors in Chicago, anyway. Not anymore. Hell, you knew this was coming."

Henry folded his arms over his muscled but weary physique. "Not so soon."

"You'll just pull down another account, anyway. TrendStar will set you up. You deserve it."

"I'm not so sure." Henry sighed. "Heard about some off-site meetings. All the big players, including the COO. Our assistant media guy told me about them, of all people."

"Meetings you should have attended?"

"As president of sales, absolutely. But the damn media assistant said they've had two of them. Last one at the Ritz. The implications . . ."

"Well, they can't fire you."

"No," Henry said, "but they can push. I'm the second-oldest guy in the Chicago division. And you know how the saying goes. Once you get near sixty . . ."

Glenn whistled at Rune, but the old horse was watching the others.

"You hearing me?" Henry asked.

"Yeah, yeah. I don't know what to say. Companies today like to keep the workforce young. Most of the guys at TrendStar are probably Charlie's age."

"Charlie," Henry said, bitterly.

"But I can't help, you understand? I mean, I *want* to retire. They won't have to push me out. That's the difference."

"There it is." The breeze picked up again, and Henry watched the pond go choppy.

"You spoken with Al lately?" Glenn asked.

"Been a few months or so."

"You should see him. He was just up here."

"Another relapse?"

"Nah. He's actually doing okay. Good, even. That's why you should see him."

Henry rolled up his sleeves. "Well, back to the working world. Need to stop by the office. I'm sure they'll catch the bad news soon enough." He started walking away, down the gravel path.

"Friends first," Glenn said. "I'm sorry. But it's not the end of the world."

"Yeah, yeah."

"And Henry?"

He turned.

"I gotta ask."

"Yes, sir."

"What the hell are you really doing? With all this Peter Pan shit?"

Henry thought about it for a moment. "Making up for lost time," he called back, before turning and walking to his Mercedes.

12:30 P.M.
WEST LOOP, CHICAGO

His office had been moved; that was the first sign. One year ago. Sure, it was another corner office, but it wasn't the same one, and the walls were smaller, and there was only one set of windows—which looked northwest, away from the skyline and the lake and the river, which were the only vistas Chicago had. All Henry possessed now was a distant view of the suburban sprawl: asphalt highways and exit ramps, neatly plotted cul-de-sacs and shopping centers, and tame green parks that littered the horizon like cemetery plots. The problem was, even this far away, he could still spot Downers Grove and the general area of his old suburban home—a home Julie still wandered in, doing who knew what. Expecting him to come back. Some days Henry would pull down the blinds on the office window, just to get it out of sight, but even in the darkened tomb of his office he could feel his house, pulsing among the thickened sprawl. Julie, waiting. Henry shuddered—so many things these days felt claustrophobic, as if his life were lived in a series of phone booths.

Henry dropped his briefcase beside the desk and sank into his burgundy swivel chair. Despite the change in venue, the interior of his corner office remained the same—framed desk photos of Charlie's high school graduation, a third-grade Charlie pulling Barkley in a red wagon along Washington Street, and Al and Glenn holding up an enormous buck they'd shot in Northern Michigan. Only the one of him and Julie at the swim-up bar in Puerto Vallarta was absent. His sales plaques lined the wall opposite the window, the last one for overall excellence stopping at 1996. He'd been forty-two, then. Christ.

He opened his laptop computer, which TrendStar still hadn't taken the time to upgrade. Waited for Outlook e-mail to load. The whole company sinking, and unless they really pulled some clever moves, reinvented themselves with more than the linguistic trickery found on the TrendStar Web site, they'd be in trouble. Survive maybe eight, ten years after he was gone. And to survive, they had to make cuts. Henry knew he was pulling down the big salary—as president of sales, he had the large base but also kept commission on his top ten clients, among them Geico, Blue Cross Blue Shield, Merrill Lynch. But Glenn was yanking Geico away, and Henry could feel the money siphoning out of his account already. Yet, all of TrendStar was feeling it. Ten years ago, they'd been fine. And then the trimming had begun. The box seats at Comiskey and Wrigley—gone. The twelfth-row, center-court Bulls tickets, which had catapulted Henry to sales stardom during the Jordan dynasty, had been traded in for alternating blocks in the two hundred level. Then they lost their ticket man altogether, and then Sales Team A and Sales Team B merged and dropped 30 percent of personnel, and the three production coordinators became one, before finally being automated. In the bigger picture, they'd gone from seven market competitors to two, nine domestic and international branches to three, with Dallas looking wobbly, uncertain. The Columbus office was still holding on, and the Chicago branch actually expanding—but much of that was because of the closures and cuts elsewhere. Everyone backing into a corner, smiling professionally. And then, Henry thought, there were people like him. Old. Out of touch (so they said). Expensive. And the two off-site meetings in which the VP of sales attended but the president did not? Wrong, Henry thought. The walls closing in.

He thought of that young blonde he had brought back to his place a week prior. Twenty-eight, twenty-nine? Average intelligence. Gold digger, sure. But a knockout. And he'd gotten her, taken her home over the slobbering mouths of men half his age. She'd seen his condo and loved it, seen him naked and cooed, missed guessing his true age by eight years. Their sex was emotionless, perfunctory, but good. He'd been able to go twice. And in the middle of the night, through a layering of watery shadows that made him feel as if he were at the bottom of a fish tank, Henry had put his arm around her delicate hips and felt her take his hand. He'd almost forgotten the feeling of another's fingers locked inside his own, and felt his throat catch blindly with need. He'd held her against him and her hand had clasped his own and those dark eels and underwater shadows had moved across the penthouse ceiling, eventually giving way to the drumming and smearing of rain. But when morning came, she was gone, and Henry wondered if it really had been a dream, if she'd clasped his hand at all.

With the sunlight, all that remained was the pride of his conquest, and truly, that was enough. A note with her phone number was taped to his granite countertop, written in pink pen. Pink! Maybe she was younger than twenty-eight. And then he'd taken a shower and leaned against the marble walls, the jets of liquid rushing across his body, and felt the same flood of relief as he did with every one-night stand. The steam rose high in the shower, fogged up the glass, made him lose a sense of the walls around him. The water scalded his skin, but he kept his back against the sleek surface of the marble and watched the steam rise and the glass disappear, and thought he could be in the clouds or fifty feet tall, that he could be anything or anywhere or anyone. And the one-night stand with the blonde had kept him in a decent mood for days; he'd held his head high at the office, walked past young, important people without giving a second thought, laughed off an aggressive comment by that prick Dorfman, the VP of sales. But now, in his office, he felt the familiar need. To be in those dim-lit clubs and feel the burn of alcohol and the wet, greedy eyes of young women who saw something important in him, something alive. God, he needed it, had to have it, not to have it was to suffocate, to lower himself into a darkened place and throw away the ladder. Christ. He would get laid tonight, and all this shit about Glenn dropping the account and Julie making desperate calls and the company having these fucking off-site meetings would go away.

1:30 P.M.
WEST LOOP, CHICAGO

After the turtle-chinned IT guy arrived and told him he'd inadvertently turned his Wi-Fi off (waddling away with what Henry believed was an eye roll), the Outlook e-mail opened. He hated using it, the same with all forms of writing. Which wasn't to say he didn't appreciate the written word. No, Henry read history books compulsively, especially old-school military history—not World War II but rather biographies of Napoleon, Genghis Kahn, and Alexander the Great. Despite this, he never found a need to actually write. What good was it in a face-to-face business, where people mattered, where force of will closed the deal, not words? But now, everyone was judging intelligence and professionalism by the grammatical skill displayed on goddamn e-mails. Well, who gave a damn about those things? Just put him in a room, sit the client down, and the sale was made. E-mails were little more than cheats and half measures. They were Post-it notes left by salesmen too scared to pick up a phone or show up outside a door. Truly, technology was a hindrance to the self-actualized man. But that wasn't the answer anyone was looking for.

The first two messages highlighted in Henry's in-box were the typical account management confirmations from payroll and marketing. No response required. And then, there, right there—a new message from the COO, Pete Vicaro, who had become one of those snobby assholes that made you call him Peter in public. Fuck that: he was Pete, Henry had known him before, when he didn't see himself as a diva, or as Chicago's dining authority (he claimed to eat at Alinea twice a month), or as a man who required two secretaries (one matronly, the other curvaceous). Henry positioned his big hands over the tiny keyboard, centered the mouse across the bolded e-mail, clicked it once, and waited for it to load.

Sent: Friday, March 18, 2011 1:15 PM
From: Vicaro, Peter
To: Brunson, Henry
Cc: Dorfman, Rex

Henry,
Heard about the Geico account. It's a hit we saw coming.
But in other news, we have 36 new accounts in from
the Dallas closures that we're going to spread through the
sales team. I wanted to personally let you know that you
will not be receiving any of these new accounts. And also,
I'm sorry to say, we've removed your prospects and
dispersed them among the rest of the squad. Let's be
honest—you've got enough heavy hitters already, and we
need to spread these out to some of the younger members
on the team.

Best,
Peter Vicaro

Chief Operating Officer
TrendStar Document Management

P.S. I got reservations at Schwa this weekend with Dan Roan
and a couple of other guys from WGN. I'll send you my
review.

Oh, fuck you, Henry thought. Have a nice dinner, you arrogant,
potbellied prick. And cc'ing Dorfman? He imagined picking that thirty-
year-old weasel up by his powder-blue tie and tossing him headfirst into
one of TrendStar's endless displays of motivational pictures. Let him
show his smirking, ironically stubbled face around the office after *that*.
But at least the cat was out of the bag. Step one of the Henry Brunson
phase-out process, beginning now. He wondered what their timetable
was. Have him out at fifty-eight? Fifty-nine? He felt the phone booth
walls shrink another inch.

He'd been a salesman for over thirty years, and despite all the
changes in the digital age, the message was still the same: *always* be
mining for clients. Always look to excavate new leads and discover
new accounts, because even the best, most profitable relationships
have a life cycle. Hell, Glenn was proof of that. Sometimes it was better pricing elsewhere, or an epic screwup on the part of TrendStar, or
simply new ownership who wanted it done differently. But the fact
remained—all accounts had a life cycle, and they eventually dissolved
into nothing. Which meant, at this point, that if TrendStar couldn't
take the kill shot and force him into retirement, they could at least
make a wound and wait for him to bleed out. No new clients. Henry
put his head against the lightly humming laptop. He felt himself an
aging, silver lion, with the hyenas circling, beginning to laugh, assuming
their attack positions. With him gone, Dorfman would scoop up the
title of president and with it, his other top accounts—Blue Cross Blue
Shield and Merrill Lynch, to be sure. The rest of the hyenas would
fight over the table scraps. But maybe he still had a couple of moves
left. He was Henry Brunson, after all. And what he needed, tonight,
remained the same. He would buy new jeans at Diesel, eat alone at
Joe's Stone Crab at his usual corner spot by the bar, get himself the

bacon-wrapped sea scallops, and begin his night with three shots of Patrón.

The office phone trilled—the sound of breaking lightbulbs cascaded over his perfect silence. Henry yanked the handset from its cradle.

"What?" he said. "What?"

"Hello to you, too, Henry."

Oh, dear God. Julie. "Listen," he said. "We've made an agreement. No communication unless absolutely necessary. You agreed to this. Didn't you agree?"

"Can you please just listen, Henry?"

He sighed. Every time he felt fully free of her, there she was, digging the talons back in. "It's not a good time, Julie. I've got work."

"Please?"

"I just—okay. You know what? You've got two minutes."

"Fine. Barkley had a phone interview."

"For teaching?"

"Yes, for teaching. You know he majored in education, right? You remember?"

"Yes, I remember. And I told him a hundred times it was a bad idea. Horrible market for jobs, miserable salary, defunct bureaucracy, not to mention all the jocks will eat the poor kid alive."

"Well, try to be happy for him. It was with Eastwick."

"No kidding? I'll have to talk to him, then. Brief him about what to do, if they call him back to come in."

"He'll be fine. He's a smart guy."

"He needs to know how to interview. How to sit. What to wear. How to answer questions. What questions to *ask*. And he's got to curb that babble. That's not going to cut it in the professional world. He can't just segue into that *Dungeons and Dragons* talk. He's got to give them a reason to hire him, beyond the fact that he's cheap."

"You sure seem to know what everyone else needs. Kind of funny that you haven't—"

"Oh, God, here we go," Henry said. "There are reasons we don't talk, Julie. There are reasons."

There was a muffled pause. And then: "I'm calling about Charlie. That's the big news. I just got the call a few minutes ago, and his plane lands today, it turns out. I know we thought it would be next week, but it looks like he's early. And that means you're going to have to change whatever your plans are for tonight."

"Look," Henry said, anger rising in his throat. "I can't tell you how many e-mails I sent that kid when he was overseas. Never got one response back. Not one. And you remember how he left it. I don't care if he's coming in right this minute, that kid has a lot to answer for."

"He was doing what he believed in. Be proud of him. Don't you understand that—"

Henry held the phone away from his ear, massaged his temples with his free hand, then returned it when it was clear she had trailed off. "Julie. You know the strings I pulled to get him that Lucent position? And the war? He never said a word about it before. Didn't know the history, the strategy, the equipment, didn't do anything but watch *Saving Private Ryan* and write those stupid movie review blogs with his friends. But he wanted a condo, and I fronted sixty-five percent of the bill. When he wanted a job, I got him a management position directly out of grad school. Directly. With his own office. And he threw it all away—spit in his father's face. Didn't even say thank you."

Julie started talking urgently again, but Henry held the phone away, let her ramble on, then returned it when he heard something about how he needed to be there *tonight*, how he should just suck it up and be home—be there waiting for the kid, despite everything.

"Julie, you know I don't operate that way. Yes, granted, he's returned from a war, but it's a mess he got himself into—and he still needs to make amends. Barkley says he's angry with me, which I think, quite frankly, is crazy. And I thought we already agreed—no more phone calls for the time being."

"No, you said I could call in an emergency and this is—"

"Catering to Charlie—the person who threw away everything—that's not an emergency. You understand? He's the one who cut ties with his father."

"Henry. He did not. And this is an emergency."

"You're a perfectly capable parent, and you're still getting my stipends, aren't you? What emergency can money not fix these days?"

"He needs a *man* to be here, and that man needs to be his father."

"If Charlie needs a man to help, he can be a man and ask for it."

Julie cursed across the static. "He can't be expected to call. You don't have to see me. Okay? You don't have to see me at all. I can run errands, I can go out, but I think you should be there tonight. But if you do want to see me we can—"

"Bad idea."

"Okay, fine. Fine. But you need to see your son, and you need to see him now. It's not a question of whether or not you want to do it."

Henry sighed. He couldn't stay in the office, not with the hyenas lurking, smelling the open wound.

"Henry?"

"Leaving now," he said. "Leaving now."

But he knew, even as he said it, that he wouldn't go home.

4:30 P.M.
LAKE SHORE DRIVE, CHICAGO

When he was behind the wheel of his obsidian-black 2010 Mercedes C350 Sport, the passing world was a flawed oyster through which Henry grudgingly had to travel. He kept the almond-mocha leather and burl walnut trim interior at a brisk sixty-nine degrees, the power seats sprawled back for full leg extension, the Bluetooth connectivity on, the panorama sunroof closed. One of the media guys had helped him with the iPod docking station and XM Satellite Radio, which he used when he wasn't listening to the pleasing drone of ESPN 1000 sports radio. And right now, turned up high, came the jangly guitar riffs of "Born to Be Wild," which he'd been listening to for decades—it never got old. Even when Charlie was a baby, during those times when Julie was at the store or out of town, Henry had taken the sudden pocket of freedom to put his old Steppenwolf cassette tape into the stereo, turn up the volume, and let the introductory rock-and-roll notes wash over his infant son's smiling face. And he swore that his baby had loved it.

But the man who leaves is always the bad guy, Henry thought bitterly as he floored the Mercedes down Chicago's most scenic expressway. Julie had already left two voice mails asking where he was. To his left, North Avenue Beach sat abandoned from the earlier storm: empty, untread bluffs, deserted sand volleyball courts, and cold green water sloshing against slabs of concrete. He was in control, he reminded himself. These were his decisions.

Everyone thought it was about the sex. But the way he felt, it was never just one thing that breaks up a marriage. And he hadn't really thought about the sex as all-important. "It will decline. A fact of life," Al had told him—and he'd been married three times. Henry the best man at all of them; by the second, it had become a joke. "They've all got natural half-lives," Al said. "A real marriage can't go more than four or five years without changing into something else. It's like a brand-new Abrams tank. You get a factory-fresh bruiser and that puppy works great. Fires shells all the time, moves fast, no engine breakdowns, no loss of radio communication to base. And then the tread wears down and the barrel gets rusted and the GPS falters, and so on, but there's a difference: you can order new parts and repair a tank, but not a relationship. Sure there's tricks. A couple new positions, some bedroom gymnastics. The old wheel barrel maneuver. That could give you an extra three months. Then you got vacations. Take the old lady to the Bahamas and recharge the batteries. Or move to a new house. Hell, ballroom-dancing lessons. There's another four months. But those are Band-Aids. Espresso shots. Eventually, everything returns to zero. Fact of life."

Henry had prepared himself for the dull ache of suburban monotony, for the *Tom and Jerry* loop of strip mall backgrounds, for the rotation of chain restaurants and jam-packed, chlorine-drenched public pools. But what he hadn't been prepared for was the cliché in Julie and the cliché inside himself. When his life became that movie, where the poor married sap in the sweater vest only got it on his birthday, from an increasingly wrinkled wife who no longer looked good in her nightgown? That was a problem. And the sex. Once a week the first few years. Which was fine—he wasn't a deviant. But then, like an old heavyweight boxer who relegates himself to easier fights in dirtier, sparsely populated arenas, Henry had gritted his teeth and settled for once a month. A month! He might as well have been single. And with his once-a-month schedule, he had grudgingly accepted the need to masturbate, which disgusted him, revolted him, the idea that he, dashing Henry Brunson, the man who left a trail of broken hearts throughout high school and college, the man who mocked self-pleasure as the crutch for those who couldn't get any, was sitting up at 1:00 A.M. at the old Dell computer, surfing for Internet porn with his aging junk in his hands? Disgusting. And still, he had to say, it hadn't been about the sex.

But when the sex (or lack thereof) was combined with the attentions of J—he didn't even want to say her name—and the shrinking office space in an out-of-touch company, when his children didn't need him anymore and the suburbs became a recycled cartoon that Al rightly mocked, when his only escape was through an imagination he didn't like to use, certain decisions had to be made. Evacuation plans, for the sake of himself. Because, in all honesty, no one was living his life but him, and taking charge was the right and necessary thing.

Henry saw his penthouse rising up in the distance, a polished, towering jewel. High above the roads and the cars and the water. This was where he belonged. And if Charlie needed him, he knew where his father lived.

8:47 P.M.
GOLD COAST, CHICAGO

Step One: Enter penthouse. Lights on. Boot up Steppenwolf's *All Time Greatest Hits*, surround sound, 75 percent volume. Begin with "Born to Be Wild." Song does not get old. Undress. Admire South American (primarily Venezuelan and Peruvian) spear and pottery collection on west wall of living room. Hold one of the spear's worn shafts and walk to full-length bathroom vanity mirror to admire physique. Pose as if ready to throw, to take down an Andean bear. Flex. Make sure abdominal muscles are divided as if by canals. Retrieve Philips Norelco BodyGroom Pro from its charging station. Trim pubic hair. Turn on shower.

Step Two: Enter shower, full pressure, full steam, both showerheads and all six jets, soap the chest, the armpits, the undercarriage, the feet, the neck, the legs. Water must scald. Lean back against the chill of the marble, let steam rise, close eyes, inhale. Try not to think. Allow a smile. Listen with approval as "Born to Be Wild" segues into the druggy fuzz

of "Magic Carpet Ride.'
cotton towel in front o
slope down your aging
static pops its way into
east onto the turquoise
dim-lit sailboats doing
emotional high of a la

Step Three: Enter
mute. No sound, eve
Then, volume at 60
in the event of a on
red comforter and r
women rendered i

12:33 A.M.
RUSH STREET, CHICA

Henry leaned back and
hours was more than
with a red purse
his cutoff, he'
ter of two
ton nos
hell

look. Listen for the beginning notes of The Enter walk-in closet. Choose fresh briefs, dark chocolate socks, alligator boots, new frayed jeans from Diesel (remove tags), pressed undershirt, navy blue button-down, and oil-black, trim-fit, linen-blend Boss sports coat. Do not get dressed. Reenter bathroom. Shave, aftershave, cologne, deodorant, toothpaste, mouthwash. Powder balls. Grudgingly acknowledge this technique is not self-taught but learned from eavesdropping at the East Bank Club.

Step Four: Dress in front of CNN as the lurching, ominous, chugging notes of "The Pusher" begin. Bob head. Watch the headlines for any notes on Afghanistan, even though Charlie is back. Slip on alligator boots last. Throw back head and howl, "God-DAMN, The Pusher man," in unison with John Kay. Take fifteen minutes to finish chapter from current book on the Persian Empire. Smile with recognition when Alexander the Great is mentioned. Turn off CD at track nine. Never finish Steppenwolf's *All Time Greatest Hits*, as this is bad luck. Steppenwolf must seem to have a catalog that never ends. Turn off lights. Admire the shadows of the penthouse; all those slabs of granite and stainless steel, the husk of darkened lake through the big windows. Exit penthouse. Remove all thoughts of TrendStar, Julie, Charlie, Glenn, and any signs of ill health from your mind. Remember that the note containing the pink phone number of the blonde whose hand you clasped remains inside your wallet. Begin night.

listened. Running out of time, and usually, two enough. The woman, who sported a short red dress and white heels, was about thirty-one (thirty-eight was decided) and drunk. A talker. Claimed to be the daughrestaurant critics in Tennessee, a foodie herself, and had a butand southern drawl that was doing wonders for him. But holy did she talk about food. They sat under the flashing blue and purlights in the corner of the club, everyone receiving bottle service from scantily clad waitresses, and in the distance, the writhing dance floor, the golden-lit bar, the vaulted ceilings. But the girl, the drunk southerner he'd had his eyes on all night, was trying to talk again.

"It's been so long since I was home," she drawled.

"Yeah?" Henry said. "Tell me a little bit about home." He pushed the Grey Goose martini closer to her side of the table, watching as she drank it.

"Oh, you wouldn't be interested," she said, pursing her lips, holding a hand over her mouth to disguise a hiccup.

Henry leaned forward, felt the swell of his chest and biceps against the fabric of the sports coat, and placed his strong fingers on her bony forearm. "I want to know everything about you," he said. He gave her a squeeze. "You need to know that."

"Oh, yeah," the girl said. "I know that. But you really want to know about my home life?"

"Sure do. Refill on that martini?"

She waved her hand. Covered her mouth as another hiccup came forth.

"Go ahead and tell me about home," Henry said, summoning the last of his patience, submerging the now urgent desire to prove his virility. He'd put his hand on her leg twice tonight, and both times she shook him off. Difficult to read.

"Are your eyes okay?" she asked.

Henry sighed. "My eyes? Yeah, my eyes are great. Just had the Lasik surgery two years ago. I've got the vision of a bald eagle."

"No, no," the girl said. "Your *eyes*. The color. They look a little yellow."

"Probably the lighting. See those gold lights above the bar?"

She hiccuped openly, her chest bouncing inside the tight red fabric that contained it, and Henry felt the frustration bubble up again. The girl shook her head. "Not the lights, Henry. Maybe you've got pink eye."

Henry massaged his forehead, reminded himself that she was at least a nine, possibly a ten without that dress. "Tell me about home," he said. "I thought you were going to tell me about home."

"Well," she said, "I'm from Tennessee, as I'm sure you've gathered, what with my parents and all. Everybody knows what they look like now, so they have to wear these disguises when they go to new restaurants. And Tennessee? You people think Tennessee is the dirty South, but it ain't really the dirty South, not like Georgia. And the worst is Mississippi. That's the highest obesity rate in America, you know that? Which reminds me of this guy from my hometown in Nashville. You listening, Henry?"

He held up his frosted glass of Stella Artois. "I am. But I can't drink all this alcohol by myself."

"Okay, okay, I'm drinking. But this guy was big. Like Mississippi obesity big. Big ole whale belly and red suspenders and shaggy muttonchops. Name was Big Freddie and he cooked ribs. He used Memphis pigs, which are the best kind, if you're from Tennessee—it's just something people know. Cooked with three kinds of grills, had these big coffee bean cans that he filled with barbecue sauce and you could see him out there all day every day, sweating, slathering all the ribs with this paintbrush he dipped in the coffee bean cans. Freddie's Slabs and Barbecue, it was called, and he had the best ribs and pulled pork in the state of Tennessee. Baked beans, brisket, you name it. You hungry yet, Henry? And why are you so interested in seeing me drink?"

Henry swore under his breath. He sheepishly smiled and gritted his teeth. Her eyes faded to the distance as she droned on and he let his gaze fall upon her ample breasts, her thin arms, the curl of hair that fell across her delicate features. He wanted to toss her on his bed like a conqueror, a barbarian in the times of old.

"Maybe you're the drunk one," the girl said. "Maybe it's those yellow eyes."

"Listen," Henry said. "I'm not drunk. What I *am* is interested in this big fat man you're talking about. What happens next?"

"What's that? The fat man? Oh, Big Freddie! The point is he got bought out. Corporation something or other, and Big Freddie made a lot of money and got to walk away. But see, the problem is that they kept Freddie's name, but they didn't get those Memphis hogs no more, and those slabs were smaller and tougher and they weren't cooked by hillbillies, which you can believe ruins any chance of a good slab, and the pulled pork barely pulled apart. Some folks said it was frozen. And so eventually people figured out Freddie was gone. And the point is, I saw him one time, after Big Freddie sold out. At a junkyard when my man at the time was dropping off his old Chevy. And the guy I was with cussed him out good and said he should be ashamed of what happened to the slab joint, but Freddie said, hey, I was getting tired of that old slab cooking and now I'm rich and I do what I want to do. But he didn't look good. That's what the point is. Big Freddie, he, you know—that grill *was* Big Freddie. It was like he got amputated without even knowing it. I like that word—*amputated*. But he left and went away from it and he just became a big fat man with no real purpose who had ruined the one good thing he had. Know what I mean? And do you like the word *amputate*, too?"

"Absolutely," Henry said. "Yes, indeed." He massaged his forehead. Yes, the girl was cute and claimed to be a model for the Food Network— but the babble about barbecue was like listening to a drunken, drawling cartoon.

"Yes, what?" the girl said.

He'd forgotten her name. He wanted to say Daisy, but that was probably because it went through his head with a southern twang. Henry fought back laughter, focused on the frustration that was bubbling up like undrinkable champagne.

"Yes, what?" she crooned. "C'mon, Henry, what'd you think about my story? About Big Freddie?"

He leaned back. "Great story. You want another drink?"

"Were you even listening, Henry?"

"Sure was. Carolina ribs. Freddie sold out. Frozen meat. How about getting out of here? I've got a collection of tribal spears and Venezuelan pottery you might like to see."

The girl, whose name he'd forgotten, appraised him. She had a funny smile on her face. He tried to decide which of them was drunker. If his eyes really were yellow.

"Well?" he said. "Want to leave? These flashing lights are killing me."

She laughed her southern belle laugh. Finished up the rest of the martini and dabbed at her chin with the napkin. Stood up and slung her red purse over the shoulder strap of her red dress.

"I think I'm going home, Henry. You seem nice."

"Believe it or not, I've got some pulled pork in the fridge."

"Right."

"Come on," he said. "We've spent all night together. I have a king-size bed. You won't even know I'm there."

The girl—her name truly escaped him—leaned in close. "Something's not right with you," she said. "There's a reason you remind me of Big Freddie."

"I've got six percent body fat," Henry said, but her back was already turned.

She walked out, and Henry sat at the tiny round table under the blue and purple lights. He didn't want his mind to go there, but he could feel it sliding down a muddy slope, and he briefly saw an image of himself and his penthouse and these clubs as if from afar and felt a lurch of panic. But then he stood up and went to the golden-lit bar and ordered two shots of Patrón and sucked on the lime and then balled the spent lime up in a cocktail napkin and tossed it over his shoulder. His brain warmed up pleasantly. There was a soft drone in the background that he couldn't quite place. Didn't matter. He forced his mouth into a smile for the red-headed bartender who knew him well. He felt for the pink phone number that was still in his wallet. Yes, he thought, he still had a couple moves left. And then he went out the doors and into the night, held his head high, breathed in the city air, and forgot about the southern girl who had turned him back.

ECOSYSTEM
EVALUATIONS

On the BNSF Railway to Downers Grove, Barkley searched for Ginny's profile on Facebook, though he didn't know her last name. He felt queasy, unprepared. Charlie was coming home *tonight*, his mother had said, blathering on the phone about schedule changes and altered timetables. He'd rushed off to take the train, his heart pounding at the thought of his brother. The plan: have dinner with the family, spend time with Charlie, and then take his mother's car into the city for Ginny's concert. And afterward—depending on how fortuitous the night was—return to Downers Grove postconcert or the following morning.

Across from him, a man in a navy business suit took a seat, crossed his legs, and removed a small paperback book from his corporate satchel. The novel's front cover displayed a man with a suave tie and a silver pistol, running from an ominous silhouette. Beach reading, Barkley scoffed. It was as if even the small population of Americans who did read were determined not to delve into real literature. Judging by the wrinkled picture, the businessman's book was about a detective, probably alcoholic, whose past was going to "catch up" with him, likely in regard to the guilt rendered by a dead partner, the love of a reformed hooker, and the obsession of a serial killer with a penchant for scrapbooking. Barkley thanked his lucky stars for being given a discerning mind. Around him, the train rattled and slowed, and the intercom intoned that they were approaching Congress Park. Still a ways to go.

Ginny's concert would be a great chance to move in a new direction. Barkley thought about what a girlfriend could do for his confidence, his sex life, his writing—even his application to high schools for an English teaching job. Teaching. Ugh. *Student* teaching had been well over a year ago, and still, no schools had even given him a whiff of a face-to-face interview. And while other friends had enjoyed jobs straight out of college, he'd been left to tread water and make excuses in the thirteen months that followed. Was he cursed? Was the economy-crushed job market for new teachers really that bad? He'd applied for positions in March and April, the entire process online now, and received nothing but confirmation e-mails and a deep swell of digital silence. Then May and June had rolled by with more applications and still no human response, and the realization sank in that he might not get a teaching job, period. His father said he had to be more aggressive in the application process, said he had to start calling and e-mailing and pounding the pavement like an honest-to-God salesman, to move beyond the online applications, but regardless, Chicago Public Schools had just laid off over a thousand more instructors, which would only make things more difficult.

In fact, all he'd gotten in months was a phone interview—no more than ten minutes long—with Eastwick High School, the castlelike Catholic school located on the south end of Downers Grove. His mother had practically exploded into confetti flakes of joy, saying she was going to call his father, to call everyone they knew, the whole time Barkley repeating again and again—*it's a phone interview, Mom, I'm not Catholic, I went to a public school, I seriously have no chance.* The interview itself, over a week ago, had been tepid and unreadable for the first eight or so minutes. His reception was bad, he'd fumbled over his words and forgotten to mention that his great-uncle had attended the school for two years. But by the end, he'd gotten something of a second wind, and made what he thought was a decent speech about literature and education and a metaphor about young minds being akin to water wells. But it was stupid to call it a speech, he thought. He likely had no chance to move forward, and the only option was to continue applying for work before the summer ran out.

But he needed a job, and he needed money. He'd checked his account balance earlier today and almost suffered a panic attack. (His monetary survival, at least for now, existed on the graces of his father's college graduation gift—a cash installment that was down to its final embers—and the paltry, bimonthly sum he received from working as a part-time ACT tutor.) Beyond that, he needed, as always, to get organized. When was the last time he'd done laundry? Weeks. There were totem poles of dirty clothes lining his studio apartment. And the White Sox comforter that Charlie had given him as a gag gift? The comforter he flaunted while telling people it was from his brother, who was "in the shit"? He hadn't washed that in a long time, if ever.

What he didn't want to think about was Charlie. Home again. He didn't want to think about how during the first twenty-two years of his life Charlie had all but ignored him, stopping only to laugh at his mismatched outfits or lack of plans on a Friday night. In those days, before Barkley established a wall of defense against those who judged who was and wasn't cool, he had simply retreated to his bedroom and his books: Hemingway and Yeats, Salinger and Faulkner—well, maybe Faulkner had gotten the best of him, but the rest he'd read. It would have been easier if that had been how it stayed, if Charlie had left and there had been no relationship at all, no sibling bond, just emptiness, absence. But during those weeks last summer between AIT and first duty, when Barkley was decompressing after college graduation, a switch flipped. Charlie started taking him to rooftop parties and small-venue concerts in the city, shooting hoops with him on their parents' net-less, garage-mounted backboard, even reading his poorly written short stories about goblins and knights—feigning interest, maybe. For a long time after Charlie shipped out, Barkley hoped he had actually earned his brother's acceptance, that he was suddenly a better, more interesting sibling. And he was, wasn't he? College was where he met his largest group of friends, when he started drinking, when he finally had something to do on Fridays, although there was no older brother around to prove it to. Barkley remembered one June night in particular before Charlie left, when he answered all his questions. They were shooting hoops, playing H-O-R-S-E, and Barkley, finally, was winning. He had his brother down to the last letter.

"You letting me win?" Barkley asked. The spotlights on the garage illuminated the asphalt driveway, and made the acrylic backboard shine and glare.

"Nope," Charlie said, his voice raw as ever. He dribbled absentmindedly between his legs, fluid without even trying. And then he threw up a shot that careened off the top of the backboard.

"What the hell was that?" Barkley whined. "I want to beat you for real."

Charlie said nothing. There was a wall of evergreens at the edge of the driveway, separating their house from the other lots, and Charlie stepped back until he was against the needles, until all Barkley saw was a shadow.

Barkley retrieved the ball and tried to pinpoint where his brother was standing. Everything around the glowing driveway was ink.

"Charlie?"

His brother never showed real emotion. Always he joked, mocking himself, mocking others, physical comedy or verbal comedy—none of it mattered. He was witty in a way that Barkley could only try to capture on paper, through stories that still didn't do his brother justice. But as Barkley approached the line of trees, he saw that Charlie was seated, looking out at the road, at the distant flare of a streetlight.

"Charlie?"

His brother finally looked. His shaggy dark hair was gone now, his face shaved, his eyes like black marbles.

"I've got this feeling," Charlie said.

Barkley waited. His brother had joined the army spontaneously, as he did many things, but had managed to make his decision appear like the only natural course of action. Real men served. Heroes were being made every day. It was a privilege to be an American. Barkley's parents had never spouted such talk, but that's the type of person Charlie was. He got ideas, believed in them, made others believe in them, too. And then, unlike the rest of the family, he followed through.

Charlie shook his head in the darkness. "I know something is going to happen, Bark. I feel it. Every day I feel it. At night I can almost hold it."

"What's going to happen?"

Charlie looked out at the streetlight. He frowned and crinkled up his eyes.

Barkley sat next to him, felt the wet grass on his rear and the needles of the evergreens against the back of his head. "What's going to happen?"

"Change. Something. I can't describe it." He massaged his eyes. "I have no idea what I'm doing, you know that?"

Barkley laughed. "Yeah, you do. I've heard your speeches on why you have to serve. Almost made me want to join."

Charlie picked a handful of grass from the ground, held it up to his mouth, and harshly blew it away. "Don't be stupid."

"I'm just saying—"

"Everything is going to change, Bark. I don't know how or what. I feel strong. I feel ready. I'm a surgeon with the fucking M4. But there's this feeling."

"It's going to be fine," Barkley said. "You're going to have like fifty pounds of medals."

"It's waiting for me—that's what I know. And I'm trying to fix what I can before it gets here."

Barkley knew his brother had fixed a couple of things already. He had gone out to Hinsdale to apologize to Karen Simon, his ex-girlfriend, a nice girl whom Barkley thought Charlie had broken up with too quickly. He paid their father back most of the money he'd lent, sent an e-mail to an old teacher, even cleaned the gutters on the house. But Barkley saw that the biggest thing Charlie had fixed was them. They were finally— what? It was okay to say it. They were brothers. And he didn't know how he felt about that, or what to say, but before long his brother was gone, across the ocean and in the shit, and the hollow feeling of his absence said it for him. All Barkley could do was wonder, every night under the weight of that White Sox comforter, if that thing waiting for his brother had found him yet.

Focus on Ginny, Barkley thought as the train rattled and swerved.

Charlie was going to be fine. He stared into his BlackBerry's tiny screen. Ginny. Focus. Maybe she shared the same last name as his teacher. He typed in *Ginny Doring*, and Facebook gave him two results, one of which depicted a middle-aged woman hugging an old man at a Greyhound bus stop, the other a close-up of a timeworn Raggedy Ann doll. Both of those had to be fails, unless Ginny thought a weird, obsolete doll's head would garner a laugh—come to think of it, maybe it was her. She would probably describe Raggedy Ann as vintage.

His BlackBerry beeped: a friend request.

"I'll be damned," Barkley said, causing the suit-and-tie businessman to frown at him. Unbelievably, Ginny had just friended him. He tried to remember the last time a female had sent him a friend request.

"Ginny Morton," Barkley said, sounding the words out. He felt the businessman watching him again.

Her profile picture was of a dark, backlit stage in midconcert. There were four musicians on it, one of whom had an arsenal of cymbals and drums and appeared to be banging away. Looked like it was all chicks. There were purple lights streaming down from the ceiling, and Barkley found what had to be Ginny on the right side, holding up an electric guitar, in the middle of a Pete Townshend power strum. Barkley chuckled to himself. He couldn't see her face clearly but imagined that it matched the mock seriousness of her rock-and-roll pose.

What else? Her band name was the Flaming Nostrils. Nostrils, he said to himself. Kind of a gross word. Flaming worked, except it copied directly off the Flaming Lips, simply choosing a different part of the face. He wondered if they were a Flaming Lips cover band, but hoped not—cover bands were notoriously uncool unless they were fucking flawless. He clicked on *Info* and checked out her likes—this was a big one—God forbid she watched reality TV on any channel but Bravo. But look here, Barkley thought. Favorite TV shows: *The Wire, Californication, Futurama.* Interesting. Wasn't that last show the cartoon that was forever being canceled and uncanceled? He pictured Ginny watching cartoons. A bowl of cereal in her lap and matching four-leaf-clover pajamas, the top two buttons of her shirt undone. And then he pictured his hand crawling forward like a pink spider, lifting open that flap of cloth—

"Now approaching Downers Grove," the voice on the speaker said, bringing Barkley back to reality, away from Ginny's shirt.

Barkley swung open the screened back door of the family's powder-blue Cape Cod, and there he was—back where everything started. His mother was at the stove in a kitchen lined with maple cabinets and stainless steel, one pot bubbling with a thick broth of meats and sauce, the other boiling water and linguine. Barkley dropped his overnight bag on the floor.

"Barkley!" she cooed. She held a wooden ladle up in the air. "Want to try?"

"Where's Charlie?"

"Upstairs," his mother said. "Give him space."

"Where am I sleeping?"

"Your old room is filled with boxes," his mother said. She was still as tiny as ever, almost like a pixie. She moved from the stainless steel fridge to the maple cabinets and back to the fridge before finally settling at the stove again. If anything, age was making her move faster, as if she were reaching the end of a race.

"So . . . couch? I get to take the family room couch? Score."

"Yes, you do. Hold on, honey." And she let go of a wooden ladle and ran forward to give him a hug. "How are you? Have you sent any work out yet? Any new stories?"

"Eh," Barkley said. "Nothing is ready yet."

"Any news on the interview?"

"The phone interview? No, still waiting."

"What about that intramural football league? Didn't you say you were going to do that, sign up, get some exercise? You could wear your old high school uniform—I still have it upstairs. Number twenty-four, right?"

"Right, Mom, twenty-four. That old uniform would be great."

In truth, he'd played only one game of varsity football during his time at Downers North High School, and that was because both Tommy Gardocki *and* Lenny Spatz were injured. He remembered wearing a helmet that seemed too loose, feeling it slide back and forth across his grimy cheeks, stirring up fresh trails of acne. His face would clear up later, by the end of high school, but not before he had lived through a dermatological house of horrors—worst on the memory list were all those secret trips he made to the bathroom, hoping to apply Retin-A face cream across skin that looked covered in barnacles.

He'd finished that day with three tackles. And yet, looking back, more than the smell of the wet grass and mud that was stuck to his face mask, more than the defensive huddles brought together by barking alpha males he could barely understand, Barkley remembered cursing himself out, berating his ever-monologuing mind—why can't I shut myself off and just play? Why can't I stop remembering that Dad is watching in the stands and that I don't want to get hit and that every play holds the risk of looking like a total idiot? And everyone around him—every single person on that testosterone-soaked field—seemed to shut off their minds just fine.

He left the kitchen and wandered toward the fringes of the living room, which was unchanged—in fact, it seemed that not even a stray pencil or discarded *Chicago* magazine had moved since he was a freshman in high school, over eight years ago. The L-shaped couch, made of wrinkled, milk chocolate leather, faced the far end of the vaulted room, across from which stood the rectangular coffee table, with an underlying shelf that held more expired magazines. Barkley saw an *Entertainment Weekly* from January 2010, *Rolling Stone* from August 2009. It wasn't that his mother didn't clean, Barkley thought, it was that she took a degree of comfort in certain things staying the same. And Barkley saw wisdom in that, too. A lot of things she did were absurd—her stubborn optimism in the face of failure, for instance, and the fact that she refused to acknowledge that Dad's leaving was a bad thing, a wrong thing. Pictures of them together were still up around the house, posing in front of red-bricked college campuses, trailing wakes of autumn leaves, more evidence of her stubborn refusal to accept reality. But the way she left the living room? There was a comforting nostalgia to that. It was like walking into the museum of his childhood. And even though his childhood hadn't necessarily made him happy, he still took comfort in the evidence that it existed, that it was *his*, and that other people had shared memories of that same, self-contained space.

He padded over to the coffee table, picked up the remote, and flicked on the television. His mother still hadn't gone for a flat screen, opting instead for a converter box, and that was a part of the living room that didn't have to stay the same. Their old Sony model had a big enough screen, maybe forty-two inches, but it had the girth and weight of a loaded safe. Dense wooden paneling made up the television's frame, adding even more to its absurd heaviness.

"Mom," he called into the kitchen, "you've got to get up-to-date with the television. Have you seen my LED? Fifty inches. And it weighs like ten pounds."

"I'm focusing on remodeling the bathroom, honey."

Barkley sighed and sank into the folds of the couch. The television's picture finally came to life and revealed the scrolling headlines of CNN. Images of the tsunami in Japan flooded the screen, and Barkley watched a helicopter-eye view of water rushing through tiny streets, picking up compact cars and vans as if they were cardboard boxes. The disaster had happened in March, he thought—and they were still talking about the clean-up strategy. No quick fixes to be found.

"Who's been watching CNN?" Barkley said. "Mom, are you watching those political talk shows again?"

Barkley felt a nagging awareness in the back of his head, a knowledge that Charlie was actually home, in this house, drifting around upstairs, *staying upstairs*—but why? They were hiding something from him. A conspiracy. And then he heard a door open above him and felt his entire body go rigid.

Charlie. He heard footsteps above; the living room ceiling creaked. A throat cleared. Knobs turned and water ran. Barkley wanted to shout hello, to bound up the stairs like a Labrador retriever, but stopped himself. The water went off. He heard the ceiling creak again, but only once. Charlie was just standing there. Barkley sat frozen, unable to operate. He decided to count to twenty, and if Charlie was still standing, he'd go upstairs and see him. But by the time he got to fifteen, the bedroom door had closed again.

The smell of pasta and Italian sausage drifted into the living room. Barkley flipped from channel to channel. Comcast SportsNet was flashing the pregame introductions for the White Sox–Indians Friday night game in Cleveland, which the rain, moving east, had delayed. Charlie would want to watch it, of course. For Barkley, the only sport that had any measure of relevance was basketball. He was only ten when Michael

Jordan's Chicago Bulls won their final championship in 1998, but it was Charlie's fanatical devotion—his door-framed poster of Pippen's dunk on Ewing in '94, his Dennis Rodman bobbleheads and color-changing collectors mugs, his VHS collection of taped games during the 1996 championship season—that made Barkley the stout follower of the Chicago Bulls that he was. He had a vague self-awareness regarding his lack of *knowledge* about basketball, an inability to describe plays and sets and zone defenses, and even accurately fathom what a pick-and-roll was, but he did appreciate the rhythm of the game. It was constant, it was fluid, it was exciting—unlike baseball, which was like golf with meathead posturing. Baseball he couldn't do. It didn't matter how much Charlie loved the White Sox or his father brayed about the Cubs.

Barkley thought again about the stray pictures around the house. It was infuriating, really, to see that his father still existed in this home, on coffee tables and wall frames, his mother displaying his likeness as if he were a wild game trophy. In the family room, there was a picture on the entertainment center to the right of the TV, a picture of his father holding a wriggling barracuda off the coast of Florida, surrounded by choppy green water. His father—tan, muscled, shaggy-haired, and smiling, everything Barkley was not—had a spare arm slung around his mother, who leaned against his tropical shirt as if he contained all the world's supply of warmth and joy. The picture must have been from the 1980s, or at most, the early 1990s. College sweethearts, married for more than thirty years, and then gone. And Dad wasn't just gone but *never in the house*. On the occasions when he'd come to pick Barkley up last summer, his father had idled by the curb, the black Mercedes purring, the windows tinted. And no one punished him for leaving. Certainly not his mother.

And, thinking about his father and the overall ignorance that permeated the house, Barkley stood up, walked over to the entertainment center, and snatched up the picture of his father with the barracuda. He had the pleasant idea of smashing it, of watching the glass shatter like ice around his feet, but something like that wouldn't destroy the picture, just the frame. Instead he tucked it under his arm and walked up the stairs toward the second floor. He reached the landing, considered his choices, thought about what he was trying to do. Just hiding the picture would be enough. Ahead of him was the hallway leading to the master bedroom, to the right was the entrance to his old room, congested with the shadows of boxes, and to the left and back was Charlie's abode. His brother. His brother was home and still hadn't come downstairs. Barkley, staring at the whitewashed door of his older brother's bedroom, carried the barracuda picture over and placed his hand on the knob. Who said he couldn't just say hello? It's what he would have done in the past, anyway. He turned the knob.

The door clicked and the wood moved outward a crack. Barkley could tell it was dark in there. He felt his heart rev up. He clutched the picture of his father against his chest, considered pulling the door closed, leaving Charlie to whatever he was doing in that darkness. But instead, Barkley peered into the room, his pulse quickening with something akin to danger.

It took him a moment to properly focus. The light was off. Charlie's bed was made, unoccupied, untouched—he hadn't even slept in it yet. But there, at the other end of the room: his brother. Charlie was on his knees, bent over prayerlike in front of a wooden stool. And there were two candles lit on either side, bouncing twin shadows of Charlie across the opposing walls. On the middle of the stool was an object. Barkley craned his neck in, mindful of the floorboard just outside the door that creaked. The object on the stool was a key chain. A red, plastic key chain.

His older brother was bent down in a kind of trance. Normally he jumped at any sound within hearing distance, but he hadn't even heard him open the door and remained hunkered over, his muscled body in a perpetual flex, hands folded in front of that key chain. Barkley noticed that as close as his hands were to the object, they did not touch it. He pulled the door shut slowly, a strange bubbling rising in the pit of his stomach. The picture frame felt heavy. There was a chill beneath his skin as he walked down the staircase and back into the living room. He placed the picture of his father, as it was, back on the entertainment center. He thought about Charlie, up there with the candles and the key chain and the prayer. He knew now that his brother had been right. Whatever had been waiting for Charlie had finally found him.

THE CORNER POCKET

Charlie lay flat on the floor beside his bed, welcoming the stiffness underneath his legs and back—lumbar support for the formerly enlisted. Everything he did now, postservice, was compared not to the experiences of his buddies (though JB had been talkative) but to wartime classics like *The Deer Hunter*, followed by one caveat—don't become the Christopher Walken guy, don't become the Christopher Walken guy! That would be a nightmare. But thinking about extremes was a good way to put his current state in perspective, to metaphysically minimize. *Honey, I Shrunk the Soldier's Guilt?* Sign him up. And in regard to the Christopher Walken guy: was he a mind-fucked idiot who, rather than reintegrating with society, disappeared into a third world gambling pit of Russian roulette? No, he wasn't that bad. Not even close. Given what had occurred, he wasn't that bad at all. He'd made deals with himself, promises he intended to keep, and that was that. Move on. That's what people in the modern world did. They moved on.

He closed his eyes, listened to the gurgle of pipes, the clatter of kitchen pots, the shuffle of Barkley's footsteps across the living room floor. It was important, he thought, to reconnect to the Charlie that existed before deployment. He wanted all of them to recognize him, see the same old joking hotshot that had left—or at least think they did. But it wasn't easy. Every time he closed his eyes, he saw the mountains, the highway, the car, the key chain. Ridiculous, really—he should just keep his eyes open, then. He should stay awake all night every night, especially if sleeping meant he'd have bush-league montages running through his skull. Jesus! But he was tired. And wherever his old self used to be, he now sensed only frayed wires, snipped away without permission.

Charlie felt his father inside him sometimes. It was a strength-giving thing, but worrisome. It became obvious during high school, and even then, he could see that however much of himself was Henry Brunson, that much of Barkley was not. Charlie hounded his younger brother for this comical deficiency, for his lack of focus, for his misunderstanding of social cues and machismo, all the while knowing Barkley possessed some internal function he himself did not. And what it was, Charlie couldn't always pinpoint. It wasn't an understanding of the physical world. Charlie had played Division III college basketball, while Barkley barely knew how to watch it. It wasn't intelligence—Charlie knew he was smart, he saw the grades, all those A's and standardized test scores scrolling across his brain like a NASDAQ report. Sense of humor? He had that in spades! Every girl he'd dated said he was *hilarious*. But what else could he be missing? Imagination? Maybe. He didn't write stories; didn't see the need to write stories when he could instead be experiencing life first-hand. Reality was the nucleus of all experience. All stories spawned from it, reacted to it, escaped from it, embraced it. So why not be at the center? Despite this thinking, he did have at least a modest grasp of what imagination could produce, and greatly appreciated television and film for the kaleidoscopic places they took the viewer. He even had that college movie review blog with Bobby Leeds, his four-year roommate—a buddy, incidentally, whose dreamy intellect and focus on the cosmos reminded him of Barkley.

The review blog was called *Cue Mark Reviews*. In 2001 at Augustana, he and Leeds were so transformed by a freshman film elective that every night the house parties ended with near-apocalyptic arguments about the medium. Once that tenth beer kicked in, they'd violently discuss which flicks held merit over others, which modern sagas exploited the classics, which acting performances were timeless and complex, while others were harnessed strictly to their time period. While Charlie yelled about De Niro in *Raging Bull*, Bobby offered him Marcello Mastroianni in *8½*. For every Brando in *Last Tango*, Bobby fired back a Maria Falconetti in *The Passion of Joan of Arc*. And if anyone listening disagreed, they were wrong. He and Bobby got into shouting matches about low-angle shots and dolly shots, about floodlights and Steadicams, all with other freshmen who didn't know any better. They skewered the sophomoric cinematography of summer action movies the other students loved, and lauded decade-old indie films they had never heard of. It was poor sport, really, just unfair. Like Green Berets attacking grunts. The issue, as always, was setting their sights higher.

By February of their sophomore year, he and Leeds sat down and began brainstorming a movie review site. They anchored themselves to their rickety kitchen table and took days to figure out the blogging basics, weeks to finally get the thing up and running. Leeds chain-smoked Marlboro Reds and fortified himself with a moat of prelaw textbooks, while Charlie nursed a Rolling Rock and punched keys on his grungy laptop—he was taking it easy during basketball season, trying to up his 10.9 points per game average at shooting guard. It was Charlie who eventually christened the blog *Cue Mark Reviews*. Why? A cue mark was the industry nickname for the tiny dot used to signal the projectionist to change reels. And after a week of sketching and finagling, followed by the recruitment of a taciturn graphic arts major, they developed a blog insignia that seemed visually appropriate: a cartoon pool cue shooting an eight ball onto a billiard table, in which all the other balls gazed upward, watching a drive-in movie. It was, as his mother said, *cute*.

Charlie and Bobby weren't sure how much to play up the billiard angle of the blog title but eventually decided on going full throttle—anything less simply wouldn't be memorable. Why not ramp up the double meanings, Charlie suggested. Continue the cue mark and billiard angle into oblivion! And so, as the blog traffic and message board posts spread like wildfire, Charlie decided he should become skilled at pool. It was the Henry Brunson in him—simply deciding to be good at something. Even as he began practicing, however, Charlie realized it was all another excuse, an excuse to dive headfirst into yet another endeavor and turn it inside out, looking for an answer. And so what? He went ahead and enlisted Hank Schumacher, the old pool shark who hovered on the second floor of the Blue Cat Brew Pub, right along Eighteenth Street, overlooking the river. For thirty bucks an hour every Tuesday and Thursday, Charlie took lessons from the old man, listening as he mumbled through handfuls of peanuts, yet offered the wisdom of a grizzled assassin on green felt. Charlie learned how everything in billiards was math, all a constant restructuring of algorithms and geometry and velocity. With chalk on his hands, he learned inside English and outside English, stop shots and throw shots, draw shots and double hits, and he knocked away at his targets while outside, the big, gray Mississippi River flowed.

They kept *Cue Mark Reviews* going past college. The war films were Charlie's favorites—taking him to a place he literally couldn't go, and doing so with such visceral cinematography that he was sure the real thing was so much more. He could put every cinematic angle into a Petri dish, he could examine the trajectories of techniques that depicted the carnage over the years, he could compare the similar tactics in *The Battle of Algiers* (1966) to *Saving Private Ryan* (1998), but he still couldn't *know*. He couldn't turn war inside out, not like he had done with billiards and basketball and film. There was no Hank Schumacher stationed in a river view pub, waiting to teach him about some previously unknowable experience. Moments in battle, being shot at, *shooting back*. And why did he feel the need for it? What was the answer he was looking for? He never had gathered that completely. Discovering the answer, he figured, would let him know more about the question.

He knew one thing: the war movies hinted at an experience only a certain percentage of humans had been privy to—terrible, in many ways, but not all, a sort of heightened living that was not possible in any other context. Watching them, he obsessed over the nature of this one particular experience that could never be known, unless witnessed firsthand. None of the movies were anything close to prowar; in fact, many showed the horror of war and the psychological fracturing that was sure to occur. But Charlie couldn't stop considering how it was impossible to turn war inside out, to understand why people like him felt a calling for it. The most intense experience men and women—no, mostly men, *mainly men*—could have in life, however troublesome, however horrifying, and he didn't have it. Instead he was taking a management training course in Mundelein, Illinois.

"Dinner's ready!" his mother called, breaking him out of his trance.

He was still on the floor, looking up at the darkened ceiling. He felt a sharp twinge in his right hand—the same hand that had been injured in the bomb blast in what felt like years ago. He thought back to that feeling of being carried away by the men, the guilt of it, yet the buried thrill that it was actually happening to him—that he was finally experiencing *something*. He remembered praying that nothing was damaged beyond repair, and then feeling disappointed when it turned out he hadn't really been hurt at all. Because that was part of war, wasn't it? The injury? The battle scar? Strange. He did have the tinnitus—an auditory memento that could last a lifetime. He felt his hand curl into a fist.

"Charlie!" his mother called.

"Just hold on a second!" he bellowed, eyes open in the darkness. "I'm almost ready!"

Don't be the Christopher Walken guy, he thought again. Don't be the cliché. No broken soldier returning home after war, no sob stories, no bullshit—it was 2011, for Christ's sake, not 1946. In his room, the candles flickered. The key chain was still on the stool, but he wouldn't think of that, *couldn't* think of that. To think of the key chain would pull him away from the old Charlie, basketball Charlie, movie-watching Charlie, crystal-clear-vision Charlie.

Rewind to preenlistment, postcollege. In Chicago, in a Wicker Park condo his father had helped him pay for, Charlie read war books intermittently (but not enough), signed up for intramural volleyball at North Avenue Beach in the summer, flag football under Lincoln Park's silver-lit grasses during the fall, and basketball, of course, year-round—pickup games and indoor skirmishes and even free throw contests (when his brother was around). He had done all these things, had stayed in decent shape, taken Karen out to the "Best New Restaurants" listed in *Chicago* magazine, kept up with the indie films and the Academy Award nominees, even visited the summer art fairs that smelled like paint and corn dogs. And his father, from the top of some ivory obelisk in which he pulled the strings of Chicago's businesses, had bartered to get him a management position at Lucent Technologies. Charlie already had the condo. He had the movie collection. The job was waiting for him—he just needed to take the corporate training course out in Mundelein. And then . . . what? Charlie realized one night, a night when he woke up covered in icy sweat, a feeling of terror in his throat, that there was no *what*. This was all there was.

Charlie had paced from room to room in his barren condominium, across cushioned, vanilla carpeting, past mahogany bookshelves and DVD libraries, out to the big windows that looked onto the frozen skyline of Chicago. The buildings out there glowed, but they seemed so cold, so vacant, so set in stone, that he honest-to-God felt dead already. This was all there was. Charlie would accept the job at Lucent—a great job by all accounts—and he would work there for four to five years, his father said, before bartering for another position and moving up yet again. And the corporate climb would continue. His father would meet him for lunch in the Loop once a week. He'd marry Karen, because Karen had always been there. He'd have two children, move to Arlington Heights or back to Downers Grove, get the kids into good suburban schools with strong athletic programs, and find a nice house amid all the others. His children would go to Midwestern universities. They would follow his lead, as he had followed his father's. And then Charlie would grow old, streaks of gray in his dark hair, wrinkles and bags emerging under his eyes. He'd retire at sixty-two. The high point would be the yearly trip to the Bahamas or Tuscany with Karen, who would have also grown old, and even more tired of him than she was now. They would have silent dinners in romantic corners of Florence, they would sip house Chianti that waiters poured from quaint, ceramic pitchers while looking past each other, into backlit side streets, anything but eye contact, anything but an acknowledgment that this was all there was, the eating and drinking and corporate climbing and retirement, anything but accepting that they were reaching the end of a road that had given them nothing. Charlie had looked out onto that Chicago skyline, and that feeling of terror had stayed with him, burrowed into his heart. Yet the next day, the next week, the next month, he'd done nothing. Changed nothing. He began taking the management training course in Mundelein. He studied for it in a plastic purple binder with colored tabs. He took Karen to the "Best New Restaurants." Had a nice dish: wood-grilled octopus. And all he felt, from movie to meal to purple binder, was a slow, boiling terror.

It was a couple of months after the feeling started when Barkley, back from college during summer break, called him and said that Dad was acting weird. Walking in and leaving. Not coming home.

"What do you mean, not coming home?" Charlie said. He sat on the edge of his almond comforter, looking out at the skyscrapers as the sun went down and reflected off their sides. The television was running in the living room—Karen watching a reality show on Creole cooking.

"I mean," Barkley said, "Dad's gone. Like all the time. It's insanely weird."

Charlie heard the voice in the living room proclaim crawfish as the chicken of the bayou. "I'm not sure what you're telling me," he said. "I'm going to need more than that. Are you telling me that he's staying at a hotel? At the office? Is he traveling for business?"

"No. I don't think so. He comes home sometimes after work. Goes upstairs and changes clothes, like I don't know, *going-out* clothes. Puts on cologne. Doesn't say hello. Then he leaves."

"Doesn't even say hello to you?"

"No. Not usually."

"What the hell? Does he have dinner?"

"No, dude, he does not have dinner. Can't you understand what I'm saying?"

Charlie felt the terror lodge itself deeper in his throat. He took a breath. "You're saying that they're separating. Or separated. Is that what you're saying?"

"Charlie, I don't fucking *know*. Why do you think I'm calling you?"

The Sears Tower, which would soon become the Willis Tower, straddled the skyline and pointed its twin white horns toward the reddening clouds. He didn't know what to say—he felt he knew nothing, had no skills in this department.

"Charlie?"

"Yeah, kid, I'm here. How you doing with all this?"

"I'm fine. Been hanging out with the college friends. But Mom's acting weird. Mom is home, like, all the time now. She keeps rearranging those old albums from when they lived in Evanston. Says she has to go grocery shopping but doesn't pull the trigger."

"Just sits in the house?"

"Yep."

"Jesus," Charlie said. He ran his hands through his shaggy hair. Someone on the television said *gator stew* and chuckled heartily.

"So what do we do?"

"It's okay," Charlie said. "I'll handle this. I'll talk to Dad."

"Go for it," Barkley said. "It'll be a miracle if he says anything."

"He'll talk."

In the Stan, there had still been times when Charlie, in his hooch, woke up in blind darkness, at 0500 or even 0400, and expected to look out from his mattress and see that frozen Chicago skyline looking back, and have the old terror return, the idea that he'd done nothing with himself, that this was all there was. But then he remembered that he *had* done something, had done a good thing and was serving his country, putting his life on the line, and felt that flood of relief, relief that he'd escaped the path of his father, that he'd paid him back for the condo loan, that he'd finished things with Karen, that he'd escaped from the mine cart track that had been laid before him. His father, who, after leaving their mother, had proved that the set track really didn't work at all. And he was finally experiencing that elusive thing, that violent adventure that many men felt a calling for, whether it was real or imagined. But the problem, really, was that Afghanistan was no place to be. And the other problem, the thing he'd only said to Barkley, was that something was waiting for him out there in the mountains. Something big.

In his bedroom, Charlie finally stood up. He had to go down there, go down and hope that the old instincts and jokes kicked in like muscle memory, that his mother and brother could, at least for this night, think they were spending time with the person they'd known. Outside his window, Charlie saw two of those idiot neighbor kids, the Waltons—in middle school when he left but now in high school—running across the front yard with what looked like cheap firecrackers. *After* the Fourth of July, of all times. Fuck. Where had he left his earplugs? He stood up and went to the bedside table, but in the corner of his eye, he could already see the sparks flying, then heard the *pop, pop, POP, POP* snapping up into the ether, and felt his hands automatically slap the sides of his face.

Charlie was immediately struck by the ringing in his ear, a microscopic version of the cymbal crash he'd experienced during the explosion. The buzzing started in his left ear and then connected to the right, and the two sounds reached a kind of pugilistic harmony, a persistent whine, like the relentless call of the cicadas he'd heard as a child, when there were so many the driveway seemed to writhe. In Afghanistan, Doc had called it tinnitus—Charlie was amazed that there really was a name for everything. And when was the ringing going to stop? Doc had hesitated then, smiled patiently. It might not be something that goes away. Tinnitus was often permanent. The key, he said, was to layer the sounds, to create an auditory harmony of a different pitch, something to drown out the low, buzzing whine. Charlie had asked him what the hell would do that, and Doc had replied, music would do it, distant gunfire would do it, but at night, the best thing was likely a tiny bedside fan. The rotation of the blades created a much more pleasing hum, a hum that was external, that would be capable of equalizing the tinnitus while he tried to sleep. Turn it on medium, he'd said, it shouldn't require much more. And, in truth, after he picked up a fan it *had* worked, and the whir of the blades was actually pleasant, another reminder of early childhood nights. But times like now, when the buzzing drone came back, Charlie realized he couldn't escape it, no matter where he went, that the buzz was *inside* him, and no other harmonies could send it away.

When the firecrackers stopped and Charlie realized he wasn't going to chase the Walton kids down and pummel them, he packed away the key chain, blew out the candles, and walked downstairs for dinner. He thought to himself, once more, like a mantra: *please, please, please, at least for tonight—don't be the Christopher Walken guy.*

MUSEUMS ARE
CRUMBLING

"Guys, last time, let's go! Dinner's ready!" Julie called, busying herself by setting ceramic plates around the Formica table. The table, she thought, was one of those relics that didn't match the rest of the updated kitchen, but like many things, it would have to wait. Bathroom first, then kitchen table, then maybe that old vault of a television out in the family room. She heard Barkley rustle against the folds of the living room couch—food got him moving every time.

Maybe at one point, when Henry was here, she didn't demand that her children *always* help her set the table, or offer to clean up, or do any of those things she knew children were supposed to do—either intrinsically or through meticulous training—for their mothers. But now, on her own and expecting at least a shred of attention and respect, the lack of care made her want to scream. Sure, Charlie had just returned. She got that. She understood. But they both knew the drill. And just because she didn't have a career (that dream long deserted) and received a hefty stipend from Henry didn't mean she wasn't still entitled to those two things: respect and attention. Hadn't she built up enough credit over the years that she could cash in on it now?

Then there was Henry. He still didn't understand why Charlie was mad at him, believed that anything he had done to his wife should have no effect on his sons—zero, zilch! *Our marriage is none of their business*, he'd said, sounding genuinely offended. And it was clear now that Henry wasn't going to show, not for dinner and not for the night. She'd left him three voice mails, each increasingly desperate, even though she knew that the more he heard that tone in her voice, the further away he went. But she couldn't help it. She didn't have time for mind games when her children were involved. And where was that anger she used to have? Her younger self would have been roaring, cursing him out, even driving to Chicago to chase him down. But now? The fuel gauge felt empty. And on the inside—nothing but the scuttling sounds of all those ingredients.

Barkley ambled in, wearing a striped blue polo that was at least two years old and which, she thought, made him look a little bit like a beach ball. He noticed both pots simmering on the stove and inhaled the steam, wafting it toward his face. He really needed some exercise, she thought—consistent, aerobic exercise. And he needed to cash in on that teaching job.

"Charlie!" she called again, still unsure of the protocol with her older son. She knew only muted facts about his service—he had been injured early but soon after recovered. Yet rather than relief, Julie took it as a preemptive warning about his total vulnerability. How else was a mother supposed to take news like this? One month in, her son nearly torn apart by an IED, no one telling her why? She found herself watching hours of CNN for headlines and updates, following the blogs of rogue embedded reporters, and seeking out every low-budget documentary she could find. She woke up in the middle of most nights gasping, checking her phone, knowing that for Charlie, it was nearly ten hours ahead, it was day, and he was walking somewhere, rifle on shoulder, sun overhead, enemies in the rocks and the huts and the caves above. How could anyone sleep, knowing this? She found herself perpetually sure that he would be dead one morning, dead any minute, that she would rise to find his gruesome execution video plastered on YouTube, one million hits and

zero good-byes. Later, when Charlie was sent into the mountain out-
posts, she was sent into another delirium—especially after seeing that
horrifying documentary of chaos, *Restrepo*, at a theater in Downers
Grove. Eventually, the only answer was to force her mind away, away
from Charlie and Henry and her own inertia and the sense of what could
and would be lost. There were ways to do this, countless ways to forget—
she simply had to choose the best one. And knowing the forces that
had ransacked her life, was anyone really going to blame her?

Charlie had finally left those mountains—still intact, she knew, still
alive—and it was there that an event had occurred. What it was she wasn't
quite sure. He had called her about it from all those miles away. He'd
told her that something had happened, and that she shouldn't question
him about it. He made her promise. Was he hurt? No, he said, he wasn't
hurt. Then he told her he was coming home.

"Mom, what kind of meat is this? Italian sausage, right?"

"Yes," she said. She tried to focus. "That's right, Italian sausage."

"From where, Jewel? Have you been to Mariano's, Mom? That's where
you get the best meat. Just an FYI. I think I'm going to learn to grill this
summer."

She nodded, felt her eyes close. She'd just been thinking about—documentaries. IEDs. Her son. A series of strange popping sounds came from
outside the house.

When she'd finally found Charlie at the airport, a good minute had
elapsed before she realized she couldn't breathe, so strong was her son's
embrace. *That's a good sign*, she'd told herself as he put his luggage into
the car. *A good sign that he's come back whole.* And then, on the ride home,
he'd pressed his face against the glass and barely said a word.

It reminded her, in its own strange way, of the studio.

In college, when her skill as a dancer had reached its zenith, Julie had
always felt that silence was its own form of communication. And silence
with movement—fast and slow, rising and crashing—not only had aesthetic value, but communicated depths of the human condition. Because
of this, what worried her about Charlie wasn't his silence, but his im-
mobility. Since the moment she'd picked him up today, he'd been a heavy
thing, inanimate, a darkened stool in the corner of a room. She tried to
feel the cotton balls. Who was she to be thinking about dance again,

anyway? It was long gone now, traded in for the other realities of life, of motherhood, of so-called domestic bliss. The image of the studio, and the movements inside it, were little more than mementos of a past self, of the yearnings and curiosities of her youth. Both of them were emptied now, replaced with broken things.

At Northwestern, Melanie had been the one dancer anywhere close to her skill level, and became her best friend for all of college and the many decades after. She was the one whom Julie would call in these times of inertia and confusion, these times of heaving sadness, and whom she wanted to call right now. And yet, just two weeks ago, Julie had sat down in the kitchen and realized that, quite simply, she and Melanie were no longer speaking. The water had been running in the sink, filling the room with liquid static. She couldn't comprehend how it had happened. There had been no fight with Melanie, no anger, no geographical separation (she still lived in Evanston), no *nothing*. But it had happened just the same. Julie had picked up the phone, held it, brought it to her ear, and realized that she couldn't even dial Melanie's number. This crucial friend, this confidante, this SOS to the outside world. Gone. They'd moved on as the years passed, space and air between them, two ships that years ago seemed parallel and then somehow drifted, docking in solitary waters.

Upstairs a bedroom door opened and closed, footsteps sounded, and Julie jolted back from her reverie. She watched Barkley sit down quickly at the kitchen table. The sound of Charlie's bare feet falling against cedar planks, the rhythm of it, the *something*, made Barkley seem to shrink and shrivel up, a human raisin. Barkley's cheeks paled and became ghostly white as the sound approached the kitchen, and Julie became worried that something was honest-to-God wrong with Barkley, when her elder son burst into the room.

He wore a maroon T-shirt that hugged the sides of his chest, the sleeves ending just past his deltoids, causing the extension cord veins of his biceps to swell on proud display. Yet his jawline, once chiseled and masculine, now looked simply gaunt. The meticulous crew cut from basic training appeared haphazard and even half-assed, and his stomach wasn't so much defined as sunken-in. He'd shipped out like a cyborg, she remembered—more than a man. He'd come back as something else.

He slammed both hands down on Barkley's shoulders. "Little brother!" he shouted, with an edge in his voice Julie couldn't pinpoint. "How are you, buddy?"

Barkley turned, stammering, unable to make eye contact. "Good, you know, I'm good, how's everything with you? It's great to see you, of course. How was life in the, uh, in the, uh, in the desert?"

Charlie raised an eyebrow. "I was in the mountains, genius."

"You're not thinking of Iraq, are you?" Julie asked.

"No! No, I am not thinking of Iraq. I thought you took a trip into the poppy fields at some point."

"True, little brother," Charlie said, giving a finger point, "I did. That's correct. It slipped my mind. I'm a bit of a jumbled mess these days. Think *A Beautiful Mind*. Russell Crowe doesn't have shit on me right now."

Barkley turned to his mother. "You see? I was right. Poppies cover the desert floor over there."

"Boom," Charlie said. "You got it. You were right."

Julie stepped in. "How about a hug from you two?"

She watched as Charlie grabbed Barkley and hauled him to his feet. He put his younger brother in a rough headlock, slapped the back of his polo, and pushed him back playfully. Barkley smiled, but Julie instead watched the strain and fatigue in Charlie's eyes, an expression that seemed oddly familiar.

"Good to see you, Bark. Damn. It's been a while. Great to see all of you."

Julie smiled and nodded. Give your elder son a chance, she thought. Give him time. And now was probably not the ideal moment to bring up his father.

"Dude," Charlie said, "Barkley. You should have sent me some of your writing. I had nothing to read out there but fucking manuals and reports. It was goddamn boring. It's not like the movies, man. There's no storming of Normandy on the border of Pakistan, you know what I'm saying? We're talking days and days of staring out raggedy windows in a COP—"

"COP?" Barkley asked. "What's that stand for? Wait, wait—Carbonation . . . Optometry . . . Prodigiousness. No, wait. Let me try again."

"Combat Outpost, ya fucking maniac. It's the name for bunker-huts we had to live in outside the wire. We'd sit up there in the mountains all day, doing nothing, playing cards, music, literally letting fucking days go by."

"Language," Julie said, feeling the need for that cotton ball lift.

"What'd I say?" Charlie asked.

"The *f*-word is too much for this house. Your father wouldn't tolerate it, either." She set a ceramic bowl that matched the cream-colored plates in front of Charlie, filled to the brim with linguine and Italian sausage bits and a thick, red sauce. She tried to remember when she'd taken her last dose. After the mall—hours ago.

"Right, sorry, Ma," Charlie said, taking a seat with the rest of them. "I've been hanging out with too many potty-mouthed nineteen-year-olds. It was worse than a dorm room up there, seriously. I think I actually regressed. Anyway, you've got to give me your new stories, Bark. What's holding you back?"

"I don't know. Nothing's ready. Revisions."

"Everyone should read Barkley's work," Julie said, setting down plates in front of Barkley and herself. Charlie dug his fork deep into the chunky red mess, then lifted up the pasta and dislodged a pillared plume of steam.

"Thanks, Mom," Barkley said, lifting up his silverware.

She sat down. They were all around the table again. It could easily have been a year ago. Not two years, because two years back Henry still lived here, and he had the presence of an orbiting planet, but one year back, sure. It could be the same. She saw Charlie, maybe fifteen pounds lighter, but still well built and staring at his meal; Barkley, who was gazing at his food and his older brother with equal intensity; and the image of her own self, closing her eyes now and breathing in the meal, feeling a soft smile ripple across her face, a smile not lifted by the puppet strings of the chemicals. Sometimes, Julie thought, you had to give the family credit. Maybe they weren't as dysfunctional as she thought.

And at that moment, Charlie, who was looking into the red sauce deeply, as if it were a murky mirror, grabbed the edges of the table with both hands, lurched forward, and vomited explosively, into his bowl and onto the floor.

Before cleaning up anything, Julie stood and took her purse to the bathroom. She popped open the vial and removed three 100-milligram pills of Zoloft—no, make that four. She cupped water into her hands and drank deeply, splashed it on her face, tried to ignore the sounds of Charlie coughing and Barkley stammering and one of them trudging upstairs. If these pills didn't work, she thought . . . but cut herself off. They would work because they had to.

W.W.S.P.D.
(WHAT WOULD SERGEANT
PLUTO DO?)

Barkley felt his mother watching him over the drone of the White Sox game, whose rain delay had finally been lifted. He could see her in his periphery, bobbing around the living room with birdlike motions, pretending to move coasters and old magazines, all while constantly readjusting the silver necklace Dad had bought her the year before he left. Something was definitely up—though how could it not be? After Charlie lunged forward and retched, the mud-colored vomit spraying the sides of the table, flecks hitting the rim of Barkley's pasta bowl, everyone reacted in unison, pushing back on their chairs and away from the table, his mother gasping, Barkley so shocked that he simply stared up at the July 2011 *Scenic Northeast* calendar on the far wall, which portrayed a rustic porch amid burgundy leaves in Vermont. Charlie, eyes glassy, went upstairs to his room, and Barkley sat silent, immobile. There was flaking paint on the side of the Vermont porch swing—it seemed smartest just to fix his eyes on that.

"Okay," Mom had said, once she returned from the bathroom. "Okay.

Let me clean this up. There's extra pasta and sauce on the stove. Go get yourself a new bowl."

"Right," Barkley said. "Not feeling too hungry about now. I think I'm just going to go watch TV."

"That sounds like a fantastic idea," she said.

Barkley watched as she lined up a cylindrical roll of double-length paper towels and disinfectant, ready to clean up the mess that Charlie had left. And, of course, it was unclear how much of a mess there really was. Barkley had always scoffed at the idea of the soldier who came home broken and hollowed out, cinematically reveling in disassociation and despondency. And he knew his older brother had made fun of that image, too. But now Charlie was home and Barkley felt he was dipping his toe into a vast, cold lake that would reveal exactly how little he knew. There was a real world out there, and Charlie had taken a taste and come back royally fucked-up and *that* was what was real, not his average day of sauntering from coffee shop to bakery, of writing emotionless, sarcastic stories about sex, of sex he wasn't having, of worrying about his potbelly. Jesus, Barkley thought, I'm a fucking fraud, and my brother is hurting bad, and no one is doing a thing.

His father hadn't called yet. Did he even know Charlie was back? Surely Dad could do something, could make sense of this. He hadn't served in the military but knew friends who had—there was that buddy of his, Al, who'd survived a tour in Vietnam. Barkley remembered being young and entranced, sitting on the kitchen counter of this very same house and listening to Al talk to Dad. By eight o'clock they'd be snapping the bottle caps off MGD longnecks and dangling deep-dish pizza over their mouths and the great Henry Brunson was relaxed, muscular, still aloof, maybe, but there. Present. Al would start talking about 'Nam and Barkley could tell that Dad was intrigued by this, by this world he hadn't inhabited, by the fact that he'd been in college while Al shipped out to the jungle. He could see his father's eyes grow large while Al spoke, sometimes retelling the same stories, like the time Sergeant Pluto (as Al called him) had shown up to weapons squad so high on crank that he didn't notice the two bullet wounds stitched and leaking across his abdomen. "Sergeant fucking Pluto," Al would say, eyes almost merry. "Strongest, craziest bastard I ever met." And then other nights he would share something that changed the mood of the house entirely, put a weight on their roof, like the story of how he'd ridden high over the jungle on a rattling transport helicopter, a Chinook, and some lunatic corporal began pushing North Vietnamese children out through the loading dock, to their deaths below. "I didn't do nothing," Al had said. "They just fell. Little kids, man, six and seven year olds, falling twenty stories. Seeing that will drive a man to suicide." And Dad had picked up Barkley right then and there, under the armpits and into the air, muttering that it was time for bed, and he'd missed the rest of the story.

Every time Al came over, which in elementary school was about once a month, Barkley knew he had about half an hour to coexist in the kitchen before he was sent upstairs to bed. Sometimes this was expedited by the stories Al chose to tell—if they were about strategy or daily life or the exploits of Sergeant Pluto, he generally could stay the full half hour, but if Al launched into the ones about the falling children or his "sucky-sucky" girlfriends in town, it was over before it began. Dad merely had to point with his thumb and grunt "Upstairs," and Barkley would hang his head and trudge toward the steps, thinking of all the stories, of all that grown-up time, that he was missing. He often heard Al's ragged, musical laughter as he reached the landing, and fresh MGD bottle caps hitting the counter like coins as he turned the handle to his door. But his bedroom: rife with plastic *Star Wars* figurines and stacks of paperback Choose Your Own Adventure books and a slanting ceiling on which the poster of a scale-covered dragon was adroitly glued. By the window was his favorite—a framed painting of the glittering constellations of space with an enormous, gaseous, red-hued planet in the foreground. Approaching this planet was a tiny spaceship, chalk white, with enough room inside for one. Barkley had always imagined himself in the cockpit of that ship, the craft vibrating gently, the vents breathing out cool streams of oxygen, the dials glowing green and luminous, and that big red planet looming straight ahead. And Barkley, in his ship, imagined getting closer still until the tendrils of orange cumulus and red fog enveloped him, until he was completely inside the planet, until it consumed him. But Al: how many story beginnings had he heard with his tiny legs hanging over the counter? Tales of crotch-sucking leeches and abandoned Vietcong tunnels and snapping AK-47 rounds, before Dad sent him away, into his room with the dragons and the spaceship? Al had spoken of long walks through jungles so hot and dense that the light from the sun came only in trickles, like holes in an attic. He spoke of patrols that felt like an unending, aching summer. He spoke of bean and ham meals in tin cans, of Kool-Aid powder mixed with everything, of the lull, always the lull, before the VC was on them, of mines blowing off appendages that didn't look real and the enemy firing through rice paddies and palm fronds and translucent walls of bleeding rain.

And now, Barkley thought, sitting outside the same kitchen in which those stories had been told so many years ago, Charlie would become Al. Eccentric Al, divorced Al, frequently jobless or part-time custodian Al, the guy who, as Barkley watched from his bedroom window, would stumble toward his bumperless gray Volvo, with Dad half carrying him, with Al, at times, pushing Dad away, sometimes shouting, sometimes laughing. And this was the model, the archetype that Charlie was destined to become. Such a destiny was made even more probable because of how much Charlie respected the guy (being the older one, he'd gotten to stay in the kitchen and hear those stories even longer). But, as he slumped down on the sagging couch with his ratty tennis shoes up on the coffee table, Barkley heard footsteps moving across the ceiling and then descending, returning to the living room. He craned his neck back and saw Charlie, face composed and clean, pulling a fresh T-shirt over his head.

"Going out?" Barkley asked.

"Yep. I'm feeling better. Feeling spry. And you're going out, too."

Barkley thought of the key chain. The candles. The disaster at dinner.

"Yo, Bark. Buckle up. We're heading to the bars."

"In Downers Grove?"

"That's right. Let's go."

But Ginny—her concert at the Empty Bottle started in two hours. "Charlie, can we do it tomorrow? There's this girl, I was actually planning on swinging back downtown for a concert, then coming back here later tonight or tomorrow morning. You could come, too, I mean, we both could go—"

Charlie's look burned holes in him. "A girl, dude? A girl? You're going out with your older brother who just got back from Stankhole, Afghanistan. The Sox are playing on my first night back, and that means it's a sign. We gonna get cray-cray, ya heard?"

Barkley was jolted by the change—his brother didn't even acknowledge the scene from dinner, where he was retching and bleary-eyed and then into thin air. His mother entered the room, paper towels in hand, head level with Charlie's chest.

"I don't think going out is a good idea," she said. "Especially if you're not feeling well. Maybe we should all take it easy on the first night back. Watch a movie. That boxed set of black-and-white musicals just came in the mail. *Singing in the Rain*, Charlie."

Charlie sighed. Ran a hand over his buzz cut. "Mom, I watched those with you when I was in kindergarten."

"Well, something else, then. You're the film guy. What do you want to watch? *Gone with the Wind*? That's what got you started on your movie kick."

"No, Ma. I need a drink. Barkley, you're coming. Let's go!"

Barkley ran his hands over his stomach. Maybe it had gotten smaller, considering he hadn't eaten the Bolognese. That was like an eight-hundred-calorie swing right there. Plus, the break from carbohydrates. But Ginny. The concert.

"Why don't we all hang out here?" his mother said. "Let's watch television. Play a board game. How about Careers? Remember how much you loved the section on computer science? I'll get the game out of the basement."

"No, it's not happening, all right? Damn. I need a drink. We won't be out late."

She followed them as they moved toward the door. "Barkley, shouldn't you be applying for teaching jobs? Taking one creative writing class is not full-time employment. Remember, just because you got a phone interview doesn't mean you have a job yet."

"Mom, you've been the biggest cheerleader of that phone interview, and now you think it's no big deal?"

Charlie swirled a ring of keys that glinted in the air like a ninja star. "Let's go. A night on the town for the brothers. Besides, Karen's working."

"The ex?" Barkley asked. "Think she's still on your side?"

"Hell, yes. Especially after shipping out."

Barkley watched as his older brother went out the screen door. He heard the lurch of the garage opening and the rumble of the car engine. He sighed, forgetting Ginny, his first real prospect in over half a year, and followed his brother into the darkness of the backyard.

In the Honda, with Charlie driving, Barkley watched his childhood blur past. He hadn't been home since May, and it always amazed him to see the cracked sidewalks he used to run across as a child, whose every fault line he had memorized. There was the needled bush all the first graders got pushed into waiting for the bus, there was the yellow fire hydrant that acted as a safe zone during summer freeze tag. Under the glow of the streetlights, each passing house appeared as if trapped in a bell jar. Soon enough, however, his reminiscence evaporated and their target, Ballydoyle Irish Pub, emerged from the harsh illumination of Main Street.

"There it is, I'll park here," Charlie said.

Charlie roughly steered the Honda into a parallel spot and killed the gas. Barkley, sitting in darkness, watched as a high school couple strolled down the sidewalk, laughing at unheard jokes, too young at this point to know the score. Charlie jerked the door open and stepped outside, heading straight for the bar. His mood was impossible to comprehend.

Inside Ballydoyle was lacquered wood, regimented bottles of vodka and whiskey, and an assortment of trinkets lining the ceiling and walls: medieval chandeliers with electric candles, leather-bound books on peeling shelves, tin water jugs, pictures of ancient ships, two swords above an obsolete fireplace, and, of course, Guinness—large Guinness mirrors and cartoonish Guinness posters and Guinness itself swelling from the tappers, the smell of it all around. On the elevated stage hoodie-wearing band technicians were assembling audio equipment.

"There's Karen," Charlie said, pointing to a lithe brunette filling up a pint of Smithwick's behind the bar. A young couple spoke in hushed tones at one end—Barkley didn't recognize them—and at the other, an older man in a brown blazer sipped whiskey without ice. The rest of the pub held thirty or so patrons.

"What's the plan?" Barkley asked, speaking over the din of Irish fiddle music.

"We're sitting at the bar. Hold on."

Karen sported a green Ballydoyle T-shirt and hair pulled into a make-shift nest. Her angular face lit up at Charlie's approach, then flushed, then recomposed.

"How you doing, babe?" Charlie asked, working extra gravel into his voice. "It's been a while."

Karen leaned over the bar and hugged him, her arms encircling his neck, one hand grazing over the back of his head. She pulled back. "How are you? Okay? Is it good to be back?"

"It's something."

"God. We were all so worried about you. But you made it. That's incredible. All in one piece, too."

"That's a matter of opinion," Charlie said. He sat down at the stool and motioned for Barkley to come forward.

"You look familiar," Karen said, grinning.

"You remember the little bro, right? Barkley? The aspiring writer?"

Barkley reddened and waved halfheartedly—he hated being addressed as aspiring anything, but writer most of all, especially because he was always asked if he'd been published yet.

Karen gave him a cockeyed smile and saluted. "Writer, huh? Been in *The New Yorker*?"

"Working on it," Barkley said, grinding his teeth.

Karen nodded and Barkley saw her lock eyes with Charlie again. He wondered what it was like to have that kind of history with another person, to have had more than just a couple of college flings in which being with another person made you feel even less like yourself. His own longest relationship had been, what, just over four months during his junior year in college? The breakup had been just after bar close at Chipotle—she'd ordered a burrito bowl, and he'd ordered nothing, positive that carnage was imminent. Pathetic. Sex, as much as he craved it, still scared him, and the threat of a bad performance in bed almost worked as a deterrent. He scanned the bar, trying to clear his head. The old man to the left sipped his whiskey, looking down. What a cliché, Barkley thought. Old men sipping whiskey. Was this the part where he looked into his glass and saw his broken dreams? To the right, the couple Barkley didn't recognize awkwardly engaged in a play fight. The guy, a couple of years younger and wearing a Cleveland Indians cap, pinched the girl just above her hip.

"Ow!" she squealed. "I hate it when you do that!"

"I can't stop," the kid bubbled. "Your reactions are hilarious."

Charlie glared at them, but Karen was talking again. "Anybody thirsty?"

"B-Team!" Charlie drawled.

B-Team, Barkley thought, cursing to himself. It was a reference to his former membership on the high school football team's second squad (rather than varsity), and a nickname that had been used derisively throughout his teenage years. Barkley had hoped Charlie had somehow forgotten it out there in the mountains, but no such luck. He shook himself off.

"Yeah, Charlie? What?"

"Sit down already. What you want to drink?"

"Got any microbrews?" Barkley asked. "There's this brewery in Indiana that's been getting some play, their stuff is generally pretty hoppy, but—"

"Good god," he said. "This is an Irish bar. Order a Guinness."

Barkley's face reddened again. "Fine. Guinness." He tried to think of something to fire back at his brother, or some way to recover in front of Karen, but couldn't—and Charlie wasn't paying attention anymore. Instead, Barkley sighed and clambered onto the padded stool, placing his elbows on the bar.

"Here you go," Karen said, sliding a Guinness his way. They went back to their hushed conversation while Barkley stared at the contours in the wood.

"Ow, stop it!" the girlfriend at the end of the bar squealed. The Cleveland boyfriend chuckled.

"This shitbird," Charlie muttered, nudging Barkley.

Karen went to help another customer. On the television above the bar, Carlos Quentin reared back and belted a three-run homer—the only score in the game's five innings. Charlie hooted and downed his beer, and the Cleveland boyfriend muttered and lowered his head.

"That's his twentieth home run of the year, Bark. Twenty big ones. Think I wasn't up-to-date on this shit?"

"That's great," Barkley said, clearing his throat. "But anyway. Charlie. It's crazy that you're back. And how long are you home for, anyway?"

"Permanent."

"Permanent? Wasn't your enlistment four years or something?"

"Not anymore," Charlie said, looking straight ahead.

A discharge then, Barkley thought. But for what? "Well, that's awesome that you're back, right? You going to live in the city?"

"Don't know. Got to have money for that. A job."

"Going back to work at Lucent Technologies?"

"Fuck that."

"Huh?"

"It doesn't happen like that. It doesn't just go back to normal. We're not resetting a video game, here. I quit that job because it made me crazy, Barkley. Imagine sitting in some fluorescent cubicle for nine hours a day, accomplishing nothing, feeling you have a bad case of blunt head trauma. It made me crazy enough to try to go across the world and get killed."

"Well, maybe now that you're over it—"

"Over it?" Charlie said. "*Over it?*"

"No, no—I mean now that you're done with Lucent. You've got to do something you like, is what I meant. Work at one of those places where the vets hang out. Bartend there, maybe."

"Dad would *hate* that. You know how much crow he'd make me eat? Blowing my entire college education and all that management training to tend bar? I'm not going to have the entire family talking shit about how I'm too broken down to get a real job."

"Well, there's a bunch of other stuff. You can basically do anything. I've watched you do it all since I was a kid. That five-minute detective movie you made as a senior in high school? With the whole film noir thing going on? Didn't you win an award?"

"A school award," Charlie grumbled. "Meaningless."

"You could restart *Cue Mark Reviews*. And you also could do stuff with sports. Come on, starting shooting guard? Two game-winners? You could coach! I can't do any of that stuff, Charlie. I can teach, *maybe*. And I can write a bunch of bullshit."

"Nah, man. You're good. You've cornered the market. You know what you want."

"Dude. Charlie. I have no idea what I want."

Charlie laughed. "Well, then, cheers to that," he said, and they clinked pint glasses and drank.

A silence followed. He felt his brother drifting and clawed through the filing cabinet of his mind, looking for another avenue of conversation. Did he *want* to talk about the war? Would it be therapeutic? His old buddy Hayward had sent him a couple of text messages asking for war stories . . .

"Hey, Charlie," Barkley said, taking a chance. "Anything crazy happen that you want to share? From overseas? My buddies are asking if anything wild went down, like in *Hurt Locker*. They want to know if you had to fight a sniper or anything like that."

"Who's saying this?"

"A couple buddies. Hayward—you know Hayward. Black kid, a little taller than me? He was in the chess club. Backup running back on JV. Anyway, I guess he's a movie buff now, like you, and saw *Hurt Locker*, and he's really into it. Wants to know about the Humvees and all that."

"The army doesn't use Humvees for patrols anymore. And I'm not here to entertain some fucking backup chess player, brother." Charlie looked away, then flagged down Karen. "A shot of Jamo," he said. His face was suddenly pained. Karen leaned in and touched his arm.

A tense silence clouded between them. Barkley cursed himself. Stupid. Too stupid. There was a rule, wasn't there? Never ask a serviceman about his experiences, not unless he volunteered. It didn't matter if he was family. That was two strikes. He remembered that when Al came over, his father had waited—always—and never prompted him to tell stories. Only when he began his descriptions of the jungle did Dad see fit to ask a question here or there. If only some of that tact had transferred from father to son.

Barkley looked above the bar at the White Sox broadcast. It was the top of the sixth, and Chicago was still up by three. Maybe that would make Charlie happy.

"Ow!" the girl sitting on the end shrieked. Her boyfriend looked up, crossed his eyes, and mimicked a cow chewing cud. To his left, Charlie threw back another shot of Jameson and yelled, "Fuck the Indians!"

"How about Karen?" Barkley said, leaning in conspiratorially. "Status? You interested again?"

"Eh," Charlie grunted, waving his hand. "Another shot! Yo, Karen, another shot!"

Nothing working, Barkley thought.

Five minutes later, Charlie was on his third beer, and Barkley saw the six empty shot glasses that he'd polished off and stacked, like a precarious building. His brother's face, after drinking like he'd surely done overseas, was dark and unreadable.

"How you feeling?" Barkley asked. "Want to go catch a movie? Isn't *Captain America* out? He's the first member of the Avengers; I'm kind of intrigued."

"Nah, no movies on the first night back. This here is what I'm talking about. Getting fucked-up with the brother. You wanna knock out this prick who keeps pinching his girlfriend?"

"Um," Barkley said, "not really, no. Probably not. Although I have gotten in some fights."

"This guy's a punk," Charlie said. "Screw it. How about two more shots for me and the bro?"

"Charlie, should I be doing something different? Like, I want you to have a good homecoming, a good first night out, but I feel like everything I'm saying is stupid. Am I being a huge idiot?"

"You're not being an idiot."

"I'm serious."

"So am I." Charlie looked at him, and the flat-eyed machismo was suddenly gone from his gaze. "Brother, you're doing a good job. It's me that's doing the bad job, man, it's me."

"Sorry I asked you about *Hurt Locker*."

Charlie laughed. "Dude, it's okay. You know I love movies; it was a smart tactic. It's just that I'm an unpredictable bastard now. I'm trying not to be too unpredictable, but this is weird, man. Being home is *weird*."

"I can't even imagine it."

Charlie looked at him again. "Here, you want a story? I mean, I've got lots of stories. I'm not trying to be the stoic soldier that can't talk about them. I went out there so I could *have* stories. Like, for example, do you want to hear about when I shipped out to one of the COPs? First time we saw real action?"

"So you definitely saw action?"

Charlie nodded, then pulled down another shot.

Karen was looking at them from the other end of the bar, whispering to one of her coworkers, but it was clear to Barkley that Charlie didn't notice. That was good—he didn't want him to see it. For the first time—possibly ever—Barkley felt protective of his older brother, and the thought of others gossiping about Charlie made him want to hurl his pint glass.

"So, a story," Charlie said, stretching back on his barstool. "Shit, I'm getting a little plastered here."

"I'm all ears," Barkley said.

"I've got a fact for you. These COPs out in the mountains, these shitty little rat nests we're supposed to live in—they cost about a million dollars apiece. Crazy, right? A million dollars for a rat nest. But you've got to have the living quarters, the guard towers, the generator, the clean water resupply, the black water removal. All those sandbags and HESCOs . . . I mean, you're building a makeshift fort out of nothing. So guess which part of the outpost is the most expensive? Come on, buddy, just guess."

Barkley imagined cold wind swirling over mountain tips that looked like great silver arrows. He imagined holding a dark gun and looking down upon a valley. Scanning for targets. He imagined the loneliness of it. "The guard towers," he guessed. "Guard towers cost the most."

Charlie flashed him the thumbs-down. "Fucking gravel, man. It costs a quarter of a million dollars just to lace a COP with gravel."

Barkley's phone buzzed. He looked down—a voice mail, from all the way back at 4:30 P.M. He hated when voice mails showed up randomly like that. But maybe it was Ginny. Could she have gotten his number? And would she realize he wasn't at the concert? Did she care? Of course she did—she'd felt their brief spark outside that bookstore, that interpersonal, subconscious feng shui. Unless, of course, she didn't feel any of it. Christ. This was possible, too. More than possible. He could be doing that neurotic thing again, the thing where the story he was telling himself was no more than a manifesto to disguise his loneliness, completely unrelated to reality. Shit. It was possible that he was totally, completely, irrevocably disillusioned and fucked—unless, of course, Ginny *had* left him a voice mail. He slid the phone out and checked the number. The area code was from the suburbs, not Chicago. Well, maybe her phone had been registered in the suburbs!

Charlie waved a hand in front of his eyes. "You okay there, little bro? You look like you just witnessed a mailman drown a litter of puppies."

"I'm fine, totally fine," he said, gathering himself again. "Where were we? The COPs? Are you serious with that statistic about the gravel? It's the most expensive?"

"Dead serious. And in terms of action? Our outpost would get hit every day. Like every single day."

"Taliban?"

"Of course. Little fuckers. Totally insane, that's what you have to remember. These guys are out of their minds. But getting hit doesn't make it an all-out assault or anything. Generally, you just get some knuckleheads firing at you from far away, trying to take one of your buddies out. Or take you out. After a while, it's normal. You're playing Texas Hold 'Em or Hearts or something, trying to shoot the moon, and you hear this whizzing sound outside, and it's like, 'Okay, we're getting hit, let's go look at it.' Weird, right?"

"Very."

Charlie took a long gulp of his beer. "But this one time, I wake up, and I hear my buddy Bruiser with the M240. This is one of the big boy guns—oil black, big-ass gold chain of bullets coming out the side. And when it fires, dude? It sounds like . . . I don't know, like a big boat engine or something. A big boat engine churning swamp water. It makes noise, is what I'm telling you. Like this—*pow-pow-pow-pow-pow!*"

"Crazy," Barkley said. He felt an internal giddiness. He saw Karen watching them from across the bar again.

"So I run out of the hooch, you know, and I snatch my sunglasses off the rail above my bed, because the sun is fucking *bright*, and the M4 is already in my hands even though I don't remember grabbing it, and when I turn the corner, Bruiser is blasting away with the 240. Campo is shouting that they're at eight thousand feet, and that's when I know, like, it's on. Because Campo—you remember him from high school?—he never shouted. Hold on a second."

"What?"

"Yo, Karen!" Charlie bellowed.

She came forward but didn't smile, like before. "Yeah, Charlie?"

"Shots," Charlie muttered, twirling his index finger. "For both of us. I'm telling a story. First story I've told since coming back. But you can't be here. Brothers only. Two shots, though."

"Let's slow down," she said. "It's getting a little loud. I don't want the manager to give you trouble."

"Okay, then. Two shots for my brother here. What I do with them is my business."

"You know, I've got this thing, Charlie—it's a job. It's not the greatest, and yes, it's just a *transitional job,* as my parents like to say, but I'd like to keep it, if that's all right with you."

"What?" Charlie growled. "You're serious? It's like that? My first night back? And after all we've been through? After keeping in touch?"

Karen raised her hands. "Whoa. I'm just saying—"

"It's cool," Barkley said, waving his hand. "It's totally cool. I don't want a shot, anyway. I just want another beer. How about a Guinness? Charlie, you want a Guinness? And what about the rest of the story?"

"Christ," Charlie said as Karen walked away. "This is what I mean about home being weird, man. Like, everywhere I look, people are morons. They're sensitive about everything, they're coddled, it's awful. I know we're in the suburbs—but you tell a war story with slightly increased volume, and you've immediately got half the stuffy little bastards scowling at you. And I was the same as them, once."

"Right, right. I can see that. It's gotta be weird. But what happened next?"

"Yeah, the story. So this whole time, I've fired back when they've fired at us, but really never hit anything. And it's so sporadic, anyway. But Bruiser's 240 is doing that *pow-pow-pow-pow,* and Campo is yelling, and I can tell that it's combat firing—even though Bruiser wants to just hold the trigger down. Oh, here she is with our beers, thank you so much, Karen, I really mean it. I'm serious."

Karen shook her head and walked away. Charlie slid one of the darkly sloshing pints toward Barkley, and he took it, glad it wasn't Jameson. On the television, the White Sox were batting in the top of the eighth, but hitting poorly. The Cleveland boyfriend was nodding, texting rapidly, mumbling, "Three up, three down. Attaboy, Smith, doin' *work*."

"Dude," Charlie said, "mistake by the Lake. Cleveland sucks. You guys are down three, and have, what—three hits all game?"

"Two innings left," the kid muttered, and pointed at the television. "The Sox love to fold late."

Charlie leaned in. "This little turd could get hurt tonight, just so you know. If you're feeling like letting loose."

"Jesus, Charlie. Not worth it. Just finish the story. And then we'll go. I'm fine, I've only had two beers."

"All right, all right. Anyway, I assess the scene, and then get behind the line of HESCOs with some of the other guys. Campo just keeps shouting instructions, saying where and how high, and then I pop up and look through the Aimpoint—"

"What's that?"

"*What's that?* Don't you play *Call of Duty?*"

"It's a scope?"

"No, dude, it's not a scope. It's a red dot optic. Got a bunch of different light settings. Very handy."

"Okay, got it, got it."

"So I look through, and I'm scanning, and I hear the 240 going POW-POW-POW-POW, you know, fucking *loud*, and I can hear everyone's bullet casings hitting the ground, just spilling all over the gravel. Very fucking hectic is what I'm saying. And then through the Aimpoint, up high, I see this sort of fallen-over tree, and see two little flashes. Seriously, it could have been light catching off a rock, and then bam!" Charlie slammed his hand on the bar top. "Right by my ear, two AK rounds, literally could have killed me right there. I dive on the ground, and Campo yells to change positions, so I'm crawling, thinking, what the fuck, the Taliban are supposed to have terrible aim and I almost just got my head blown off."

"Holy shit," Barkley said. "So the shots were, like, a couple inches away?"

"No, man. Like a millimeter away. I could feel the heat of the bullet on my skin. *Right* next to my head. That's my entire life, that's me sitting next to you having a Guinness or me in some box draped with an American flag. One millimeter. That's what gets you thinking."

"What happened next?"

"We drove them back. I popped up from the line of HESCOs, looked back for that fallen tree, saw some of them running. For the M4, you've got semiauto or burst, and I kept it on semi, and everyone else is firing, but I've got this guy keyed in, and I lead him just *so*, and then, once again, *bam!*" Charlie hit the bar top again, causing nearly everyone in range to look at him. "Right as I fire, it feels like destiny. Kill shot. The hajji kind of spins, and it looks like mud shoots into the air, but it's not mud, obviously. And he's down. Just lying there, man."

Barkley watched Charlie take a long gulp of beer, and the motion, the fixed eyes on the ceiling, the extended head tilt, the way the liquid just disappeared as if something in Charlie was bottomless—Barkley saw Al, at the kitchen table, with the MGDs.

"You know what it's like?" Charlie asked. "I'll tell you. I kept thinking, the entire time, *what's it going to be like when I kill someone?* If I get the chance, that is. And you kind of expect that some sort of shock is going to go through you, something crazy, I don't know, like a sound track or an eerie violin concerto or some kind of full-body heat wave. But in reality, little brother? I pulled the trigger, the guy fell down. That's it. There was nothing. The universe rolled on. It isn't until later that you feel the effects."

"What effects?"

Charlie tapped his temple. "It's the thinking that gets you. The doing? It was an empty moment. Guy falls down. Life goes on. But then, thinking, thinking, and more thinking. That's the problem."

Barkley stared at his Guinness. His brother had killed a man. At least one man, maybe more. It was bizarre to think about, to put into compartments, to file away. It was a category that men fell into—those who killed, and those who did not. And now he and Charlie were on separate sides of the moat. Charlie the jock, the movie guy, the finance major, the joker, their father's favorite—at least most of the time. And now . . . what was he? He imagined pulling a trigger and seeing a distant soldier fall. An empty moment, Charlie had said. Could that be true? What he wanted to think, if the empty moment theory was accurate, was maybe that the bullet was something else, like a note or a letter, and the killer simply its courier. Maybe the person delivering it didn't feel anything, just like a postman wouldn't feel anything dropping a message into a mail slot. Maybe all the emotion went into the person receiving the bullet, to the one experiencing that other unspoken event, that final journey. And maybe no one found out what it all meant until they got their own letter, until they received their final delivery by way of bullet, or sickness, or the winding down of their temporary clock. It was conceivable, he thought, that all those empty moments *did* add up to something. A person just didn't find out what it was until the end.

Then again, maybe he was just rambling.

What Barkley really wanted was someone to talk to. He wanted to leave, and more than that, he wanted to discuss all of this. Not with Charlie—that was too dangerous, especially if he said the wrong thing. Not with Hayward, not his father, not his college buddies. The face that kept coming back was Ginny's, which was, admittedly, absurd—he didn't know her at all. But what would she say? She was smart, he knew that. And clever. And funny in a weird sort of way. Never before had he really wanted to know what a girl would have to *say*. Which meant he was either a shallow bastard, or he was hanging out with the wrong types of girls. Or, he thought, just not hanging out with girls, period.

"All right, Karen," Charlie said, waving his arm, "you can come back, the story is over. But can you bring those shots now?"

"Charlie . . ."

"Come on, girl. We have history. Do you really care if I get plastered? On my first night back? Pretty sure it's required."

She leaned in. "It's just that you keep talking about getting in a fight, and I can't let that happen. I'm trying to watch out for you."

"Right, right, I keep forgetting. Back in the States, these are the things people care about. Whether or not somebody takes a shot, or throws a punch. It's all a *tremendously* big deal. Okay, Karen. Okay. I get it. You're still one of the lambs who don't know any better."

"Jesus," Karen said. "You know what? Two shots coming up. But you're seriously pushing it."

"You see how she's looking at me?" Charlie said, raising his voice, forcing the younger couple to glance up at him. "You see how they judge us? Once we've killed—"

"Two shots of Jameson," Karen said, sliding them toward Charlie. "Drink up. And keep your voice down."

Barkley and Karen looked at each other. Karen shook her head, quickly and discreetly. Charlie slid a shot in front of Barkley, then slid one in front of himself. And the way he did it—that forceful slide across the bar top, the fixed stare on his face—once again Barkley saw Al, passing a frosted beer to Dad.

"Drink it!" Charlie bellowed.

"Don't be so loud—please?" Karen pleaded.

"It's like walking on eggshells back in the States," Charlie said. "I've seen eighteen-year-old kids so fucked-up you'd think they'd vomit their guts out, yet here, one shot of Jamo is this big, gigantic secret. Because all we're all concerned about are regulations. Toe the line, stay calm, stay classy, it doesn't matter what's going on in the rest of the world."

Karen raised both hands and walked away. The old man was looking at them. The PDA couple was looking at them. The guy with gray stubble trying to order a Smithwick's was looking at them. Charlie pointed at Barkley. "Take that shot. Cheers, motherfucker. To coming home."

They clinked glasses and Barkley felt the watery burn of whiskey slide down his throat and send mist immediately into his brain. "Ugh," he managed.

"Woo!" Charlie shouted. "That's the spirit. I'll order another."

Cleveland Boyfriend made a sour face in their direction. "Maybe we should go," he said, loud enough for everyone to hear. "It sucks in here tonight."

Charlie, for a solitary moment, looked suddenly lost and adrift. His eyes watered, focused on something above the bar and likely, Barkley thought, not even in the room. But then they cleared again, as if he'd remembered something. He jabbed a finger at the kid. "What're you talking about, shithead? I've been watching you all night."

The kid rolled his eyes. His girlfriend tugged at his arm, trying to move him to the other side of the bar.

"Hey," Charlie said, standing up. "Any problem you've got can be handled outside. No, it's okay. Seriously. Come on, Cleveland, let's go outside. Whoever wins buys the other guy a beer. You ever even been in a fight, little man? Or does your girlfriend carry Mace to protect your pathetic ass?"

Karen came back to the bar, but this time snapped her fingers at Barkley. "Hey, microbrew," she said. "Come over to the end of the bar for a second."

Barkley got off the stool and shuffled down to the end, where the old man was staring back into his whiskey. Karen's jaw was tight.

"You gotta keep your brother in line," she said, putting a hand on his shoulder. "Like, right now. I don't want this to get bad, but I can't serve him any more."

Barkley stared at her round nose and light blue eyes. "What can I do?"

"Tell him you have to go home. Seriously. Or say something else—you're his brother. I don't want to send him out, and I don't want the bouncers to do it, but I can see where this is going. Especially if he keeps this tough guy act up."

He *is* a tough guy, Barkley wanted to say, but he wasn't sure if he was just being protective again. "What's the deal with you two, anyway? Are you and he an item or something?"

"Or something." Her eyes were unreadable in the dim lights.

"Right."

"I just want Charlie to be okay. And the first step is getting him out of here."

A reverberating slam came from the bar top and Barkley turned to see that his older brother had ordered whiskey from another waitress, polished it off, and brought the shot down like a gavel. The waitress had fled.

"What the hell was that about?" Charlie shouted as Barkley returned.

"What? Listen, I think—"

"Answer the question, man. You and Karen. You two conniving or what? Huh?"

"Um, no," Barkley said. "Just talking."

Charlie burst out laughing. "You fucking rascal. Trying to move in. I love it. Go ahead, buddy. Anything for my brother. Anything. I'd die for you."

"Maybe we could go," Barkley said, watching as the young couple stood up and went to the back end of the pub. The White Sox game was over—they'd won. Barkley could see the girlfriend consoling, whispering, leading him away. The boyfriend appeared to feverishly disagree with the change of location.

"That fucker didn't want to fight," Charlie bellowed, letting his voice carry. "This is all a show, her leading him away, like he's this Doberman on a leash. What I'd do is I'd take my hand, like this? See how I'm not closing it into a fist? And then, *bam*, I'd jam it right under his jaw, dislocate that shit immediately. I'd do it for the home team, brother—hell, I'd do it for Mark Buehrle. Let's go White Sox!"

"Yeah," Barkley intoned, "I'd be cool with leaving about now."

Barkley had seen his older brother crazy enough to fight just once: after getting elbowed in the face during a conference basketball game between DGN and York. The ref had blown the whistle for a flagrant, but Charlie was back on his feet immediately, holding the ball behind his back with one hand—Barkley had always remembered that one particular detail, as if he only needed one arm to fight—and then Charlie had pressed his face right up against the York forward's nose and everyone on the Downers side stood up and hollered. Barkley remembered thinking: awesome. That's my brother. But that feeling seemed so far away now.

Charlie was yelling. "We're not going anywhere, kid. I'm drinking with my brother tonight. And before that, we're going to beat that Cleveland-loving shithead's ass."

"Tell me you're kidding. Right? You're joking. I'm serious, now."

Charlie looked at him, and once again he seemed suddenly different. His eyes softened, and he gave a lopsided grin. "All right, little brother, all right. I'm kidding."

"You won't get in a fight, right?"

He looked down at his beer. "No. No fights. I'll be a good kid. Just one more drink and I'm out of here."

Barkley thought again of the voice mail. It could be Ginny, couldn't it? Or something else? He pulled out his phone as Charlie snatched a leftover beer.

"All right, Charlie. One more beer and we go. I don't need one. I'm just going to go check this voice mail, all right?"

Charlie waved him off, and Barkley strode purposefully to the men's room, eager for a pocket of quiet. Fluorescent lights surrounded him. If Ginny was tracking him down, if she *had* called him, well—that was a very good sign. And he needed to explain the situation. He put the phone to his ear.

You have one new message, the automated female voice said. Barkley listened over the din of music and patrons talking and something outside the bathroom clattering. Through the wall, he heard his brother laugh.

"That's enough!" somebody shouted.

Shit, Barkley thought. The voice mail was muffled. Was that Charlie out there? But the voice he had heard—familiar. Important. And definitely not Ginny. Barkley pressed four to listen to the message again.

He heard Charlie yelling through the wall. Something else clattered. A pint glass? Barkley, heart jumping, squinted and concentrated to hear the message: "We're—appy—invite—view—wick—" And then, air sucking into his lungs, he understood. He shoved the phone back into his pocket and, hearing the bellowing of his brother, ran back into the bar.

It was too late. Charlie was walking toward Cleveland, too fast to be denied; a waitress blocked his path momentarily but was knocked aside. Behind the bar, Karen was hissing urgently and the patrons in the bar were all standing up and staring. A pint of beer slid off the bar and smashed.

"You know what? Let's go!" Cleveland shouted, raising his hands. Charlie circled him and laughed harshly.

"Charlie!" Barkley yelled, waving at his brother. "Charlie, stop! I've got crazy news!"

"Do something, Barkley!" Karen yelled, but it was happening too fast.

He saw the blur of Charlie's movement, and even drunk—plastered— his brother was far quicker and stronger than the younger man. Cleveland tried to shove him backward, but suddenly Charlie had the kid by the neck, pinned against the edge of the bar, arm wrenched behind his back, as if he were cuffing a crook. Barkley ran forward, slipped on the shattered glass, got up again, and saw two hulking bouncers closing in from the side. Shit.

"Charlie!" he called out. "Stop! Listen!"

Charlie looked up, cocked his arm to throw a punch, and Barkley—unsure of how to prevent disaster—tackled him. He put everything into it, all four years of backup football, the urging sounds of his obese coaches, the times with the tackling dummies, the wrestling matches against college friends, the techniques from Bears games with his father, any anger he could muster, any fear—and he rammed directly into his older brother's sternum. He saw a burst of weeping stars, felt his nose pinch and eyes tear, sensed the muscled torso of Charlie resisting, resisting, before finally giving way, and then gravity took them both and it was the cold tiled floor, his head striking it like a cowbell, so dirty, Barkley thought, before refocusing and realizing that Charlie had already climbed on top of him, knee on his chest, hands pinning his wrists, eyes staring darkly into his own.

"And just what the shit was that, little brother?"

"Charlie," Barkley said, breathing heavily, realizing he couldn't move. "Don't do anything. I've got news. Very good news. Just listen!"

"And I'm trying to hit somebody, can't you understand that? Just what the fuck is so important?"

The bouncers were on them then, grabbing at Charlie, trying to drag him back, but now Karen stepped in front of them. "Stop! Andy, Bruce, stop! That's my ex, okay? He just got back from overseas. It's his first night back. Literally his first night back. He's fine. Let's cut him some slack."

"Some slack?" the Cleveland boyfriend whined, sitting on the floor and massaging his wrist. "Give *that* guy some slack?"

"Just be quiet," Barkley said. "Please. I've got this. Charlie, can you hear me? Can you focus?"

His brother tore his gaze from the bouncers and stared back at him. His eyes were red, skin suddenly blotchy, a glaze of perspiration clinging to his cheeks. Barkley felt the pressure on his wrists increase, the knee dig in deeper to his sternum.

"What's so important, B-Team? What?"

"I've got the final interview at Eastwick High School, Charlie. I'm the last of two candidates."

"Eastwick?"

"The most famous high school in the state of Illinois? Do you know what this means? Can you imagine that? Come on, imagine it—*me* as a teacher there. Me!"

And it was only then that he heard his older brother's laughter, felt the pressure on his body release, and realized they were going to make it out of there without the help of a police cruiser.

"Un-fucking-believable, brother," Charlie said merrily, slumped somewhere in the back of the Honda. "Eastwick. Crazy old Hogwarts of a Catholic high school. Shiiiiiiit. Gotta get the job, man. Gotta get the job. Mom will love it. And you can send kids to the dean every day, just to mess with them. Every fucking day."

"One of the most famous schools in the state," Barkley marveled as he drove down Kenyon and turned at Washington. "I mean, the phone interview—I didn't think anything would come of it, but this? This is the final round. She said it was between me and one other candidate. Some girl from Kansas. That's home field advantage for me, right? For the first time ever?"

"It's unbelievable," Charlie said, leaning back and grinning. "You've got the home field advantage. You're one millimeter from being a beast. Who'd have thought?"

"Not me," Barkley admitted.

"And by the way, brother—I had you on the ropes after that sneak attack. You were going down."

"What?"

"I had you pinned, you know."

"Yeah, Charlie, I know."

"Things are changing," he mumbled, but Barkley didn't know to which of them he was referring.

He smiled. Sitting in the driver's seat, he felt a kind of dazed wonder at the machinations of life and destiny. First, the mere fact that such an esteemed school wanted to give him a final interview. *Him*, of all people. And secondly, the way that late-arriving voice mail had changed everything about Charlie's mood—had taken the fight right out of him, imbued him with the enthusiasm of a puppy. It was almost the way he used to be. Barkley whistled. "I don't have the job yet, but how crazy would that be?"

"Crazy as fuck," Charlie said softly, from somewhere in the backseat.

When they got home, the house was dark. Their mother, thankfully, was asleep. Charlie blundered to the couch to watch television, and watching the way he walked—the stumbling half step, the ragged laughter, seemingly to himself—Barkley again thought of his father's old friend. With the couch taken, Barkley went up to his former bedroom, still cluttered with shadows and boxes. He felt for the light switch, but it didn't work. Drunk, he thought. Maybe he really was drunk. But an interview. He wobbled around the room, heard fragile glasswork shaking in the corrugated containers. He eventually found himself by the window, the same place he used to look out as Al stumbled from their house so many years ago. Dad shouting for Al to hand over the keys. Al shouting back that he wouldn't get them. The same old song and dance. Barkley placed his hand on the area of drywall where the poster of the spaceship used to be, where that little white ship seemed destined for a red, unknowable planet. He laid his forehead against the windowpane. His mind swam. He imagined himself in the vessel again, saw those glowing green dials, felt the cold oxygen streaming from overhead vents. Saw that big, red, gaseous planet, ready to take him in.

HOW MANY TOURS
IF YOUR DREAMS REPEAT?

"Charlie?"

He jolted. Moaned. Heard himself cough. His rifle disappeared, his hands floated away into moths, the mountains melted. His eyes weren't even *open*. Wired shut more like it, layers of cobwebs, muted orange light pressing against his lids. Christ. Where was he? The cushions under him like dough, all wrong. Had to be rigid, a plank, a board. Where was his rifle? Gone. He raised his hands to feel that plywood, the hook that held his sunglasses, found it gone as well. Empty air in between.

"Can I turn on the TV?"

His brother. A pair of scissors began cutting through the webs. The realization was like falling. The couch. Home already. No. He felt the weight lowering itself back into his chest. An anvil. And in the dream, he'd begun to believe, really believe, that he'd have a chance to do it again. The mountains were his dreams. Always. Charlie groaned again. A musical chime sounded and ESPN began blaring. White Sox won. Carlos Quentin. He kept his eyes shut and felt the cushions by his feet sink down as Barkley got comfortable.

Everything was different now, a funhouse mirror of domestic life. The familiar passageways of his old suburban home were far too clean and close to sea level, the filtered air an unreality, the common appliances luxurious and absurd. He had walked into the downstairs bathroom and saw the remodeled sink with its silver knobs and porcelain basin and found himself expecting, even longing for, the white PVC pipes that jutted up from the rocky ground at the COP, where Sergeant Wynn had said, simply, "This is where you piss," and moved on. And receiving a wake-up call at 0500 by a tug on the leg and a whispering of "Brunson" was infinitely preferable to finding himself on bloated couch cushions, daylight flooding in, pillows all around, with no urgency at all, no purpose. It was how he'd felt before he left, but worse.

"Sox *and* Cubs won last night, huh?" Barkley said. "Dad's probably pretty happy about that."

He felt his brother testing him. After last night, they would all want to know the same thing: how much of the old Charlie was gone? And the new Charlie didn't have an answer to that question yet, because that thing inside him—wait. He'd forgotten. The key chain. *Her* key chain. How could he have forgotten? Last night, every night, that was part of the deal, the only thing he could do, it was the only thread he had, the only penance, the only way to validate his continued existence. And he'd forgotten. How? Charlie snapped his eyes open and jumped up and he heard his brother talking behind him but he kept his head down and went up the stairs and into his room where the gray blinds were drawn and the light was blotted out, everything still dark, and he pulled open his solid oak bedside drawer and clutched the key chain in his hands, pressed it to him, fell to his knees, heard himself blubbering. He wouldn't light the candles this time, he wouldn't pray, he wouldn't go down on his knees in front of the stool, no, he would clutch it to him, he would get into this old bed that was his and yet not his anymore and he would clutch the key chain and not let go and hold it until the hard plastic edges cut into his hands and he bled, yes, he thought, bleeding was integral now, penance, always penance, always the anvil that never left, couldn't leave. Damn it, he thought. He was hungover. He was hungover and he was being the Christopher Walken guy, he was doing the cliché, and he didn't know how to stop. Charlie pushed himself under the covers and mashed his face into his pillow and held the key chain tighter and tighter until there was only the sensation of plastic digging into the lines and ridges of his palms, until the pinching of the key chain was reality, until again, mercifully, he slept. And when he slept—his memory went, as usual, to the olive tree.

The olive tree was haggard, thorny roots digging through rock and top-soil and grasping the ledge like a talon. The tree swung over the side, the trunk leaning precariously, and Charlie thought, absurdly, of an old woman doing the limbo, ignorant of the abyss below her. In this dream that was actually reality, Campo was next to the tree, he was in the shadows of its withered leaves, face and body obscured. It was dusk and the sky was purple and at least twenty of them were rounding out a full day of patrol. There had been another *shura* with the village elders, elders who always wanted compensation for dead farm animals blown apart by American air support or for chicken wire fences torn in half by mortars or occasionally for the wall of a home that had caved in, injuring their people. More often than not, though, they just wanted money, and would sit on the gray floor in their dirty robes and pull at their dirty beards and try to get the highest price, the largest compensation they could haggle. It was three months after that IED blast (old news now), and Charlie would instead remember his first real firefight, his first kill, and think, bizarrely, that he'd rather have more of that action than this bullshit, these *shuras* that were really nothing more than shakedowns and empty promises, the elders nodding and insisting that they would inform the Americans about Taliban locations and ambush threats. But the *shura* was over, and Campo had been shaking his head the whole walk out of the stone village, saying it was fucked-up, it was fucked-up because the *shura* had been too easy, too quick, and those dirty bastards had agreed to American compensation for a dead goat and a maimed cow far too easily, and the elders were *never* that agreeable. Always they bartered for more money, their faces stoic, carved out of rock. Wrong, Campo kept saying, it's all wrong, and when the sky turned purple he went by the olive tree and looked over the ledge at the higher mountains and Wynn said, *let's move,* and Charlie turned back to the olive tree and

Campo was still shaking his head and that's when the ambush came alive around them.

The dream slowed down here. Splintered leaves and rocks shredded Charlie's vision, mortars thundered, lights flashed, and then he was down, his tinnitus kicking in, the sound of a hospital EKG flatlining. He was behind a rock with JB and they both had their heads down against the dirt. He looked up for Campo, but tracer fire was coming down from both directions, kicking up gravel and rocks and skin from the olive tree. Charlie looked again. He saw Campo, thirty feet away, lose his footing but grab hold of one of the boughs. His M4 fell, harmless, a hollow twig down the side of the mountain. More gunfire kicked up. Mortars fell; plumes of craters and rock bits falling on them like wild surf at sea. Charlie fired back, fired at nothing, each pull on the M4 unleashing a metallic clap that was almost indistinguishable from the rest. Next to him, more soldiers opened up. The mountainside across from them, three hundred meters away, lit up with enough muzzle flares to put them in a basketball arena, the flickering barrels acting as camera flashes. Above, Bruiser's machine gun thundered, spraying continuously, every fifth round a tracer, no more bursts but rather constant, unending bullets glowing and extinguishing into the hillside across from them. Charlie fired blindly, blindly, aiming for muzzle flares, forgetting to look through his Aimpoint, then remembering, still seeing nothing, and then bullet spray all around him and he ate dirt, hunkered behind the rock, waited for it to stop. When he rose again and looked at the olive tree, Campo was gone. More bark and skin and leaves had fallen from the shredded branches, but Campo—Charlie thought, he must've gotten back to cover. But where was cover? He couldn't have—and then bullet spray made him put his head down again, and he felt tiny white rocks pressing against his lips and teeth, felt the spray of dirt, heard the pop and snap of rounds moving over his head.

Eventually, the infantry pushed forward. They moved five feet. Then fifteen. Assumed new positions of cover. The soldiers with 203s looped grenades into the darkened hills. Mortars from the COP began thudding, and even in darkness, Charlie could see white phosphorus spilling across the mountainside like vaporized milk. The tide was turning. His senses were back. Through his Aimpoint he could see them fleeing. He fired, three-round bursts, again and again, emptied his clip. Put in another. Moved forward. The M4 shook, rattled. Empty. Another magazine. Soldiers around him, moving forward, taking orders. Wynn barking to target their exit routes, their exit routes, goddammit, not their firing positions. Radios blared. Air support finally coming. Somebody yelled. A soldier fifty feet away from him dropped. Lucky shot. They were winning. New positions. There was a woodpile, get behind it. In the distance, the roar of the Apaches. Get those fuckers. More mortars, white sparks, flames, phosphorus. Apaches close now. Coming down from the east. JB's knee, to the right of him, exploded. He fell down shrieking, rolling, shards of kneecap sticking through his pants like teeth. Charlie bellowed for a medic. They took him away. Charlie felt nothing, only knowledge, cold knowledge: JB was hurt, he was out, it was time to move, to fight, to finish them. Charlie looked through the Aimpoint again. More movement, less muzzle flare. They were fleeing. He pulled the trigger repeatedly; hit one of the tiny, faraway fuckers in the hand, another in the throat. Magazine empty. Slap another in. Fire, feel the jolt, the blaze, the M4 shaking, and then the air around him was vibrating, the sound of an enormous fan filling the sky, and the black shadows of the Apaches, three of them, in from the east, oh yes, clear to fire, no collateral damage, open up on those fuckers. The miniguns roared from high in the sky and the canopy in the Taliban area collapsed, broke apart like papier-mâché, bloomed an umbrella of dust. Then the rockets fired, concussions felt from here even, from where Charlie stood. The hill across from them lit up. Reports came in on the radio. Charlie thought of Campo but couldn't, wouldn't compute. They were winning. His M4 thudded. He emptied another magazine.

"Been in there for eight hours. Barkley said he started a—no, I wasn't there. Of course he's tired. No, you said I could call in an emergency and this is—no, I understand that. Henry. He did not. And this is an emergency."

Charlie massaged his eyes with balled-up fists. The rumble of the mountains faded into the outline of sunlight against his shuttered blinds. It happened mostly the same way every time, although in each dream, he was given a chance—a small opening to run to that tree. And, of course, in the dream he never took that chance. Too dangerous. Was there something wrong with his imagination? Wasn't he supposed to dream about alternate realities, new possibilities, new places? But every dream unfolded his old life, and he found himself helpless to change it. Sure, a grenade might explode at a different time or a different place, his M4 might aim for different sections of the mountain, but JB always lost his leg from the knee down, and they always got ambushed beside that olive tree, and Campo, Campo—

"He needs a *man* to help, and that man needs to be his father. No, that's just not true. I have said this before because it's been true before, and now he really needs you."

Charlie pushed his face on the contours of the pillow. Like everything in the house, it was laced with nostalgia: the same blue cushion he'd used since middle school, riddled with all the familiar dents and burrows where he'd pressed his face, upset over a hundred teenage issues. But then, his life got easier, didn't it? He was good-looking enough, a three-year starter in basketball, and smart—a strong student from the beginning. Years later, when Charlie returned from college, he had pressed his face into this same pillow because of the lack of issues, because of the emptiness, because of the ease of living in America and the fact that all the mystery was gone. And there was his father, urging him on, commanding him to follow, to get the job, the condo, the marriage, on and on, not knowing that regardless of money, Charlie was already spent.

His mother droned on; Charlie squeezed the key chain hard against his palm. Eventually, a light trickle of blood came forth. It wasn't enough. And, he thought, before the key chain, there was Campo, always Campo.

The search lasted eight hours, into the heart of night. They returned to the sight of the ambush, set up a perimeter, and began by spreading out and combing the road toward town, toward the *shura* that had really been a trap. The worst-case scenario, Wynn told them, was the Taliban taking him alive. They would search all night if they had to. Apaches buzzed overhead, scouring the terrain with night vision and infrared radar. The soldiers asked questions, pushed bearded hajjis against stone and clay walls, demanded answers, roughed them up, said where the fuck is Campo, you dirty bastard fucks. But Campo wasn't in the town. And he wasn't up the mountain. So they'd retraced their steps, the night sky growing luminous, and then they found the olive tree and made their way down, over the edge, to the rocky outcropping sixty feet below. Charlie's ears hummed through it all, the tinnitus drone pulsating, promising to go away and then swinging back with more electric power than before.

They found his body just after dawn. It had been moved. Bruiser got there first, and Charlie knew it was Campo because Bruiser was swearing, again and again, saying *fuck no*, and then, before Charlie rounded the rocky bend, he heard Bruiser vomit. When he finally saw Campo's body, his best friend almost looked peaceful. Campo was on his back across the gray rocks, palms skyward, feet splayed awkwardly, one boot against some loose shrubbery. It was as if he were peacefully drunk, or waking up from a hangover. But Charlie felt the cold knowledge pass over him like a shadow: dead. Gone. Just like that. He might have died from the fall. But maybe not, Charlie thought, because as he approached the body, with his heart pumping chilled blood into his capillaries and appendages and eyes, it was clear that something was wrong with Campo's face. His face was . . . red. Broken. Bruiser was bent over, holding up the dog tags. Charlie stepped forward until he was finally standing in front of the body, and then he saw what the Taliban had done. He saw. There were bullet casings littered around Campo's face like dead hornets. And it became clear, to Charlie, that the Taliban had fired on his mouth and nose and skull until nothing remained, had fired their guns on his face until it was a murky soup, until it was caved in and chunky-red and indistinguishable, like his mother's Bolognese—that was exactly what it looked like—and the thought made him want to keel over and vomit right then and there, on top of the body, but he'd held back, his body begging him to release the nausea, his stomach pulsing, his chilled blood stabbing inside his veins like icicles. But he held his hand over his mouth and turned away and saved it, stored it up, used it as fuel for the hatred he knew would be needed. When Charlie could breathe again, he looked at the sky first. No clouds. Ocean blue. His blood felt cold and he could feel it moving underneath his skin. Then he took a breath and looked back at the body. Cleared his head. Examined it. Told himself he could do it, that he had to do it. He tried to concentrate. In the shadows, Bruiser was crying.

The Taliban had fired until there was nothing left. They had done it—why? To inhibit the army's ability to identity their man, to send a message, had they done it out of anger, out of spite, out of sport? Just to do it? Charlie didn't know for sure. But, looking at the red mess that used to be Campo's face, he did know for sure how *he* felt. The Taliban, he understood, with utter clarity, were not people. They were disease. They were insanity and ugliness. And the hatred that had been circling him harmlessly for months suddenly dropped inside his soul like a hot coal. It burned in him so deep that he wanted to see whole towns and villages nuked, generations of men hung, turbans set aflame, heads removed, scalps stripped away like Velcro, sloping farms and goat-filled hillsides and rattling jingle markets napalmed, again and again, until all of Afghanistan looked, from the night sky, like an enormous candlelight vigil, a burning, flaming, ruined country begging for forgiveness, for what they'd done. He wanted to kill and to torture, and torture slowly, using old weapons, using shards of glass and bent nails torn from two-by-fours and Phillips-head screwdrivers from his father's old tool belt. He wanted to break laws and annihilate treaties. He wanted to hear their screams and leave them wounded and leaking on cement floors in cells without windows. He wanted to cut those motherfuckers' hearts out. They were worse than animals. They were animals twisted with dogma, made dangerous, made rabid. They were human beasts mired in insanity, unsalvageable, irredeemable. Kill 'em all, Charlie thought, looking at the caved-in, ruined face of Eddie Campo, as the tinnitus bore on at a higher, sharper pitch. It was that simple. Kill them all.

FATHER BURNHAM'S SMILE

Late again. Barkley punched the accelerator, and the Honda shot down block after suburban block, his mottled briefcase bouncing in the passenger seat, as if resisting the trip. The radio was blaring Rihanna—he hammered it with his fist, turned it off. Swerved around a Volvo, then again around a rusted pickup. A white Cadillac, puttering at fifteen miles an hour, veered into his lane.

"Shit!" he shouted. "Piece of shit!"

Barkley hit the brakes, jerked the minivan into the right lane, and plowed forward and around the Cadillac. His briefcase crashed to the floor, lurching open and spilling papers. He took a second to glare at the glassy-eyed senior citizen behind the wheel.

"Fucking old people!" Barkley screamed. "Worse than teenage girls!"

Nine minutes until the interview. But, he thought, but—you were supposed to be there early. His father had said so—called him last night, shocking him with his voice, blaring cold, calculated wisdom into his ears. *Get there early*, that was the first thing he'd grunted. He'd forced him to rehearse, given him practice questions. Examples: Why did he want to teach? What was the transition from public to private school going to be like? What's an example of an effective lesson plan? What's something he's not good at? What are his goals? On and on. Barkley had been grilled for over an hour, his father merciless and demeaning but effective, and then the phone call had abruptly ended. A blip on the radar screen, dissolving.

And here he was, late, breaking the first rule. Stop sign ahead, he rolled through it, hit the accelerator, got the van back up to forty-five. Why was he never on schedule? He did it every time. Hated himself for it, then began to hate the world, as if it conspired against him. Why hadn't he gotten dressed an hour earlier? Even half an hour would have sufficed. He felt for the knot on his black-and-blue tie. Loose. Felt his button-down. One button undone. His cuffs—still flapping. No time. He saw a red light ahead, then peeled around the bend of another street, knowing it ran parallel. Swerved left at the next turn. Gunned it. Six minutes.

Approaching Eastwick High School in the Odyssey, Barkley saw a sidewall that would have befitted an ancient fortress: precisely cut slabs of limestone framed amid slender, wrought iron windows. Castlelike ramparts made a chiseled outline above the leafy elms, and beyond it stretched Eastwick's famous clock tower. Barkley felt relief. He'd been jittery for days—and it wasn't just the thought that his future depended on this interview, or that he had no idea how to deal with the rigid Catholic school system. Instead it was the knowledge that Charlie was out of commission, and hadn't left his room for days. All he'd done was drink beer and watch movies—entering the rest of the house only to grab dinner or use the bathroom. And for some reason, a reason he couldn't pinpoint, Charlie's collapse meant that he had to get this job. Had to.

He swung the minivan into a parallel spot across from Eastwick and jerked the brakes hard enough to make the tires squeal. Four minutes. Barkley noted that his palms were already lined with sweat. Had to fix the tie. He pulled down the rearview mirror. Jerked the knot tighter. Opened his mouth. Teeth were clean, though the sides of his molars had a slight sheen of yellow, like the rusting edges of his apartment bathtub.

"Why didn't I use Crest Whitestrips!" he howled.

Three minutes. He fixed the cuffs while biting his lip. Checked the mirror again. Nose clear. Skin looked good—what else was missing? Hair fine. He smoothed it out, noting that his sheen of strawberry blond was turning darker as he entered his midtwenties. The button! He found it, fumbled with the translucent little disk, his fingers impossibly greasy, then finally slipped it through the opening. He wiped his palms across his khaki pants and kicked the door open.

Barkley jumped out of the car, felt the humid summer air, whirled around, grabbed the briefcase, and through the reflection in the windows made sure his aqua-blue shirt was tucked in at the back. The side view showed him that his minor potbelly hadn't changed in size, even though he hadn't eaten his mother's pasta in days. Was it considered a gut at this point? Two minutes! He ran toward the school, a place he'd never even considered attending, what with a well-regarded public school, Downers Grove North, right next door and free. Barkley cursed as he shuffled, held on firmly to the briefcase, and burst through Eastwick's front doors.

Hallowed silence swallowed him, as if he'd been pulled into a vacuum. The entranceway blossomed into a glass-domed atrium, and across the echoing marble floor was an enormous rendering of Eastwick's emblem, a silver E bisected with a black cross, beneath which a billowing scroll of Latin phrases unfurled. No students present—the atrium eerily quiet. Summer school already in session. Barkley hustled up to the tiny window that peeked into the receptionist's office. There was a sign-in sheet. Name: Barkley W. Brunson. Time of Arrival: 8:29 A.M. Reason for Visit: Interview for English teacher position. He breathed out explosively: less than one minute to spare. The receptionist inside the fluorescent office cocked an eyebrow in his direction.

Student teaching had occurred two springs ago, and it hadn't gone well. Being in front of the students was fine—dealing with the attention-deficit cousins on his mother's side had prepared him for every manner of maniac. It was simply a question of organization and drive. Every day after school, instead of lesson planning, Barkley had gone back to his apartment and played video games. After an hour or so, the sky outside would turn burnt orange, and he would feel a tightening in his chest, a knowledge that a window of opportunity was closing, but still, despite this knowledge, he pushed on—just two more levels of *Modern Warfare*, he had to beat the sequence with the burning cars on the highway.

Then the sky would shift from burnt orange to deep blue, and Barkley would finally pause the game to jot down a few notes. *Tomorrow,* he would write. *Chapter 4,* Slaughterhouse Five, *ask about YOUTH vs. ADULTHOOD?? Give examples. Relate to high school. Compare with the transition from 8th grade to freshman year? Yes. Two, three examples, then read from text, put kids into groups.* Group work: a get-out-of-teaching-free card. And after completing those notes, Barkley would reward himself with a Three Floyds microbrew, then another, check Facebook, and soon enough the sky was not deep blue but dark purple, and when the city around him lit up, inky black. No stars. Barkley might have made a couple more notes, *read from page 56, give excerpt about Dresden infrastructure,* before downing another beer, killing a few more fictional soldiers with his digital machine gun, and by then he was tired and half drunk, and figured the rest of the lesson could be completed in the morning. But the next day he was always up late, taking a shower late, getting to school late, and running into the classroom in a state of partial panic, the vise in his chest turning into jittery, unwinding springs. There would be loose-leaf papers in his hands atop his scuffed blue folder, and atop the papers would be his copy of *Slaughterhouse Five,* open facedown and bent along the spine, and then there was the sea of student faces, appraising him, and he'd think, he'd think, *why didn't I prepare?* And after an awkward lesson that was mainly saved from embarrassment by splitting the class into haphazard group activities, in which the students clearly weren't working but at least weren't challenging him, Barkley would think, tonight, I will really plan out a quality lesson, I will do good work. But by the time he got home, he saw the Playstation 3 and the Toshiba laptop and the DVR and it started all over again.

"I'll escort you when it's time," the bun-haired receptionist said.

Barkley nodded and backed away. This time, he thought, if he got this particular job, it would be different. It was no longer possible to mess around, to be the old Barkley. He'd spent a whole year after college *not* teaching, and taking that writing class without writing a single thing that was even remotely praiseworthy, and it just wasn't working out. He calmed himself. Absorbed the rest of the atrium—it was minimalist but impressive. To his left were two industrial-size glass trophy cases, with silver water polo awards gleaming like fine china. The interior walls of the atrium were laced with old and new brickwork, some portions caked in dusty mortar, others the color of fine red wine. On the marble floor, illumination from the skylight played across Eastwick's stoic insignia. There *was* something different about the place. The old building, its palatial infrastructure, the trees and the trophies and the actual, honest-to-God personality—it was the opposite of that stripped-away, public school student teaching job he'd had, where the hallways had felt antiseptic, devoid of humanity.

"Barkley?" the receptionist said. "They're ready for you upstairs."

They? "Great," Barkley said. "Thank you. Thank you very, very much."

"I'll lead you up there now."

With that, the receptionist strode through a second set of glass doors and into Eastwick's hallowed bowels, with Barkley firmly in tow. In the hallway, he saw polished white floors and whitewashed brick walls, and up ahead, glass windows looking out onto a lush, triangular courtyard. They turned right at a stainless steel maintenance elevator and approached the entrance to a large, red-carpeted room.

"The library," she said, stopping. "Just had a two-hundred-thousand-dollar renovation, thanks to the donations of some powerful alumni. Did you know we have a Heisman winner?"

"I didn't."

"We do. See that glass skylight? Part of the renovation. And all those Dell computers along the fringes are new, too. Students can come in and work at those tables in the middle, as they're doing now for summer school. All the books are on those walls there, and then over there. Faculty workroom off to the side."

Barkley observed the scattering of male students in white dress shirts and black ties and female students in white dress shirts and gray skirts. He didn't understand why, in a school that wanted to exercise professionalism and chastity, *skirts* would be required. How was he, Barkley, or any male for that matter, supposed to concentrate? Not when every class had fifteen pairs of bare female legs slung out in front of him. No, he thought, don't even—

"Let's continue," the receptionist said. "We're short on time."

They moved again along the corridor and into a shadowy stairwell. Up one echoing flight and then out the double doors and into another long hallway lined with blue and yellow lockers—Eastwick's team colors for over a hundred years. It was unearthly quiet, Barkley thought. Most of the classroom doors stood open, and inside, elderly teachers stood firmly in front of wooden podiums and lectured in low tones. The students looked down and flipped pages in their textbooks, notebooks, folders. Pens moved, scratching soundlessly. Barkley felt himself swallow and realized the sound was actually audible. What was this place?

They followed the blue-and-yellow hallway to the end, then turned right and wound through the labyrinthine, brick-walled, quietly murmuring intestines of Eastwick's administration offices. The receptionist moved in quick strides, the hem of her dress swinging just around her ankles. She offered commentary here and there, and Barkley responded with the necessary pleasantries. They walked up a second staircase, passed the colorful shadows of the chapel, and finally stopped in an empty room with a long, bare desk, at least eight swivel chairs, and a stark crucifix on the far wall.

"This is where I leave you," she said. She offered a close-lipped smile. "Good luck."

"Thanks," Barkley said, but she had already stepped away.

Barkley couldn't help but stare at the rigid white crucifix, which, at a public school, would have been replaced with something else. A star-spangled flag, maybe. Or the earnest watercolor of a student. Maybe there was something to that idea—a way to use it in the interview. But too late: there were two sharp knocks on the door, and a grandmotherly woman in a maroon dress entered the conference room, making a beeline straight for him. Her glasses were perched high on her nose, frumpy, still-brown short hair parted down the middle, and wrinkled jowls swung from both sides of her face. She was full of excitement—or maybe agitation—it was difficult to tell. Barkley wondered if this was the department chair he had spoken with during the phone interview. Gleaming over the fabric of her dress was a small, silver crucifix. He felt his throat catch as she stopped in front of him.

"Barkley Brunson?" She held her hand out. "Margaret Carey. Chair of English. How are you?"

Barkley lurched forward to shake her hand. "Great to finally meet you. I'm—I'm doing well. Excited." Already stuttering, he thought.

She pointed toward the swivel chair at the head of the table. "Sit, Barkley."

"Great, sounds good." He sank down and she did the same, lowering herself into the adjacent seat and pushing her glasses to the bridge of her nose.

"You like sports, Barkley? Are you interested in coaching?"

"Yes, I love sports." Partially true. He looked up at the white ceiling, felt his hands clench.

Carey nodded. "And you are not an Eastwick alum, is that correct?"

"It is. I mean, that's correct. I—I attended Downers Grove North, just on the other side of town."

She wrinkled her nose. "Pretty wild over there, isn't it?"

"No discipline at all," Barkley agreed, wondering, *is this the angle to take?* He felt his breathing relax, his hands partially unclench.

Carey inhaled stiffly. "I tried my hand at public school teaching in the early days, and it just didn't work. And that was Hinsdale Central—supposed to be one of the better ones. You'll see that the children here, at a Catholic institution, follow instructions, engage in orderly behavior, and respect their teachers. The hallways are *silent.* But it's a different world out there." She motioned toward the monstrosities that lay outside the walls of Eastwick.

"I can imagine," Barkley said. "Discipline is huge for me. I can't tolerate unruly students."

Carey nodded again, holding his gaze. "Well, I want you to know that—on paper—your résumé makes you a strong candidate for this job. It really is all those creative writing classes on your college transcripts. The school is making a shift from reading to writing pedagogy, and I agree with this. Reading comprehension is well and good, but the high-functioning students must learn first and foremost how to impart their thoughts into meaningful sentences, with clarity."

"Yes, I absolutely agree."

"Now," Carey said, "what you have are two interviews. One with me, and one with the president, who is a Dominican priest. You should assume that he'll ask about your affiliation."

"My affiliation?" Barkley asked. He wanted to say that he wasn't even Catholic but didn't know if that mattered to Margaret Carey, too. Maybe they all cared. If anything, their mother had brought them up Lutheran, but neither he nor his brother had been to church in years. The only religion that made any sense was Buddhism, but he could only remember about three of the steps in the Eightfold Path, and wasn't there something about the Wheel of Dharma and reincarnating into woodland animals?

"It's possible that he'll ask you. Did you research Eastwick at all?" Carey asked.

"Oh, I've been on the Web site," Barkley said eagerly. "I checked out a bunch of the links, absolutely. Saw you guys won water polo again this year."

"We always win, Barkley. It's one of our many claims to fame. But in regard to the president, you should know that he'll ask you about the Dominican faith. He'll also ask you about how it feels to work at a religious institution, especially since you're coming from a public school."

"For the public to private transition? I've actually got an answer. I planned for that question."

From her briefcase, Margaret Carey pulled out a manila envelope and began spreading pages and data sheets around the table. Barkley recognized his undergraduate transcripts, his double-sided, ivory card stock résumé, his Type 09 Illinois teaching certificate.

"How's the year been treating you?" Barkley asked, raising his voice to a higher pitch.

Carey said nothing. She moved the sheets around the table as if she were trying to solve a puzzle. She pushed her glasses to the bridge of her nose again. Barkley noticed tiny, flesh-colored pockmarks on the sides of her cheeks—the faded craters of childhood acne, most likely.

"I need to know that I can trust you," Carey said suddenly. She was looking at him now, black eyes magnified behind the rims of her glasses.

"Oh," Barkley said. "Well, I certainly think you can."

Carey's gaze remained fixed.

"I mean," Barkley said, "in what regard? As a teacher? An employee? I think I'm trustworthy in all those areas."

"Barkley, I need to know that you'll do what I say. That you'll do what I ask. For instance, we have a policy in this school regarding plagiarism. If a student is caught, they receive no credit on the assignment, and the issue must be brought to the department chair. That means me. If a student is caught plagiarizing twice, they're gone."

"Out of Eastwick? For good?"

"Permanently. But sometimes these issues aren't reported. I've got teachers out there who want to give the students a break. Consider their backgrounds, they say. Some of them think the freshman should get freebies because they're new. And then I've got teachers who don't want to report the seniors. They're already gone, they say. Don't ruin collegiate futures over one mistake, they say. Everyone wants to handle these issues separately, inside their own classroom. Let me be clear: that doesn't work for me. So what I mean, Barkley, when I say I need to trust you, is I need to know you will follow my prerogatives. Explicitly."

"Of course," Barkley said. "Of course, I will."

Carey held up her hand. "Let me finish. We can't have every teacher creating their own autonomous governments out there. Some teachers— and this frequently includes the *young* teachers—think they don't need to follow these rules. But this isn't the thirteen colonies. I have one set of regulations, and I expect those under me to follow them. And in these aims, in the aims of a cohesive, comprehensive curriculum and an academic directive, I need to know that I can trust you, and that you will obey my prerogatives."

"Absolutely," Barkley said. "And I've got to tell you, I agree with the plagiarism issue completely. It's always been a big deal to me. It's one of my per-rog-as, I mean, one of my pet peeves. I caught a kid doing that once when I was student teaching."

Margaret Carey stared at him, then pursed her lips and shook her head from side to side. Barkley felt as if he was at the end of the road. This strange-looking old woman hated him. Across the table, Carey took Barkley's college transcripts and held them in both hands. They were close enough that Barkley could see the grades, mostly B's with some A's in Contemporary American Literature, Creative Writing, and South American Literature. An A- in Eastern Religions. And then he remembered the D. Oh, dear God, the D. Who knew what Carey would do when she saw it? Had she already seen it? Was this why she was mad? Would she send him away immediately? Complain about her prerogatives for teacher grade-point average not being followed?

Barkley squinted and stared at the transcript. The D loomed enormous, bursting off the page like a great white whale. He couldn't possibly explain how he got a D in a class called Age of Dinosaurs, couldn't explain that the title was a red herring, that it was a trick, that there were no dinosaurs. The class was all about memorizing ridiculous knee bones and exoskeleton spinal columns and all he'd wanted was to hear about a tyrannosaurus rex fighting a triceratops and the damn professor hadn't even shown a damn picture of a dinosaur the entire time. But that would be babble. All that remained was this gross, enormous, pornographic D, sitting legs spread on the transcript, begging anyone looking not to hire him. This one tragic mistake, after haunting him for years, was finally going to obliterate him.

"Well," Margaret Carey said, "I think you'd be a perfect fit here."

Barkley stared at the bridge of her thick, doughy nose. He nodded slowly. A perfect fit. She smiled, and the woman's teeth, twisting at odd angles, looked like tiny revolving doors. A perfect fit?

"This is all I need, Barkley. Your résumé is excellent. Your phone interview told me everything I need to know about your passion for education. You've taken six creative writing classes, and that's important to us. It's important to me. Writing is the departmental focus of English this year. It has to be the focus. Can we agree on that?"

"Absolutely."

"Will you follow my prerogatives? Do you agree that each classroom is not one of the thirteen colonies?"

"Yes. Of course."

"Then this was a productive meeting," Carey said, rising up. Barkley followed suit, and they shook hands.

"Thank you, Mrs. Carey."

She nodded, looked at him briefly, and then placed the manila folder back into her briefcase. She smiled. "Call me Margaret. We'll be in touch." And with that, she exited the room.

He'd made it. Part one complete. It was like playacting or something. Pretending he was somebody else. His brother or father, most likely. Yet Margaret Carey had accepted him, maybe even liked him. He looked around, trying to stay in the present, away from his ever-chattering mind, which snapped its beak constantly, like a voracious bird. And this bare-bones office: a room without memory, a room where meeting after meeting took place, only to be erased and cleaned out for the next. People probably got berated here. Or planned departmental curricula. Or got hired. Fired, even. Maybe all of those things occurred. He wondered if, months down the road, Margaret Carey would strain her memory, riding home one night from Eastwick in her rickety Lincoln, and think, *who was that potbellied kid we had in the conference room? The one who didn't get the job? The one who had the D in Age of Dinosaurs?* No, Barkley thought. He couldn't think like that.

He sighed, massaged his forehead, and considered. He pressed his index fingers against his temples. Spun once on the swivel chair. All that was left now was the Emperor, or whatever they called him. The president. The priest. It was like he was being visited by the ghosts of Christmas. And wasn't the last guy the scary one? All gnarled and bony and shrouded in a cloak? Did he have a scythe? Dickens had written that story, Barkley remembered. He really didn't like Dickens. Sentences so dense you needed a Weedwacker to cut through. What he wanted, what he craved in a book, was literature that didn't forget to entertain. *That* would be enjoyable to teach. Something with flow, something with set pieces and symbolism to boot.

Barkley looked around the room again. So bare. The white crucifix loomed over him. He had momentum going, didn't he? Just needed to follow through—which had been his problem since childhood. To drop the ball here, to come this close to what seemed like a successful interview, well, no. He couldn't do that. He couldn't go back to the way things were, shuffling around in his studio apartment, taking a single writing class, hoping for a woman or a job to jump into his lap. For once in his life, he had to follow through.

The president was going to ask him about the Dominican faith. His father had helped him come up with a plan for that. Yes. About public schools. The transition to Catholic. It had sounded so good when he'd structured it last night. His windows had been open and a breeze had swung in and coiled around him and made him sure his father's plan would work.

The office door opened, and a man with combed-over chestnut hair and a meticulous goatee, and wearing a flowing white robe, entered.

Some dark red beads were hanging down from his arm. Barkley rose from the table. What were the beads called? They looked like something stolen from an abacus.

"Barkley Brunson," the white-robed man said. An arm emerged from the gown like an animatronic limb.

Barkley stood and shook the man's hand. He had pale green irises. Strangely green, and unblinking. Barkley tried to read them for strangeness, for possible priestly creepiness, but caught nothing.

"I'm Father Burnham," he said calmly. "I'd like to tell you a little bit about my function here at Eastwick, and then I'll ask you some questions. Does that sound acceptable?"

"Of course."

"Fantastic. Let's sit. Now, I have the title of president, but my main focus, besides teaching a theology class spring semester, is my role as Eastwick's primary fund-raiser." He leaned forward, offered a mild smile. "Private schools like Eastwick require money from donors to stay afloat, to stay affluent, to offer the best experience and education to the students. Without the income from property taxes that public schools generate, fund-raising is absolutely crucial for us. Sure, we've got the fifteen-thousand-dollar yearly tuition from all students—but think of the expenses that goes toward. Administration salaries, teacher salaries, cafeteria food, athletic equipment. Library renovations and computer labs and school supplies. At a certain point, yearly tuition is not enough to keep our school running as well as it could. So my role, beyond Dominican leadership and theological instruction, is to visit both organizations and individuals, and continue the quest to keep Eastwick one of the top-funded private schools in the country. Making sense so far?"

"Yes," Barkley said.

"And one of the main effects of my role here is that you won't see me as much as you'll see, say, Principal Finn or Margaret Carey. I'm out in the field frequently. Of course, that doesn't mean I'm not available. I don't want anyone to come to that conclusion."

"I can tell you keep the lines of communication open," Barkley said, feeling horribly artificial.

Father Burnham gave his mild smile. "With that said, with your understanding of the needs of a private school like Eastwick in place, how do you see yourself fitting in here? Or more explicitly, your résumé describes you as a K through twelve public school student who went to a public university and student taught at a public, suburban high school. How do you feel about making a transition to faith-based education for the first time in your life?"

Barkley felt the seriousness of the question drop a shadow over the room. He knew his response was important, and Father Burnham wasn't grading him just on the right answer, but also on how he answered. This determined if he was right for the job. The man's green eyes appraised him, and Barkley swallowed, thought back to his father's phone call, and the sound of his voice, growling, *not good enough, Barkley. You need more. More.*

"Well?" Father Burnham asked.

"I've been in public schools my entire life," Barkley said, saying a private prayer for his own verbal dexterity. "It's true. And there's a positive to that experience. The rationale behind it, behind the absence of religion in a public school, is that it welcomes all faiths and modes of philosophy. It excludes no one and doesn't make a single student uncomfortable. At Downers North, we all walked those hallways knowing we could think whatever we wanted and go in whichever direction we wanted. That's what the public schools were said to offer, and to a certain extent, they did."

Burnham nodded.

"But," Barkley said, "there was always something missing. There was something else in play all those years. I felt it, and I know the other students felt it as well."

Burnham leaned forward, ever so slightly. Barkley took a breath.

"Because the absence of religion is just that: an absence. And absences, in my opinion, are always felt. Even by those of us who didn't have a faith-based upbringing in the first place. The thing is, freedom of religion is one thing, but a total absence of religion, especially during those crucial, formative years when young adults *need* guidance, when they *need* a moral philosophy, when they *need* a helping hand and something to believe in—that's different. Having a religious presence can save a lot of students from depression and a poor family life and bad decisions. I can't tell you how many public school students I know who could have benefited from a faith-based academic environment, simply because that type of guidance gives students who are changing, or who are lost, or who are in turmoil—it gives them something to believe in. A compass to follow, if you will. And isn't that why schools exist in the first place? To guide and mold young adults into the best possible versions of themselves? I believe that a school with faith-based education is a school that's operating at its full potential. And full potential, in my mind, is an institution doing everything in its power to better prepare young people for the future. So I have to say, in all honesty, that even though I've attended public schools devoid of religious guidance throughout my formative years, I've been waiting for this opportunity my entire life. Because this is the place where the best education possible occurs, it's the place where faith-based education makes young adults *better*, where it supports them, and it's the place where, quite frankly, I've always wanted to be."

Barkley sank back in his chair and let out a breath. It was the most operatic, self-contained moment of beautiful bullshit he had ever spouted, and he hadn't even stuttered or trailed off, and somewhere deep down, he might even have been convinced by the words. But around him, as if the weather of the room were clearing, he felt the energy shift, the shadows dissolve, and the mild smile on Father Burnham's face become large.

THE CHEDDAR
CHEESE MAN

"It's gallstones," Henry said, hunched over the doctor's table. "My buddy, Glenn, he says it's open and shut. And don't you have those electromagnetic whatchamacallits? The machines that pulverize the stones, no surgery needed? That's what I'm looking to do here. Can't afford to be lying on the butcher's block. Time-wise, I mean. My insurance covers everything. But time-wise. Gotta be out there. My window is limited."

Dr. Pashad smiled at him. The office was small. Certificates lined the walls, laden with emphatic, flourishing signatures and official-looking gold stars. Henry liked to see the certificates. It wasn't pompous, like some easily offended ninnies thought; it was reassuring. He wanted every inch of the walls to be covered in certificates, in commendations, in awards. It was the aura that mattered, and Pashad had it, cultivated it, and made him feel as if he was in the dexterous hands of a medical master.

"We'll know for sure on Wednesday," Pashad said in his smooth but vaguely clipped English. "The blood tests confirm that it's not malaria, or any other parasitic disease. But of course, that wasn't expected in the first place."

"So it's gallstones, correct?" Henry said. "Everyone is saying gallstones. This fucking skin of mine—" He held up his yellowed arms again, as if Pashad had forgotten. "And my *eyes*."

"The most common symptom of gallstones *is* the jaundice, Mr. Brunson." He held up a finger. "But not all jaundice is caused by gallstones. The ultrasound of the gallbladder will determine that."

"But it's what you're expecting, right?"

Pashad gave Henry a long look. "Mr. Brunson, I wouldn't be shocked if that was the cause. However—"

"Exactly what Glenn told me," Henry said, whistling.

Dr. Pashad smoothed out his lab coat and opened the door. "We'll know for sure on Wednesday. And remember: no food or drink for the twelve hours before the appointment."

"What about my eyes? I swear they look like wheels of cheese in the dark."

"Mr. Brunson, tests first, solutions later. All in good time."

"Those damn gallstones."

Pashad chuckled stiffly. "See you on Wednesday, Mr. Brunson."

In the climate-controlled contours of the Mercedes, Henry marveled at the way his life was turning. Only the beginning of August, and Trend-Star had already moved Dorfman into the refurbished corner office, with a penthouse-worthy view of Lake Michigan. The company had approved Dorfman's request for a leviathan Mac desktop and a leather swivel chair with eight comfort settings and some kind of cherrywood desk, all while Henry sat using the same equipment he'd been stuck with for eight years. Julie was leaving two voice mails a day again. And his eyes—his eyes and skin—that floozy in the red dress had been right: he was turning into the cheddar cheese man. Gallstones. Fuck it, give him kidney stones, he'd piss the pebbly bastards out just like he did before, when he was thirty-two. But now, when he got dressed, he actually found himself considering, *what color would work best with yellow?* The answer, incidentally, was a dark, autumnal red. Which, also incidentally, is what he wore when Chelsea came over. Chelsea of pink phone number fame, Chelsea who after three visits in one week was becoming his first regular, Chelsea whom he still knew almost nothing about. He knew she'd come from the West Coast; not California, but somewhere in Oregon or Washington.

He knew she liked thunderstorms, became a little kid when she heard the sounds. He knew she liked how his penthouse stood above everything, for the same reasons he did.

Chelsea arrived just past eleven every night, smelling vaguely of alcohol and unfiltered cigarettes. Their sex would begin immediately. No hellos, no pleasantries—she would toss her purse onto the kitchen's granite countertop and roll her jacket onto the floor and come toward him with immediate, feverish need. They tried every position, fucking in the most ridiculously acute and obtuse angles, using any kind of apparatus they could think of. In the bedroom, the bathroom, the shower, the Jacuzzi, halfway out the balcony, on almost every elevated surface the penthouse had. But it was all a sideshow. The reason he kept calling Chelsea back was because of what came after—the fact that he knew she would stay over, instead of leaving like all the others. They would lie in bed, side by side, and she would take his hand in the shadows and clasp it with an intensity that shocked him. She was thinking of something else, he decided. Who knew what it was? But their hand-holding did the trick, and even as he knew it wasn't good for either of them, he let it continue, on into each night, until he fell asleep. Sometimes her long, pink fingernails would dig into the tops of his hands, and he didn't mind at all.

In the mornings, she was gone.

His iPhone buzzed as he merged onto the Eisenhower Expressway, heading east—a text message from Barkley. *Got the job!!!* it said. Henry chuckled to himself. Damn right you did. After being prepped by the grand master. But he had the mindfulness to write back, *Congrats, kid. Let's buy you some professional clothes sometime soon.*

Charlie was another story. It was a stalemate—trench warfare between father and son. Sure, the kid was mad at him for leaving their mother, for his romantic excursions (which weren't his business), for his anger and lack of support regarding the war. But Henry was angry, too. The kid had burned the bridge on his contacts at Lucent, thrown away a job that hadn't been easy to pull strings for. He'd tossed himself into danger without talking to the family about it, without being open to what actually was *best*. And he hadn't even responded to his e-mails while over there in those mountain shitholes. Ignoring his own father—not acceptable. And so Henry would not budge, would not compromise the simple law that no one pushed Henry Brunson around. If Charlie wanted to see him, to talk to him, he would have to be the one to make the move.

But now came an idea that had been floating in his mind for days, an answer to Julie and Charlie, without having to move a muscle. Henry hit the number for Al's cell phone, a number he hadn't called in at least three months.

"Al," he said as the familiar voice mail greeting came up. "How are you, buddy? Hey listen. Remember all those deep-dish pizzas and beers I bought you back in the day? Well, I've finally got a way for you to pay me back."

CUTTING THE WIRE

Rock bottom actually felt soft, Julie decided. It was a feeling of losing bones, of everything hard and rigid and supportive slipping away, floating across a still pond, one by one. First went her tibias and phalanges and vertebrae, gliding across the water like ivory lily pads and stark-white buoys, and then her spinal column sank to the bottom like a two-by-four, and then her breastbone and hip bone and rib cage and finally her skull, all of it slipping away across the pond, across the still water, until what remained was a husk on the shore: a woman of no resistance.

Rock bottom was giving up, but when you got there, it didn't feel like *giving* anything. It felt as if a burglary had taken place; as if she had walked into her foyer and saw the broken glass and the torn-up living room and the places where the television and couch and table used to be and instead there was nothing, just empty space and more broken glass and frayed wires hanging limply from the walls. Her stone bridge was falling away and looking more and more like a plank, and now there was no feeling but the Zoloft, the Zoloft, and the promise of silence. Because even with her pills, the soothing feeling of cotton balls on her brain and belly wasn't so much cotton balls anymore but simple white masses that blocked the smell of her own helplessness, that came at her like clouds of blinding snow. Everything felt like winter now, everything that had been her and her purpose was gone, lost under piles of rising white powder. Lost at the bottom of the still pond, now freezing over, under a carapace of ice.

Elmhurst was only a fifteen-minute drive from Downers Grove, and she found the old limestone quarry along West Avenue and Second Street, about a half mile west of downtown. The quarry, she'd read, was about 150 feet deep, full of sharp edges and cracked creases and stunted cliffs. Did anyone care where she was going? Henry was gone, she knew that now. If he wouldn't visit his eldest son, he certainly wouldn't return to a wife he'd left of his own volition. But it was more than Henry—even her children didn't look at her expectantly anymore, simply brushed right past her. Charlie had flatly told her, just last night, that he didn't need her help. No, that wasn't quite it. He stayed in his room with his laptop and his movies and he told her, over and over again, that she *couldn't* help. That she couldn't even understand. It had been two straight weeks of this. So what else was there? Her neighbors were boring and self-involved, and offered nothing like the connection she'd had with Melanie. But she and Melanie were no longer talking. So again: what else was there?

There was a black iron fence that wrapped around even the most desolate edges of the quarry. Skinny trees and shrubbery blocked most of the view, but through the leaves and fence she could see the gaping hole in the ground and all those shades of jagged white. She parked the Honda and walked over to the fence, each step widening the view through the shrubs of the crater that lay before her. In her left hand she held the small silver necklace that Henry had bought her, supposedly during a business trip in San Antonio. She reached the fence and looked through the openings at the deep stone ridges that fell back into the hole. There were tiny orange construction machines moving at the bottom. Julie cocked her arm back and tossed the necklace over the side.

"Damn, lady. You don't like silver?"

Julie turned. There was a short, red-haired teenager standing against the fence some twenty feet away, smoking a cigarette. He shook his head at her.

"Not worth that much," Julie called back. She felt herself shivering against the contact of a stranger. If she could just keep smiling a little longer—

"I mean, there are easier ways," he said. "Like garbage cans. Or thrift stores. Like that one on York Road? The one with all the pocket watches and panda dolls in the windows? That's where I got these." And he lifted up his white shoes and showed them to her.

"Shoes?" she asked. "At a thrift shop?" She looked back through the holes in the fence, at the crater beyond.

"Unbelievable," the kid said. "Converse All Stars. Right on York Road. The place with the pandas, I'm serious."

Julie smiled stiffly and looked at the fence again. She'd have to walk around, away from this child, and find another place to climb over. Was there barbed wire everywhere? Had they put it up to stop people like her?

"I should apologize," the kid said. "I'm a little stoned. I got grounded. Fucked up a summer school math test. Who really needs the slope intercept formula, can you tell me that?"

"I don't know."

"And now I'm, like, on the run or something. Not like running away. Just avoiding. And when I get grounded, I get stoned, and when I get stoned, I talk to people. Like what I'm doing now. I mean, I have no idea who you are. You could report me. You're not going to report me, are you?"

"It's okay," Julie said. She thought that if she didn't look at him, maybe he'd drift away into the atmosphere, or turn into a pile of leaves. She closed her eyes and tried to feel the cotton balls.

"Are you going to report me?"

Julie finally turned. The red-haired kid was still leaning against the fence. He wore ratty cargo shorts and a gray T-shirt with the black sketching of a sword, and his cigarette was a glowing nub.

"No," she said. "I don't care. It doesn't matter to me. Keep smoking for all I care."

"I will," he said. "I'm planning on smoking for another two hours."

"That's good."

"Thanks for not reporting me."

"Listen," Julie said. "I have to go."

But where could she go? Around the fence. But the other sides of the fence were busier—more traffic on the roads. In her purse were the wire cutters. The cutters would work for the barbed wire. And she could climb the fence. She'd been athletic in her day. Not a jock, in the end, but a dancer. Flexible. Strong legs. Good balance. Dancing had been an outlet, but getting there had not been easy. Her parents had signed her up for pottery when she was in third grade, but that hadn't worked. She had too much energy just to sit in a smock and paint stupid clay jars in bold, obvious colors like the rest of the art kids. And in fourth grade her parents signed her up for violin and she *hated* violin. She hated the way the chin rest jammed into her neck and bruised her and made it look like she was active and physical like the boys who got to play football in Washington Park. In her case the bruises didn't earn her anything, she still didn't get to move or run around, she was just sitting there in that plastic black chair with that chicken scratch music next to other girls with pale skin and straight hair and boring dresses who didn't want to be active at all. God, she'd hated violin. She hated pottery, too, but violin more; she hated having to cut her fingernails so short and the way her back hurt after a practice and the calluses on her hand and of course those unearned bruises, and who could forget the shrieking eel music and the methodical children who seemed to have no thoughts but the ones their parents wanted? In the fifth grade she'd screamed at her mother and taken a black pen and drawn all over the violin and thrown it behind the shed where her father kept his lawn equipment. That got her grounded, and when she was finally released she went out to Washington Park and demanded to play football and at first Teddy and Walt and the other boys refused to hit her or play her tough, but she remembered her first touchdown, she remembered catching that short pass and then pushing Walt to the muddy ground and outrunning Teddy the rest of the way, hooting and hollering and running backward, and after that, after *that*, they had played her tough, and all summer she'd come home with fresh bruises that made her heart sing.

It was during the end of that summer before sixth grade, after she got her rear molar knocked out during a scrum against the middle school brats, that her parents told her enough was enough, and dropped her off at the dance studio. She didn't even know what dancing was, then. The studio was full of lightly colored wooden floors and horizontal support beams that ran along the edges. There were mirrors behind those beams and also a high ceiling, and the teacher was a woman who had the most shockingly beautiful body Julie had ever seen. Miss Pelletier, they called her, and the first dancing style she learned was jazz, and then tap, and then ballet (which she hated), and then, as she grew older, modern dance, creative dance, dance through feeling and emotion and movement, and sometimes and then frequently more times she danced alone by herself on a dark stage with a single light that shone down, illuminating. Finally her parents, her parents in that audience with the rest of the crowd holding their programs, watched how their daughter could be good at something and love it, too, how she could be a woman and at the same time be moving and active, and after college, it was this movement that she missed, that she missed so desperately it hurt. She had always wanted to teach dance, to be back in that studio that smelled of polished wood and hand chalk, but there had been Henry, and Henry had been more, done more, said more, convinced her, yes, he'd convinced her to give up the studio that was in her heart and to put himself in its place. He'd asked to become her new dream, and she'd said yes. And now, all of this led to the quarry, to the drop, to the cotton balls that felt like winter, to the need for sweet silence now that the dream in her heart had left.

"Ma'am?"

Julie realized her eyes were closed. She should have come when it was dark, she knew, but she'd wanted to see the crater, she'd wanted to really look at it. But now it was only five o'clock and the sun was still up and this child, this child.

"Hey, ma'am? Excuse me."

Julie sighed. She opened her eyes. The red-haired teenager was standing closer to her now.

"You all right?"

"Fine."

"I mean, you're standing there with a pair of pliers in your hand. You breaking in or something?"

Julie tried to feel anger but really, honestly, couldn't. She couldn't muster anything anymore. "Go away, now," she said.

"Hey."

She shook her head. "I just need some time alone."

"With those pliers."

"Maybe you could come back in half an hour."

The kid flicked his cigarette into the grass. "You know," he said, "I've got a sister who works at a bookshop. And she reads all these books and she tells me that almost all of great literature only becomes great when people start making life-or-death decisions. Like, for example, *Lord of the Flies*. It doesn't become top-notch until Piggy dies, until the stakes are raised to life or death."

"Debatable," Julie said, thinking back. "Debatable."

"I'm just talking about my sister, here. But she thinks that when you add in death, literature picks up steam. You know? It kind of seals the deal. It adds weight. Without the threat of death, it's like, okay, it's a good book. But add death and it's a great book. Isn't that weird?"

Julie looked at the kid. He smelled like decent marijuana. Not good, but okay. She'd smoked with her friends sporadically in college and then with Henry and then Henry had said they were adults and they shouldn't be smoking anymore.

"What are you going to do with those pliers?" the kid asked.

"I need you to go away, now. Please."

He pulled a white pack out of his pocket and withdrew a cigarette that looked like a long piece of chalk.

"If you're going to smoke another one of those, maybe you can do it somewhere else," Julie said. The cotton balls, she thought to herself, but she couldn't find them. Even the cotton balls were gone. She squeezed the rubber handles of the wire cutters.

"I'm not leaving," the kid said. "What are you going to do with those? Go over the fence? Into the quarry? Why? People have jumped from there, you know. I'm taking Intro to Philosophy. We talked about this kind of thing. Are you trying to get into the quarry?"

"No."

He crossed his arms. "Then what?"

Julie wanted him to leave so badly and she didn't know why he wouldn't and she didn't even know this child and it made her feel so powerless that this kid, this damn kid, she couldn't even overpower him or get him to move she was nothing, she was spent, she was all exhaust fumes and fading ether, she wanted the kid to turn into a pile of dried leaves and blow away and she couldn't move him and there was nothing left to her, she was sure of it. She felt the tears on her face then, she felt them leaking hot and wet and trickling salt into her mouth, and she felt her nose running and she felt this kid move forward and say hushed words to her and put his arm around her shoulders and then she cried more because she couldn't even remember the last time someone had *touched* her like that. This kid had his arm around her and she felt herself shaking and then drop down into the grass with the stiff metal of the fence against her back. She just wanted it to be over and to give up and to split apart and fade away and the kid had his arm around her and she was so far gone that she wasn't even embarrassed, didn't even care, she felt her cheeks turn to slippery water and her body shake and she knew the Zoloft hadn't been letting her cry and now she sat with her back against the side of that fence with the teenage kid holding his arm around her and she cried and cried and cried, and she cried for her children who didn't need her anymore and her husband who was lost, she saw that now, she felt pity for him, she saw outside herself and above the corn maze for the first time in a long time, she saw how lost her once sweet Henry was, and she wept over her knowledge that he would never be back and that she didn't want him back because what he'd been and what he was now were so different, and he'd betrayed her, and her friends, she wept for her friends who seemed to see life no more than three feet beyond them and certainly not out of their own backyards, these neighborhood friends who watched over their children like birds of prey but still seemed to see nothing and feel nothing and think nothing. And at last she wept for the dance studio that had been in her heart and then lost so many years ago, how she missed the studio and had thrown it so far away and put Henry in its place, how she had chosen another person over herself, how this was only fair, how it was fair, she deserved it, and she thought of the studio and the sweet smell of that wood and those support beams and the silhouettes of the dancers moving in the mirrors and in the shadows on the floor and she felt herself her true self and knew she was still lost in that room. It was only fair, and she felt the grass beneath her and the fence against her back and the arm of the teenager around her shoulders and a cool, solid feeling entered her body, ran through her limbs and muscles and heart, and she felt herself crying but saw from above and yes, she agreed, it was only fair, she had loved someone more than herself and this is where the path led, she deserved it, it was fair, and, unbelievably, through all the fog and desperation she saw the old dance studio again and saw that there was a bridge after all, there were planks leading to all other places, planks all around her, but there was still one bridge that remained, a real bridge, and she didn't need anyone else to get there and she knew then that nothing in the world mattered more than getting across it, just crossing it, and she felt her hands relax and finally drop the wire cutters.

There was a long moment of silence before Julie heard the overhead passing of a jet and the distant whine of car engines and the rattling of a drill down in the quarry.

"Ma'am?" the kid said.

She could hear him now. She felt how wet her cheeks were. She tasted the salt on her lips.

"What do you want me to do?" he asked. "I'm really, really sorry, ma'am. I'm really sorry."

Julie stood up slowly and picked up the wire cutters and even the touch of them felt wrong so she handed them to the kid, to the kid who had put his arm around her.

"What do you want me to do?" he asked.

"I don't know," she said, wiping her eyes. "Throw them over the edge. Will you?"

"Sure. I mean, I can definitely do that. But we could easily trade these in to the panda store, get you something better in return. I can do that, too. I can trade them in for you."

Julie laughed. "No," she said. "Over the edge they go. Throw them as far as you can, please."

She kept her eyes on the road. The kid stood up, then grunted as he hurled the wire cutters into the air. She closed her eyes—was it possible to hear them strike the bottom? She imagined them circling through space. She waited to hear the sound.

AN M79 MAN IN
A CLUTTERED OFFICE

"The people running the country know history, but they don't appreci-ate it," Al said, scratching his mustache. "They don't *feel* it anymore. They don't feel for the way America was in the 1800s, after winning her inde-pendence, or even in the early 1900s, when anything was possible. Once you understand that, and get past the heartbreak of it, it's possible to see with clarity."

"The heartbreak," Charlie repeated, settling down into his chair. It was uncomfortable, he thought, being away from his room. And he needed a drink.

"Yes. Do your reading on Thomas Jefferson and John Adams and Thomas Paine and Ben Franklin. These aren't cartoon characters. They are brilliant minds, devoted people who would die to create the perfect society. Think of it: to fix all the mistakes in our shared human past, and place into action the systematic minutiae and large-scale ide-alism required to craft a society in its greatest, purest form. Free, pros-perous, welcoming of new and old ideas, both powerful and benevolent. Jefferson himself said, 'Peace, commerce, and honest friendship with all nations—entangling alliances with none.' Think of it: this place, all of it, was *engineered* by brilliant minds. The fact that this country ever got made in the first place is a miracle, and that it existed as it was intended, without much subterfuge or sabotage for so long, is truly remarkable. And then Lincoln, Lincoln, now, there were a lot of reasons for that war, but the end result, which many more died for, brought us even closer to our original philosophy. And then you have Martin Luther King, using his ideals to bring America as close to the cutting edge of a moral society as possible. And with America on the cusp of really making it, really being free, you know, you have Vietnam. And that's where the heartbreak really begins, and where the subterfuge and sabotage began to change this country for good."

"Because we didn't win the war? Because we withdrew?"

Al waved his hand. "It was the methodology of the whole thing. The CIA and the Defense Department, acting like they're on top of Olympus. The deceit with the Gulf of Tonkin alone—with Johnson perverting public opinion—do I have to say more? Sure, we've always had a degree of propaganda in our military machine, a need to sell war bonds and recruit soldiers, but outright lies that cost tens of thousands of American lives? It was just the beginning, too. And on the flip side of what we've done abroad, you've got the entertainment and commercial industry, babysitting citizens that know less and less about the world beyond their borders. Of course, Charlie, this is only my opinion. You can look outside and see one hundred happy customers sipping their Starbucks. But is this what the creators of our country imagined? Are we still functioning under the principles of the ideal human society? Do our leaders *feel* the beauty and brilliance of what went into creating this place? I say, no. I say, every day we move closer and closer to becoming the big, honking wheel of death that the world will eventually have to mercy kill. And the citizens inside—more and more illiterate, lacking ideals, lacking purpose, each young mind given the keys to ambivalence and the spare cash and toys to stay there. Stars and Stripes, you say? How about Xbox, Taco Bell, and Twitter? With distractions like that, the days fall away like dominoes."

Charlie looked around Al's study, at the trinkets and photographs, at the piles of yellowed newspaper and VHS tapes and DVD documentaries. A single window looked out onto the neighbor's yard and sprinkler system. When the voice mail had come from Al, saying his father wanted them to speak, it was the one true thing, the only thing, that had gotten him out of the house. Years ago, the old vet had come across as little more than a loopy friend of his father, telling stories that always had sad endings. Now he seemed like the only voice capable of knowledge, or worthy of respect.

"I don't know what to say," Charlie said.

Al leaned forward. "That's the problem. That's the stage you have to get out of. I was there once. You come home and there's so much in your head and heart that you don't know where to go with it. But you've gotten out of the bedroom, that's step one. And now we need to get you talking, forming opinions again. What you have to understand is that the men who serve know *more*, not less, than the average citizen. Our opinions count for more, you get me?"

"Then why don't you do something, Al? Speak up? Write a book? Someone with your intellect, with your experience, all the reading you've done—"

"Charlie." Al sighed. "One thing I've learned to accept, about myself as a man, is that I'm damaged goods. So far corkscrewed in the wrong direction that only death will release the twisted pressure inside."

"But don't you think people need to hear this stuff?"

"Seriously, Charlie. I'm fucked-up good. But at least now I'm *functioning* fucked-up. That didn't use to be the case. It's taken me a long time to get here, but now I can live each day with a modicum of basic happiness, regardless of the madness and sadness around it. And I can learn, and read, and even synthesize. Maybe I can write. But, Charlie, this all comes from knowing I'm a lost cause. Too fucked-up to move beyond myself. If I tried to get involved, if I got my emotions riled up and going again like I did when I was young, it would all lead to the same thing."

"And what's that?"

"Killing myself," Al said simply. He patted his chest. "I can't let emotion into this place anymore. Too many things don't work. Too many cogs and wheels busted beyond repair. And nobody wants to see me go back to the way I used to be. God." Al looked pained, and his face bunched up and he leaned forward in a grimace.

Charlie moved to put a hand on his shoulder but watched as Al breathed in and out, closed his eyes, and eventually made the creases in his face dissolve.

"I'm good," he said, finally. "I just can't go beyond the place I've made for myself."

"But all that knowledge," Charlie said. "All those beliefs. That *purpose*. I've been looking for it my whole life, and you've found it."

Al smiled but looked tired. "I have found it, and I'm happy to keep it to myself. But you—you're going to be fine. You're still close to the man you've always been. And you haven't done anything since getting back to the States, you haven't driven yourself further into that hole. There's still time. You see? You can be the person you wish I was. Just skip all the fucking cocaine and the fighting and the divorces. Follow your gut instincts."

"My gut is what I can't find anymore."

"No, no, it just seems like that. Your real gut can still talk to you. It feels lighter, cooler than that red mess of rage and guilt you're mired in. Follow that lightness. It's always there. Took me thirty years to realize that it was, but it is. It really is."

Charlie shook his head. "I hear what you're saying. But all the shit that's happened—it's like I can see myself on the other side of this canyon, but I can't get across. The people in my life, that's the person they want. And I don't know who this is." He patted himself on the heart. "I don't know what this thing is that's looking through my eyes. I can see myself across that gap, and I know I can't get to him. So what's left? When I think about it too much I just want to beat the shit out of someone."

"Yeah," Al said, nodding. "Been there. Done that, in fact, many times. But still—it doesn't fix anything."

"And the guilt, the fucking guilt over what I've done. I'm a monster, Al. And to not feel bad every second of every day is to be OK with what the monster has done. To accept him. To not feel bad is to . . . to forgive his existence. Guilt is the only thing that keeps me human."

"Guilt," Al spat, "is the stupidest fucking thing in the world."

"But as penance—"

"True penance is when you do something productive. But once you understand your actions are wrong, guilt is just about the most pointless thing in the world. It's a mental block, and an idiotic one. Absolutely idiotic."

"How? What the hell is wrong with guilt? And what the fuck does it block?"

"Happiness. It blocks even the smallest amount of happiness. And true progress. True acceptance. It blocks all of it. Guilt is nonsensical self-hatred. It does nothing but damage the person who already knows he's wrong."

"That's your opinion."

"Charlie, it's one I'm right about. I've lived this life, too, remember."

"No offense, Al, but if I lose the guilt I lose myself."

"You've already lost yourself, or so you said. All guilt does, all it's ever done, is halt the progress, halt the recovery, of the individual. It prevents the healing of broken men and women. I'm serious. Once you understand that, the truth that guilt has no purpose in a functioning human life, you'll move on. But as long as you tell yourself you require it as some sort of punitive medicine, you'll stay in this funk, thinking you're a monster. You think you need it to stop hating yourself, but guilt *is* hate. Yeah, yeah. I'm like a walking pop psychology book. But this is from experience, Charlie. It doesn't matter if it's from the jungle or the desert. Knowledge is knowledge."

"It's still your opinion. But I'll think about it."

"Or, if you can, you talk about it. That's real therapy. They've got sessions—"

"And why can't I just talk to you?"

"Beyond this? I'm not certified, kid. And I can't promise you'll get the answer you like. I don't give hugs. Or, correction, I've given about three in the last twenty or so years. So, I'm not the most compassionate bastard to be listening to troubled souls."

"But if I want to talk?"

Al shrugged. "Those of us who've served are a special breed. And one of the things that makes us special is that we don't surprise one another. Anything you tell me, either I've done it, I've seen it, or I've had a friend who experienced it. Shit, kid. Everything we've seen or done has happened a million times before. God created man, man created war, war changed man. It's a story as old as time. If you want to talk, go ahead."

"I do, I think. I want to talk about what happened after Campo died."

Al lifted a cigarette from his coat pocket, leaned forward, and lit it. "You want one?"

"Nah. Campo smoked, I didn't. And then pretty soon after he died I was going through a pack a week, and then a pack a day. Psychologist over there even recommended it."

"Good enough reason to start. Sure you don't want one?"

Charlie saw Campo in his mind's eye, saw the way he was lying across the rocks. Saw the remains of his face, only for a moment. He leaned forward and put a hand over his mouth, felt hot needles in his eyes.

"You okay, kid?"

Charlie choked back a sob. "His face was shot to hell. I mean, I can barely describe it. Jesus. His fucking face. My fucking friend. And I told him nothing, nothing about how much he did for me. What kind of guy he was. And he had a wife. A wife. Oh, Jesus Christ. My goddamn best friend in the whole army. My buddy since middle school. And no one *pays* for it. No one even cares."

"You care. Shit, I'm sure all of you care."

Charlie was silent. He brought his hands up to his eyes, smeared the wetness around.

"You'll notice," Al said, "that you're not getting a hug. Tears or no tears. I warned you. I'm a heartless fucking bastard."

Charlie laughed, coughed, balled up his eyes again. "Jesus. I didn't expect that so soon. I mean, I've got my brother asking if I've fought any goddamn snipers, like in *The Hurt Locker.*"

"Shit, you know how many questions I got about *Platoon?* Or if I ever knew a drill sergeant like the one in *Full Metal Jacket?* Regular civilians are educated by entertainment, they can't help it. Doesn't make them any less stupid, though. No offense to your brother."

"Nah, none taken. And I was the same as him once—I went to war partially because of war movies, if you can believe that sort of idiocy. My father thinks I'm an idiot for serving my country."

"Charlie," Al said. "You *are* an idiot for serving your country. Same as me. I mean, what the fuck are we doing out there? It's the same thing with Vietnam. Why were people risking their lives and dying for some goofy, dysfunctional bastards in the middle of a rain forest?"

"So you regret serving, then?"

"Didn't say that. I just said we're idiots. But that doesn't make us any less brave. Fuck it if we aren't the bravest motherfuckers on the planet."

"And stupid?"

"Sure. And stupid. But our kind of stupidity is something special, don't you agree?"

Charlie smiled. "Yeah."

"So talk. After your buddy passed away . . ."

Charlie looked at the ground. The lurch of trembling emotions had vanished, and he saw clearly into his past, as if it were unfolding in front of him. "So, when he was gone, it was like my reason for joining the army was totally forgotten. Or changed. I mean, I joined so I could do something good, with meaning, with actual merit. Experience that rare thing. And I know I was starting to lose that over time, I mean, days and days of downtime, and then attack, and then more downtime. So many hours of quiet, and then ambush. Killing. It's hard to keep your reasons straight. And the fucking adrenaline of the violence, it's—"

"Exciting?" Al asked, smiling.

"Fuck, yes. When you're not shitting yourself, it's a goddamn rush, I'm not kidding. Now, getting shot at, well that sucks, I'm not saying I want to get shot or I think taking a bullet is great. And mortar fire— that's the worst. But in a sense, it's the ultimate contest. The ultimate stakes. Kill or be killed. And when you first play it, after you get over that panic of *holy shit, they're shooting at me, my life could go black any minute,* you realize it's the absolute pinnacle. Nothing in this world is more intense. And horrible, of course. But *hitting* one of those bastards, dropping him—"

"Bliss," Al said. "Nobody understands it back here. In fact, you flat out can't talk like that or they think you're damaged goods."

"We are damaged goods. You even said so."

"But that doesn't make the excitement of killing any less true. Sure, not everyone felt it. I had guys in my squad lamenting, torturing themselves about it. Others were scared to death about taking a bullet, losing their friends. But those of us who got it, who accepted it?" Al whistled. "Damn. A whole new world."

"Didn't you feel bad?"

"Sure, maybe at first. A little. But once they kill one of your guys, you realize the stakes. No more feeling bad. I mean, there was this one time, up in the Mekong, after my buddy went down, this kid, funniest kid in the platoon. Everybody called him Gnocchi—long story. But he got taken out by these bastards who were up high with a .30 caliber, who had us pinned, and I was an M79 man, you dig? My first shot was a panic, way off, hit the tops of the trees. I remember all these leaves and branches raining down. And then I loaded another grenade, and you know how the M79 has that aluminum popping sound, like uncorking a champagne bottle? Well, I fired, and there was the *pop*, and then, one second of waiting, and *bam*! I literally saw the gook bastard blown in half. His torso went about fifteen feet in the air. And you know what? It. Felt. Good."

"Truth," Charlie said. "And you don't expect it to be that way. To be that simple."

"Which isn't to say, 'Hi, I'm Al, and I love killing people.' I'm no sociopath. But the unparalleled rush. What really kills the spirit is the downtime. Thinking about what you've done is exponentially worse than actually doing it. And then, of course, the self-hatred—but all of it comes from the thinking, not the doing."

Charlie snapped his fingers. "It's kind of like the realization is what fucks you up the most. The idea that taking a life can be exciting *and* horrible. Because you're not supposed to like it. And even though it's the truth, it still breaks apart everything you knew about the world. About being human. It shatters you. And the time in between is awful. I mean, every day we were afraid of getting hit by the Taliban's fucking plunging fire coming down those mountains. We were afraid of the mortars, shit yeah. I mean, what the point of those HESCOs was, I'll never know, because the bastards were *above* us. They'd just shoot right over the fucking top of them. But, yeah. We never asked for more fighting. During downtime, we were crossing our fingers not to get hit again. Praying to live just another day, thinking of our women, our high school friends, our family. Praying for life. But once we were in the shit, really in it, with those bullets snapping back and forth—it was different. We learned the secret."

Al's eyes widened. "It's the biggest shot of adrenaline the human body can handle without dying. And what's adrenaline? Essentially, a drug. So sure, you feel horrible about what you're doing in the abstract sense, and in the battles you fear for your life in the logistical sense, but once that adrenaline kicks in—"

"It's like tripping balls, but seeing clearly," Charlie finished. "Once I got used to it, I'd get this, like, Spider-Man super-sense. And you're right, it wasn't till after, till the downtime, that you really feel bad. Till the self-hatred kicks in. Thinking about all of it, what you've done, what you've become, driving yourself crazy. But it's like we hated ourselves for learning the truth."

"Until your friends die," Al said. "Then you can hate them even more than you hate yourself."

Charlie was quiet for a long time. He listened to the ticking of Al's grandfather clock, to the next-door neighbor's sprinkler stuttering and twitching its way around their yard. Finally, he looked up. "About two weeks after Campo died, we got ambushed again. I mean, basically, we wanted this to happen. It sounds crazy, but that was our actual strategy. Patrol around until they hit us. Then we fire back, call in air support, and try to take them out before they get away. And air support was a whole 'nother nightmare. Clearances had to be made. Confirmations. Fucking bureaucracy, man. There had to be a perfect understanding about collateral damage—what towns were nearby? What farms? What property? How would the villages respond? Would the elders go against us, begin siding with the Taliban? Sometimes, by the time air support got there, the hajji fucks would be driven back, and we'd get some kills. But other times the Apaches were, like, fifteen minutes late, and the bastards were already gone, and we just ended up firing on empty mountainside."

"You're bringing back memories," Al said. "Gotta love the chain of command taking you down to the pace of escargot."

"So, anyway, we get ambushed. Same kind of thing as when Campo died, but we're better prepared this time, and they're worse for wear. I mean, some of those hajjis must have been new recruits, the way they were spending ammunition, running the wrong fucking way. Dumb asses to the end. And my buddy Bruiser and I, we catch up to one of the bastards, in one of those wooded areas up the mountain, above another identical village. He's hurt, bleeding, and the fight is pretty much over and elsewhere. Green everywhere, like a real forest. And he was lying against this big white rock. I can still see it. A rock shaped like a giant turtle shell. And I remember I started asking him—*you kill my buddy? You kill Campo?* And I was spitting on him and kicking him and I heard my buddy Bruiser telling me to stop, but something in me was already different. I—I took my pistol out, and I got real close, and I put the barrel right underneath his chin. I told Bruiser to stay the fuck back. And I asked this guy again, *you kill my buddy?* And he spit at me. Spit blood, but he was hurt and it just dribbled down his chin. And I thought, you know what, I'm doing the world a favor. These guys are fucking animals. I heard this voice in my head trying to pull me back, pleading with me not to do it, but I squeezed the grip of that black M9 and pressed the barrel harder underneath his chin, and then . . . I told Bruiser to go take a walk. And he saw what I meant to do, but he saw my eyes, and he walked away. And I waited a couple minutes, the barrel of my gun under this guy's chin, and this piece of shit is still staring daggers at me, talking shit in another language, and I said, *this is for Campo you fucking asshole,* and I just did it. Like flipping a light switch. I pulled the trigger and the pistol jumped and his head split open like a . . . like a coconut. The rock behind him took most of the mess. And it wasn't until later that night, when I was alone, when I saw how Bruiser was looking at me, that I realized what it meant. What I had become. I was a murderer, Al. I still am."

Silence drifted into the room. This is where I should cry, Charlie thought, but he felt sluggish and hollow. The sprinkler outside kept stuttering.

"Most people are never really challenged," Al said. "Never. Maybe once in their lives, they're at a drugstore when it gets robbed, and they have to make a violent decision. Or maybe they just lie down on their stomachs and get robbed with the rest. But we had to make violent decisions *every single day*. There's no way to have a perfect record, Charlie. No way. The longer you're over there, the greater the chance of an imperfect human making a perfect mistake."

"I hear you. But honestly, I have no idea if you've ever done anything. Not really bad. Not like me."

Al closed his eyes, held them that way for a moment, and opened them again.

"I'm sorry," Charlie said. "I didn't mean anything by that. I'm being an asshole."

"No," Al said. "You just want evidence. That's fine. Listen, I won't even get into the fact that I was involved in every manner of fucked-up shit in that jungle. I won't talk about the executions and torture I saw and let happen and sometimes even participated in. No. Let's talk after the war. Let's talk away from the place where killing is encouraged. Let's talk normal society. Let's talk cocaine, fucked out of my mind, cheating on every girl that ever cared for me."

"I've already done the cheating. And that's *before* deployment."

Al laughed. "Christ, kid, you want to swap stories? Okay. Here's one. It was my fiancée and I's anniversary. This is after my first divorce with Patty, another girl who really loved me. God knows why. Maybe I'd place us in 1984 or so. Before the Bears won the Super Bowl. Your dad and I measure everything by the Bears, if you hadn't noticed. Anyway, I'm strung out on fucking coke, but I'm out—for some reason, I was always out—I don't know why I didn't smarten up and buy a couple eight balls. But of course my fiancée at the time, Samantha, a total doll, a wonderful woman, is tolerating me. Tolerating my habits. Because when I was lucid, when I snapped out of that shit, I was good. Smart. Decent-looking guy, despite all the drugs and drinking. Always had the mustache. Anyway, I'm in the passenger seat of Samantha's bright blue 1983 Toyota Cressida—a good car in those days—with our new puppy in the backseat. Black Lab. I don't even want to say its name. But I start telling Samantha how I've got to stop by my dealer's house, that we have to stop now, even though we're late for a fancy Italian dinner in the city. And she's yelling at me, telling me to get my shit together, and I'm cursing her back, saying I'm strung out you fucking slut and I need another hit. And then she says how since we got the new dog, we can't afford my habits anymore. That I've gotta quit because of how much the visits to the vet and the Kibbles and Bits are going to cost. And here I am, strung out, and she's telling me this, and I, I, fuck, I lose it. I lose it, Charlie. I say, this fucking puppy is more important than my happiness? And she says, it's more important than your druggy-ass, addictive habits, that's right, you piece of shit. And the next thing I know, I take the black Lab in both hands—we're going about fifty miles an hour now—and I just . . . I throw it out the window. I throw my black Lab puppy out the window of our speeding car."

"Jesus," Charlie said.

Al closed his eyes, inhaled, exhaled slowly, and opened them again. "Relationship over *like that*. Any semblance of stability over *like that*."

"How did you live with yourself?"

Al ran his hands across the top of the desk. "I didn't. Couldn't. One week later I tried to hang myself. The rope broke. Then I took a bunch of pills and woke up in the emergency room. Your dad came and got me and dragged me into rehab. Released three months later, relapsed a year after that. Married and divorced again in '89. Then for the hat trick in '93. Gone to rehab seven different times in three different states. Almost killed a guy before the Bulls fifth championship, out in Skokie, of all places. I was forty-four then. Already an old man. He bumped into me, an accident, and I punched him until one of his teeth was lodged inside my knuckle. Ruined more friendships than I can remember. Got stabbed when I was fifty-two, trying to feel up some Latin guy's girl on a dance floor. Four-inch switchblade. Got me three times before we were pulled apart. Ruptured my spleen. Punctured a lung. But in the hospital, Charlie? I finally, finally, saw the light. I understood what I've been trying so hard to tell you. Finally, after all those months in the hospital, I was sober. For good. So trust me, Charlie. You don't want this life. You don't want any part of it."

Charlie listened to the *chick-chick-whir* of the sprinkler system.

"So now it's your turn to finish. What about the key chain, Charlie? What's going on with the key chain?"

He shook his head. "I can't. I just can't. Even you will know I'm irredeemable."

"That's not true. You know I don't think that. I *can't* think that."

Charlie stood up. He was shaking with each inhalation, gripping the key chain tightly in his pocket, trying to make it cut his skin again. If only he could bleed, bleed into his pocket where Al wouldn't have to see.

"Charlie, now is not the time to run out. Get this shit off your chest. What happened with the key chain?"

Charlie backed away. He held up his left hand. "I can't, Al. I can't."

"Charlie," Al said. He brought his thumb and index finger an inch apart. "You're this close. This fucking close."

"I'm out of here."

"You put your head down now, Charlie—you're just asking for more suffering. And there's no need for it. I know what it's like, how you feel guilty both because of what happened *and* because your guilt is naturally fading away. You want to hold on to it, but it's not natural. It's not natural, Charlie."

"It is for me. You don't understand the full story. I haven't even told you the worst thing."

"Let's get some air. We don't have to sit in this damn study. Here, let me grab us a couple 7-Ups. I can't drink beer anymore, you know. Makes me crazy. Kind of proud of those stupid AA badges."

Charlie waited for Al to duck down, to peer into the tiny fridge beside his desk, and then he turned around and ran, across the maroon carpeting of the hallway, over the burgundy rug in the foyer, past the ruby-red welcome mat, and out the door to his car, away. And as he drove, all he heard in his mind were Al's words, *you're this close,* and the fact that he knew, he *knew,* he didn't deserve it. Not even close.

RAIN DANCE, PART TWO

Barkley looked up at the sign for the Myopic Books and marveled at the sheer force of the rain that seemed to be not just falling but firing, sending geyserlike machine-gun bursts across the sidewalks and streets. He held the blue plastic folder tight against his chest, under the protection of his umbrella, and in his little pocket of safety, the rain drummed hard and struck the umbrella like slabs of falling poultry. His shoes were damp, but they were new shoes, sleek black New Balance running shoes with swaths of white that still sparkled, even in the rain. He moved under the entranceway and looked back at the bubbling rainwater that was now rolling in waves against the sides of the curb. It was even worse than last time. But at least he was dry. He opened the door.

"I'm starting to think you like coming here," Doring said, scratching his graying half beard as Barkley let himself in. "But it's the end of the summer semester—one more absence at DePaul and I've got to drop you a letter grade."

The stillness of the place, complete with particles of dust settling like snow upon haphazard hills of used books, was again comforting. There was something infinitely nostalgic about a place so crammed with stories and silence.

"I don't know," Barkley said. "It just makes sense to be doing this in a bookstore, doesn't it?"

He swung his eyes around for Ginny. Doring manning the register. Where was she? Had she quit? Why hadn't he grown a pair and just Facebooked her? He was better than that now, wasn't he? These days, every action he took had to be graded and judged, each decision examined like a jeweler holding up a rare stone, so that he could determine whether or not his actions were furthering his newfound autonomy and confidence, or detracting from it. And this here, he thought, this idea to come to the Myopic Books looking for Ginny was a positive, but not messaging her beforehand was a fault. A truly confident individual, one who grabbed life by the balls, would have made that move, would have guaranteed her presence.

"Where's your cash register girl?" Barkley asked.

Doring squinted at him. "She's grabbing a smoke. You must have walked right past her."

"Really?" Barkley looked back at the pockmarked door, heard the rain drumming against the windows.

"Let's go," Doring said. "I'm short on time."

"One second."

"Hey—"

Think, Barkley thought, think—and then, moving toward the door, he considered, brilliantly: *don't think*. He turned the knob, ignored Doring, and pulled back the curtain on the rain-splattered world that surrounded him.

"How'd I miss you?" he asked. She was right there where she'd been before, red hair down, puffing away, wearing another disturbingly tight sweater.

"Writer guy?"

"It's me."

"The white knight that would save me from any molester?"

"So, you *do* remember me."

"Yes. And I *do* remember inviting you to my concert. But tragically, you bailed."

"Oh," Barkley said. "About that. Right. Been meaning to address that."

Ginny blew smoke in the air. "Unless you were lurking in the crowd and then decided to slink away unnoticed, which is actually more disturbing. Have you been following me? Tracking me since our last meeting?"

"No!"

"Are you some kind of ninja-stalker?"

"Stop!"

"Hmmm . . . well, anyway. You should have seen my solo. I was tearing it up. And then, as usual, there were the old guys in the crowd. Have you ever noticed that all old guys think it's *hilarious* to request 'Free Bird'? They request it and then high-five their old guy friends and laugh their asses off. Every time."

"Actually," Barkley said, "I do think it's funny if you request 'Free Bird' during a nonguitar event. Like a piano recital. Or, um, I don't know, like a Scottish funeral or something? With the bagpipes?"

Ginny squinted at him. "You'd request 'Free Bird' during a funeral? Sick bastard."

"No, no. Not at the eulogy! I'm talking about the bagpipes. If there are bagpipes. Imagine it."

"Sick. Bastard."

"Well, not as sick as playing the molestation card to strangers."

"Uh-huh. So what's your excuse for missing my concert?"

"Oh, right. Well, my brother came back. Like that day. The day of the concert. I'm serious. Back from Afghanistan."

She raised an eyebrow. "No shit? He was in the war?"

"Yeah. Nobody knows what to do with him. It's kind of a problem."

"Damn. Like PTSD?"

"No clue. No one is talking. And he wanted to go out to the bars in Downers Grove that night, and yeah, that's why no concert. I would have rather gone to the concert, seriously. My bro almost got us into a fight. He's crazy now."

Ginny looked at him thoughtfully. "He's your brother."

"I know he's my brother."

"I feel bad for him," she said.

Barkley laughed. "You don't even know him."

"I don't have to! He just got back from fucking Afghanistan! That's insane. It's probably impossible to adjust. And he's got you talking about Free Bird funerals to keep him company."

Barkley felt a dry feeling in his throat. "I'm trying," he said. "I really am trying with him. No one knows what to do. But I'm trying."

She winced. "That's my bad. I'm sure you are. I shouldn't be joking."

"Nah, it's all right."

Barkley shut up, felt himself hit a speed bump on his runway toward fledgling confidence. It was his second conversation with her, and he'd gotten serious. Why was he such an idiot? If only there was a way to steer things back to normal—he looked at Ginny, but she was looking away, she was looking at the heavy rain falling across the street and the water leaping up across the asphalt and the cars zooming by, wipers slashing, headlights blurry. She took a drag on her cigarette and the nub glowed; then she looked back at him and nodded again.

"I'm sorry about your brother," she said. "That's tough. It's got to be tough. I joke around, but I get it. You know?"

"Yeah," Barkley said. "Listen. You want to grab a beer? Maybe tomorrow? Or are you busy? Maybe the next day?"

Ginny flicked her cigarette. "How about later in the week? Three days from now."

"Sure. Yes. I got a job, by the way. I'm an English teacher now. I start on the twenty-second."

She smirked. "That's going to be entertaining. But you better get your ass in there. My uncle hates people making him wait."

"Shit," Barkley said, and then, looking at Ginny, he felt an abrupt sense of warmth, as if an oven had been opened. There was an urge to rush forward and gush romantic platitudes, to let his jubilation tumble forward, unchecked. But he held back, restrained himself, thinking that every mature action was a tiny scaffold that supported the new Barkley, the Barkley that could actually do a few things right.

"Guess I'll see you later, Ginny."

"You'll be needing my number," she said expressionlessly.

Back at his apartment, when the conference was over and Doring had denounced another one of Barkley's short story drafts—this one about a futuristic sniper in a clone war, tormented by memories of a lacrosse-playing bombshell who had scorned him—Barkley sat, very quietly and very still, at the mail-strewn IKEA table of his studio apartment, trying to wrap his head around the implications of his new life. He was a teacher now. That was enough to make his hands shake. He would be judged by children. His stories were getting assassinated by his writing teacher; likely, he thought, with good cause. But he was sure he had at least one good story in him. And lastly, most absurdly, was the fact that a girl was actually interested in him. Well, that was underselling it. This one, this unknown, undeniably *cool* entity from a bookstore—there was a pull he felt when he talked to her, a kind of magnetism between minds. Unless he'd been imagining it, concocting pink-hued mirages for himself like some hapless sorcerer's apprentice. That had happened before, too— imagined "connections," on a deep and cellular level, with countless girls—Allison Ward in eighth grade, the engaged Julie Hempley (his sophomore honors English teacher), Sasha Gomez (among her hundred other admirers) in early college, the mysterious, shy-but-possibly-sneaky-yet-still-bookish-while-wearing-bewitching-dark-eye-makeup Kathryn Palazzi (in his creative writing classes), not to mention the girl on the 151 bus between Diversey and Webster, the girl reading Franzen on the Brown Line to Sedgwick, the woman at the gym he rarely went to who'd looked up at him intently from the elliptical machine not once but *twice*, the bartender at his favorite beer snobbery oasis, Hopleaf, and, of course, the thousands of pretty girls he had passed on sidewalks and pathways over the years, whose every nanosecond of eye contact triggered in him a deeply complex, heart-convulsing, imagined destiny of unrequited love turned passionate, golden-tinged future.

On the way home, riding that train, he couldn't help but think of Ray-Fi Twenty-Two, his fictionalized sniper from 2056, looking out across midnight purple rocks at the vast expanse of halogen-lit pod cities, still troubled by memories of a besieged youth. Doring had said the story lacked connections between Ray-Fi's memories and his current predicament, scanning a night-vision scope for enemy targets on a rocky moon. The train rattled, and Barkley thought of the red planet from his own childhood. And wasn't it all connected? Maybe it was Doring who didn't understand. All anyone did was scan for targets, point and shoot, point and shoot, until they either hit something, or ran out of ammunition. And for once in his life, he felt like he had an extra bullet in the chamber.

MISE-EN-SCÈNE

Julie sat on the mattress in her room with the blinds drawn and the red drapes closed like thick curtains in an aging theater, and her feeling in the darkness was that she couldn't tell if the curtains signified the end of a play or simply the break between acts. But she wanted it dark, she knew that. She wanted the darkness all around her, no distractions, only herself: her bare toes pressed against the surface of the carpeting, her bottom against the silky, unwashed sheets and the comforter that had become prickly from lack of care. She sat there with that good secret feeling still humming. The feeling that had sprung up at the quarry—a cool breeze in her solar plexus, a sense that change was possible, even around the corner—was practically howling.

In the shadows she could see the outline of framed pictures of her and Henry, one on the wall by the windows and another propped atop the armoire and a third on the bedside table, close enough to touch. The dark shapes of the frames stood there in the blackness like the mounted heads of long-dead animals. They were little more than aging taxidermy now; they held no power and no comfort and existed merely as relics and ghosts, only there to catch the corners of her mind.

In her hands, she held the translucent orange bottle of Zoloft. She felt the label and ran her thumb along the rumpled corners. She shook the vial, and the pills rattled like strange, precious eggs. The window. Open the window and let them scatter. But the sunlight, no, she wasn't ready. She had to be sure. There had to be a plan. Another act. She had come back from the quarry, yes, she had come back and it had felt good and the light, cool feeling still existed in her body and even in the marrows of her bones but she had to be sure it wasn't cowardice that had brought her back, but purpose—a real bridge.

She glanced at the picture frame on the darkened table next to the bed. She knew it was of her and Henry in college, his big arm slung around her lazily, his smile wide, an autumn tree behind them with leaves so orange they seemed to be glowing.

When Julie first met Henry, he'd been playing intramural baseball in a long green park by the edge of the water near Evanston, Illinois. She had stopped at a dive bar to get a drink with Melanie because it was Friday and why not and when they left it was into the amber rays of five o'clock, the soft edge of humidity, and the haze of impending summer break. Across the street were some boys playing baseball, shouting and whooping. The baseball diamond was a perfect burnt orange, like the dust at the bottom of a canyon, and beyond it that lush runway of manicured outfield and the deep blue line of Lake Michigan, dotted with white triangles she knew to be sails. Julie and Melanie crossed the street and saw that it was a full game, a serious game, the players wearing their gear: cleats and socks and elbow braces. They were likely students at Northwestern, like herself, because two of them had caps with the Wildcat logo on the front.

One of the players hit a looping pop fly and a man with a barrel chest held his gloved arm up and caught it at first base, caught the ball as if it belonged to him, as if he were in his own backyard. He tossed it back to the pitcher and said something Julie couldn't hear, but the pitcher simply grinned and shook his head. The first baseman's face was clean-shaven, strong-jawed and tan, his hair was a shaggy brown, and his eyes were a crystalline blue, with a flicker of mischief that showed, even from where she stood, just how much in his life he'd already gotten away with.

Julie and Melanie walked to the chain-link fence that separated them from the baseball field. They approached in their pastel spring skirts and she knew they were young and attractive, their bodies toned by hours in the studio, and the first baseman who'd caught the ball was already looking at them, flashing teeth as white as the sails on the lake. The teams switched sides and he trotted over, the inning complete, and Melanie nudged her and whispered *look at this one* but Julie was already looking, she saw him, she saw his easy gait and that flicker across his grinning eyes. One of the other players was shouting something but the comment was lost in the breeze. The tall, chiseled one yelled a retort through cupped hands, jogged backward, turned around, and suddenly he was there on the other side of the fence beaming down at them.

"Hello, girls," he said.

Julie felt Melanie's elbow in the side of her ribs, but she knew not to say anything back to this one, she knew to return his eye contact and keep her admiration for everything that was shining and glinting off him a secret, to send it off into the breeze.

"Come to watch the game?" he asked.

"Just passing by," Julie said.

"Where from?"

"A bar."

He winked. "Are you two properly sloshed?"

Melanie giggled and held her thumb and forefinger an inch apart. Julie rolled her eyes.

"By the way," he said. "I'm Henry. I'm a junior at Northwestern. And I'm going to hit a home run for this one right here." And he put his fingers through the rusted openings in the fence and pointed at Julie.

"Bullshit," Julie said.

Melanie giggled again.

"Don't believe me?"

"Can't say I do, Hank."

"It's Henry."

"You sure?"

"Henry's more dashing. Don't you think? And I'm going to hit a home run for you, okay?"

"Would you?" Melanie asked, faking a swoon.

Julie frowned at him, kept frowning, and bottled down the wild joy that seemed to be rising up inside her like a buoy.

"Don't encourage him," Julie said, biting back a smile.

"I don't need encouragement," Henry chirped. "I encourage myself. It's a habit."

"I can tell."

"And what's your name, feisty one?"

"Julie."

"You watch, Julie. Just watch, all right? I'm going to put this thing into orbit."

And with that he trotted back to the dugout with the other players and he kicked dirt in the air and clapped powdery hand chalk against his palms and slapped his teammates on the back. One of them said something and Henry threw his head back and guffawed and through the holes in the fence, fighting against that helium bubble of joy, Julie saw it all. This man knew some kind of secret—she was sure of it.

Henry went up to the plate, twirling the wooden bat, tapping it against the dirt three times, four times, the bat knocking hollowly against the ground; then Henry twirling it again, making a spectacle. Finally, he set his legs, and the bat moved up behind his right shoulder and Julie could see the concentration in his stance, the full power of his attention and what it meant. The pitcher wound up and threw a high fastball and Henry swung with powerful, controlled violence—his big shoulders contorting against the fabric of the uniform, triceps flexing into thick sinews of muscle—and he crushed the ball. There was a resounding *whap* and the white sphere shot up toward the right field line, rose higher and higher in the air, a spitball against blue sky, still shrinking, and Henry stood at the plate frozen, the wooden bat held outward like a thrust sword. Julie watched the ball go higher and higher, rising as if it couldn't possibly fall, and then saw it fade to the right, disappearing from view.

"Shit," Henry said.

"Yeah, that's a foul ball," the catcher drawled. "But damned if that isn't the loudest foul ball I've ever seen. Over four hundred feet there, big guy. Probably hit one of the sailboats."

Henry spat. Julie watched from the fence. Her fingers curled around the metal openings. Finally, he flashed that smile like the sails on the lake. "Close enough," he said, looking back.

Years later, in her bedroom, Julie gently placed the picture frame face-down against the desk. She closed her eyes and opened them. Squeezed the bottle and relaxed. There were other memories in the room, she knew, but she didn't have to relive them all. The trips to New York, to Buenos Aires, to their wedding at the Drake. Pictures of all those early years in Downers Grove, with Henry holding Charlie up high in the backyard, pointing at the passing jets, naming the make and model of each and every one. These memories, all of them, they all meshed together in the shadows, but they didn't hold a candle to those college years when she really had his attention—before the work, before other women, those times in college when they had lain in bed and talked, arms slung around each other, the bedside fan whirring through the humidity. She had listened to him speak and seen how *smart* he was and how good he wanted to be. The real Henry, the one who even wrote her poetry.

But there were signs of trouble even then. In college, when it was late at night, Henry was always talking about the strange feeling inside him, the termites, he called them, a feeling of something inside him that was not good, not helpful, always hungry. The termites. And he'd told her, he'd told her point-blank—*you're the only one who can make them go away.* He held her close when he said the words. She smelled his after-shave. She felt his bristles against her cheek. She felt his arms, which were like warm stone, all of him warm, as if beneath his skin was a hearth, always burning. And despite the termites he was happy most of the time, walking around campus with his shoulders rolled back, owning the world. Everyone wanted to be around Henry. And no one knew about his feeling but her.

Later, when they had children who were getting older, when she felt him fading away, he wouldn't even acknowledge what he'd talked about in college. She'd mentioned the termites during an argument, and Henry had looked at her with revulsion, scrunching his eyes up in disgust, like she'd lifted up a rock and reminded him of all the creepy crawly things he didn't want to see. He'd snorted at her and busted open the screen door and walked out of the house and from the kitchen she heard the Bentley roar to life, then the Steppenwolf CD start, then the car rocket out of the driveway. He was gone for three days, the first time he'd left and not come back. In 2003, she thought. The beginning. She'd never mentioned the termites again.

On the desk, she lifted up her phone. No new messages.

It was what she deserved, she knew. But now she had her own feeling. She would dance for herself and feel her bare feet on the wooden floor of a studio. She would once again feel the release that came with the bends and lines of her form, the expression as she moved through her emotions like a fish on a current, the overhead light beaming down.

Julie rose up from the bed and tore open the curtains and white morning fired through, blinded her, but it didn't matter, it was time, she felt that cool feeling in her bones now and something about the termites and the foul ball and the whole spectacles of these pictures of Henry like stuffed animal heads seemed suddenly ridiculous, even funny. She laughed. The white morning light was all around. She pulled the curtains wider. She shook the pills. Cranked open the window. A late summer breeze pushed through. And so she cranked open the window farther and the August air came in and the chirping sparrows filled her eardrums. She didn't need the cotton balls or Henry. She stuck her hand out the window and felt the breeze and the little pills fell not like snowflakes but like hail, too heavy to catch the air. She watched them rattle off the side of the house and scatter into the green bushes that wrapped around the siding. She let the bottle go, too, an orange blur, down to the ground with the rest of them. She turned around and flicked on the lights, knowing that the first step across the bridge, the first scene of the next act, was making a phone call.

"Hello," she said, when she heard the familiar voice on the other line. "Yes, it really is me. Now I know it's been a while, but I'll buy you a steak dinner tonight if you drop everything and meet me at the scene of the crime."

Before leaving, she checked on her son. Charlie was in his room, lying on his bed—which was progress over the floor, she guessed—but he also had his Sperrys on and the blinds lowered. Not worth saying anything about the shoes. Balanced on his stomach was his old silver laptop. The screen bathed his face in a theatrical glow. Julie propped the door open farther, knocked twice. He looked at her as if through a distant dream.

"Hey, there," she said. "Going out at all today?"

Charlie stared at the screen. Music and noise came forth.

"What are you watching?"

Charlie pursed his lips. "*Goodfellas*. But it's not like before."

"Oh yeah? Director's cut or something?"

"No."

"New high-definition transfer?"

He paused the movie. Took a breath. Looked straight ahead. "No, same cut, same everything. You wouldn't understand, Mom."

There it was again. *She wouldn't understand.* It was strange. She felt liberated without her pills, but also defenseless—a gladiator minus the armor. Charlie and his swirling negativity, the whole pit he was mired in, it all seemed like quicksand. She wanted to run, to hold on to the vapors of her own good feeling and let no one get in the way. But she stayed put.

"I wouldn't understand? Try me, Charlie."

"Just forget it. You haven't even seen *Goodfellas*. You wouldn't understand."

"I said try me, didn't I? Give me a chance."

He sighed, eyes still fixed on the screen. "I just watched the most famous scene in the movie, Mom. Henry Hill—this is the main mobster character—he takes Karen on their first date. They go to the Copacabana, which is the hippest club in the business, impossible for a normal person to get into without waiting in line for hours. But that's just the setup, okay? Because Henry Hill takes Karen in the back entrance, and he knows everybody, and he's paying them off, handing them wads of cash, and the camera follows as they do what they want to do. It's like it's a tour of the Copacabana, but also of the mob, of the power and allure of the mob, and it's almost a POV tour, but not quite. It's like we're *with them*. It's all one take, one long Steadicam shot, and Scorsese's got the camera following close behind, you understand? Pretty much continuous over-the-shoulder shots, the way Aronofsky likes to do it now, but with a little more distance, and with 'Then He Kissed Me' by the Crystals playing in the background, which is *perfect* for their first date.

And that's still not all of it—there's also the ambient sounds from the club and the people and the kitchen, and the scene itself goes on for three minutes, *three minutes* of a single take as Henry Hill leads Karen through the back entrance and the bustling kitchen and the main room of the Copacabana, where they get the best seat in the house. He knows everybody, and he's laughing, shaking everyone's hand. And the whole time we follow them, feeling what Karen's feeling."

Julie felt a vague recognition, though Charlie was right—she hadn't seen the movie. "What is she feeling?" she asked.

"The thrill of it all. The thrill of being with someone who commands that sort of respect, someone who gains access to the better life. But there's a million moving parts in this sequence, Mom—there's Scorsese's use of mise-en-scène and there's the music and there's the colors and the fact that it's all one take and that the Steadicam makes it seem like you're *there*, makes you feel Karen's excitement, and Mom, Mom, it's everything that actually thrills people, everything, it's the sum total of the romance people feel about the Mafia, about the life of the gangster, about why they feel it, why they seek it out and commit to it even though they know it's totally and completely wrong. Do you understand? Do you understand what I'm saying?"

Julie stared at her son. He was breathing heavily, tiny pellets of sweat lining his brow. "I think I understand," she said. And it was true—there was a sluggish sense of déjà vu pulling at her, tugging her down. Making her wish for the cotton balls all over again. "And do you like the scene yourself, Charlie? Is it as good as they say?"

"It used to be my favorite scene, of any movie, ever."

"And now?"

He held eye contact with her for the first time. "Right now I don't feel a single thing watching it. I feel nothing. I've watched it three times now. This used to thrill me, Mom. Every time I watched it I wanted to go make my own movie, get my own camera, thrill someone else. All the romance of an entire way of life, of an idea, all of it captured in a single scene, my all-time favorite scene, and I feel *nothing*. What the fuck's the point of that?"

"Of what, honey? What's the point of what?" She thought of her pills, lying there behind the bushes. Technically, they weren't gone.

"Of what? Of *anything*. This is my favorite scene. This is why I started writing movie blogs. This scene, right here, the Copacabana, Henry Hill, 'Then He Kissed Me,' three minutes of Steadicam, the thrill of the gangster, all of it. And I don't feel a single thing watching it. It's just white noise. I keep thinking what I'm sure a lot of people think: it's only a movie. It's not art, it's not powerful, it's not important. It's old news. This used to light a fire under my ass, and now I feel like I'm reading the fucking *Wall Street Journal*."

"I'm sorry, honey. I really am. And I guess you're right—I don't know exactly what to say. Maybe you've seen it too many times."

"You know it's not that. You know it."

"Maybe you should talk to someone. You know, depending on the reason for your discharge . . ."

"I told you I don't want to talk about that."

"I know, honey. But depending on the reason, you might be eligible for benefits from the VA. Real benefits. Real treatment. You don't have to tell me about it, but it might be worth it to—"

"Please don't start, Mom. Please. Al already did everything he could do, and nothing's working."

She sighed. She thought again of the desire to be selfish, to not let anyone get in the way. "I have to go meet a friend," she said, finally.

"Okay."

She walked over to the window, found the cord, and pulled up the blinds. August light flooded the room. Charlie cursed behind her.

"Right now, Charlie, this is about all I can do for you. And about me not understanding what you're feeling?" She straightened up, offered him a small smile. "I might understand more than you think."

It was nearly sunset when Julie arrived, and the great lake beyond was windblown and barren, absent all vessels and lined with slashes of froth. The outfield was threadbare, too, stamped and browned by the heat of summer. But the diamond looked good—it still had that orange dust she remembered from those years before, when Henry rocketed a foul ball as if he were trying to strike a satellite. She strode across the diamond, across that orange that could have dusted a canyon floor. She made her way to the pitcher's mound, stood at the top, faced home plate. Alongside her good, buzzing feeling and the image of the studio was an almost equal desire to retrieve the pills she had tossed out the window. Did she even have a plan without them? No, she only had an idea. An idea was not a plan. And it was possible— probable, even—that there was no true way to get what she wanted, no way to find a studio or to dance or to retrieve any of the old emotions she had barred away for years. She focused instead on the baseball diamond.

As a child, Julie was naturally skilled at almost every sport, and she'd thrived upon dropping the jaws of all the clumsy elementary school boys in the neighborhood. Ice-in-the-veins jump shot, jitterbug touchdown runs, wicked slap shots at a goalie's throat—she'd done it all, even loved it all, until she found dance. Still, baseball had never been her favorite—too much standing around, too much waiting for the next big thing. She'd always wanted to move, move, move. She did like the role of the pitcher, though, the person in charge, always planning the next step, a sequence of movements that would ultimately lead to victory. She imagined hurling a fastball from the mound, scorching a strikeout that sent the batter spinning, collapsing into a bowlegged heap. Screw it: she imagined beaning the invisible batter, covering his muscled body with welt upon welt until he hunkered down, held up his hands, and said *no more, no more, enough is enough.*

"The scene of the crime," a female voice said from behind her. "Well, well, well. *CSI: Failed Relationships,* eh?"

Julie spun around, only to be grabbed and embraced by Melanie, her former best friend. Melanie brought her in tight, and Julie wondered again how they had somehow, some way grown apart.

"Scene of the crime," Julie repeated, extending the hug, breathing into her hair. "You've still got a sense of humor, I guess."

Melanie pushed her back, put her hands on her hips. "This is where you met the big lug. I was there for the whole thing. A witness. Julie went gaga for the big galoot."

"Big galoot, sure," Julie said, chuckling. "You were swooning for him long before I was."

Melanie sniffed. "My taste buds were underdeveloped at that time. I went for John Ashmore that year, too, don't you remember? The Hemorrhoid King?"

"Ugh. And the following summer you dated Jamie Dickson."

Melanie scrunched up her face. "Uhhh . . . Hi, Melanie." She waddled around in a circle. "Will you pick out which turtleneck I should wear, Melanie? Is this cornflower blue or cobalt blue, Melanie?"

"God, he was colorblind, too?"

"Colorblind, asthma, psoriasis, a serial waddler—am I missing anything?"

"Let me think," Julie said. "I guess you can add millionaire to that list. Gazillionaire, even. That guy's probably running half the country now."

"Not even. Last I heard it was a midrange suburban bank in Willowbrook."

"That's *it*? We should go open an account."

"Perfect," Melanie said. "Ask to see him personally. Deposit a nickel a day."

Julie laughed at that, all the while taking in the way Melanie looked, which was somewhere between adorable and exquisite. She was still slender, her movements youthful. Julie noted her elegant neck and dangling earrings, the licorice smile that never showed teeth. She wore smooth pants and a cream-colored blouse. At fifty-seven, her oval face had a few creases, but the effect here was also elegant, as if a silk curtain had merely been rippled in the breeze.

"You look," Julie said, "absolutely stunning."

Melanie smirked and did a curtsey. "Not so bad yourself, madam."

"Well, that's where you're wrong. We can both see that, clear as day. I'm an old bag lady now."

"Julie, you look great. And we're both on the cusp of sixty, here. Things change. It can't be like college forever."

"It's true, though. *You* look great. How do you do it?"

Melanie shrugged. "The short answer is a glass of wine and a decent book. It didn't use to be that way. Remember college? I was running around like a madwoman. But then, you find the right guy, have a couple kids—"

"It can't be just that. A million people find a guy and have kids. You ended up dancing professionally—that had to be part of it."

"Well, it could have been you, too, if you'd wanted it. Not a lot of money in the gig, of course. And what else was I going to do? Billy didn't want me sitting at home alone, losing my mind."

"You still call him Billy?"

"Julie, did my husband ever look like a stolid old *Bill* to you? Or a *William*? He's as goofy as they come—who do you think is running the show back there, anyway?"

And you used to be my sidekick, Julie wanted to say, but didn't. Beyond her, the wind picked up, and Lake Michigan's choppy waves leaped upon each other, churning bubbled spray into the air. To the west, the sun hung a notch lower in the sky. And suddenly, abruptly, Julie remembered why she'd lost touch with her old friend in the first place. She'd seen Melanie's rise in autonomy just as distinctly as she'd witnessed her own decline, many years ago. It wasn't one incident but many—the excited voice Melanie had used to describe her latest performance in New York, the sound of her husband laughing with (and caring for) their children, that one vacation in '91 to the Outer Banks, where Melanie, plain and simple, had not only stunned the other husbands in her turquoise bikini, but also walked off not giving a damn about it. There was a period of slow horror during that trip, when Julie, planted in her lawn chair, square feet dug into wet sand, had finally understood how surely their lives had been switched. She, the tomboy queen of elementary school, the dancing star of high school, the girl who got the guy in college, she who had been so sure of herself during the first half of life, was fading, grinding into the granules of the sand, no longer anything close to airborne. And Melanie, she understood—Melanie, her sidekick, her second banana—had taken her place. She'd climbed the pitcher's mound, not giving a shit who thought she could do it. She'd followed through with dance, married Billy, been happy, stayed happy, and made that awkward, declining leap into womanhood look like it was some kind of reboot, a renaissance. And then, returning from the Outer Banks and knowing the score, Julie had phased her out. She'd simply stopped returning her calls, until the calls stopped coming.

"What it is," Julie said, shaking herself, "is that you've been given the fine wine treatment over the years, and I've aged like a gallon of milk."

Melanie stared at her, her smile gone. "But at least I thought we'd still be friends, Julie. No matter what, wine or milk or whatever, I thought we'd be that."

"Look—"

"But you stopped everything, didn't you? You stopped all communication. And that's fine, I saw it coming. I was shocked that you called me today, but mostly I'm mad at myself for coming to meet you so easily. I dropped everything, went right back to it. Here in this old ballpark, which is clearly about Henry, not us. Never us. You're not perfect, you know that? You think you're the victim—but the choices are yours. They always have been."

"Of course, I know that—"

"You were my best friend, and then you got Henry, and you *disappeared*. Off the map! He turned you into his lackey, just like I told you he would. You never wanted to hear a word about it. Henry was a superstar, sure. But even then we knew he had issues. We saw the way he looked at other girls. How he never really listened. You didn't want to hear about it. And even when I heard he'd left you—what, two years ago?—even then, I still felt bad. I find that very, very strange. Uneven, considering."

Julie stayed silent and kept her eyes on the lake, on the dark and rolling waves. She *would not* cry. She wanted to tell Melanie how far gone she'd really been—maybe still was. She wanted to tell her about the quarry, about the drop that had opened up and pulled at her like nothing had in years. She needed Melanie to know that it wasn't personal, that what had consumed her wasn't Henry at all, but an avalanche of the spirit. She wasn't going to cry again. And somewhat lucidly, she understood that not all of her goals could be accomplished at once—that all things would, even if she stayed focused, take a good deal of time.

"Melanie, look. Listen." The wind blew around them harder now. Julie held her hair out of her eyes. "I'm sorry, Melanie. Let's just start there, okay?"

Melanie pursed her lips, looked out at the water and then back. "How bad did this guy get to you, anyway?"

"Bad," Julie said, feeling wetness in her eyes again. She fought it back. And then her face moved into that automatic mask of smile, her lips opened, and she spit out gibberish. "But I'm doing fine, now," she said. "I'm much better. I've adjusted."

Melanie nodded. Julie felt sick.

"Jesus. I lied just now," she blurted, causing her old friend to look up. "I'm not doing fine. I know you can see it on my face."

"Well, I am sorry for you, Julie. You know I am."

"I have no idea why I lied. It's become a reflex or something. But you're right, I keep acting like it's all about me, and not about us. And Melanie, it *is* about us. You're the first person I called when I realized I had to do something. To change something. I've been wanting to call you forever."

"So the marriage is kaput? No chance of him coming back?"

Julie stared at the water. Behind them, the sun lowered itself another degree, almost behind the buildings. "There's no marriage left to speak of. He left two years ago, like you said. And I still hear about people seeing him. Every once in a while, our neighbors go downtown, and tell me they saw Henry. They used to give details, Henry at the clubs, Henry in Viagra Triangle, Henry with bimbos half his age. But now, not so many details. I can tell they're trying to spare me the embarrassment. Who goes running wild at the cusp of sixty? What kind of man?"

Melanie shrugged. "Many kinds, unfortunately. Thankfully, I got lucky with Billy. He was one of my good decisions. Not to rub it in, of course. I did date Jamie Dickson."

Julie shook her head and grinned. "God, those turtlenecks . . ."

"And so what, Julie? Who cares about Henry? He doesn't want to be with you? *Good*. Read him his Miranda rights and keep him the hell out."

"Well, that's the attitude I've needed for years. But the problem . . ." She sighed and looked away. "Do you want to sit down on that bench? I have no idea why we're standing here on a pitcher's mound."

"Because it's the scene of the crime, very weighty and all. But sure."

They walked over, sat down, and Julie eyed the section of the fence where she had intertwined her fingers, where Henry had looked at her and said, *I'm going to hit a home run for this one right here.*

"This *is* where it all began," Melanie said. "We came out here buzzed, remember? Vodka tonics. Happy hour."

"I feel like I was buzzed the entire time I was with him. That was part of the problem."

"Classic alpha male, Julie. And he was *big*, physically big. I know Billy was practically afraid of him, desperately wanted the guy to like him.

And I kept telling Billy, 'Baby, Henry doesn't care about you or anybody else.' But he had that effect on people."

"He cared about me," Julie said. "At least for a while, he did." The gusts of wind came back, tossed her hair around.

"It's for the best," Melanie said, leaning back. "Once you get over the Henry hype, you understand it's for the best. He's overrated. I used to try to hint that to you."

"Yeah, but you weren't with him, you don't know what it was like. He could become the center of your world, without even trying. And then, the minute you thought you had him pegged, he'd say something so smart, something so out of left field, that the mystique was back all over again."

"Yeah, yeah. Parlor tricks, Julie. I knew a guy in New York who memorized quotations from, like, Sun Tzu and Sitting Bull and a million others. He was nothing more than a drunken oaf, but each night he'd start talking to a girl, get serious, give those doe eyes, and quote, I don't know, Dostoyevsky or Amelia Earhart or something. And then he'd look into the distance and take a long sip of his drink."

"And then he'd get laid?"

Melanie nodded. "And then he'd get laid."

Julie laughed. Even without rose-colored glasses, though, she knew that Henry was bigger than that, better. Maybe even the real deal. But there was no telling Melanie about it—they'd been on opposite sides of the fence when it came to Henry for decades. Real deal or not, however, it didn't make Henry any less of an asshole, or a bad husband, or an absentee father. And it didn't make her problem any less immediate.

"So what's the issue? You said on the phone that you had something important to talk about? Beyond Henry?"

Julie nodded. "I'm actually coming to terms with him, I really am. It's just that I can't be cooped up in that house any longer. He's everywhere. And the house is too big, even with my son back. And what I used to do, all I used to do—is dance. That's what I loved—what I love still."

"Me, too," Melanie said as the sky turned blue around them, furrowed with deep swaths of maroon. "But how can I help you?"

Julie had been thinking about this for days. It simply felt good to get out, to take a trip to the lake, to have the promise of conversation. That was the first step.

"I want to dance again," Julie said.

"Mmmm . . ." Melanie countered, rolling her eyes. "Don't I, too? But I can hardly complete a plié, much less a grand-plié. As Miss Pelletier used to say, 'You can't call back the clock for dinner.' Am I right?"

"Well, I don't need to be hanging from a ceiling and rappelling or anything. I don't even need to be the one dancing. I mean, I *do* want to dance. But I just want to be out there. Involved. I want to be in the studio again. *That's* the endgame."

"Ah." Thick clouds congealed on the horizon, and the lake went from dark blue to purple. Julie squinted and could barely make out the lines of froth.

"Not ideal, I know. But there has to be a way, doesn't there?"

Melanie smiled. "Well, I still have connections, of course. I could make some calls. If we're friends again, that is."

Julie slung an arm around her. "Just give me a chance, all right?"

Melanie nodded. "But let's be serious. I can't get you into high school or college dance programs—you need more experience. They'll want certifications you don't have. Student teaching. Certification takes years. And it's been a long time since you were actually in a studio."

"Well, I've got some ideas, myself. About how to get back into it. Thought I'd run them by you."

"Sure. And don't you owe me dinner or something? It's getting a little chilly out here. And there's tons more gossip to get you caught up on."

"Yes, dinner. Yes, gossip. But in a minute, okay? Would you mind just sitting here a little longer?"

Melanie smiled at her. "What's cooking in that brain of yours?"

Julie looked straight ahead, at the shadowed baseball diamond, the tangled outfield, the bruise of lake. "I just want to stay here a little longer, is all. I want to see what this place looks like at night."

"Okay, Julie."

"Will you stay with me?"

She felt her old friend hunker down. Beyond them, the sky darkened, and the lake became a distant object, a black sketch. Shadows crossed

the field. Soon there were only the headlights of the passing cars behind them, of a thousand journeyers on their solitary tracks. Julie closed
her eyes. She felt Melanie next to her on the bench, the chilled summer
wind, the movements of their hair. She thought of the studio, and of her
feet upon the floor. When she opened her eyes again, the field was gone,
dissolved into another night. It was something only for dreamers, Julie
thought. Something for the lost.

THE LEGEND OF
CANDACE BRANDT

"So," Ginny said, leaning across from Barkley at the candlelit table beside the bar. "This little place was an astute choice."

"Even the name is classy, right? The Black Duck. But why so astute?"

"You're saying you don't know? That us walking in here was pure chance?"

"Oh, I *know*," Barkley said. "This is what I'm good at. Premeditated astute choices. The problem is in the moment. Then I'm like a clown doing pratfalls. But, okay, so this place—why such a good choice?"

"You want me to tell you what you already know?"

"I just want to hear what you think. It's a test."

"I'm not being tested!"

"Come on!" Barkley said. "Tell me why I did good. I *did* put some thought into this, I swear."

"You had to, after missing that concert. I'm not a forgiving ginger, Barkley."

He finally laughed, breaking their poker-faced banter. She looked good—black sweater, tiny gold earrings that winked in the candlelight.

Her dark red hair had been straightened and smoothed, framing a face that was gentle and rough, depending on the angle. And seeing her was a relief; the past three days had been filled with corkscrews of fretting. His old high school buddy, Hayward, had come into town from his film-editing job in Brooklyn, and Tuesday had been a welcome reprieve, drinking at the Map Room and reliving the old times. But as usual with their sessions of reminiscence, his old friend had steered the conversation back to his fateful high school night with Candace Brandt. *What are you going to do,* he'd asked. *Afraid the Twenty-Second Man will come back in full force, if the occasion beckons?* And Barkley had laughed and flipped Hayward off, all the while feeling his insides bubble like a cauldron with all the wrong ingredients. His mind had been circling the memory idly, not committed, and his old buddy had turned on the tractor beam. What if Ginny *did* want to go home with him? Or take him to her place? Since Tuesday, he'd been frantic, scrolling through Web site after Web site of sexual how-to's.

"The danger with a first date," Ginny was saying, "is finding the balance between too casual and too serious. Like, you couldn't take me to some black-and-white-tiled diner. And not a sports bar with chicken wings. Those are moves that say, *I don't care.*"

"But I like chicken wings."

"Shut up. And you also couldn't take me to a French bistro with Pouilly-Fuissé and trembling accordion music. So, Barkley, this is an astute choice because you have achieved the much-coveted 'balance.' Move ahead one space on the dating game board of life. Are you happy?"

"Yes!" Barkley cried, finally breaking loose of his wax statue demeanor. "You got it. See, I scouted this place. Like, this *is* a bar. Which means casual, no pressure. There's a bar right over there. But it's also a nice bar, nice wood. What's the dark wood—mahogany?"

"Not all nice wood is mahogany."

"Whatever. And there's also low lighting. Candles. So it's intimate. But there's still sports playing on those two televisions. So it's also casual. And it's not like full-on entrées here, but it's also trendy, you know? I mean, look at the appetizers."

"Bacon-wrapped scallops. I've been staring at those. I want them."

"Let's get them," Barkley said, wondering what it would do to his stomach. Scallops. Those were fish, right? And fish were healthy, right? But didn't scallops look like giant gumdrops of fat?

Ginny was waving the waiter over. "An order of the bacon-wrapped scallops, please. What are they called? Ah, the Angels on Horseback. I mean, that's very epic. I'm impressed without taking a bite."

The waiter smiled benignly and walked away.

"Where were we?" Ginny asked, staring him down.

Barkley, for a moment, panicked, feeling awash in some vast, attention-deficit ocean. He considered what a mudslide back to the old Barkley would be like—the stammering, the nonsense, the false confidence. But the difference was that this felt normal. Easy. With Ginny, thoughts and words finally, miraculously met each other halfway. And also, he thought, this was the new Barkley, he came equipped with a life raft, and he could get through one date unscathed.

"We were talking about classiness," he offered. "And moving ahead one space. And—"

"You know," Ginny said, "I'm not sure if this is the right time to tell you. But the waiter touched me after he took my order. Down there."

"Do you want me to throw this candle at you?"

"Don't throw things at girls," she said. "It's immature. My little brother still does that, and he's in high school. But let's switch tracks. You have a new job. Where are you teaching?"

"Eastwick High School," Barkley said, feeling an injection of back-straightening pride.

"Damn, they're pretty badass, aren't they? I went to a Catholic school. Immaculate Conception in Elmhurst, you know it? I mean, it's not like Hogwarts, the way Eastwick is, but we had priests in robes."

"Could they cast spells? And damn, you went to IC? That's right near my hood. I grew up in Downers Grove. DGN, myself."

"God, I hate being from the suburbs," Ginny said. "We're all such pussies, you know? How do you experience anything legitimate when you're surrounded by strip malls? And even more so with private schools. My brother switched to public and goes to York, thinks he's a badass, and he's still wrong."

"Yeah," Barkley said. "I feel like there's nowhere to prove yourself any-more. That's one of the problems for our generation."

"Oh yeah?"

"Think about it—2011. Everyone is coddled now. Plugged in. Where can you go to be tough in your youthful years? To do something truly challenging?"

"City schools. Get your education on the South Side. Or the West Side."

"Right. Or after high school, you join the army. Seriously, think about it. The only options are to throw yourself into danger, or accept that the only dangers left are abstractions. And technology—I know they say it made the world flat, but it also compartmentalized each person, you know? Protected them from any real danger. Like, it made the world flat, but with millions of little cubicles."

"Sterile, fluorescent-lit cubicles," Ginny said, nodding. "With iPads and DVRs. Even toddlers get tablets now."

"You get everything you could ever want, minus challenges."

"So, go to school on the West Side of Chicago."

"Right," Barkley said, feeling his face get hot, as if he was onto something just out of reach. "Go to school on the West Side. It's like the Wild West we heard about as kids. And why is it wild? Less technology, more crime. Fewer resources, more danger. And it's obvious that we've already been domesticated, because we're scared shitless of it."

"What about war? Some people aren't scared. They want to join. Hell, I thought about it as a kid. I wanted to be a GI Jane helicopter pilot once."

Barkley tapped his fork on the table. "People join the war because it's still being romanticized. They think there are answers out there. Bad neighborhoods aren't romanticized, but war is. And it has to be, right? That's the difference. The end result—I don't know. Ask my brother. But he doesn't seem happy about it."

"It's a problem for everyone, I think. Although lots of people don't know it's a problem. My mom, she's been sucked into all of it. She's got all of the handsets, all of the gizmos, all of the binge-worthy TV shows queued up on Netflix. But my dad—he's this woodsman type from Wisconsin. I think you'd like him. He's having none of it. Goes into the forest and hunts with a bow and arrow. Drags a moose back by the antlers."

"Man crush," Barkley said. "Immediately. But that's it, don't you think? And that example there—you're going to call me sexist, but hear me out—I think it's more a problem for guys than girls, this whole technology-infused pleasure-world, because it's like, guys have testosterone. Guys have the urge to commit violence and put themselves in perilous situations. It's our DNA. And now, with the way society is, it's gone. And what are we supposed to do? This is why we all sit in theaters frothing at the mouth while some ninja wearing sunglasses kills a thousand people. Or we write stories about it. You should see my stories from high school. The body count is almost pornographic."

"Well," Ginny said. "You're a sexist pig. No, not really, but, oh look—"

She leaned back as the smiling waiter set down the ceramic plate that held their appetizers—Angels on Horseback, Barkley remembered, eyeing the steaming scallops in their bacon-wrapped choke holds. He watched as Ginny popped one in.

"Down the hatch!" she cried, causing the waiter to give a double take.

"I think he's one of our domesticated types," Barkley said, nodding.

"Oh, fuck him very much. These bad boys are delightful."

"You were saying? You were saying something, weren't you?"

She swallowed. "Yeah, the testosterone thing. It's true. For girls, it's a different effect, though. If technology makes men stifled, it makes girls more insecure. And competitive. Both. I mean, back in the day, you'd compare yourselves to your peers, sure. Every girl does, it's a tale as old as time. How each girl looks, what she wears, who her friends are, which boys she's talking to. But at least you could turn away from it—take a break once you were out of school. Right now, though, there's no turning away from comparisons. Between passing periods you're looking at Facebook albums of girls prettier than you, doing what you weren't doing last Saturday night, wearing what you don't have, hanging out with boys who don't know your name. You go home and it's more of the same: Facebook and Twitter and Instagram, and hundreds of television shows with girls who are mutants—real fucking mutants, I'm serious—in their comic-book sexiness, most of which is concocted by surgeons. Literally, girls are assaulted by social comparison *every second of the day*. It's frightening. And they either get buried under their insecurities, or they fight back, or they don't care."

"And which one are you?" Barkley asked.

"The woodsman—woodswoman—in me doesn't give a shit. I go my

own way. One of the reasons I refuse to play rhythm guitar. And the other part, well, I was insecure for a while in middle school, but who isn't? And then I fought back. I'm not perfect by any means, but I do have my assets, my perks, and I'm not going to shy away from what's working."

Barkley knocked one of the scallops on its side. "I think a lot is working," he said. "For you, I mean."

Her green eyes flashed at him, and then softened. "You know," she said, "I've told a lot of guys to fuck off in my time. But there's something about your delivery . . . I don't know. You're kind of cheesy, but it works."

"So you're not going to tell me to fuck off?"

"Let's get out of here, shall we? I've got beer at my apartment."

Barkley yanked out his debit card and waved it at the waiter.

Ginny lived in the upper level of a Wicker Park brownstone owned by one Ken Tanwabe, a Japanese bonds broker who had left for England a summer ago. They climbed the steps while Barkley, buzzed and feeling a whooshing sound in his head, made sure his legs didn't give out. Back to her place, back to her place—he could hear Hayward laughing in anticipation all the way from Brooklyn.

"How'd you score this sweet little residence?" Barkley asked, rubbing his sweaty palms together. "Do you pay the rent in gold doubloons?"

"Tanwabe's son played bass guitar with me during my freshman and sophomore years at Michigan State. I was out for beers in the city with him—the son—talking about how I wanted to move out of Lakeview, and he's like, 'My dad would totally let you rent out his place for three hundred a month.' A refurbished brownstone for three hundred, Barkley. Fully furnished. All I have to do is feed his Lake Kutubu rainbow fish."

"You serious?"

"Oh, deadly."

"I'm paying seven hundred for a rectangle and a bed."

Ginny shrugged at him. "Gotta hang out with the Japanese more."

The upper level was immaculate and traditional—a maple and bamboo *getabako* by the entranceway for placing the shoes, *fusuma* partitions dividing up the living room, their wooden understructures attached to rails, the papery constructions depicting cherry blossoms and tranquil limestone fountains. Ginny explained it all, led him across the straw tatami mats to an American-style, black-and-gold couch across from a television. All around the walls and ceiling were more trinkets: a chandelier made of carved wooden monkeys and a pagoda, two jade Buddhas, a golden plate with delicate inscriptions, pictures of family members. On the wall between the two bedrooms was the bubbling blue aquarium, where Ken Tanwabe's Lake Kutubu fish circled and danced.

"You actually live in this palace," Barkley said, sitting down gingerly.

She handed him a Pabst Blue Ribbon and reclined on the couch beside him. "I don't drink these ironically," she said. "My dad drinks them. His dad drank them. That's kind of the deal."

"Your inner woodswoman, huh?"

"Proud of it."

"So how does all of this Japanese stuff jibe with your individuality?"

"Oh, I like different cultures. And different people. And options. And this right here, this Ken Tanwabe palace—it's a window. You know? You can't get enough windows."

"Windows through the cubicles," Barkley intoned, before realizing he was trying too hard. "Shit," he said. "That's pretentious. I suck."

She grinned at him. "Pretty bad."

"God. You know, I'm going to be honest. I'm lost at this point. I don't know what the next move is. Spontaneous decision making. I warned you earlier."

Ginny leaned in close, and Barkley felt their forearms touch, and the tips of their knees, and the soft particles of her hair against his cheek.

"You fret a lot, don't you?" she asked.

Barkley felt the sweat on his hands again. "I don't know."

"You're clamming up, and you don't need to."

"I'm not. I'm definitely not."

"Here, touch my hand. Like this. See, our little convo on testosterone-stifling moved you ahead at least five spaces on the dating board of life. That's why we're back here."

He stared at her, feeling hopeless yet combustible, as if he were doused in lighter fluid and waiting for the sound of a struck match. He saw a flash of his decade-old encounter with Candace Brandt, and abruptly realized he could only touch Ginny's hands with the tops of his own—his palms were greased with a film akin to olive oil. "I've got no reason to clam up," he said. "No reason at all."

"Yeah," she said, leaning closer. "But you're acting like a big wuss. What are you afraid of? What is it?"

He looked at his faded jeans. "Nothing, of course. I'm just naturally . . . shy. It's nothing!"

"Oh, it's something," she said, suddenly leaning back. "Come on, I can sense it. I can see those wheels spinning. What's the situation?"

Barkley laughed. "Are you psychic or something?"

She pushed her index fingers against her temple. "Yes. I should sit in the Lotus position more. Charge for services. Now what's the situation?"

"It's nothing. A very old, goofy memory is all. And my buddy's been bringing it up ever since he heard about us going out, trying to get me freaked-out."

Ginny cackled. "Oh my God, you've got a full-blown story, don't you? I can feel it! Tell me."

"No!"

She downed her beer and strode over to the kitchen, leaving Barkley with the ghost of her hand against his own.

"What's it have to do with?" she called from the kitchen.

"Nothing."

"Is it about getting beat up by an Amazonian?"

"No."

"Is it sexual?"

"I don't know."

"So, it's definitely sexual."

Barkley looked up from his lap. "How did we get to this? Let's talk about the technology stuff again."

Ginny pranced back into the room, holding two more beers. "Nope. This is far more entertaining. See, you could have kissed me two seconds ago, but you didn't, and now it's therapy time. I want the story. Will you tell me the story?"

"Oh, God. I've told, like, two people the real story since high school."

"Ah, a high school story! This is going to be amazing. Can you please tell me?" She cracked open a beer for him.

"No, let's go back to that thing about kissing."

"Um, no. You can earn that with a tale of adventure. Please go? Begin!"

Barkley sighed. "No judgments?"

"You big ginormous wuss! Tell me!"

"Okay, but you have to remember that I was a sophomore in high school at the time. I mean, that's pretty young. I was just a kid!"

"Jeez, away with the disclaimers, please. So you were a sophomore, probably with zero sexual experience, and something happened. Correct so far?"

"Correct."

"All right, set the scene."

"Okay. I can't believe we're really doing this. But, yeah. Wow. So there was this big high school party. We're at this giant house in Downers Grove—me and my buddy Hayward—the Spumonti family mansion. It's this beast of a domicile with like three stories and an indoor pool and a furnished basement. The dad was like the VP of an insurance agency or something. Maybe State Farm. Anyway, John Spumonti was a senior when I was a sophomore. Totally a Gatsby. Threw a lot of parties, barely drank. Wanted to be an engineer. I think he went to Wisconsin. Whatever. Anyway, the basement was furnished with all these cool trinkets, like Dolby surround sound and a *Ghostbusters* pinball machine, a *Jurassic Park* pinball machine—"

"I've seen that one before! With the T. rex."

"Yes, there is a T. rex involved, I believe. But anyway, the party is mainly in this basement, and it's a lot of upperclassmen—we're there strictly because we're on the sophomore football team, and one of our friends had gotten moved up to varsity and invited us. We really have no business being there. But everyone is drunk, and John Spumonti is only playing Goo Goo Dolls—"

"Ouch. 'Iris'? 'Broadway'? That was all over the airwaves back then."

"I think I heard 'Black Balloon' about fifty times. If we're going late 1990s, you'd think we could get some Third Eye Blind. I will defend Third Eye Blind until the end, just so you know."

"Well, if you want to step onto that ledge, my friend . . ."

"Ha-ha. So anyway, we clearly don't belong. I'm drinking Busch Light, and it's probably my third time ever consuming alcohol. All beer tastes terrible at this point. Hayward and I are standing in the corner of the basement by the pinball machines, trying not to be stupid, but the entire time we're discussing whether or not Ra's al Ghul is an 'admirable' Batman villain. What a joke! Anyway, lots of people start coming into the basement—you've got the varsity wrestling squad, who are seriously a bunch of animals, then some of the two-sport athletes, then a parade of future sorority girls, and the whole time I'm running in and out of the basement bathroom, trying to make sure I don't look weird, trying to fix my hair, but then I'm afraid to dry my hands off because the bathroom has one of those stupid ornamental-type towels—you know what I'm talking about? The trendy little ones hanging off ornate hooks you're afraid to use? Well, yeah, so that was basically the first two hours or so of this party. Hayward and I getting drunk on Busch Light together, debating Batman, whispering about girls."

"God, you were such a *stud*!" Ginny yelled.

"Do you want this story or not?"

"This is quite the buildup. Yes, yes, I want the story!"

"So this girl walks in, and she is screaming and shouting. Just losing her mind."

"Name?"

Barkley sighed. "I'm not going there."

"Why? Because I'm going to Facebook her tomorrow morning?"

"Well, come to think of it, *yes*, that's an excellent reason why."

"Just go. Name. It's not fun if she's an anonymous blob."

Barkley wondered, briefly, if he should twist the story, or change it, or add in details to make his sophomore self look better. It *was* a funny story, but it had also been decidedly unfunny to be the recipient of the story's experience, at least in the long run. But no, if anything, the roll he was on tonight centered on truth telling, dating etiquette be damned. And how many rules had he broken already? Getting nervous, having sweaty palms, talking about past experiences with girls, discussing philosophy . . . he'd pretty much done a faux pas world tour. Yet it felt like he knew this girl, and none of those rules really mattered.

"Okay," he said. "She walks in, and her name is Candace Brandt."

"Ooooh."

"Now, I don't know if that name echoes in eternity like it did for all of us at Downers North, but this girl was legendary. Candace Brandt. She was one of those girls who you had to say the first and last name for."

"Describe. Full description. Do your writer thing."

"Yeah, right, the writing that your uncle skewers. But okay—Candace Brandt comes in, and she's wearing like the tightest white skirt of all time, to the point where she looks like an upright sushi roll or something. Purple heels—tacky, but it worked. Don't remember the shirt, but it was some kind of tank top, used to show . . . you know."

"To what? Reveal her assets?"

"Yes, correct."

"And are these assets what she is known for?"

Barkley leaned forward, spread his hands wide. "She is legendary for these assets. Not that I've had my eye on her or anything. This girl is on another level, totally off my radar. Now, at this time, her reputation is beginning a slight downward spiral. She'd been with this football player Gardocki for about a year, and then with at least two of the wrestlers, and is currently with this maniac Benny Alvarez, who . . . wait for it . . . plays lead guitar."

"Ah! Well, male lead guitarists are very different from female lead guitarists. First and foremost, not being nearly as stable. That's lesson one."

"That actually sounds pretty accurate. This guy Alvarez was crazy, like ADHD meets Jason. He broke all the windows of the science lab when Mr. Mortier failed him."

"Mr. Mortier tends to deserve it, I hear."

"You must be having fun with this. All right, so fast-forward. Candace Brandt doesn't have the same reputation as she did maybe the year before, but it's still there, and she's still got that *name*. And for some reason, she sits down next to me on the couch."

"The couch? I thought you and this Hayward were standing by the pinball machines."

"Well, we're fast-forwarding here. Things get fuzzy, okay? People are drinking. Time goes by, alcoholic consumption increases. So now it's later in the night, around two A.M., party still pretty big. Hayward and I are on the couch, and there's like, *South Park* and *The Jeffersons* on—somebody keeps flipping back and forth with the channels. The point is I'm distracted, and suddenly Candace Brandt is sitting right next to me."

Ginny slapped her hands against her knees. "What happened? Did she talk to you? Did you hit on her with Batman lines? Please tell me you said, 'I am the night.' That actually would have worked on me at the bookstore, I'm not even kidding."

Barkley shook his head. "See, that's the world I want to believe in. But anyway, she sits down next to me, and yes, she actually talks to me. But she's also drunk and angry. Her boyfriend Benny Alvarez is apparently not returning her calls—very likely cheating on her and letting her know about it. And so she looks at me and says, 'Have you seen Benny?' And I'm too startled to really know how to respond, so she's saying it again, 'Have you seen Benny, have you seen Benny?' like a mantra, and Hayward is nudging me, and then she's saying 'Hello? Hello?' Finally I blurt out that, no, I have not seen this guy, I've never even really met him. Which gets her angrier."

"Ah! Then what?"

"This dude Benny Alvarez sends her like the world's most vindictive text message. Or something. I have no idea what it actually said, but she reads it and literally goes ballistic. She starts screaming 'Fuck this asshole!' and 'I'm gonna tear his balls off,' you know, really heinous, outrageously violent comments, and her friends are swooning over her, trying to talk to her, but she's shooing them away, and Hayward and I are just sitting there, like, *rigid*. Like, we've got Candace Brandt not only sitting next to us, but Candace Brandt in killer dragon lady mode, wanting blood. So then she turns to me and asks what my name is. I manage to burp out that I'm Barkley Brunson. She asks me if I'm a freshman. I say, no, ma'am. Clearly this was her fear. Even blackout drunk, she wasn't going to get with a freshman."

"A strong goal for a strong-minded woman."

"Right."

"Is this where it gets traumatic? Do you need another beer?"

Barkley massaged his forehead. "Yes to another beer. Yes to about to get traumatic."

Twin snaps came from the kitchen, and seconds later Ginny dangled a fresh Pabst in front of him. He took it, drank deeply. Ginny sat next to him again, grinning.

"Okay, big boy, let's have the story. What's next? She's pissed off, she asks if you're a freshman, you say no . . . go!"

Barkley shook his head, then forced down another gulp of beer. "Well, I tell her I'm not a freshman, but then she's immediately talking to one of her girlfriends again. *South Park* is back on. Then Candace gets another brutal text from Benny Alvarez. And this time, Ginny? Nuclear explosion. I'm not going to repeat what she said. She literally tears her phone in half, rips out the battery, throws the pieces in her purse. She yells at her friends to leave her alone, and now the room is clearing a little, because everyone's a little afraid, and she zips up her purse, slams it next to her on the couch, looks at me, and asks, almost like a taunt— 'You want to fuck?'"

"Stop!" Ginny screamed. "No, way. Dragon lady tried to bed you? Stop!" She threw her head back and cackled.

Barkley chugged down the rest of his beer, nodded and smiled. "I don't even answer her, I'm too shocked. She has to be talking to someone else, right? But she's just staring at me. Then she says it again, and Hayward is nudging me, saying, 'Dude. Dude. *Dude.*' And then I get it together, realize what's happening, and tell her that yes, of course, sure, absolutely."

Ginny put her hand over her mouth. "I'm so frightened right now, Barkley. This is going to get dark, isn't it? It's going to get twisted. I can't take it."

"Should I stop?"

She punched him in the arm. "Continue, you fool! Go."

Barkley shrugged. "Well, she tells me she's going to some random bedroom. She says to meet her there in five. I'm beyond nervous. I don't even know what's happening. What to do. I'd tried to put on a condom once before, as practice, but those clamped ridges? It was like trying to slip on a mousetrap. I couldn't do it. So I'm freaking out about that, and the whole time, I'm also thinking, Why didn't I just read that damn blue sex ed book they handed out in sixth grade?"

"The *Michael Book*! Where was the *Michael Book*?"

"So I go into this bedroom, and it's almost pitch-black," Barkley said. "That's the first thing that sucks. I can't see her, I can't really see anything, and the only light is from this halogen patio bulb outside the window, but it's blocked by a bunch of curtains that are thicker than Kevlar. Candace practically tackles me—this girl is rough. I mean, this isn't romantic. I am a pawn in a revenge sex scheme against a sociopath.

There is no kissing. Zero. She tears off my jeans, then practically throws me on the bed like a shot-putter."

Ginny covered her eyes, but motioned for him to continue.

"So, like, she slaps a condom packet against my chest, but I couldn't put this thing on in a brightly lit bathroom, much less a bottomless, lightless abyss with a dragon woman. I mean, the pressure is insane—it's like I'm holding the world's most expensive wet wipe in my hands."

"And?"

"And she is just cursing at me, eventually pushes me down against the bed and puts the condom on *for* me—so brutal, like an angry mother putting a soccer sock over a shin guard. And then, well, it happened. We had sex, and I lost my virginity. I guess that's the cool part, right? That I tagged a legendary unicorn with my first try. However, the experience itself sucked. I couldn't see her, and the entire time I was just holding on for dear life and trying not to pass gas. Seriously, that was the hardest part. Air bubbles all over the place. And the traumatic part . . . I mean, it was my first time. I wasn't in it for the marathon distance."

"Oh," Ginny said, trying not to laugh. "So you were a sprinter. Are we talking the two-hundred-meter dash? The one hundred?"

Barkley gave a thumbs-down. "More like the forty. Or the ten-yard bag race."

Ginny covered her face with her hands.

"Basically, the gist is this: I had about twenty-four hours to gloat with all of my sophomore friends. That was cool. Then word got out about my 'performance,' thanks to Candace Brandt. End result? I was bestowed with the nickname 'the Twenty-Second Man' until that broad graduated."

"Stop. She did not call you that."

Barkley nodded. "It was awful. The Twenty-Second Man. Luckily, the fact that those twenty seconds occurred with Candace Brandt gave me some slack, and my friends didn't care, as long as they could taunt me about it. But still. That became my actual nickname for a while, and my buddies still use it to get me nervous."

Barkley's lips felt dry. There were six empty beers on the coffee table, and Ginny was curled on the couch, convulsing with laughter.

"Holy shit," she said. "You're like an abused puppy dog! I feel so bad—the Twenty-Second Man! You're a legend!"

"Great, isn't it?"

"Yes."

"Now you understand my situation?"

"Well, that settles it," Ginny said, regaining her composure.

"Settles what?"

"You've earned a second date. Plus, maybe a little make-out session for right now."

"I—we're what?"

"You're not afraid of a little romantic CPR, are you? You're an abused puppy dog and you need a good experience."

"Pity make-out?" Barkley said, feeling weak.

She finished her beer and squeezed his arm. "Let's go rustle around on Tanwabe's massive bed."

"Look," Barkley said, "I think—"

Ginny leaned over and kissed him, roughly, forcefully, and his thoughts fell away.

"It would be a shame if you didn't get over this by the time you're thirty," she said. "You're an adult now. You're in control. Who cares about some hilarious high school experience?"

"Right. You're right, of course."

"And one thing you should know?" she said, pulling back. "We're on the same team."

"Right. I know."

"I'm serious. We're on the same team. Say it back to me."

"We're on the same team," Barkley said, trying to believe.

Ginny stood up and left him there on the couch. Bubbling from the aquarium took over his hearing. The *fusuma* were all around him, all of those cherry blossom partitions and ancient tower walls. But the door to the bedroom was open, and eventually Barkley stood up, looked away from the revolutions of the Lake Kutubu rainbow fish, and followed her in.

GERMAN
ENGINEERING

Henry Brunson got out of his Mercedes and walked to the doctor's office, looking at his phone. It was a hot day in mid-August, and inside the automatic doors it was air-conditioned and cool and also antiseptic.

"I'll take you to his office," the nurse said brightly. "He's running a little behind."

Henry grunted. Twenty minutes later, he still sat hunched and unattended in Dr. Pashad's office, scowling at the cardboard box that held the latex gloves. All those fancy certificates with blue borders and gold stars were little more than decoys, he thought. As were the tiny framed photographs of Pashad's family: a gaunt eighteen-year-old son in a graduation robe, arm around his father; a woman with dark eyes holding a bottle of Pinot Noir, wedding ring glinting from the flash of the camera. Simple decoys. There was a tiny basin for hand washing by the door to the office, and next to the basin was the white box from which a single rubber glove sprouted like a grotesque flower. *That* was the real truth of the place. There was something horribly unnatural about the glove, Henry thought, and underneath that unnaturalness was a hint of lurking malevolence, as if it promised to visit you later, when you were lying naked on a cutting block.

Henry glared at the certificates. He felt the space of Pashad's office now: the constrictive parameters, the low ceiling, and the scent of rubbing alcohol and disinfectant bouncing off the walls. How had he ever felt comforted by this place?

The door opened. Pashad entered, wearing his doctor's whites, skin looking a little tighter than before, stretched taut like those latex gloves.

"Sorry about the wait, Mr. Brunson."

"Just give me good news," Henry said.

He'd weighed himself two weeks ago and come in at 210. His natural weight, carefully balanced with whey protein isolate and omega-3 fish oils and hours on the plate-loaded bench press and treadmill, was 215. It had been 215 for two years straight, and it was a good weight, the right weight. But two weeks ago, 210. And today, the nurse had told him he'd dropped another two. Worse yet, his pectorals looked smaller, flatter, and his biceps didn't have the same melon swell, and the soreness, the soreness from working out, continued for days, his whole body a bruise.

Pashad pulled a swivel chair out from the desk with the photographs and sat down in front of him.

"My skin," Henry said. "My weight. I'm supposed to be maintaining a level of athleticism here. It's more than inconvenient. It's a pain in the ass."

Pashad had a manila folder in front of him, and ran his hands over the folder while the tip of his tongue pushed again his cheek. Henry noticed both of these nervous gestures from the hundreds of boardroom meetings he'd attended over the years. Some scratched the back of their heads. Some picked fingernails. Bit lips. Rolled their tongues around in their mouths, bounced their knee, moved their hands around the surface of something solid.

"It's bad news," Henry said. "Isn't it?"

"Mr. Brunson—"

"So, not gallstones?"

"It's—Mr. Brunson, it's more serious than that. I've looked at the ultrasound."

Henry felt anger flush his face like red dye. "Well, I hope you looked at the ultrasound. You're getting paid to look at the ultrasound. And then I needed the CT scan. And the ERCP. Have you looked at the results of those as well? No one tells me anything, and now you need to inform me that you've actually reviewed them?"

"I understand that this is a sensitive issue, and you have to understand that we needed to be sure—"

"I've dealt with my share of sensitive issues, Doctor. I've practically kept an entire company afloat for the past ten years, by the virtue of my sales. I've got a son who just returned from Afghanistan. Don't tell me what's sensitive. I want the information, do you understand?"

Pashad's fingers stopped moving across the folder. "It's pancreatic cancer, Mr. Brunson."

Henry smelled the rubbing alcohol again. He felt a rush of strange wind against his skull, then stifled it, stifled it strong and fast, and looked past the doctor, at the framed photograph of the son with his arm around the father. He wondered, trying to focus, how long ago the picture was taken. Five years? Before 2000? And where? There was a white building in the background. A golden dome with pillars and a long spread of green lawn. Greek Revival. The son was smiling, but his eyes were unreadable. Henry was usually good at reading eyes. It let him know, at the din of the halftime show at the Bulls game, with the crowd's roar softened to a lull, or at a dinner at MK or Blackbird or Tru, during those moments between courses—the eyes let him know where the client stood, how much he could say, how many points, how much pressure; a person's eyes were everything. And he was an expert, a professional who knew when to lean in and utter tight, controlled phrases under his breath, lodging a doorjamb of pressure into the client's brain so that he was pleasantly trapped, so there was only one course of action: agreement, agreement, agreement.

But he couldn't read the eyes of the young man in the graduation robe with his arm around his father. He had to focus. The doctor wasn't important right now. The son's eyes were dark eyes, black eyes, eyes like those of the woman with the bottle of wine. He wondered where the son was now. How often they saw each other. If they saw each other. Did they only meet when the father demanded it, getting together on some rain-swept Tuesday in the Chicago suburbs, sitting bent and awkward over a deli luncheon table, not finding the words? Or did they golf regularly, laughing between the sloping hills and sand traps, heading afterward to the clubhouse to watch Cubs baseball? He wanted to know.

"Mr. Brunson?"

"Yes. Doctor."

"The ultrasound revealed an abnormality in the pancreas. This is why the CT scan was so important. It allowed us to be sure—it used multiple X-ray images and a computer generator to give us cross-sectional views of the pancreas and surrounding organs. A pancreatic mass was found, a suspicion of pancreatic cancer raised, and the ERCP confirmed this. So it *is* pancreatic cancer. I know this is difficult to hear. But, Mr. Brunson, even though I know this sounds like very bad news, it's not all bad news, there's a silver lining—"

"Your son," Henry said. "That's your son in that picture?"

"My son? Well, yes. Jeremy."

"That's a fine-looking high school to graduate from. Private?"

"Well, it's a college, actually. The University of Iowa. He went there to write. But in regards to the silver lining, with the pancreas—"

"I thought he was eighteen. Your son."

"He's boyish, Mr. Brunson. Youthful."

"And writing? No medicine for your son?"

Pashad looked confused.

"I mean," Henry said, "you must have encouraged medicine. But he wanted to write. This must have been a source of discomfort. Expectations being what they are. Especially in a medical household."

Pashad ran his hands across the folder again. "Children are destined to go against their fathers, Mr. Brunson. My father was involved in religion. It's a normal cycle. And my son is relatively happy, it seems."

"Happy," Henry said, turning the word over, and then looked by the basin and saw that single latex glove sprouting forth from the cardboard box. He cleared his throat, rolled his shoulders back.

"Mr. Brunson?"

"I'm all right. I'm fine. I apologize for that. You were talking about a silver lining. Let's hear it."

"I understand this is a shock. A terrible shock. But there is hope. Based

on the CT scan, the mass in the pancreas appears not to have metastasized."

"Metastasized?"

"Moved to other organs. When this happens, the situation is more
immediate. Sometimes it appears in the liver. That makes the situation
much more strenuous. And, to be totally honest, when patients come in
already showing signs of jaundice, the chance of metastasis is high. But
the good news is that on the CT scan, the liver looks clean. And this
gives us options. If you want it, we can be more aggressive."

"Life expectancy?" Henry felt the wind against his face again.

Pashad held up a hand. "If you'd like the aggressive route, the procedure I'm going to recommend is the Whipple. I'll be putting you in
contact with the best oncologist at Northwest Community Hospital,
Dr. Fredrickson. He's already seen the CT scans. Given your age and
outstanding health outside the diagnosis, you should be an excellent
candidate for both the procedure and the recovery. But the Whipple
procedure is not to be taken lightly—it's a long surgery, and they'll be
removing the head of the pancreas, the gall bladder, the duodenum,
and a portion of the bile duct. We'll put a stent in the bile duct, which
takes care of the jaundice. With me so far?"

"Life expectancy, Doctor."

"All right. It's really across the board. With today's Whipple, twenty
percent of patients live beyond five years. One in five. But the number
is skewed. It doesn't account for the patient's age or general health. You
need to factor in all those individuals who acquire pancreatic cancer later
in life—in their seventies and eighties and nineties. Some of those individuals simply die from old age, other causes. And like I said, you're in
excellent health."

"One in five," Henry repeated.

"Make it longer than five years, yes. But again, that covers all ages of
diagnosis. There is hope with this procedure, Mr. Brunson."

Henry stared at the gloves. "And that means eighty percent live less
than five years. And if it covers all ages, it covers those who get it at
thirty, forty, and fifty. Those who are younger than me. Am I right?"

"I think the most important thing, Mr. Brunson, is putting you in contact with Dr. Fredrickson. And we'll move forward from there."

Henry walked out into the vast expanse of parking lots and parking garages and slowly moving cars and the sun was hot against his skin, hot on his neck, hot across his cheeks and nose and hands. He breathed in the air. A soft breeze blew back, ruffled his hair, played against his white button-down and softly swaying tie. He closed his eyes, and the sunlight was orange against his eyelids. He opened them, breathed in again, smelled pollen and asphalt and the fresh scent of leafy air, of air surrounded by the ancient oaks and elms of the suburbs. The sky was blue, butane blue, the blue of a Bunsen burner. A single jet pulled a ribbon of white across the sky, cutting across that blue like a speedboat over Lake Michigan. More cars drove past. He looked at the trees. He saw squirrels, birds. A boy across the street passed on a silver bicycle. Someone was hammering in the distance. A sprinkler system clicked and whirred. An old woman with a floral dress was using a walker. A mother in light blue jeans was pulling her son by the arm. Another car passed. He breathed in the air. The sun was hot. The sky was blue. He smelled, felt, breathed, found that he was sitting down on the curb in front of the automatic doors to the doctor's office, closing his eyes and opening them, marveling at how much he had missed.

But in the car, turning the ignition, Henry felt his hands shaking. He tried to remember the color of the sky and the way the air had smelled, had just smelled not five minutes ago, but now he was inside the Mercedes and the sunroof was closed and he had forgotten and all the thoughts began cascading inside his brain. The Whipple procedure. A ridiculous name. Whipple. "Born to Be Wild" came on and Henry punched the dashboard twice, three times, until the radio turned off. Even with the Whipple, he was gone. He felt a tremor. He'd always known that somehow he would die, could die, but now death had a stamp of authenticity, a guarantee from some biological CEO—his ticket was punched, he was at the station, he was waiting for the train. And it didn't matter how high his penthouse reached. He could call Charlie. Yes. He *should* call Charlie. He was dying now. Was he dying? There was a procedure. There was still a way out. Through the windshield, he saw all the oaks and elms. He had just felt something outside, something real and different from the way he had felt in a while, but now that feeling was gone and he wanted to get it back, but he felt constrained inside the Mercedes, suffocated by all those dark colors and padded leather, and so he pulled over at a small pub in downtown Arlington Heights that appeared to be open. He kicked open the car door and slammed it, stood in the street, tried to breathe the air, but once again felt nothing, just confusion, just the tremor, a sensation of falling.

A neon sign for Coors Light stood in the window, and inside was a simple wooden bar with padded stools and three or four men sitting on those stools drinking whiskey or beer. Henry felt himself squat down and heard himself order bourbon, straight, and then tasted the bourbon going down the hatch like coal into a furnace. He received another, then another. He ordered without feeling. He ordered again.

"Jeez, pal," a voice next to him cracked. "You're thirsty."

"Parched," Henry said. He kept his eyes on the glass. There was a path, he thought, a narrow path he could be taking upon receiving this news, and it felt like he had almost grasped it, let it slip, and that he should be working to grasp it again. And he knew that drinking like this was wrong. This was the other path. But he tossed his head back and finished another round off.

"Not working today?"

Henry looked. It was a heavyset man two stools to his right, wearing a faded brown sports jacket, one hand around a pint of amber beer, the other hand absentmindedly stroking his bald head. He was burly, a couple inches shorter than Henry, maybe heavier, some fat, some muscle. Henry had been sizing up other men his whole life—he enjoyed it, enjoyed the mathematics of it, the complex predictions of a violent altercation, the promise of using that energy that all men kept so tightly bottled. He'd probably been in six or seven real fights in his life and won all but one. Two were college brawls, under the streetlights after midnight, with the football and rugby players from his fraternity, the SAEs, fighting with him side by side. Those were the fun ones. Hitting the pavement and rolling onto the drunken assholes who had started it and then getting up and throwing a punch so hard that the poor sap in front of them spit and spun and fell, and feeling that circle of people gathering around the fight, laughing and cheering, and then the moments afterward, standing tall like heroes while the losers retreated. Henry remembered how he and his friends stood while watching them walk away—button-downs and rugby shirts torn, blood on their knuckles, the evening air alive, breathing deeply, alive.

"Taking a sabbatical?" the balding man asked.

"You could say that."

"That's the way. Let loose. Work too much and you end up being retired, wondering where your family went, and what to do with all that money."

"Sage advice," Henry said. "Very sage. Have you read Socrates?"

"No."

"I can tell."

The balding man went quiet.

"Another," Henry said to the bartender.

"What did you mean by that?" the balding man asked.

"Never mind. What do you do?"

"I drink, mostly. I drink all over. Not just here."

"Career?" Henry asked, staring down at his glass.

"I was an electrician for twenty years. Now, I work security."

"Mall cop?"

"You're busting my balls, aren't you?"

Henry sighed. "It's been a day," he said. "Still wrapping my head around it."

"Cheers to that. I'm Sil, by the way."

"Henry."

They didn't bother shaking hands. Henry looked up at the tiny television to the side of the bar, which was playing a daytime soap opera.

"You watching this?" Henry asked.

"Nah."

"Hey, bartender. Can we change this?"

"Sports?" the bartender asked.

"History Channel."

The television screen went through a series of permutations before finally settling on archival footage of the Third Reich marching, and, seconds later, Adolf Hitler, shouting.

"You get off on this sort of thing?" Sil asked.

"This sort of thing is the history of the human race," Henry said. The bartender set down another glass of bourbon, and Henry noted that the man was too small and skinny to size up seriously, just a small man with a thin mustache and carefully combed dark hair. Henry tossed the bourbon down the hatch again, waving immediately for another.

"World War Two, huh?"

He looked at the screen, his brain finally, finally, fuzzy. There were fighter planes soaring through a black-and-white sky, turning and banking, heading for a distant dogfight.

"Are those F-somethings?" Sil asked, scratching his head. "American fighters? Or P-somethings?"

Henry loosened his tie. "That's the Luftwaffe."

"Germans. The bastards."

"Some would argue the greatest military force of all time. Those planes there—Messerschmitt Bf 109s."

"Not as good as American planes."

The bartender slid another bourbon in front of Henry, and a beer in front of Sil.

"Well," Henry said, "by '43 we were mass-producing the P-51, and that really might have been the finest plane. But the Bf 109s were there at the beginning. And you have the best fighter pilot of all time flying them, statistically anyway. Erich Hartmann. Heard of him?"

"If he's German, then shit no. Who wants to know?"

"He's the number one ace of all time."

"He's the number one asshole."

Henry felt his teeth clamp. "You've got to think broader than that. What if Babe Ruth was from China? Would you hate him then? No, you acknowledge the skill. Three hundred and fifty-two victories—think about that. It's a lot. Never shot down once."

"And you like that. You like it when the Germans win."

"I like my history. And I appreciate anybody who refuses to lose."

Sil grunted. "They all die eventually. Even your Germans."

"Not easily."

"And you're like that, huh? That's you? The tough guy?"

Henry pictured himself blocking a right cross from Sil. All fat guys tried to power punch you, came at you with their best hand, went right for the nose. And Sil was drinking with his right, and he'd punch with his right, and the punch would be a cross. Henry determined that he would block the punch instead of sidestepping it. He'd raise his left arm up and block the punch and then come at him with his right—but he didn't want to hit him, not right away. Instead he'd take him by the throat and push him backward. A quick shove, giving them space, giving them both time to raise their fists, and then the fight would begin.

But, as he raised the glass to his lips and blinked through the rising sensation of white noise in his brain, he realized, as if he'd been stabbed, that he was dying. Cancer. Had it really happened? He could keep drinking. He could get so drunk that maybe he'd forget that it happened. He was dying. He felt something inside him, something long inside him, wanting to tear itself out.

"You okay, pal?" Sil asked.

"Just shut up, all right?"

He pictured a casket. He pictured darkness. It was what he always thought of when he thought about death—blackness, pitch-blackness, a wide, long cave of infinite ink. But it was his own son Barkley who'd said to him at sixteen years of age, sitting in the living room reading a fantasy novel, that blackness after death wasn't possible. Henry had been uncorking a bottle of wine. He'd asked his son why, bemused, and his son had said that the people who feared blackness were the people who feared not existing, who were afraid there was nothing on the other side. And Henry had said, yes, so what, what's your point, and Barkley had said that if there wasn't an afterlife, there would be no need to fear the blackness—because even blackness was *something*. And no afterlife meant no more existence, meant nonexistence, meant nothingness, and blackness was still indeed something. If you stop existing, Barkley said, flipping a page, you won't even know it. It won't feel like anything. You'll be gone. And Henry had always thought this was the most astute thing his youngest son had ever said, and he'd loved the nonchalance with which he'd said it. But Henry, pouring himself that glass of red, had simply nodded and asked him to turn the channel to the Bulls game.

"What's going on, pal?" Sil again.

"I recommended shutting up, that's what's going on."

Sil was grumbling, but Henry was thinking how he wanted to call Barkley, how maybe his son had figured something else out, how he'd know something—the kid was smart like that, smart in ways he didn't expect, lighting matches in the darkest corners of the mind, while all the while being blind to the obvious. He wanted to talk to him. To call him. But the father couldn't call the son. No, that conversation could never happen. Never. Barkley couldn't see him like this. And so, even though Barkley had lit the match that illuminated Henry's fear of the blackness, he still feared it, and he feared not existing, and he feared the afterlife, childish though it seemed to even believe in. The afterlife seemed dreadfully long. And what was there to do? And did it really go on forever, without reprieve? And he was supposed to choose between that and the nonexistence and the blackness?

Fuck it.

"Stand up," Henry said.

Sil looked up from his beer.

"Stand your ass up, fat man. Let's get this over with."

"Now, hold on a second," the bartender said.

"We won't break anything," Henry spat, climbing off his stool. He unbuttoned his cuffs, rolled up his sleeves while Sil sat there staring at him, looking fatter than before.

"What is this?" he asked.

Henry clenched his fists, watching the cords of veins bulge forth from his forearms. His body was sore, and his stomach hurt, and he had the jaundice, but he was still 208 pounds and angry and he was still Henry Brunson.

"We don't need to do this," Sil said. "You're pushing me, but we don't need to."

"Damn right we do. Get off your ass, mall cop."

"Aw, hell, that's it!"

Sil came off the stool, came right for him, low to the ground, growling. Henry struck him across the face immediately, a perfectly placed right cross, and the fat bastard went reeling into the bar, cheek rippling from the blow, a single flailing arm knocking over an empty pint glass.

"Hey!" the bartender shouted.

Henry laughed, came in close, and delivered two swift shots to Sil's kidneys, his knuckles punching up into fabric and cushioned blubber. Then he reared up and kicked him in the stomach and sent him sprawling on the ground.

"That's the way!" Henry yelled. "You feel that? Now get up. Get up!"

But Sil was slow getting up. His hands went to the stool for balance. His face flushed. He spit.

"Let's go, fat man!"

Sil stood shakily. Henry realized, with disgust, that the fat man was too drunk, too stupid—he wouldn't be the challenge, wouldn't be what he needed.

"Come on," Henry said. "Come get me, you little shit!"

"Stop this," the bartender said. "Stop it, now, I'm warning you!"

But Sil was charging again. He was slow, lumbering, eye movements as glacial as his mechanics. Henry considered letting himself get punched. It would feel good. He wanted to get punched. The sting of knuckles, the rattling shot to the skull and brain, the adrenaline that seemed to jar loose the senses, zooming everything in. He wanted the fat man to hit him. But it had to be earned. And so he stepped aside as Sil came close, slung his arm around his neck, a headlock, and wrenched him toward the ground. Sil wheeled and fell like a wrangled buffalo, the stools shaking in response.

When Henry stood back up, he saw something in the corner of his eye, the bartender holding something red, and then there was the sound of aerosol spraying at full volume, and Henry's eyes exploded into white-hot needles. He bucked his head back, pinwheeled, heard himself screaming. Everything was stabbing pain and it was like his eyes were being gutted, and there was hot water leaking and needles in his eyes and he couldn't breathe—he was hacking, coughing, falling onto the floor, pulling the padded stool with him, the stool clattering, his hands pawing at the slippery tiles on the floor.

"I can't see!" he shouted. "Help! I can't see!"

"It'll pass," the bartender said. "Just lie there."

Henry flailed on the cold tiled floor. He groaned and pressed his palms to his eyes and felt the needles and his running nose and the water leaking and the urge to vomit. He wondered where the fat man was. Where his family was. All of his sight was white and pink and bright orange, it was total blindness, he couldn't see a single fucking thing in front of him.

II

FIRSTS AND LASTS

CLASSROOM-BANTER LINGUISTICS: A FALL SEMESTER ELECTIVE

He'd been shaking for days, imagining the moment.

The dented oak door of room 115 stood in front of him, and through the tiny square window, the heads of students. Juniors. Sixteen and seventeen. Twenty feet away, now. He walked forward, the knot of his tie a rough knuckle against his throat. Fifteen feet. There was a male student in the front of the class, fist-bumping a seated kid with shaggy hair. Ten feet away. Barkley felt sand in his throat. A blonde sat on the teacher's desk, slinking her legs out from her skirt. The fist-bumping kid reached over to grab her thigh and she slapped him, lightly, twice against the cheek. Five feet away. The door ajar. Was he late? Two feet. One. The bell above the door trilled. His ears buzzed, vibrating as if a humming beetle were tunneling into his skull. The standing kid shouted something. The blond girl walked to the back of the class. The ringing stopped. Barkley pushed the cold handle and the oak door swung open and he stepped inside, moving slowly, fixing a smile on his lips as all those faces turned.

The day had begun at 4:00 A.M. Barkley had been tormented by sweat-filled dreams of running through Downers Grove backyards in his underwear, dodging the broad reflective windows of other families who could look out and see him. In this universe, all the houses had wooden stilts, and the grass was yellow, chest high, swaying like brittle wheat before a storm. But the houses kept rising on those stilts, higher and higher above the grass, and all through the dream he could feel the families watching, no matter how fast he ran. He woke in a wrenching panic, cheeks cold and damp, not in Downers Grove but Chicago, the white moonlight intruding upon the darkened floor.

There was no getting back to sleep, so he stayed up and turned on the television, stomach lurching as he imagined his first class staring back at him. He would have minutes—maybe five minutes—before they formed an initial opinion. He would see their opinions forming under their skin, rippling like tectonic plates. He took a scalding shower and ran his face against the fire, imagining, over and over again, his first class staring with cold, vacant eyes, doll's eyes, shark's eyes, judging him, vigilant against imposters. The water pounded his scalp. He imagined a downpour on a tin roof. Coffee. He needed coffee.

He went to the Starbucks on Diversey at five-thirty, ordering a regular with two shots of espresso. He slipped the cardboard sleeve onto the smooth white cup. He should have stayed at Ginny's, where her presence increased his confidence, but she'd insisted instead he get a good night's sleep away from her, at his own place. Well, she'd been wrong, dead wrong, and now he wanted to tell her that, wanted to text her how wrong she'd been, absolutely. He looked around the Starbucks. Bleary-eyed worker bees stood in an awkwardly bent line, all suits and ties, blouses and skirts, dress pants and cuff links, newspapers and iPhones. Dawn beginning to break behind the buildings. Where to? The welcome presentation in the Eastwick auditorium at 8:00 A.M. Eastwick a forty-minute drive from Lincoln Park. He had some time. He would drink his coffee. He would take a walk, postponing the inevitable. And then he would drive.

But time was water through his hands. By 6:45 A.M. he was on North Avenue heading west, aiming for the highway. His "new" used car, a white 2001 Ford Taurus, the price tag partially footed by his father, hummed raggedly. Coffee bounced in the cup holder. Getting closer. What would he say to his students? *Hello, I'm Mr. Brunson.* Was there a joke to go with that? Brunson sounds like . . . what? Munson. Fun Son. Blumpkin. No. All bathroom humor off-limits, like wearing an electric dog collar that zapped the vocal cords. And what would they say to him? Nothing? Respond with a silence so deep he could hear the popping of pipes, the clicking of hallway heels?

During student teaching, a couple of the kids had made paper airplanes ironically, not even throwing them, and that hadn't been a problem, not with the three-hundred-pound observing teacher roaming like a predator on the fringes. But now he'd be on his own. And how would they look at him? Would they see his potbelly first? See him as the former high school dork? Or would they think of him as creative, intelligent? Handsome? He steered the Taurus onto the Eisenhower Expressway. The floor rumbled as he crossed the exit ramp. Coffee bubbled from the plastic opening. He wasn't ready. Had never *been* ready. He was just doing it to do it, because nothing else made sense. Was he supposed to be marooned in some corporate office lined with gray cubicles and short-circuiting fax machines and motivational windsurfing pictures? *Dare to Achieve.* Achieve what, carpal tunnel syndrome? No. He brought the Taurus up to seventy, switched to the left lane, passed a junk food–toting semi with snarling graffiti on the sides. Charlie had almost gone corporate. Some of Barkley's friends were doing that now. They talked about the zombified daze they suffered from the buzzing computer screens, the way time seemed stuck in cement, and the never-ending plastic pinch of telephone headsets, strapped and unrelenting on their craniums. No, corporate life wasn't for him.

Maybe he could avoid Eastwick altogether. Turn around, head west, and escape to California. Yes. Drop everything and get a job at some surf shop, selling sunglasses and board shorts to laid-back people who said *bro* and *chill* and didn't judge at all. It sounded great, didn't it? There'd be a thatched roof over the shop and tiki torches on the fringes and the frothy blue line of the Pacific in the distance. He could do that, right? Right? No. Of course he couldn't. Barkley had tried that once in college, as he drove his friends back from the mall and they approached the exit ramp that would take them back to campus. *Let's just drive past it,* Barkley had said. *Go to California.* His buddies had laughed and said *yeah, yeah, Vegas, too,* and they'd started quoting *Swingers*, started talking about how they could all just miss a week of classes, how it wouldn't matter, how Timmy Calmus had an uncle in San Jose, how amazing it would be to get out of that midwestern winter, on and on they had plotted, *Vegas, baby, Cali, baby, we're so fucking money, baby*, until the square green exit sign was finally visible and Barkley was sure they'd actually pass it. But it was Timmy Calmus who cleared his throat first, who started talking about a quiz he had in Cognitive Psychology. Then Chubs—Chubs of all people, the binge drinker of the group, the one who'd wet the apartment carpet three times in two years—had said he was supposed to go shoot clay pigeons with the ridiculous hicks he'd met at the townie bar the week before. And sure enough, by the time they were a quarter mile away, everyone in the car was shouting for Barkley to *get off at the fucking exit, are you fucking nuts, we're not going to California, just turn, dude, turn!* So, of course they didn't go. Of course Barkley took the exit, just like he was supposed to. People followed the tracks in front of them, onward, onward, just as he was doing now.

He increased the speed to seventy-five. He wasn't meant for cubicles or surf shops. Hayward was a film editor, but that required cinematic smarts and a different degree. Barkley's math skills had deserted him after geometry, and that meant no engineering, no accounting, no finance, no Board of Trade. Too lazy to be a lawyer. Too white-collar to go blue-collar. And so this was it. The town at the edge of the abyss. He would teach. The car jumped as it hit a pothole; coffee shot up and hit the ceiling, and Barkley imagined himself in the classroom, speaking with a particular brand of confidence, sliding together the perfect order of syllables that would somehow make the students like him, make him a success. But the problem was, he couldn't see those syllables clearly enough—they were fuzzed out by some sort of static, by the curse of his imperfection, his lack of confidence, his lack of *something*. And so he drove forward, turned the radio to 94.7, heard the twang of CCR, of "Green River," and he hoped.

Minutes later, his phone rang. Ginny.

"Hello," he said, trying to steady his voice.

"Are you ready to kick some ass today or what?"

Barkley looked out at the vast swarms of highway traffic. "I'm freaking out here. Drop something wise on the situation, will you?"

Ginny cleared her throat. "You are tall, dark, and handsome. You have the mind of a poet. You are hung like a bridge troll. You—"

"A *bridge troll?*"

"Sorry, *Lord of the Rings* is marathoning on HBO."

"Oh my God, not helping!"

"Come on, Barkley! You're going to smoke it. You're a beast. Go get it. Do it for Gimli. I mean Gandalf. Damn it, I mean—"

"I'm going to trip you when we meet up later today. First thing."

"Oh stop it. You're going to kill it today. Go get it done. And have fun, all right? First days are great. I know you can do it."

"Gotta go," Barkley said as he steered the car toward the exit ramp. "I'll talk to you when it's over."

7:15 A.M. He could see the school from where he parked three blocks away, and he tried to take it all in. Red brick turrets and wide wooden doors and bronze statues of scholars with quill pens commanded the block, and all around him, Barkley saw tired schoolchildren walking slump-shouldered into the building, heavy bags slung along their backs, and parents in purring luxury SUVs calling out to them about summer reading lists and homeroom teachers and permission slips, and the instructors themselves walking bleary-eyed into the side entrance, past the multibraceleted mothers with chic strollers on the sidewalk, past the skateboarding middle school brats with black nails who were ditching class, past the dog walkers, the Hispanic gardeners, the fluttering, hopping sparrows, the shadows of the buildings, the drug dealers in the alley, the football jocks, the preps, the nerds, the going-nowheres, the future politicians, the entire multifaceted herd—and Barkley, out of the car now, made his way left and right, nodded here and there, stepped over cracks in the sidewalk and then yellow lines in the parking lot, and tossed his empty coffee into the rotund garbage can by the door. His knees threatened to buckle. All he could hope was that on this day, in this place, finally, he would be a part of that herd, a welcome statistic in the matrix, a cog that made sense. No longer the new guy, he thought, no longer the outsider or the nonconformist, and he opened the side door and the wide, white hallway spread before him.

7:55 A.M. Barkley sat in a creaking red chair in the Eastwick auditorium balcony, under graying rafters with hulking black speakers lurching from the corners. He sat there along with the rest of the teachers, all of whom were wearing ties and sports coats or fancy skirts and blouses, all of whom looked down at the projection screen with varying degrees of patience as it flicked from captioned picture to captioned picture, a disjointed effort to begin the school year with aplomb. Below the teachers, who hovered on the balcony, Barkley could hear the oceanic murmur of the student body, reaching over rows and passing notes, texting and whispering and laughing. Immediately after the presentation, those students would come flooding out of the lower-level auditorium and into *his* classroom, and they would listen for *his* homework, and they would call *him* Mr. Brunson. So he watched the slideshow, and hoped it would never end, hoped the administrators would find an extra slide, then another, something to keep him prisoner on the rickety balcony, anything to postpone his demise.

The projection screen below clicked; the audience was now looking at an Eastwick water polo forward rising from chlorinated water to hurl a shot at a Brother Rice goalie. *Leadership,* the caption read, before switching to a picture of a tearful brunette accepting an award. Barkley looked away, tried to catch the eye of a younger female teacher on the other side of the balcony. Why was he sitting alone? He should have coordinated, made himself look more connected.

Principal Finn, he remembered, was gone—and in his place, interim principal Bill Grumpson, who wasn't really grumpy as much as he was old and hobbled and halfway gone. After Barkley first spoke with him at teacher orientation, he'd surmised that inside his skull was little more than a graying, arthritic gerbil, shuffling slowly on its metal wheel, trying to get comfortable with all the intravenous tubes hooked into its sides. Two days into last week's summer training sessions for new teachers, Bill Grumpson had fallen down the athletic stairwell by the wrestling room and was now hobbling around in a medieval-looking gray knee brace. In his new principal's office, rumor had it, the phone was never answered, and papers were already forming into swaying towers on his desk.

A stout, middle-aged balding man lowered himself into the empty seat to Barkley's left and sighed heavily. "This is what happens when teachers don't have pensions, new guy. The relics start taking over the school."

"Huh?"

"The screen. Look at the screen."

The projection showed three graying men who all looked to be over eighty, with their arms around each other. *Commitment* was bolded under the picture.

"Ha," Barkley said.

"What's your name again?"

"Barkley. Barkley Brunson. English department."

"Is that how you like it said? Not a shortened version, like a 'Bark' or a 'Barkinator' or something like that?"

"Nah," Barkley said, finally looking up at the man. He was about forty, with a barrel chest and stocky arms and a bit of a belly. "Barkley is perfect. And you are?"

"Mike Dobbs. Science department. I think we might get along. Know why?"

Barkley wondered if he was being hit on.

"You're not getting hit on, you meathead. We'll get along because I think you're starting to see how crazy this place is. Grumpson? Have you seen that guy yet?"

"Knee brace," Barkley said, afraid to go further.

"Totally fucking senile," Dobbs whispered. "Literally installed as a figurehead. Nobody wants to take the heat following a guy like Finn. There'd be no way to win."

"So Finn *was* good," Barkley said.

"Oh, shit yeah," Dobbs said. "Actually sane. His brain worked. He cared about the teachers. You know, if I had a problem with some prick in administration who was constantly giving me bad observation reviews, I could go to Finn, and he'd actually handle it like a diplomat. But now there's no one to go to. And who the fuck's pulling the strings? That's what everyone wants to know. Sorry, I curse like a sailor."

Barkley shrugged, adjusted himself on the chair. The slideshow below continued, showing pictures of scarf-snuggled students singing fiercely earnest Christmas carols next to the inscription *Christian Spirit*.

"Maybe," Barkley said, testing the water, "it's being run by committee? A democracy sort of thing?"

Dobbs rolled his eyes as the slideshow switched to a blue-jerseyed

Eastwick point guard sinking a fadeaway jump shot. *Willpower!* Then a shot of the same point guard firing a bounce pass to a driving teammate. *Teamwork!*

"Absolutely not," Dobbs whispered. "The power circle here is notorious. No way they'd give up control."

"And you're sure it's not Grumpson?"

"No chance. Yesterday I watched him try to open the principal's office with his car keys. Three times!"

"Shhh . . . ," one of the teachers to Barkley's right hissed. She had blond hair and narrow shoulders and looked to be in her midforties.

Dobbs raised his hand in feigned acquiescence, then lowered his voice to Barkley's range. "Another tight ass. Just got to let these people exist, and stay out of their way."

"I've heard that."

"But who else? Shit. On one hand, you've got the dean, you met the dean yet?"

"No."

"Danny Peters. When this guy was a history teacher, he was smoking bowls in his car on the way to work. Laid-back son of a bitch. Now he's got the disposition of a terminator."

"So maybe him?"

"Eh, but then you've got the good-old-boys club, which is the athletic director, the assistant principal, and the lady helming your ship."

"Margaret Carey?"

"Yeah, buddy. The department chair of English. Administration cronies love her. She's seventy years old and says a prayer before every class, the definition of old school. Batshit crazy, too."

"You sure?" Barkley whispered. "She had me over to her house this summer to go over curriculum, a few days after I got hired. Offered oatmeal cookies."

Dobbs chuckled and shook his head. "Just look out, buddy. That's all I'm going to say." The slideshow clicked and the audience looked at a photograph of Bill Grumpson, pre–knee brace, shaking a red-robed graduate's hand. *Fruition,* the caption read, and Barkley raised an eyebrow.

Maybe Dobbs was misinformed, Barkley thought. Margaret Carey had been singing his praises, to his face, ever since he came in for that interview. She was the one who'd pushed for his hiring—and had told him, point-blank, that he seemed like the ideal candidate to follow her lead and learn the ways of the department. Barkley had done little else, save nod vigorously. And maybe she had been a little aggressive during that summer meeting (heavily line-editing his unit plans, quizzing him on how to keep the students *silent* in class), but she'd still baked him those cookies. And if she wanted a follower and he got a job out of it, he was on board, absolutely. How hard could it be?

"You nervous?" Dobbs asked, eyes gleaming.

"I don't know. Well, yeah. But aren't I supposed to be?" And then, as if the act of admitting it had detonated a precarious dam between his lucidity and the bogeyman that was his fear, Barkley felt like throwing up. How much time did he have? Ten minutes? Ten minutes to his first class? He tasted bile in the back of his throat.

Dobbs laughed, shaking his head.

"You're loving this," Barkley said.

"No, no, buddy. I'm just remembering my first day. You're going to be fine. You know what you got to do? You need the right attitude."

"And?"

"And it's a system I figured out. The way you treat your class. Certified to work. Are you ready?"

Barkley squinted up at him as his stomach lurched again. "I guess."

"You treat your class the way you would treat a chick. A chick you just met at the bar. Hear me out, all right? Now, I don't mean you act the way a goofball would act. That's part of it. You don't grovel, you don't overextend, you don't try too hard, you don't use scare tactics, you don't think about your own weaknesses. You act the way a real fucking playboy would act. All right?"

"All right."

"Say you meet this girl, she's hot, and you *want* her to like you. If she likes you, she does the things you want. Just like, you know, if the class likes you, they shut up and do what they're supposed to do. So you treat your class like a player would a chick at the bar."

"Well," Barkley said, "I'm not saying I'm not a player, but—"

"Right, right, so you're saying, what would a player do? And here's the answer. A player looks at that chick and *knows* he's in charge. He makes fun of the chick instead of groveling at her feet. He definitely doesn't threaten. And he knows that the secret is holding back, and what's more, what's *more*—"

A song began playing throughout the auditorium. Was that Sarah McLachlan? Barkley looked at the projection screen and saw a beautifully framed shot of Eastwick High School, in all its palatial, multiturreted glory, from what appeared to be the dry cleaners across the street. Superimposed over the picture: *Let's Show the World What the Eastwick Panthers Can Do in 2011!!!*

Father Burnham appeared at the podium, still clad in his white robe, rosary beads dangling, and tapped the microphone twice. The murmuring student body went quiet.

"Let us begin the school year with a prayer," he said. "The Lord's Prayer. Our Father—"

And the student body and many of the teachers spoke the words with him, the sound rising up into a single, reverberating baritone, a collective incantation—*thy kingdom come, thy will be done*—Barkley looked around him, Dobbs was silent, lips pursed, the teacher who had hushed them was speaking with her eyes closed—*give us this day our daily bread*—the first-year teacher he'd tried to make eye contact with was also speaking, and there was a tiny cross flat against her neck, she knew what to do—*and forgive us our trespasses*—he remembered the words vaguely, from Sunday school as a child, but he couldn't keep up, and that theater bulb three down from the speaker in the corner was flickering—*but deliver us from evil*—he couldn't tell if Father Burnham's eyes were closed, or whether or not you were supposed to close your eyes, his uncle at Thanksgiving did it with his eyes open—*in the name of the Father, and of the Son*—but he had his eyes wide open, wasn't ready to close them, had never really been ready, and was vaguely aware that this meant something—*Amen.*

Father Burnham seemed to glide away, and then a taller man with a receding hairline and rigid cheekbones mounted the podium.

"Peters," Dobbs muttered.

"Now," Peters said, "I want everyone to have a great year. And I don't want to hear about a single behavioral disturbance on our first day of classes, or there will be consequences you haven't seen before. I'm talking Saturday school, do you understand? You will represent what it means to be an Eastwick Panther in this first week of classes. And I don't want writing on the desks! All summer, our custodians wasted their time erasing the marks *you* all made on school property. That is not what being an Eastwick Panther is all about. That is acting like a juvenile delinquent. Represent your school, ladies and gentlemen."

There was a collective snickering below.

"Oh, good, you think it's funny?" Peters bellowed. "Well, I want you all to know that we are looking for people to make an example of this year. You want to be the one who gets caught, be my guest. I'm looking forward to it. Or, you could all do your school proud, and represent the Eastwick Panthers with dignity, and make this the school year everyone here deserves. Think about the tuition your parents are paying, folks. Do everyone proud, or we will make an example out of you."

"On that note," Dobbs said, making a farting sound.

Peters cleared his throat as two more administrators came to the sides of the podium. "Now, we will dismiss you *by year*, and you will head to your lockers, get the appropriate materials, and get to class *on time*. You all have fifteen minutes, and that should be more than enough. I don't care if it's the first day of school, ladies and gentlemen, if you do not get to class on time, there will be a JUG waiting for you. Your teachers have been instructed to follow this directive. If you are one second late, that's a tardy, and a tardy on the first day of school is a JUG. Furthermore, if any teacher sees you with a cell phone, the phone will be confiscated, and you will have a JUG."

"I still can't believe they call it that," Barkley said.

"It's the world's most awkward acronym," Dobbs said. "Justice Under God. The Catholic way of saying, 'You have detention.' And yes, they are unaware that it's ridiculous."

Barkley allowed himself to smile. Dobbs was possibly off the deep end himself, but at least he was funny and seemed to know the deal.

"Seniors," Peters said, "you may gather your things and leave via the two rear exits. It is eight-thirty A.M. Classes begin at eight-forty-five; we will be on a Liturgy Assembly Schedule. If you have questions about this schedule, freshmen, the alternate timetables are posted in the classrooms. Teachers, you may also leave. Juniors, please gather your things."

The faculty stood up as a unit, a few immediately rushing for the door, likely to print out last-minute syllabi and documents. Dobbs rose from his chair and groaned, arching his back and stretching his arms behind his head.

"What were you saying before?" Barkley asked.

"About Peters?"

"No, no. About the attitude. The classroom attitude?"

"Not following."

"What you just said! About the chick in the bar!"

"Oh, right, right. I don't know, I think I said all of it. You'll be fine. Good luck, buddy, I gotta go grab a biology book from my car."

Danny Peters, still at the podium, cleared his throat again. "Sophomores, please gather your things. You now have thirteen minutes."

8:43 A.M. It was amazing to think that, after all he had done to actually prepare, for the first time in his life, really—the hours spent crafting a syllabus that was both astute and creative, the clothing outlets he had perused for the perfect outfit with Ginny, the tireless practicing of his introductory speech in front of the mirror—it was remarkable that despite all these precautions, he, the teacher, was unable to find his own classroom. He'd taken what he thought was a shortcut, cutting out of the auditorium balcony, and instead of following the teachers out across the gymnasium balcony and onto the second floor, he took a winding staircase down to what he surmised would be the first floor and the relative location of room 115. But the staircase dropped him off at a white hallway in which a series of red pipes were running along the auditorium-side wall, a hallway that curved and buckled and then became a ramp that led to some kind of second gymnasium, much smaller than the first, which was filled with rolled-up green wrestling mats and no electricity. Ringworm, he'd thought, disgustedly, before realizing that the door had locked behind him, and the only hope was the double doors on the other side of the tiny gym, which, when he burst through, revealed a dark staircase leading up through the music department. Luckily, it was unlocked, but by this time it was 8:39, and he was in some type of high-ceilinged music room, with chimes and cellos and a harp and three snare drums

pushed off to the side, away from a series of benches meant for a practice orchestra. Barkley barreled out through yet another set of doors,
found himself in a side hallway, and finally recognized the main office
and the central walkway that went past the library. Now, here he was,
at 8:43, briefcase in hand, hustling through what had to be the tenth pair
of double doors, finding the right staircase, already feeling a slathering
of cold sweat underneath his arms and across his forehead.

At 8:44 he found the one-hundred-level classrooms, saw all the blue
and yellow lockers, saw that, to his right and three classrooms down, was
room 115. He felt the wave of nausea again, the loose hinges that were his
knees, the damp wetness in his armpits, this was it, it was actually happening. The door stood right there, ajar, right in front of him. And so he
moved toward it, saw the students in the window, the fist-bumping kid
and the blonde sitting on the desk, heard the awful trilling of the bell, felt
his ears ring, and walked into the room, listening as it went silent.

He stood in front of the class for a moment. All the guys wore white
shirts and ties. All the girls wore white or gray shirts with plaid skirts.
There were twenty-nine students in this class, American Literature for
juniors. Nonhonors. They were staring at him. The kid with shaggy hair
in the front, the one who had received a fist bump, appeared to be
smirking. The blonde had gone to the back of the classroom and was
whispering to a shorter brunette. The shouter from the front of the
class, medium build with a crew cut and a ridiculous tie depicting Wolverine fighting Batman, was sitting against the windowsill, blatantly out
of his seat. First, Barkley thought, he had to put his briefcase on the
desk and get out the folder, which held the syllabi. The syllabi would
take ten minutes of the class period. But he should speak—

"Hi," Barkley blurted, at medium volume. Then, again, louder: "Hello,
class!"

They were silent, except for the blonde in the back who laughed, quietly. About him? Her hair was curling over the side of her face, shielding an eye from view. She put her hand casually over her mouth and
the brunette bit her lip.

Wolverine-Batman Tie, still standing against the window, said, "Hello
to you, too, good sir!" in a voice that sounded like a Broadway vibrato.
The class cackled.

Barkley sighed, irritated, and suddenly the nausea disappeared. They were all a million versions of himself at that age—the same insecurities, the same awkward stages of development. He imagined Charlie, pre-enlistment, and considered how he would have acted with a classroom full of Barkleys. Why was he scared right now? He'd seen the template for how to control a high school student countless times before, simply sitting in the family's living room and listening to his brother talk.

"You," Barkley said, pointing to Wolverine Tie. "Take a seat."

"Carter's in my seat."

Testing his defenses. It was like those movie scenes in a prison where the new guy arrives and has to immediately bludgeon an inmate with a lunch tray, or lose respect.

Barkley cleared his throat. "We don't have seats yet, Wolverine. Oh, wait, yes we do, look at this one right up front."

"Next to Shuman? Tight. I can handle Shuman. Shuman, can you handle me? Can you handle this? Tickle fight! Hey, Shuman—"

"Thanks for telegraphing that," Barkley said. "But no, not next to Shuman. This one, over here by the door. There you go, you just chill over there, all right, Wolverine?"

Shuman, the kid with shaggy hair, guffawed. "He's calling you Wolverine."

"I like Wolverine," Wolverine said. "That's fierce."

Barkley thought about it, gaining steam. "Nah, Wolverine has to be earned. You're more of a raccoon right now. Or a tabby."

The class laughed at that one, mildly, and even Wolverine smirked up at him, maybe glad to have someone that could fight back.

"Okay," Barkley said, "I'm going to do a roll call, and for now, these are your seats, but we'll see. Probably have to mix some of it up. Oh, and I'm Mr. Brunson. Want me to write that on the board?"

"Yes, please," Wolverine said. "In cursive."

You little twat, Barkley thought. But he couldn't get angry. If he got angry, that showed a chink in the armor, and then it would be open season. He thought of telling Wolverine himself to write it, but that would give the kid an audience, and he'd probably misspell the name on purpose.

"Actually," Barkley said. "Cursive is for raccoons. Which means you.

Which means for the homework assignment tonight, I want you to write in cursive."

"Are you serious?"

"Oh, totally, freakishly serious," Barkley said, and felt the invisible particles that made up the aura in the classroom, that somehow controlled the metaphysical vibe, slowly siding with him.

"I don't even remember how to write in cursive!"

"Google it, Raccoon!" he shouted cheerily, and that earned him another laugh, including one from the blonde in the back, whom he felt watching his every move.

"You just got owned," Shuman said.

"I can't believe I have to write in cursive. Harsh, man. Harsh."

Barkley wrote his name on the board in big, block letters. "It's not harsh, it's cause-effect. I'm rewarding you for bringing up a delightful style of writing." He turned around and faced the class. "So, I'm Mr. Brunson, which I admit, sounds weird to say—"

"You look kind of like a student," Shuman said. "Not a 'mister.' You're a young gun."

Barkley pointed at him. "That I am. But I'm still Mr. Brunson, and let's find out who you all are."

He unfurled the first of the attendance sheets he'd found in his mailbox. Cleared his throat, felt them watching him, sitting still, actually listening. Was he in the zone?

"All right, starting at the top. Jennifer Alston?"

A large, overweight girl sitting behind Wolverine slowly raised her hand. Shuman looked like he wanted to make a comment, but Barkley glared at him immediately, and he went back to writing on his hand.

"Todd Brennan."

A gawky individual in the back raised his hand.

"He's got two first names, and he's my very best friend," Wolverine sang. "Two first names and he's my very best friend."

It was clear, looking back and forth between the utterly dorky Todd Brennan and the almost predatorily confident Wolverine, that there was absolutely zero friendship in existence. But Barkley let it pass, thinking, *pick your battles, pick your battles.*

He made it through the *C*'s and the *F*'s without incident, then hit the

G's, which gave him Jeremiah Gilroy, an African American individual sitting in the exact center of the class, drawing some kind of gothic squid in his notebook, not hearing his name being called.

"Gilroy," Barkley said again, "Gilroy, I think I know your dad. Isn't your dad that real estate agent in Lincoln Park? What's his name? Yale Gilroy?"

Jeremiah finally looked up. "That's him," he said, and went back to drawing.

"Gilroy is an original G, Mr. Brunson," Wolverine said. "And speaking of O.G.'s, anybody got some of that O.G. Kush?"

Fuck, Barkley thought—he was talking about pot. He'd actually smoked a few weeks ago when Chubs came into town from Providence, and it *was* pretty good, even though he handled marijuana horribly, lost all social skills, but the issue at hand was Wolverine—

"I wonder if Mr. Brunson . . . um . . . partakes," Wolverine said, whistling to himself.

Shuman shook his head in wonderment, and the blonde in the back groaned.

"You're such an idiot!" she shouted.

"I'm with her," Barkley said. "You just moved from a raccoon to a small woodland animal. You're a squirrel now, Wolverine. A baby squirrel. And don't forget that cursive homework, I want it impeccable."

Wolverine threw up his hands but said nothing. It was over. Barkley continued with the roll call, knowing he was in control, feeling that he was in control; maybe Dobbs was right, maybe that *was* the attitude to have.

It turned out that Wolverine's real name was Steven Mann, but Barkley liked Wolverine better and decided outright that Mann was out the window. The blonde in the back was Elise Rossi, and when called, she raised her hand off the table, just barely, and tilted her head at him, just barely. The brunette next to her was Maggie Tolliver, and she raised her hand higher, more agreeable, but he was already forgetting the names as soon as they came up, and soon enough, roll call was over, and he was handing out the syllabi, still feeling good, still in control.

He split the class into partner groups, each with the task of interviewing the other, and then presenting the information to the other students. A simple introductory exercise, one that had undoubtedly been used by countless teachers before, but Barkley just wanted the day to go smoothly; he wanted to get from A to B without his ship striking an iceberg. He was fine with predictable on the first day, as long as the pieces he presented fit together.

With the forty-five-minute periods shortened to forty minutes due to the Liturgy Assembly Schedule, class was over at 9:25, and so after the partner interviews, which got a little out of hand, a little loud, but still seemed to stay under his general control, Barkley waited until 9:20 to give the homework.

"First-day homework," Shuman said, sighing. He was taller than Wolverine, hawk-nosed and lanky, and would have been more intimidating if it weren't for the simple fact that he didn't seem to care. School was school, his look seemed to say. Surprise me or don't.

"An easy assignment," Barkley announced. "This will be the first entry in your notebooks."

A collective sigh rose up but faded quickly—they were groaning as a reflex, a learned response.

"Just listen," Barkley said. "This is pretty cool. I thought about this one."

Another groan, followed by a cackle from Wolverine.

Barkley allowed himself to smile. "All right, here's the deal. We've dispensed with the introductions, so we can do something creative. Here's what I'm looking for: step one, what is your greatest fear? Seriously. What are you afraid of? Aliens? Drowning? Tornadoes? Dark alleys? Once you've got that down, I want two solid paragraphs in your notebooks written in *first person*, as if you *are* that fear. For example—"

"I don't get it," Todd Brennan said.

"Derp, derp?" Wolverine called back to him.

"That's *South Park*," Barkley said, and judging by Wolverine's thoughtful expression, his knowledge of the word's cartoonish roots might have gained him a small foothold of respect.

"What's the rest of the assignment, Mr. Barkles?" Maggie Tolliver asked.

"Just hold on, guys. All right? And that's Mr. Brunson. So you're writing about your greatest fear. From the first-person perspective. Which *means*, for example, if Maggie's greatest fear is spiders, she writes from the first-person perspective as if she *were* the spider. Understand? You're showing me why this fear is scary, by becoming the fear. She can talk about having eight weird legs, creeping all over walls, making webs, hiding in the corner of the bathroom, and so forth. Sound good? The goal is to make it a story, told by your greatest fear. You can even add yourself as a secondary character if you'd like. Then we'll share them tomorrow."

"Not terrible," Shuman admitted.

"That's what I like to hear. Okay, good first class, and—"

The bell shrieked, and the room immediately erupted into dialogue and laughter and hurriedly zipping backpacks. Half the class ran out in what seemed like a panic, the other half walked casually, with a few remaining in their seats, likely waiting for people they knew in the next class. Barkley went to his desk and got out twenty-eight more syllabi for period two. The key, here, right now, was to continue being in this zone, this zone where he was acting and reacting but not getting lost in neurotic thoughts that turned his acuity into molasses. He smelled a slight whiff of perfume, a scent that, strangely, made him think of tangerines, tumbling across a grocery aisle.

"Mr., um, Brunson?"

He turned. It was the blond student from the back of the class, what was her name—Rossi? Elise Rossi. She was almost as tall as he was and had somehow styled her hair so it always fell, in a strawberry-blond wash, over one side of her face. She had piercing blue eyes and tiny, almost imperceptible freckles that somehow appeared stylish, like a garnish. It was a trick he knew would not have worked on others.

"Yes, ma'am? What can I do for you, Elise?"

"Ew, that's weird that you remembered my name."

"What?" Barkley stammered. "That's what I'm supposed to do. That's my job."

"Creeper!" she sang. "Cree-eeper!"

"Um, you better be joking, Rossi. Seriously. Calling me a creeper on the first day of class? I'm going to be sick."

She laughed. "I'm only joking. Way to tweak, Mr. Brunson."

"Okay, well, you'd tweak, too, if you were me. What can I do for you?"

"How long does this assignment have to be? Like half a page? Or can I do a third of a page?"

Barkley hesitated. "Well, in the syllabus it says that all notebook entries have to be at least half a page, so yeah. There's your answer."

"But I mean, if I only did a third, would that be okay? How many points would I get off?"

"Just do the assignment, all right?"

"Ugh, whatever. See you tomorrow, Mr. Barkles."

"It's *Brunson*."

"See, I'm not a creeper. I didn't remember your name."

New classmates for period two began trickling in. They seemed louder than the previous class, and Barkley tried to gear up and get his focus back.

"Elise!" one of the male students shouted. "You see the pictures from Hogan's thing last weekend?"

"I better not be in them," she said, taking out her phone and turning her back on Barkley.

Three minutes until the bell. Barkley cleared his throat. "Hey, uh, Elise, you gotta put that away. We're under some pretty strict instructions—"

"But you don't care, do you, Barkles?" she said, her back still turned to him. "One second."

Jesus, he thought, he was having a good day, a good time, and then this little wench was blatantly disrespecting him, and in front of the next class, too.

"Elise, phone, put it away, or just leave, all right?"

"But *Barkles* . . . ," she said, still typing into her phone. "I'm almost there." He saw the blue heading of Facebook appear.

"Now."

"I just gotta see these pictures. If I got tagged, it's going to be really embarrassing."

The male student was looking at him suspiciously. Fuck, Barkley thought. What was he supposed to do, stand here and get made an ass of?

"Oh, no," she said. "How many am I in? *Eleven?* I don't even remember these! When was this taken? And whose bathroom is that?"

"Elise!"

She turned.

"All right, I'm supposed to give you a JUG for taking out your phone, but instead, let's compromise. I want you to clean off the eraser board."

"But you're just going to rewrite it all for period two!"

"Do it, will you?"

"I'm leaving. I'm going to be late."

"No, Elise, you're not leaving. You need to respect what I'm saying, here."

"I'm not erasing some board on the first day of classes! Can't you just be cool? I'll be tardy to my next class and get a JUG there!"

"It's, like, four things you have to erase. And I'll write you a pass."

"I'm leaving."

"If you leave, you're definitely getting a JUG."

"I have two minutes, Barkles—"

"Just stop. Here, I'm actually going to hand you the eraser."

Barkley turned his back for one moment, lifting the eraser off the metal shelf that ran along the bottom of the board. When he turned back, Elise was gone, but he heard her laughter echoing in the hallway. The kid with the buzz cut was staring back at him.

"She definitely just ran out on you, Mr. B."

"I can't believe that. Is that normally her style?"

"You could say that. I'm John, by the way."

"Okay, John," Barkley said. "Nice to meet you. Why don't you go ahead and get seated? We're about to start."

He saw that the rest of the class was staring at him, too.

"She's getting a JUG!" he called out. "Just so you all know. I'm writing her up for sure."

But later, after the school day was over and Barkley's mind felt like a bowl of tepid oatmeal, he thought about how easy it would be not to write anyone up, to pretend it hadn't happened. He'd be more likable that way, and he wouldn't feel bad for being stuck-up, and he could just go home after this first day that felt like both a whirlwind and a marathon. Drinks—he needed drinks. Did teachers become alcoholics the way doctors became pill poppers?

Still, sitting at his desk in the empty classroom, looking out at green leaves that pressed against the windowpanes, it nagged at him. If he didn't follow through now, she'd be walking over him all year, sitting in the back, laughing at his every mistake. And the others would follow suit. But if he wrote her up—on the first day of school—she might hate him. And he really didn't want Elise Rossi to hate him. No, there was nothing fun about the popular girl hating the new teacher, and that could be like a virus that would spread—some mutating, airborne pathogen that could make others hate him, too.

In the end, he went for it: pulled out the triple-layered JUG form, each sheet the bright pastel of board game currency. He wrote in her name and the date and period, and described the altercation. *Elise was using her phone in the classroom despite explicit instructions to put it away.* Explicit sounded good, made him seem like a disciplinarian. *Upon request for her to stay after class and clean the eraser board, she instead ran away.* He laughed out loud, writing the last bit. Then he stood up, and uncertain about his destiny as a teacher and what the verdict of taking the authoritarian route would be, he walked out of his classroom, up the staircase to the administration offices, and dropped off the JUG slip in a bin he'd been shown during teacher orientation.

"Already, huh?" the secretary behind the desk said, adjusting her bun.

"I guess," Barkley said. "Got to start out strong, right?"

He walked out, through the hallways and down the staircases and into the parking lot that held his car, happy and relieved, uncertain and fearful, relaxed and numb. He got into the Taurus, turned on the ignition, and saw a folded note resting underneath his windshield wiper.

"Shit," he muttered.

If it was something heinous from a student—an insult about his pot-belly, a drawing of a bulbous penis, some bizarre scrawled-out rumor—he'd be put over the edge, end up binge drinking into a stupor. Barkley rolled down the window, took the paper from underneath the wiper, and, wincing in expectation, unfolded it.

Barkinator—heard you did good today. Kids seemed to like you. That's what I call treating the class like a chick! Keep it up, buddy.—Dobbs

Barkley felt a twinge of lightness in his chest, and nodded to himself. He pulled out of the parking spot, hit the accelerator, and put the note in his pocket as the scenery slid by. Keep it up, buddy, keep it up. It was a beginning. And it would start all over again tomorrow, and then the next day, and the next. But this one was over, he thought. And it was his.

THREE DIRECTORS

Charlie reclined in bed with his trusty laptop entrenched in the folds of his stomach. Home again. He'd put on weight during the past month's impromptu vacation—not a lot, but after thirty days of pilsner lager and gamy meat and no exercise in Eastern Europe, it could happen to anyone. He placed his hands on his cheeks and felt again the shocking thickness of his beard. It was an aesthetic that had worked for a while, giving him an imagined capacity for wisdom that he hadn't felt as a clean-shaven soldier. But now, back in his childhood room, it felt like a nagging reminder—yet another growth that a quick shave wouldn't wash away. And all of the country seemed covered in these growths as well, if not beards then overblown muscles or swollen bellies or ridiculous bling. A spiritual gentrification scuttling across the forty-eight states, and all the while it felt like Americans were covering up some kind of truth, something that would have been nakedly obvious if not for this self-conscious evolution and the image of progress. There was a knock at the door.

"Mom?"

"Yes, honey. Mind if I come in?"

"Sure."

His mother sat on the side of the bed and offered a noncommittal smile. She wore black workout pants and an old Northwestern T-shirt and looked different from before. A change in posture, maybe. He didn't know. He stayed quiet. His head had finally cleared, and he considered all the nonsense he had shoved down his esophagus in Budapest— MDMA and painkillers, mushrooms and whiskey, absinthe and acid. It was truly idiotic. He had finally seen the city, but he had not taken it in like a lover of architecture, not like someone with an eye for Gothic facades and baroque trimmings, but rather a blind man, running on a wheel.

A week into their trip, even Bobby Leeds, his best friend and travel buddy, had developed a hangdog, defeated expression that showed how exactly he understood: this vacation wasn't going to help or cure or fix *anything.*

"Charlie?"

He stared at the ceiling, massaged his cheeks. His beard was tangled, snaking across his face like that kudzu he'd seen enveloping telephone poles across the highways from Illinois to Kentucky, when he and Karen had driven once to Louisville. What year had that road trip been? 2005? 2006? After college. He and Karen had borrowed a car and driven across state borders and cabled bridges, the light flickering through the trees and upon the movements of the water. All the while, Charlie had kept his eye on that swarming green plant, snaking across poles and shacks and depots, consuming everything.

"I think it's time you and I had a talk, Charlie. A real talk."

Had he really been in Eastern Europe for the past month? Memorized every bridge and street in Budapest? Ditched his friend? It was already mid-September, for Christ's sake. Yet now the experience was dissolved, the memory flapping from his mind like a startled pigeon. He had always loved traveling, the thrill of departure before a new journey, the chance of some new experience or revelation. And even back during that car ride with Karen, swinging through Kentucky and heading south, even then, he'd been looking for an answer that wasn't behind any door.

His mother's cool hand was on his head. "This can't continue, Charlie," she said, and she spoke with a degree of authority he hadn't heard in years. "You're smarter than this. Nothing can get you down, remember? Nothing has ever been able to get my boy down."

Charlie cleared his throat. "Until now, you mean."

"Well, that's only because you're letting it. And not communicating. And growing this tremendous beard."

"I knew I'd catch flak for that."

"Seriously, honey. I would be up for any kind of communication. Quite honestly, I'd just like to hear about your trip."

Charlie closed his eyes, tried to see the shadows of the buildings again. "Budapest is unlike anything else, Mom. It's crumbling and growing at the same time. Towers and cobblestones and secret nooks and candlelit bars. And all those bridges going across the river."

"Which part did you like the best?"

Charlie shook his head. "It doesn't matter, I could hardly enjoy it, anyway. I went there for Campo, though. He was the reason for the whole trip . . ."

"I know he was. And was it like he said it would be?"

Charlie thought back and remembered the final night of his trip—three weeks after he'd ditched Bobby at the airport and gone off on his own. Their vacation had started simply enough. With excitement, even. Leeds had visited Downers Grove in August, and Charlie, intoxicated, could tell that Bobby was mortified by the apocalyptic feel around the house. Charlie heard him talking to his mother, and so he turned up the volume on *Breaking Bad*, a show that gave him a kind of masochistic pleasure, a sense that downward trajectories could still be cinematic, even symphonic. A couple of days later, however, Bobby was calling him, chatting with him, talking about getting out of Illinois and going on a trip together. Didn't Charlie still have money saved up? Well, sure. Didn't he want to get the hell out and go to Prague and Budapest and Istanbul, cities built for Cold War thrillers and film noir? Eastern Europe, baby—cheap food, Gothic jigsaws of centuries-old architecture, and beautiful girls so numerous they didn't even know they were beautiful. Sure, Charlie had said. But not Prague. Not Istanbul. Only Budapest, the city Campo had talked about all the time in Afghanistan, as if it were some kind of oasis. And for a moment, Charlie felt like he had with Karen before those road trips, that sense that anything was possible, that a revelation was just around the corner.

The vacation had been fun for a while—reliving old times with Bobby under the shadows of Heroes' Square, discussing a reboot of *Cue Mark Reviews* with the sun glinting off the spire of Matthias Church. Fumbling over guidebooks and hitting on girls and even getting laid (in a cafeteria-loud hostel, with an Irish girl who couldn't stop laughing). And he could feel Bobby watching him throughout, cataloging his progress, wondering about the chances of a relapse, the possibility that he'd go back to that exoskeleton he'd discovered in Downers Grove. Would Charlie feel better, return to his preenlistment self? It was the million-dollar question, but what no one understood was that the question was rigged. Charlie, on a conscious and clear level, understood that he didn't *want* to. He didn't *want* to adjust. At Szimpla, just before bar close, he'd finally understood. There was only one true way that he could right the wrongs he'd committed, but he was too much of a coward to make the leap.

It was supposed to be a weeklong trip, Bobby cashing in on his vacation time, but Charlie had left the airport when his best friend went to grab a magazine. He'd left a note in his chair, simply saying, *I'm sorry. Not ready.* And no, he wasn't ready yet. It was possible that he didn't ever want to come back, to return to this America where something was irrevocably wrong and no one wanted to do anything about it. And moreover, what was there to return to? His bedroom. His laptop. His movies, which felt so pointless and insubstantial—expired coupons for the mind. So he left Bobby at the airport and returned to the center of Budapest, to the place that Campo had loved so much. He checked into a hostel and it had been three more weeks of wandering around the city and going to bars, three weeks of drugs, three weeks of trying to turn the truths about himself into something else.

On his last night abroad, Charlie had gone walking alone through the Budapest streets. September was already halfway gone. His family had left him e-mails. Bobby had left him e-mails. Even Karen. It didn't matter. He was there because of Campo—and so Charlie walked.

He started down the trendy Andrássy út, flask in hand. Past museums and monoliths, beyond old mansions with flaking skin and cracked concrete, and then into a network of beer gardens and alfresco dining that seemed lit by something primordial. And Charlie, already drunk, swerved past St. Stephen's Basilica, its massive dome flanked by identical clock towers, and yelled up at the church and the photo-snapping tourists. He fell once, skinned his knee, then muttered something to a Hungarian girl with a cargo shorts–wearing boyfriend, said he'd like a piece of that, but they'd ignored him. They all ignored him, moving back and forth into that network of red lights and clinking wineglasses, moved the way seaweed moves, swaying in an undercurrent.

Charlie kept walking, and ran a hand across his growing beard, which had at first seemed artistic, then intellectual, then simply mangy. Fuck it. Through narrow streets he saw pink on the horizon. Then a sloping, green hill. The Buda side of the Danube, waiting for him. Sun disappearing. Going dark. The night made everything new. He approached the Chain Bridge as it lit up, as white bulbs struck out across the cables. He walked past the lion statues that seemed freshly carved, past the glowing cables that lit his way, and stood at the center of the bridge, staring at the sprawl of the Danube. Every night he'd done this, waiting for something to happen. The buildings were sparkling now, the sun gone, sky purple. On Castle Hill was the Royal Palace, the rows of pillars bathed in gold, while across the river the Parliament Building fanned its white-thorned spires in holy light. It didn't matter, Charlie thought, that the dome on the Royal Palace was half black from damage and time's passage, or that the Parliament Building was strangled by catwalks and construction girders. Here, night was a Band-Aid, a cool washcloth for a fevered head.

He pulled at the greasy hair above his eyes and watched the boats move across the Danube, away into dusk. Slowly and steadily they moved, glowing faintly like sunken fireflies. Budapest was always better at night, when the cracked facades of the monuments smoothed into gold and white illuminations, each broken treasure new again. He took a final shot, then tossed the flask into the river. It fell quickly, and the splash was soundless over the whir of the boats. Why the Chain Bridge? Why Budapest? It was silly to think that he'd find something here, but Campo had gone backpacking through Eastern Europe, the summer before his enlistment, and Budapest was all he ever talked about—especially the nights after shit had gotten bad. *Just stand on that Chain Bridge,* he'd repeated, again and again, almost like a lullaby, likely to himself. *Just stand on that Chain Bridge.* He could still hear Campo's voice, swirling in the darkness of those Afghanistan nights that stretched their legs into forever. *You can't have any problems as that sun goes down, as those boats go by. Trust me.*

What had Campo seen out here? What had he understood? Charlie gripped the edges of the guardrail. Campo had been here. His hands had been where Charlie's were now. He had looked out, Charlie thought, out across the water, and he had seen *something.* Understood something. Every night Charlie had come here to see what it was. Beautiful? Yes. Shadows and light? Of course. Five kinds of architecture, rising and reaching, silhouetted against fading sky? Another yes—yes to it all. But that moment, that moment that would make a man reminisce all through a war, through two tours? That was something Charlie couldn't find.

He heard himself belch, and behind him, a British man drawled, "There's an American for you."

Charlie whirled, fist raised, shrieking, "The *fuck* you say to me?"

But no one was there. About ten feet away, a squat American woman in a floral print dress waddled hurriedly past, followed by a teenager who kept his head down. The mushrooms were kicking in. He'd taken a whole bag, he remembered, washing them down with the vodka he couldn't taste. He had a sense of summer passing him by, of hours becoming days and flaking apart like so many monuments. The Chain Bridge rose up out of the water. The firefly boats formed into a glowing scarab. In the Danube he saw a sunken palace made of fishtails and coral thrones. He laughed to himself. Pain, pain, go away. In the sky, past the Parliament Building whose spires were now revolving, he saw space, fell into space, watched the thousand-year histories of every burning star. The planets stretched, and Charlie saw purple gas clouds light up like stained glass, light up from the glow behind the black curtain, the white light from which everything rose and fell. He had to become someone else. In space, he connected the pearls that made Sagittarius, the Big Dipper, then Campo, then the girl. And past them all he went, away from his body, toward a chandelier of comets that told him Charlie had done those horrible things, but he hadn't, that he wasn't Charlie anymore, no, he was free, he was energy, he was lifting, he was light.

When he woke up slumped under a rotting staircase leading up the Buda hills, the light was gone and the anvil was back and his skin was paler than before. Scratches up and down his arms. It was two in the morning. On the Danube, the boats had disappeared and the water was dark, still. But he had felt transcendence, and so he made his way to the bars.

Four in the morning, now. He vomited in a bathroom without a sink. He slapped two French girls on the ass after they gave him a number with only four digits. Beside a taxicab in an ugly section of Pest, he bumped into a towering Australian who was shouting into an old Nokia cell phone, bellowing about missing microwaves.

"Sorry, bud," Charlie mumbled, looking ahead at three Hungarian girls, who were in turn looking back at him, and at the swirl of drunks spilling from the bar.

"Fuck you say?" the Australian shouted.

"My bad, my bad."

"What?"

"Don't worry about it."

"What's that? Fucking what?" the Australian still had the phone against his ear but was now pursuing Charlie in earnest. Six foot five, maybe taller, a monster. A wave of drunks separated them. Charlie lost his thoughts in the movements of scarves and skirts and car exhaust and rank perfume. He looked again for the Hungarian girls. Two giant hands gripped his shoulders.

The Australian shoved him into a wall. Charlie felt his forehead smack the old bricks, felt his skin shred, heard the tinnitus's electric shriek, and noticed that his hands were up, up, up, but now his skull was banging against the bricks again, the Australian shouting, "What?" until a brilliant Roman candle of rage bloomed inside him.

Charlie wheeled, threw a punch, then another. He fought drunkenly, angrily, stupidly. The Australian came back and battered him, knocked him back against the wall. Charlie landed a right cross, but then the towering shithead had him in a headlock, swollen arms crushing his neck, his windpipe, some fucking idiots behind them cheering—Charlie thrashed and kicked and spat, bucked his head up and struck the Australian under the chin, which got him free and gave him room. But he was shoved back into the wall again, punched again, then again, until he slipped and fell and rolled, mouth against dirty cement and spilled beer and a crumpled gum wrapper, the big fucker screaming at him, and Charlie, weak now, too weak, unable to move. He waited for a finishing hit that never came. He pulled himself up. The drunks moved past him as if he were empty luggage, old groceries. He got a cab. Returned to his hostel. Imagined taking the Australian and smashing his head through a plate glass window. He laughed out loud at the image. He bumped into a wall. Fell into his bunk and used the pillow as gauze for his leaking face and throbbing mind. And then—blackness.

In the morning, he felt rejuvenated.

The big lug had truly hammered him—knocked out two of his molars, fucked up his ears, bludgeoned his body until half of it was a bruise. The skin on his forehead was split by a scabby wake the brick wall had left behind. He looked into the mirror and coughed, laughed. If there had been no drugs in his system, well . . . it could have gone the other way. But even in a loss, the fight had been therapeutic, so different from that altercation Barkley had prevented. The fighting, in no uncertain terms, had woken him up. Snapped him back to reality. And reality told him, with real clarity, that he needed to leave. He called his father, finally, after thirty-two days abroad, who flew him home. He returned to Downers Grove bearded and without a suitcase, returned to his room, said nothing and did nothing, resumed the old position, all the while considering that the highlight of his escape had been the beatdown handed to him by a hulking Australian, the feeling of his head striking bricks, of his fist smacking skin. And what any of it meant was lost to him.

In his bedroom, Charlie sighed and looked at his mother. "Standing on that Chain Bridge, Mom? Sure. It was almost like Campo said it would be. But I was acting like a total loser out there. I let Bobby go home without me, you know—there's no excuse. But I wasn't capable of anything else. I tried to get to the bottom of things out there, but the bottom just kept getting lower."

"You know, Charlie, what you're going through isn't strange. It isn't abnormal, and you're not a loser. I've been doing a lot of reading, and it's pretty clear that no one comes home from service to an easy adjust-ment. Everyone has some degree of difficulty, and pain, and resentment. What you're feeling—what all of your friends are probably feeling—it's normal. Most likely it needs to be felt. Talk to the VA or don't, but you absolutely need to stop beating yourself up over it."

He rose up on his elbows. "But I was supposed to be better than that, Mom. I was supposed to be *smart* out there."

"You are smart, Charlie. You do have an open mind. But no one— and that includes you—is exempt from the effects of their experiences. I'm not, as much as I'd like to be."

"True, I guess."

"Everyone is affected. We can't even imagine what you went through— and I know you don't want to talk about it. But we're all so proud of you, Charlie. The whole neighborhood is."

He looked up at her. "You're seriously proud of me?"

"*Of course.* Everyone is. Beyond proud. You served your country. You're a hero to your family. You did something a lot of people no lon-ger have the courage to do."

"Dad doesn't feel that way."

"Well, I'm not Dad. And believe me, he is proud—he just doesn't want to admit he was wrong."

Charlie looked out the open window. The sun was already low in the sky, another day gone by, fallen away without resistance.

"So what's the problem, Charlie? You might not want to talk, and I've tried to give you space, but we have to find a way to move forward. We need to help you move forward."

Charlie took a breath. He breathed out shakily. "I've done things, Mom. Things that, if you knew about, you wouldn't want to see me anymore. You wouldn't want me in this house. You would literally dis-own me."

"Now you're talking crazy."

"I'm not."

"Try me."

He closed his eyes. "Please, Mom. Talk about something else. I'll get through this, but please just talk about something else."

"Movies?"

"Not movies. I told you, they hardly work for me anymore. What about around here? What else happened while I was gone?"

His mother drummed her fingers lightly across his forehead, in the same musical manner she used to when he was a child, when it was time to hear a story, the next chapter in *Hatchet* or *The Giver*, maybe. "Well, let's see. I'm working on something—top secret, though."

"Top secret?"

"Of course."

"What are you, a triple agent or something?"

She smiled. "I'm just waiting until everything is in place, that's all. But other than that, your father is still downtown—I haven't spoken with him in a while. Barkley is teaching at Eastwick; school's a few weeks in. He really seems to like it. And he has a girlfriend."

Charlie almost spit. "B-Team is *dating?*"

Julie chuckled. "Remember those dinner dates he went on just before you left? I think he was staying quiet until it was for sure, but those two have been official since the end of August. She's a great girl, Charlie. I was planning on inviting them over for dinner, now that you're home. What do you think?"

"Sure, sure," Charlie said, thinking, *good for him, the old B-Team outkicking his coverage.*

"Any requests for tonight? I'm meeting some old college friends later tonight, but before that I can go chicken Parm or I can go fancy French. What'll it be?"

Charlie forced a smile on his face. "Chicken Parm would be perfect, Mom. Perfect. I'll be downstairs in a bit, okay?"

Her fingers danced across his forehead again, then lifted. "Sounds good, honey. See you downstairs."

Within moments, he was alone again, and he let his smile drop away. It was almost time.

In the following weeks, it would seem to Charlie like there were three films playing in his head, and none of them could be turned off. The first film was the present moment—and he could imagine a team of screenwriters planning to perpetuate it, sitting in a cluttered room, drawing up cheesy diagrams. In this case, the present moment consisted of a beige-tinted long shot, filmed by a director with a stationary camera and an eye for the inescapably mundane. Time passed and nothing changed. Hair follicles and flakes of lint hung in the soft-focus air. Outside, cars moved back and forth, back and forth, endlessly circling the Downers Grove set. The dedication to static minutiae was impeccable: a pencil left on the upstairs computer desk last Thursday would remain there to-day, just as the continual aches inside his rib cage, or the groaning dis-comfort that came from being inside himself, was present from the moment he awoke to the moment he closed his eyes.

The second film, always playing, was Charlie's knowledge of film. The light off the Waltons' illuminated pool at night recalled the ending of *Sunset Boulevard*—the shadows of the Aquabot pool cleaner reminiscent of William Holden's floating body. His own suburban inertia brought to mind *American Beauty*, and he saw Downers Grove as filmed from above by Conrad Hall, and imagined Sam Mendes calling for yet another postdeath voice-over. When he thought about the horrors he had experienced and then fled from, it was Brando's cadences as Colonel Kurtz that both affirmed and mocked his realization, and he saw himself on that movie set of broken temples and stinking bodies, that set in the Philippines disguised as Cambodia. No thought, no observation, no feeling came without its requisite cinematic companion—and the knowledge that, at least at this point in history, he could not escape the cliché.

The third movie, playing behind doors he couldn't always close, was his personal hell, his montage of horror and lost camaraderie from Afghanistan. These movies were not shot with artistry. No talented director was at the helm. There was no sound track, no expert lighting, no film grain, no tracking shots. His memories came to him in fits and spurts, sometimes the benign image of a fellow soldier laying down a poker hand, while other times the ruptured face of Campo, or his own acts of mur-der, or the sounds of falling mortars. The truth was forced into his mind without alternatives. He was a murderer, and neither denial nor running was an option. The buzzing in his ears would return at night, remind-ing him, as always, that something was amiss. And did the rest of the country hear it, too? Did they hear the same hum in their heads, in the middle of the night in the heart of suburbia, that distant octave that said something inward was askew, that what was once vast and plentiful had been hollowed out? Did they hear the sound?

In his room, it was 6:00 P.M.—time for the ritual, the one habit he couldn't forget. He rose up and removed the key chain from his bedside drawer. He laid it carefully upon the stool beyond the edge of the bed. With his lighter, he set the two tea candles aflame, and watched them flicker and bounce the light and shadows off the wall. This here, his mind told him—this had been done before, filmed before, analyzed before. He couldn't escape it, couldn't escape the thought that he was self-pitying and false, but it didn't matter. The ritual had to be done with honesty. It had to be done with a true desire for penance. He wouldn't run from the truth. Budapest and the Chain Bridge were no different from his bed, from the movies that could no longer set him free. So he would stay. This would be his ritual, his schedule, his daily guarantee. He didn't want to feel better. He didn't want to run. He wanted what he deserved, and that was this, only this.

SANCTUARY

When Julie saw it, it was one of those double-take moments—like see-ing an old friend scooting by on a red trolley, like passing a sandwich shop from her Ohio youth, or hearing a song, maybe something by Alice Cooper, that triggered a surge of memories she'd long forgotten were hers. This was the feeling Julie got as she passed Links Hall on Sheffield and Clark.

It started as a pleasing, absentminded kind of search. Just driving, em-bracing the journey, with her true goal shrouded on the horizon. She liked that the search was hazy, similar to that fuzz she used to feel from the pills. Except, of course, the fuzz out here was real—it came from the wind and the buildings and the lake, not the prescription. And it wasn't like giving up the pills had been easy. For every two good days, she had one bad, suddenly cowed by the facts of her life. In these cases, it was a simple declaration of those facts that bowled her over: no husband (scratch that, husband on the lam), oldest child hurting, she herself stuck in the suburbs, devoid of career. But there was a difference—some internal compass had been triggered, and that helpless sense of inertia had passed, giving way to solid ground.

And here she was, in her Honda, taking the Eisenhower east into Chicago, that great maw of city opening infinitely wide. It wasn't like being swallowed, she realized, it was like leaving the mouth of the fish that had already taken her in. And so the skyline got ever closer, the Trump and Willis and Hancock gleaming, and she was out, out in whatever new adventure this would be.

Sometimes it seemed as if the freeing thing and the damning thing were one and the same. Start with the good, she thought, keeping her hands loose on the steering wheel, allowing an overpolished red Corvette to swing through her lane and then blast off into the far left. The good thing was being unconstrained. If she wanted to glide off at any of these exits, she could do it. Go to Kenwood and Hyde Park, try to swing by Obama's house, see if Secret Service agents stopped her? Done. She could do it. Museum of Science and Industry, the last surviving building from the 1893 Chicago World Fair? Absolutely. She was in. Stop for lunch at Blackbird or Ria or Trattoria No. 10 and watch thousand-dollar suits slam power lunches and broker deals with foreign businessmen? Beyond easy; she'd done it before. Or she could sneak away to some of her old favorites: 90 Miles, the little Cuban shack on Armitage, where she could chomp down on a pork and plantain sandwich and watch the traffic pass; or Yoshi's Café, that old Lakeview classic on Halsted and Aldine, where she could order the tofu-stuffed kabocha pumpkin, swirl her chardonnay, and feel at one with the metropolis that made all worries disappear. All of these she could do, and more, which, of course, led to the bad thing.

The Eisenhower merged into Congress Parkway, and Julie kept on driving straight east, through the tunnel under the Chicago Stock Exchange, up toward the Congress Hotel, whose employees picketed in a small, sagging circle. Past them she went, straight into the green sprawl that led to Grant Park, before swinging left on Columbus, then right on Jackson, running parallel to the symphonic sprays of Buckingham Fountain. She couldn't remember the last time she'd been down here alone. In 2010, maybe, when she'd come down to deliver a care package of comics and cupcakes to Barkley's new apartment.

When she passed North Avenue Beach and Castaways, the submerged-in-sand, shipwrecked boat bar Charlie used to talk about, Julie found herself contemplating the bad thing again: she had no income but that which Henry allotted her. She could move past him, get over him, have new adventures beyond him, but the shadow of his financial support might as well have been a tattoo. It was cast over her surroundings and each new place she went, a depressing monolith of forced and accepted dependence. It was this thought, truly this thought, that made her at times want to spiral back to the way she had been, to retreat to her room in Downers Grove, to slam those cotton ball pills down her throat and feel light and fuzzy and allow the knowledge of it all to fade away. The ability to forget unwanted truths was what the pills promised, and many times, that was more than enough.

Some nights she still spent crying, pulling out the old albums that just the day before she'd stuffed into a closet, determined to never unearth them again. Just last night, she'd made herself one vodka tonic—one!—and by the time she finished, all the old emotions had dug into her like shrapnel. The need to feel the cotton balls? Check. The gaping hole of Henry's absence? Check. That draining, helpless sensation that she had no control—would never have control? Big check.

Yet, something was different now. Every urge to lie down was followed not by that wavering, jelly-legged sensation of giving up, but by a seething burn deep inside her chest. And so dance, and the studio, remained her bridge. It was something she knew she could do, knew could be hers. Meager income, however much—hers. Would it pay enough to get her on her own? Likely not. Not at first, at least. And she understood what Melanie would say. She would harp on Julie to get out there and work two jobs, three jobs, anything to get out from under Henry's shadow. Work at the Gap, at Famous Footwear, anything. You might think it demeaning, Melanie would say, but being on your own is bliss in comparison. And in the meantime—pull the trigger, hire a lawyer, and find a way to divorce the man.

Maybe. Maybe she would do that. But she would also keep her eye on the target at hand.

She took the Belmont exit and found herself coasting down the streets of East Lakeview. On the passenger seat was the list that she and Melanie had made at a recent lunch, places where studio space could be rented, with one choice in particular circled twice. But Julie had just wanted to drive today, this third Wednesday of September—just drive. After seeing the baseball diamond, the scene of the crime, she had returned to Downers Grove ready to make changes, emotions be damned. She'd spent the rest of August and half of September getting back in shape: watching old videos from the Netherlands Dance Theater, taking a Pilates class on Tuesdays and Thursdays, grunting out that P90X tape at home. What a workout! Sweat running down her arms and neck, endorphins buzzing in her chest. She felt giddy over the newfound planning, even picked out favorite outfits to wear on each day of specialized exercise. And now, finding herself on Clark, Julie realized her target was nearby, and as she passed Sheffield, off to the right, there it was—the double take, the instant laughter, the knowledge that this was her new direction. Links Hall. She parked, fed the meter, and ran to take a look.

The building was nothing spectacular. "Links Hall" was engraved in the stone crest at the top, and below it she saw a gray-blue exterior with unwashed screens and hazy windows. No movement inside. On the second level were posted advertisements for all sorts of activities, and Julie immediately saw the ones of women in leotards and tights, legs swung up high in the air, creative release blossoming on their faces. She felt her heart thump and resisted an urge to burst inside, hugging and kissing whomever she could find. On the street, a gaggle of drunken Cubs fans stumbled toward Houndstooth Saloon, and a CTA 22 bus smoked and lurched down the street, pallid faces gazing past her through the windows. Julie shook herself and walked toward the black door with a sign that read ENTER HERE FOR PERFORMANCE.

The door lurched open like the entrance to a freighter ship. Inside, marble stairs led up to a rickety-looking second floor. She took the steps two at a time, almost stumbling twice, stifling her laughter. A reverent quiet seemed to seep from the crevices of the building. No people anywhere. At the top of the landing, old wood made up a narrow hallway. There were pamphlet-riddled bulletin boards between unmarked oak doors with frosted glass. She glanced at some of the advertisements. *Jon Walz DJ Raffle. Dance Crash presents KTF. Flamenco by Rudy Rabby. Free Bollywood Dance Workshop.* There was a black-and-white framed placard announcing, "The 1993 Ruth Page Award is presented to Bob Eisen in recognition of his contribution as choreographer of the year." Halfway down the corridor she saw a sign marked WEST HALL, with a rusted horse-shoe hanging below the letters. Below that, two double doors, no windows, shut tight. She tried the knob—locked.

All the rooms were in the two hundreds, with some of the numbers chipped or missing. Farther down she saw a ladies' bathroom, the door propped open, ceramic tiles and an arched skylight illuminating chipped stucco walls. Still no movement anywhere; the entire place frozen in time. She rounded the bend, looking at the office doors. No labels, only numbers, all closed. At the end of the hallway, the final door was actually marked—"207 Links Hall." She turned the knob and went inside.

It was a small office, with a plywood desk topped with a boxy old computer. Sitting at the desk, with his back to her, was a man with graying brown hair, eyeglasses, and a somewhat athletic build. She cleared her throat.

"Hello? Am I in the right place? Sir?"

When he swiveled, Julie saw the man was sporting a mustache that she instantly liked: not too thick, not pencil thin, it was the comfortable mustache of a man who knew exactly who he was. He had blue eyes and a nose that looked to have been broken at least once. He smiled up at her.

"Hi," he said, pushing up his glasses. "Welcome to Links Hall. Glad you found your way in. It's a little tricky, I know. But we've got classes, workshops, creative space for rent. What can I do you for?"

Julie inhaled, and smiled. "It actually smells like a dance studio," she said. "It's unmistakable. Can you tell?"

"You bet I can tell. My wife used to run this place. When she retired, I couldn't get used to how different she smelled. So I started working here, just to reset the equilibrium."

"I forgot how much I missed that part of it."

"It's a great place. Been going strong since the 1970s. Have you seen the West Hall studio?"

"It was locked."

"You'll love it, I promise. Great condition. You looking to rent space?"

Julie examined him more carefully. "Yes, in a way. But if I might ask, if you're not originally involved in dance, what did you do before working here, mister, um . . . ?"

"Schoenwetter. Jack Schoenwetter. Chicago Fire Department for twenty-eight years. Me and my brother both. We're retired, but I still help run that boxing tournament between the CPD and CFD."

Julie did the acronym math in her head. "Wait. The police have a boxing tournament against the firefighters? Real boxing?"

Jack leaned back. "Oh, absolutely. It'll have you in hysterics. Lotta hoopla between the two forces. My brother, he's the fighter. I fought for a bit, but work better as a trainer. So when I'm not here, I'm down at Hamlin Park, training young kids to fight. It's strange, you know? I married a dancer, so I appreciate both the grace and the grease stains."

"That's a nice way to put it. I was a dancer, too, once."

"Oh right, of course. Where at?"

"Out in the suburbs, then at Northwestern. At least for part of my time there." She wondered if she was pushing the boundaries of casual banter, if it would be better to switch gears. "But about that space for rent—what are we looking at, price-wise?"

Schoenwetter leaned back. "Well, if you're doing private activities, like an audition, the rates are hourly, and they go up as it gets later. Five bucks an hour from five to nine in the morning, twelve bucks an hour from nine until six. And that figure increases to . . . let's see, fifteen an hour up until midnight, then thirty bucks if you're wanting to come in the wee hours—just because we have to have a member of staff present."

"No, no, I'm definitely not looking for an audition, although I'd probably want to rent the space for myself a couple times. To practice. But I'm looking to teach a dance class, Mr. Schoenwetter."

"Call me Jack. And that's fantastic! What in?"

Julie leaned against the wall and stretched her quadriceps, which were still sore from her morning routine. "Well," she said, "I'm still getting down the particulars, but I would like it to be a contemporary dance class for women, and here's the kicker, Jack—only women over forty allowed."

"Like an exclusive tree house."

"*Exactly* like an exclusive tree house. But really, I'm thinking it'll be more of a return-to-roots type of program. Hopefully most of these ladies will have danced before, or maybe they're just starting, but the main thing is they're looking for a way to regain contact with themselves, to express themselves through movement, synergy, music, silence. Body-mind awareness for women who have fallen out of touch, or for those who want to increase it. And, of course, it's fantastic exercise, too."

"That sounds like a solid foundation for a tree house to me," Jack said, flashing a grin. "Will you be carding these ladies at the door? Checking for fake IDs? You need to make sure young hooligans aren't sneaking in."

"I was hoping you could be the bouncer."

"Yeah, call my brother for that one. But really, this sounds like a great idea for a dance class. It could work very well."

"You should invite your wife."

"Right, right. Well, that's a bit of a long shot."

"Oh," Julie said. "She's flat-out retired, huh? Done with all of it?"

"A little more than that."

Julie leaned forward. "She *hates* it now?"

"Ha, no. She's out of the picture. Passed away, as they say."

Julie put her hand over her mouth. "Oh my God. I am so, so sorry. I had no idea—"

He chuckled and waved his hand. "I put the ball on the tee. Led you right into it, the way I was talking. And I don't mind, it's been almost six years now."

"Well, I am sorry."

"You know, that's quite all right." Jack brought his hand up to his mustache and tapped his foot. "But actually, changing the subject—seeing as how neither of us is wearing jewelry—I don't suppose you'd like to grab lunch sometime around here? Not today, mind you, but another time? There's a ton of places. Yoshi's—you heard of Yoshi's? About four blocks from here, Chicago staple. Or am I babbling? I'm being forward. That's the fire department in me. So blunt, it actually takes away a man's understanding of tact. And here I am, looking at your face, and it's clear that, yep, this was a bad idea. Totally unprofessional."

"No," Julie said, feeling a hot rain coursing inside her cheeks. Yet, despite the embarrassment, she felt a certain levitation of her stomach, as if from the drop on a roller coaster. Being asked on a *date*. Julie understood, as if from far away, that this was happening now, and for the first time since 1973 she had the option of saying yes. Truly, the first time since she stood in a summer skirt outside a baseball diamond near Evanston, Illinois.

"No, as in denied," Jack said, sighing. "Well, I'm out of practice."

Julie looked at him a little closer. He was down-to-earth and at ease with himself, but a little more dog-eared than she was used to. Henry would never have worn a rumpled plaid shirt like that, much less anything that didn't come personally fitted. And Jack was wearing tennis shoes, which immediately made her think of what Henry would say— Henry, who thought his Bally chestnut derbies were casual simply because they weren't Oxfords. And yet, along with Jack's lack of tailored aesthetic there was also an almost palpable aura of *zero bullshit*. Julie smiled.

"No, as in, it's not a bad idea, Jack. Not a bad idea at all. I'm glad you asked. And this is going to sound strange, but before we talk about that, can you just tell me a little more about the studio?"

"Sure, sure, absolutely. The studio. Wow, get it together, Jack." He cleared his throat. "Okay, well, if you want to teach a class, that's twenty bucks an hour for the rented space. Plus, upon request, we can get you an extra half hour free, either before or after, to cover the get-in, get-out. This also provides for use of the dressing room, the watercooler, or whatever else you might think you need."

Julie nodded. "That's perfect. Perfect. Can I see the studio?"

"Absolutely—there's a second entrance to West Hall right outside this door. Should be unlocked. Go ahead, nobody's using it. Take as long as you like."

Julie turned and went past him, and tried to hold back a smile.

Outside Jack's office was a blue door propped open about an inch. She swung it open, smelled wood and dust and pure open space. The door closed behind her and she stood there, taking it in slowly. There were no mirrors on the walls, which she liked—mirrors were a distraction. The ceilings were high, covered with exposed white bulbs and rows of black tech lights. Two sets of windows peeked out at the city, revealing a willow tree, curving El tracks, and a rusted fire escape that folded against the building like a resting bird. Off to the right were rows of black seats. But what grabbed her, here and now and always, was that wide-open space, and that beautiful floor. It was made of sprung, smoothed-out, glistening maple wood, so polished that it could have been clear water. She bent down and ran her fingers across it. She thought of all the dancers moving in this space, changing places within the group, fast and flowing, music and no music, lunging and floating, finally fluttering to the floor like those one-winged samara seeds, those maple keys that took to the air so often in her youth. It was as if, from the last day she danced as a junior at Northwestern in 1974, her true self had been stuffed in a cooler, and thirty-seven years had passed while her spirit was kept on ice. Now, finally, walking across this silent open space, across this still water smoothed into wood, she was home.

"I'll take it," she said, back in Jack's office. "I want to do it."

"The date?"

"The studio space. Can you give me a couple months to prepare and advertise? How does that work? Can I use the bulletin boards?"

"Sure, sure. You can absolutely use the bulletin boards. Make some advertisements for the class and we'll put them up. You can also have something on our Web site. Anything beyond that is up to you."

Julie wanted to lean forward, grab Jack by the collar, and shout, *my life is changing right now, can't you tell?* She was so excited she wanted to throttle him, to make sure he knew. But she held back, letting the feeling bunch up inside her—more fuel for the months to come.

"Thank you for the help," Julie said. "It was great to see the studio space. I'll be in touch about dates and availabilities. And also those advertisements."

"Okay, glad to help. Thanks for coming in." He was looking at the floor balefully, like a puppy who had misbehaved. He sighed and pushed his glasses up to his nose. "Sorry about the mishap," he said.

"Jack," Julie said. "That's a yes on that date."

On the walk to her car, every surface she moved across—each marble step on the staircase out of Links Hall, each sidewalk square on Sheffield, each chunk of asphalt on Clark—it all felt the same. Her feet seemed to glide, and everything she touched was like maple wood, polished and sprung.

LITTLE WORLDS

When the woman in red pulled him into her home, index finger held taut against her lips, Henry knew he was dreaming. A strange dream—a heavy dream—as if an unknowable force was pressed against the bubble of synapses that kept his world together. A cold breeze was blowing. The woman in red pulled him inside, and Henry felt the sky darkening, the shadows stretching into vast bruises across the front lawn. The shadows zipped closed around him. The woman in red pulled him inside.

"I'm dreaming," Henry said, though his lips didn't move.

"Shhh . . ."

The door closed behind them.

In the house, an obsidian grand piano stood alone in a crystal parlor, draped with the shadows of fallen leaves. The house was old, cavernous, coal mine black, the woman in red merely a sketch. More dark leaves scattered as they walked, fell from the ceiling like black stars. As his eyes adjusted, he saw the piano in the parlor turn to face him, revealing a maw of cracked, ivory teeth.

"Piano can't play," the woman sang. "Piano can't play with others."

"Stop that," Henry growled.

She led him up the stairs. Sparks of light illuminated their footsteps. The woman in red, he remembered, she was the first, the very first—what year had it been? 1996. Joyce. He had behaved himself before then. They reached the landing. There was a long hallway. At the end, he knew, was the bedroom. She was taking him back to the bedroom.

"You were the first," he said.

"I know."

"I used to be good. You started this. *You* changed everything."

She hummed a tune to herself.

"Before you, it was all Julie. She was my world. You understand, Joyce?"

"Piano can't play with others," Joyce said.

The hallway seemed to stretch on and on, a horizontal mine shaft with framed pictures and polished floors. Henry remembered himself at forty-two years of age, feeling old for the first time, seeing Joyce, who lived in the neighborhood, her head held high at her husband's wake.

I'm so sorry for your loss, Henry had said, touching her hand.

But at the wake, he found himself seeing only the slope of her neck and the smoothness of her hands and the green flashes that were her eyes. He found himself thinking of his own age. Forty-two. New lines in his face every day. Joyce's husband dead at forty-seven, playing tennis at the Hinsdale Golf Club, surrounded by greenery and the smell of fairways. He'd fallen like he'd been shot, the trainer said. Tennis racket bouncing, head thumping, then both silent on the dark clay court.

And Joyce had her head held high that day. She didn't cry. Only smiled with her closest friends—didn't fake a thing. Her face was more elegant than Julie's. Higher cheekbones, he decided, and long, wavy hair. He was forty-two, couldn't get the number out of his head. He'd seen Joyce's toughness and liked it and wanted that toughness pointed toward him, pointed as if he were her sun. Forty-two. He wanted to black the numbers out.

In the hallway, the woman in red kept humming.

"It's all your fault," Henry said.

The door to the bedroom loomed ahead.

He'd made her love him, eventually. And what he'd done really wasn't that bad, was it? Not in the great scheme of things. He'd seen Joyce's

bare body, had allowed her fingers to grope him like cold, probing soldiers, so strange and deliberate was her desire. He had returned this need,
had enjoyed it, maybe even more than she, and he hadn't even felt bad
for weeks, marveling at how strong and watertight his psychology was.

But after the affair was over and no one the wiser, the guilt began to
rattle around Henry's brain and body like a marble. It made him crazy,
trying to get rid of it. Sometimes, from the right angle, lying on the couch
maybe with Julie's head against him, the marble would roll into a small
divot inside his foot or the soft back of his knee, and for a while, he
couldn't feel it. It was almost like it hadn't happened. Old feelings, random, loose, breezy joy at the smallest things—a humorous commercial
about baby powder, the feeling of Julie's pulse against his arm, a young
Barkley bursting into the room wearing his green ninja headband, doing
high karate kicks and then stumbling—all came together and Henry
found himself laughing again, really feeling good, finally feeling *light*.

But then, eventually, the marble always popped out of place, and
Henry would feel it rolling around him again, ping-ponging off his bones
and organs, reminding him of what he'd done. Joyce. Especially in those
moments when he'd forgotten and had regained that bounce in his step,
the marble would rattle free, letting him know that something was off,
that an injustice had been done. It was remarkable, really, that he couldn't
seem to get over it, couldn't pluck the marble out—whose color he imagined was aqua blue with swirls of sand and white, a tiny Earth inside him,
a whole little world he couldn't destroy.

In the end, the only thing that made sense was to add more marbles.

At the end of the hallway, Joyce led him toward the door. She turned
the knob, pressed her cold fingers against the small of his back, and pushed
him inside. He expected her to undress him, as she had in all the other
dreams, to come at him with that strange need, those cold fingers, that
desire that had nothing to do with him. But instead, she simply pushed
him forward. The room emitted a soft blue light. Old posters on the
walls. There was a boy on a twin bed, and when Henry first saw him,
he thought it was Charlie, and felt a rush of warmth, as if he'd sunk into
a bathtub.

"Charlie," he said. "That's my boy, Charlie."

The woman in red laughed.

When he reached the bed, Henry pulled back, shocked. The boy's hair was all wrong, shaggy and falling over his ears, and his skin was a darker brown, and his face, more square—and then Henry tensed up and stepped away, because he knew now what he was looking at.

"Why would you do this?" he said to Joyce.

She stood beside him, cold palm on the small of his back. Her fingers didn't probe like they had before—they pushed, and held him in place.

"Why?" he asked again.

The boy on the bed was himself. Henry Brunson, twelve years old, in the months after his father died. In the blue light of the room, he saw that it was now populated with the trinkets and arrangements of his youth—curling posters of Bill George and Doug Atkins on the far wall, a framed bedside photo of his father holding two meaty arms around him at Wrigley Field, and stacks of board games to the right of the bed: the dark brown rectangle of Clue, followed by a tattered Monopoly, then Stratego, which was new and exciting and difficult for his friends to play, yet a game that Henry excelled at, even beating his own father. On the floor was a small stack of books. Henry saw two by Jack London, the two novels he used to take everywhere, before he stopped reading. *White Fang* and *The Call of the Wild*. On his bedside table—

And then Henry saw light and the dream was gone and there was a man with a hawk nose and intense, steely blue eyes bending over him, and a piercing beep like something from a submarine, all surrounded by pockmarked white walls. He was lying down, he realized, but then he was plunged under again, dropped into a vast, blue fish tank, sinking to the bottom amid a thousand broken necklaces of bubbles. He found himself again. Yes, here he was, sinking to the bottom, feet touching, space clearing, back in his old room as a boy.

He blinked. On the nightstand, dwarfing the framed photo and other harmless trinkets, was the bedside fan: a tall, square, pale blue plastic cage with a dirtied knob on top. It would start with a dull lurch and then speed up like an engine-fed propeller, dousing him in sound and a thickening breeze. He'd turn it on high at night. He'd turn it on high, and that wind tunnel sound would carry him away, humming and fading as he drifted into darkness, his bed becoming sky. Even as a boy, he had wondered if his own death would be the same: a wind, wide and loose, blowing. Fading away. Into the blackness, he thought, shivering, though Barkley had said it couldn't exist. More dark leaves fell from the ceiling.

"It's always been there," Joyce told him.

"What has?"

Her hand moved him closer; he was gliding now, moving across the floor. Moving toward his old self. The bedside fan was on. It hummed and rattled and sent wind against the sleeping boy's face. And in his hand, in the boy's left hand, was the marble. Dark blue with swirls of sand and white.

"It's always been there," she said, patting his hand.

She smiled. More leaves blew past his ankles. The fan droned, hummed, took over the room. It's always been there, Henry thought. He felt the heaviness of the dream, that safe pressing against the grid of synapses holding the place together. But the fan, the whir, stronger still. He heard the submarine beeping again, felt a sense of lifting, and at the same time that heaviness crushing the boyhood room around him.

The world became light again. Fuzzy light, with blurred movement. A terrible knowledge in that light. Beeping monitors and soft, clicking, metallic tools. Milky eyes that wouldn't meet his own. He was in a hospital. There had been an operation. Had they opened him up and seen the marbles, all of those tiny worlds, lodged inside of him? Had they seen the termites scurry beneath his stomach and pancreas, burying themselves away from the light?

"Where am I?" Henry asked, but realized his lips weren't moving.

More shuffling, more beeping, the harsh light becoming normal. Why was he here? He'd been opened up. There was cancer. They had to take out the cancer. The knowledge was like falling.

The Whipple Procedure—his way out. Cut the head off the pancreas. Snip around all those other organs. His thoughts were separate islands, strung wide like clotheslines across a vast lawn. He tried to feel his incision, to see if it hurt, but felt a heavy numbness, a thick cushion of dense, artificial cloud.

There was a blue curtain hanging in the room. He was sectioned off. The beeping was coming from behind him, but he was too tired to move his head. There were tubes, and he couldn't feel his stomach—

"Mr. Brunson? How are you feeling? Are you well enough to talk?"

"Who's there?"

The hawk-nosed face bent over him. The sharp blue eyes met his own. This was Dr. Pashad? No. This was Fredrickson.

"How did it go?" Henry asked, weakly, his lips feeling dry. Then, sensing hesitation, and gathering strength: "Tell me."

Fredrickson sighed. "I hate giving bad news," he said.

"No."

"I'm very sorry. You see, the problem was—"

"But how?"

"That's what I want to explain, Mr. Brunson."

He felt a nurse's hands on him, adjusting a tube, checking something—his pulse? His wound? Her fingers were chilly, and even through the latex gloves, the touch reminded him of Joyce. All those years ago, sliding out of her robe in the dim light of the bedroom, her cold fingers probing his chest, feeling his beating heart.

"We made the incision," Fredrickson said, "under the assumption that the cancer was isolated in the pancreas. But, Henry—when we made the incision, little pieces of shrapnel, too small for the CT scan to pick up, had metastasized into your liver."

"Shrapnel?" Clouds, he thought. Marbles.

"Small bits of cancerous mass. It's traveled to other organs. Which means, by law, that I had to cancel the procedure. It's malpractice to complete the Whipple if the cancer has metastasized. I'm sorry, Mr. Brunson. I really wanted to hit a home run here. We thought the CT had picked up everything."

Henry breathed in and out, finding himself drifting, those clotheslines stretching wider, across the endless lawn. "How much. Time. Is left?"

Fredrickson looked across him, at someone else. A slight shake of the head. Henry felt a tremendous weight upon his consciousness.

"I'm going to be honest with you, Mr. Brunson. The life expectancy changes with the cancellation of the Whipple. There will be chemo, and it will be up to you how much and of what type. Positive attitude is the name of the game now. As is spending time with those you care about."

He took a breath. "How much. Time. How many. Months."

The cold hands went back to his neck, to a tube coming out of his hand.

"It could be anything. I've had other patients go full speed ahead, with a positive attitude, which is so important, and go a year and a half, even longer. Anything is possible. Then again, I've had patients throw in the towel and slip away in a few months. We have to be honest here. Much of it is up to you. Positivity. It's the name of the game."

Henry felt himself going back into the fish tank. Blue water and bubbles filled the hospital room.

"Mr. Brunson? I understand that you don't have family here at the hospital. Would you like us to call someone?"

Henry asked if the doctor had seen anything strange.

"What's that? Strange?"

"Inside me," Henry said as the water rose higher, pooling around his body. "Anything. Strange. Or round."

"Can't say that I have. Beyond what I've already told you. Would you like us to call someone?"

Nodding was moving a mountain. No one knew, he thought. No one knew about his illness.

"Mr. Brunson?"

"Barkley. Call Barkley. He's. My son."

Fredrickson said something else, but the water had filled the room now. It was up to his nose, submerging him, tinting the world blue. It was cool, over his head, and when he went under, he heard the fan—the big, plastic fan from his boyhood home.

"It's always been here," Henry said, to the doctor, through the bubbles.

He was back in the darkened house, in the hallway. The bedroom door was closed, tightly shut, even though he could hear the fan. It wasn't time for that yet. The door stayed closed.

From the landing, he saw Joyce, his woman in red. She was standing in the open doorway, watching him as the leaves slid by her ankles.

"Wait," Henry said. "Hold on."

He didn't pay attention to the stairs or the parlor or the pictures on the wall. He made it down to Joyce, and grabbed her arm, saw that she was fading back.

"Time to go," she said. "Piano can't play with others."

Henry looked at her green eyes, wavy hair, red dress.

"I have to go," she said, taking another step back.

"Tell me why, Joyce."

She stared at him.

"Why me? Why did you choose me?"

More leaves slid past her ankles, spilled into the house like newspaper.

"Why did you let me in, Joyce? Why did you ever say yes?"

She put her hand on his heart. Her fingertips traced a circle. "You were alive," she said. Her lips went to his ear. "Alive, alive, alive."

ECLIPSE

It was 12:15 P.M., and Barkley was sitting under the fluorescents of the teachers' cafeteria, sifting through a crumpled green salad in a Styrofoam bowl, when Eastwick's west wall shook from rumbling impact. The lights flickered, and Barkley fumbled, his plastic fork skittering across the table. There was a subsequent boom, and then a third, and the fluorescent lights went out for good.

The room had only one window, and in the darkness, Barkley saw the silhouettes of Mike Dobbs and Father Daniels, sitting there silently across the table, blackened lunch trays stretching like trapdoors. They had just been talking about . . . what?

"Fuckin' tornado?" Dobbs barked.

"No tornado," Father Daniels said. "Can't figure it. Pipe, maybe."

"Bigger than a pipe."

"That was, like, dragon-big," Barkley said.

There were noises in the hallway, rapid footsteps, and Barkley could already hear the students shouting in the various classrooms, jubilantly accepting their gift of darkness. There was another boom, this one from outside of the school.

"Thunder," Father Daniels said. "Looks like we're getting hit today after all."

A month into teaching, Barkley found that he lived and died by the climate of each day's lesson. He drove home in a state of euphoria if his instruction had gone well—if the lesson had been timed out correctly, if the students had listened, if he had obtained that magical moment that made him feel as if he'd entered some educational faerie meadow of possibility—the *it* moment, he called it. *It* was a moment in time, a special moment, when all the students were quiet, just as he was finishing some point about motifs or symbols or character development, lassoing all the elements together and driving home the final point. It was that moment when the students actually went silent (heads turned toward the board, eyes up, alert yet dreamy, a collective awareness blooming over their desks and unfolding over the classroom), and in their silence, in that slow-motion sequence of instructional-intellectual symbiosis, Barkley *felt* his students learning. It wasn't the memorization of rote knowledge he was sensing; that could occur any time, any day, any classroom with PowerPoint and a notebook. These were meaningful events, little paradigm shifts hitting their minds like rain across a spring garden. It was a small amount, sure, but it still meant something, and he knew that it did, and even though the moment usually lasted no longer than a minute, in that silence of real learning Barkley felt an afterglow from some kind of educational nirvana, a feeling of truly having achieved, and the rest of his evening was bliss.

This had happened maybe once a week.

Too many things had to go right: the lesson had to be planned out, there had to be meaning and depth in what was discussed, Barkley himself had to have gotten over six hours of sleep and a decent breakfast and coffee, and he had to be having a good day, feeling reasonably confident and assured. The students had to behave, and they had to be having good enough days themselves, and the school day had to be sedate and not a Friday and not usually a Monday, but if all these events occurred, yes, if they occurred, the feeling of real, euphoric learning was possible, attainable.

Most of the days were war zones, mortar fire falling on both sides of the battlefield. Barkley had to accept that he wasn't a disciplinarian—the kids had figured this out, too—and with this knowledge came the fact that he'd be able to connect with the students, but would constantly be working harder to control the classroom. Wolverine existed as either an aid to the fun or an uprising to be stifled. Elise Rossi, after serving her JUG, had been warm and cold, offering him pocket-size challenges through which he could momentarily win her approval or lose it—the best bet here seemed to be to simply ignore her, but that laser beam stare from the back of class said otherwise. And though he felt relief when her gaze finally left him, with that relief was a tiny, eight-legged creature whose genus he didn't want to identify, but knew was a warped form of jealousy. Whom was her attention on, when not upon him? And then he would wash away the thoughts as first period ended, and this was the benefit of being a teacher, class after class, each exfoliating the other away, until all that was left was a sense of the net gain or net loss.

If he went home with the euphoric feeling one day, chances were the next would be the teaching gallows. In his delight at his own abilities, he'd take some time off planning, congratulate himself, go to dinner with Ginny on half-priced-wine night at Gaslight, see his friends, sometimes just watch television shows or play his video games. And the next day would be a grind, the students resistant, somehow sensing the scatter-shot nature of his lesson plan, he himself realizing too late that he hadn't prepared for that moment of educational checkmate when the class had no choice *but* to learn. No, the day would be a collection of hodgepodge minilessons, stitched together without forethought, the connective tissue prosthetic, the students seeing the cogs and resisting, resisting. And just as the real moment of collective learning was euphoric, so was the moment of detachment and disengagement deflating—Barkley would drive home in an icy, murderous mood, half depressed, half outraged at his own misfirings. And for one whole month it had gone like this, yet one thing had become clear: he *could* teach, and the students did respond to him, and he did have moments of genuine learning and connection. But with this, a second thing revealed itself: he had a rogues' gallery of weaknesses, among them discipline, planning, organization, pacing, and a certain bureaucratic conditioning that made some people born to ascend to the administration offices, and others, like him, destined to remain in the classroom. And this rogues' gallery of deficiencies, depending on the day, could act as common criminals, easy to stifle and of little trouble, and other days, like when the students had almost overrun him in a discussion about the dress code, like enigmatic supervillains.

The lights flickered on again, and Barkley found his eyes drawn to the neon green of the salad. Two weeks of lunchtime greens without dessert, and he'd lost only three pounds. Still, he noticed that his cheekbones were beginning to show again, unearthed from his skin like buried structures in a sandstorm.

"Here we go," Dobbs said. "Let there be light. It was a tease. It's always a tease."

Barkley grinned at him. "Thought you were getting a day off?"

And then there was a concussive boom that felt like the end of a sentence, and the cafeteria plunged back into blackness. The students in the surrounding rooms roared again.

"That sounded pretty fatal," Dobbs said, rising.

Father Daniels followed suit. "The intercoms aren't working if the power's off. But teachers are instructed to, what, wait five minutes? Ten minutes in the event of a power outage? Then we meet in the auditorium."

"Go now, or later?" Barkley asked.

"Let's head there now. Have to wake up Father Lupas from his stupor."

Father Lupas was one of the many priests who, Father Daniels said, struggled with addictions to the bottle. This was commonplace but quietly accepted in the Catholic world. Daniels stated that a large percentage of the priests he'd worked with over the years had endured some sort of bout with alcoholism. And why? It was the only loophole the Bible allowed. No sex, that was for certain. No violence. No stealing or lawbreaking or acts of vandalism. But a drink was allowed. And from that allowance spawned a shaky bridge to escape and release. Father Daniels, in his early thirties and popular with the kids (showing 1990s action movies in his theology class), openly admitted that two of the priests in his order had been to rehab clinics.

"Does the public know this?" Barkley had asked.

Father Daniels ran a hand through his close-cropped chestnut hair. "You're going to get a large percentage who want to be ignorant of it, who are outraged just by someone saying the words. To many people, the Catholic world has to be pristine, Photoshopped and airbrushed like a magazine cover, even if that doesn't match reality. *I'm* a devout believer, mind you, and most of the priests are, too, but it's important to recognize that God is pristine, not Catholicism. Everything human has its flaws, and this particular branch is lined with drinking problems. But to answer your question, most of the public is insulated from the facts. There are those other scandals that come out, but the drinking—it's how the normal priests escape. Some just drink to drink. Some become fine wine connoisseurs. Some, like me, just want a good beer. Which I'll be getting at the Black Sabbath concert this weekend."

"You're kidding," Barkley had said.

"Why? I saw an Eastwick parent at Iron Maiden a month ago, and I held up my beer to toast her, and she seemed shocked. But why? People forget that we're the same as them. We're people, too, just with different goals, different vows. Why wouldn't I like good music and good beer?"

Barkley had wanted to probe further, to ask about the even darker underbelly of the Catholic world, but he saw that Father Daniels was interested primarily in harmless reveals, watercooler gossip among the who's who of the Catholic orders. To mention that dark side, and the priests who'd been bent by more than just harmless escapisms, would likely close Father Daniels to him for good. And having a priest on his side certainly couldn't hurt—hadn't hurt.

The Eastwick hallways were dark, only the rectangular windows above the lockers letting in a rainy light. Thunder cracked again, and soon the storm was hitting the school in earnest. Barkley first ran into John Byzantine from his second-period class, apologized, caught up to Dobbs, and then ran smack into Elise Rossi, knocking her books into the darkness, causing her eyes to smolder.

"Sorry," Barkley said.

"Not in the mood," she said, grunting.

"Wow. You've been in a weird mood today. You know that?"

She rolled her eyes. "I have not."

"You didn't have your homework, didn't say a word all class, and are staring daggers left and right. C'mon, Rossi. Get it together."

She glowered at him, her hair a curtain.

"Rossi, come on, what's the deal? You look like you want to hurt someone."

"Are we finished? Can I go?"

Barkley, stung, felt Dobbs watching him. "Yeah, we're done, Elise. Bring your homework in tomorrow."

She strode away, and Dobbs said nothing, but Barkley could feel him smirking.

"What?" Barkley said, dodging a portly kid lugging a cello case in the darkness.

Dobbs laughed.

"What's so funny?"

"Jailbait, my friend."

"What's that supposed to mean?"

"That girl," Dobbs said, "is an expert game-player. A savant. You know anything about her?"

"Not really. Maybe after parent-teacher conferences."

"Yeah, her mom might show. Listen, I had Rossi last year. She's tough. But she's not your typical Barbie. And a lot of that is coming from home."

"Okay," Barkley said. "I think I get it."

"I'd just as soon keep my distance," Dobbs said.

"Obviously."

"It's tempting, I know."

"What are you hinting at?"

"Just that, as a young teacher, it's tempting to try to make an alliance. Why not, right? But it just—it never works out the way you think it will. Especially when you're an idealist."

"I'm not an idealist!" Barkley cried defensively, causing Wolverine and two of his cronies to look up from their lockers and guffaw.

"Mr. B., you're, like, *such* an idealist," Wolverine crooned. "Oh my God, you just believe in the magic of teaching. You are an expert mind-molder, Mr. B.! I swear by it!"

"I'm going to stuff you in that locker," Barkley called back, leaving them behind. Ahead, the darkened auditorium beckoned. Margaret Carey met them at the entrance.

"Blown transformer," she said. "And we've got a fallen tree that struck the school. School's out early—they're gathering the buses now."

"Score," Dobbs said. "Do we call it an act of God?"

Margaret Carey wrinkled her nose. "Too funny, Mike. Anyway, they're going to make the announcement, but you could all start packing up and get out early. Only the phones are working."

"Amen," Dobbs cracked.

Barkley turned to leave, but Carey discreetly hooked her arm around his elbow. He looked down at her—he was taller, after all—but it still felt like he was looking *up*. She pulled him in close.

"I've been looking at your daily lesson plans, Barkley. The past two weeks in particular."

"Oh? What did you think?"

"You need to utilize more grammar in these plans. On a daily basis. There should be an opening exercise or, at the very least, a grammar warm-up."

Barkley looked down at her wrinkled hand, which remained hooked around his elbow. "I've got a grammar refresher unit starting in two weeks, actually. It's pretty good—I got it from my observing instructor during student teaching. Really helps with the first-quarter essays."

Carey stared at him. Students and teachers moved past them like water around a heavy rock.

"More grammar," Barkley said, nodding. "Maybe I could begin the grammar warm-ups now. That's what you're saying, right? Leading up to the grammar unit?"

She pursed her lips.

"On a daily basis," he added. "Grammar warm-ups on a daily basis. Starting tomorrow."

And, as if the sun had suddenly crested through the clouds, Margaret Carey smiled warmly and released her grip. "I'm looking forward to my formal observation, Barkley. I'm sure it'll be a positive one."

As she walked away, Barkley cleared his mind and took the athletic stairwell down two flights, into the polished basement area where Eastwick's Olympic swimming pool was nested. Four glass doors led into it, and Barkley eyed the glassy, lavender water, the roped-off lanes, the massive scoreboard, the flanking stands that filled for each and every water polo meet, all covered in a blanket of dark. Every year, Eastwick was in the running for the state title, and never before had Barkley seen such an obsession for the sport. His own office was located adjacent to the pool entrance—a narrow room with three desks, a printer, and two shelves of tattered dictionaries and thesauruses. He turned around and—again—smacked into Elise Rossi, who was on another warpath. Her books and papers fell, clattering and fluttering to the white-tiled floor.

"Are you serious?" she said. "Really?"

"Here," Barkley said. "Let me help. My bad. I'm sorry."

"Twice in one day. Just my luck."

"What's that supposed to mean?"

She flattened out her gray skirt, said nothing. The normally bright hallway was empty, only the watery lapping from Eastwick's pool taking away from the stillness.

"Aren't you supposed to be in the auditorium?" he asked.

"Aren't you?"

"Look. Elise. Is everything okay?" He bent down and gathered her things and handed them back to her.

She took them and looked away. At the ground, the pool, the wall.

"Hey," Barkley said. Through the office door, he heard his phone ringing.

"Can I go?"

"Yeah, you can go, Elise. Have I done something to upset you?"

He felt her blue lasers on him again, tried to shrug off the strange feeling of being caught in a net.

"No, you haven't done anything," she said flatly.

The phone kept ringing.

"Then what? You got something on your mind?"

She sighed, and Barkley saw, for the first time, a weight behind her eyes, a heaviness to her normally lithe movements.

"Look," she said. She took in a breath. "The reason I didn't have my homework—there's a reason. I know you marked me off, but there's a reason."

"Okay."

"But I'm not supposed to tell anyone."

"Elise. It's all right. I mean—do you want to hint at it? I don't know. I can't tell you to say something you're not supposed to say."

She groaned, and then abruptly turned and put her forehead against the door to his office. The phone trilled again. Her eyes were closed, and Barkley felt panic and empathy creeping across his insides, twisting like opposing vines.

"Look," Barkley said. "It's all right. I mean—"

"The reason I didn't have my homework last night is that I couldn't *get* my homework."

"Okay."

She kept her head against the door. "My homework was at my house. And the thing is, I'm not living at my house right now. Okay?"

"Hey," Barkley said. "Hey."

"So, I couldn't just go get it—because I'm not living there, you understand? You get what I'm saying? I can't go back there." She took a sharp intake of breath and kept her head against the door, eyes closed, blond hair spilling and swaying.

"I'm sorry," Barkley said. Should he touch her? Put his arm around her? But he couldn't.

"No," she said. "I don't care. It doesn't matter."

Barkley stepped closer, a foot away from her, maybe less. He remembered back when Hayward's uncle had died, in 2005, how everyone had rushed forward to show support, calling, sending e-mails, and Barkley himself had written something, and it came out sounding horribly florid and false. He'd danced around the issue, unsure of how to address it. But one of their friends—Mark—who had also had a recent death in the family, had struck the right note. He'd simply said, *Look, man. I know it's bad. I know it's rough. Let me know if you want to talk about it.* And Barkley had understood, right there, that this was the route to take. Acknowledging that it was indeed bad, empathizing with the truth of it.

"Elise," he said. "Elise."

"What?" The phone rang again.

He struggled for the right words, restrained himself from touching her shoulder, even though it felt hopelessly cold to leave her there, on an island.

"I get it," he said, leaning in. "It sucks. It really, really sucks. And I'm sorry. I've had some crazy stuff happen with my family, too."

"Yeah?" she said. She pulled away from the door as the phone trilled yet another time. "Are you going to get that?"

"You know what—sure, let me get rid of it. Just stay right there. No, go ahead, come into the office. Here."

The office was a cave. He swam through the blackness, picked up the phone, his heart kicking a strange beat. "Barkley Brunson," he said. "Can I help you?"

"Barkley."

"Yes?"

"Barkley." It was a gravelly voice, from somewhere far away.

"Yes? Who's calling?"

"It's your father," the impossibly gnarled whisper said. "Your father."

The door to the office opened and closed again. "You can't see any-thing in here," Elise said, and Barkley felt something like poison seeping into his body.

"Dad," he intoned, trying to right himself. "I'm at work."

There was breathing on the other end, and then—"I'm at Northwest Community Hospital. They've been trying to call you."

Barkley felt a strange bubbling coursing through him, a change in the gradation of the floor. And Elise was in here—

"What?" he said. "Who tried to call?"

"The doctors. I need you now. You need to come now, and you can't call your mother, you understand?"

"What's happened?"

He heard Elise moving closer, standing next to his desk.

"It's cancer, Barkley. The operation couldn't be completed. There's marbles."

"What operation? Why wasn't I told?" And he realized the word, *cancer*, had been left behind somewhere, stuck between his ribs, twisted.

"Come now," said the voice that had to be someone else. "You need to come now." And then—dial tone.

He placed the phone back in the cradle, felt the room revolving, moving under his feet. His father—and then he sensed Elise in the darkness with him, heard her breathing, could feel the heat on the side of his face.

"It's so dark in here," she said.

He turned the word, *cancer,* over in his mind again.

"Is everything all right?"

"No," Barkley said. "No, I don't think it is."

He felt her step closer, saw her eyes in the darkness, and felt the urge, the powerful urge, to make contact with another person.

"What's wrong?" she whispered.

"My dad," Barkley said. "I have to go."

"We're both having bad days, aren't we, Mr. B.?"

He shook himself. Through the tiny window of his office door, he could see the movements of the swimming pool.

"Mr. B.?"

"I have to go," he said. "And so do you."

He found himself breathing again. He'd been holding his breath, but now he was breathing, and *seeing.* What was he doing in here? He strode forward and found the cold steel of the knob, opened the office door, held it wide.

"Look," he said shakily. "I've got to go, you've got to go. Bring me the homework when you can. No points off."

Northwest Community Hospital was a conglomeration of white buildings and honeycombed windows and hulking gray parking garages. Barkley drove with the radio off, thinking, driving, thinking, but his thoughts were flakes of paint, chipped and useless. He pulled out of the rain and into the parking garage, found the elevator, the room number. In the oncology department, the nurse led him to the room with the curtained blue partition, and pulled it aside to reveal his father.

His father, Henry Brunson, had been a monolith since childhood. Even his absences left a crater, a kind of inverted electrical loss. The hulking presence and baritone voice, that smell of Cohibas and aftershave—every particle was a clenched fist. And now, in front of Barkley, was something else entirely.

The machines clicked and stuttered, whirred and beeped, flicked their metallic tongues and knocked their plastic heels. Barkley saw that his father, sunken and asleep, was part of these machines now, the tubes and blinking lights and heart monitors and IV bags, all the assortment of switches and dials that made him seem part of the hospital itself—as if indigenous life were evolving from the wires, growing bold, mutating into something human. Barkley realized, vaguely, that the nurse was speaking to him. She spoke in hushed tones. Pancreatic cancer. There had been a surgery, but then a complication. Or, not a complication, a discovery. More cancer. And now the expectancy changed. Did he know any of this? He didn't. He knew nothing of this. She kept talking while Barkley's head spun. But with those science fiction machines whirring and beeping and clicking, his father did wake up, and Barkley saw the knowledge in his eyes, the stillness in his face, the skin that was carved out of bark.

"Barkley," his father said.

He stood there. So many monitors. Tubes.

"Barkley."

"Dad?"

"Get over here."

Barkley sprung forward, as he always did. Eager. He hadn't seen his father in over a month, and though his gray-brown hair was still full, his blue eyes were milky, and the stubble on his face grungy and patchwork—nothing he would normally have allowed. He still had the strong jaw, but the cheekbones were tauter than before, and the bulging muscles of his body flattened, as though the hospital gown were a punctured and deflating balloon.

"What's happening, Dad? What is this?"

His father closed and opened his eyes. "It's cancer, Barkley. I can't believe it either. I'm going to have to beat it the old-fashioned way. I don't really have a choice."

"Dad."

"I'm going to have to hit back, you understand?"

"Dad, how long have you known about this? How long has this been happening?"

His father turned to look at him. His eyes focused and refocused. "Do you remember when I took you to see the horses?"

"The racetrack? Arlington racetrack?"

"It's right around the corner," his father said. "You were eight."

"Sure, Dad. I remember. I bet on that big dark horse. What was his name? Eclipse. I used to love that word."

"Do you remember the woman we met there?"

Barkley shakily thought back. All he recalled was sunlight flickering through trees, the thump of hooves, and his father's giant palm on his shoulder, squeezing when the horses thundered. Had there been a woman? Did he remember another voice?

"Was Glenn there?"

His father sighed. "No, Glenn's got the ranch. The ranch, Barkley."

"Charlie's girlfriend?"

"Charlie was twelve."

"Oh, right. I'm a little out of sorts."

"You're being a numskull, Barkley."

He looked out the window. Rivulets of water smeared the glass.

"How long has it been storming?" his father asked.

"A few hours now. Power at Eastwick went out. School got canceled."

The old man closed his eyes.

"Dad, what are we going to do? We have to tell Mom. And Charlie. Everyone needs to be here."

His father shook his head. "I'm tired. And you won't tell anyone."

"Dad, I don't—is it going to be okay?"

"Chemo," his father said. "Months."

"Months of chemo? Or they're talking to you about months?"

The monitors beeped.

"Dad?"

"At the racetrack, Barkley, there was a woman named Joyce. Do you remember Joyce?"

"No," Barkley said.

"You met her. You liked her."

"Okay, Dad. I met her. I'm sure I liked her."

"I'm going back to sleep, now."

"Okay. I'm going to talk to the nurse."

"Barkley?"

He looked at his father, saw his body as that deflating balloon.

"Barkley, tell me about the blackness."

"The what?"

The blue eyes were on him now. "The blackness," he said again. "After dying."

"It's not possible," Barkley said, automatically. Had he said this to his father, once? There was a vague memory. He'd made the argument to many.

"Explain, Barkley. Tell me about the blackness."

"Black nothingness after death? How people are afraid of it? It's philosophically impossible. It can't happen."

"Tell me why. Tell me one more time."

"Because . . ." And he wanted to say, *Even blackness is something. And something means existence. If there's truly nothing after death, you won't even know it. You won't see blackness. You'll be gone.* But he couldn't say this to his father—couldn't talk about death here, now.

"Tell me," his father said. "You're the teacher. Teach."

Barkley thought of himself in his office, in that cave of ink, reaching for the ringing phone. And in this dream, the power to the landline was cut, too, and there was silence and blackness all around. Only himself. He stood there in his dream of night, he stood there closing his eyes and shutting his ears, wishing for that one good thing that couldn't exist.

DEATH MATCH
(WITH PAINT)

In the ravine was a blanket of pale yellow leaves that led to a small, reflecting creek, surrounded by birch trees and hollow logs. Charlie, from his elevated position, watched the lone figure traipsing along the bottom. It was Hayward's friend. Mark-something. Moving slow, kicking up leaves like confetti after a party. Stupid. Charlie put the stock of the weapon against his shoulder. He assessed, internally, that the paintball gun weighed just over six pounds. The M4 weighed 6.9 with a full magazine. He would have to adjust for the change in weight. Key chain in his left pants pocket, pressed against his thigh. Ignore it. *Have fun*, his brother kept telling him. That's why he was out here. Fun. He brought his finger up to the trigger, traced the lone figure through the scope above the gray barrel. Fifty yards away. The goofball was still kicking up shredded ribbons of yellow leaves, swinging his gun around brazenly, hoping to star in an action movie. Charlie bit back a laugh.

The wind blew, and Charlie felt old sparks warming in his heart, a sudden dampness on his palms and forearms. Mark-something had stopped by a gnarled and bumpy log. It was better this way. For all of his suffering, for all of the notions that he was fucked-up beyond reprieve, Charlie had at least learned. He'd learned about the reality beyond the wire, beyond America's mammoth pop culture filtration system. He keyed his target. And lacing his skin: cold sweat. Anticipatory sweat. Good sweat. He smelled the white bark of the birch trees. The crisp tautness of the autumn air. In the tree, to his three o'clock, a squirrel danced across a white branch and fluffed a tail like a spinning gown. Charlie looked through the scope again. He smiled, the laughter bubbling in his throat, and pulled the trigger.

Barkley was lying flat on the side of a hollowed, rotting-out log, half buried in wet leaves, paintball gun tight against his chest, when Mark Harrington thudded by. And Harrington—for all the good taste he'd shown in addressing the passing of Hayward's uncle—was acting like a moron here, strutting around ridiculously, holding his gun single-handed like Arnold Schwarzenegger. Even his paintball mask was partially off, tilted back like a baseball cap. Barkley inched forward along the side of the log. What he would do was spring forward, popping just high enough to put two paintballs into Harrington's back, and then drop back ninja-style. Or maybe he'd snipe him in the back of the head. Harrington would be mad, and it would hurt, but he also deserved it for all the posturing.

Barkley had never played paintball before. Well, he'd played once, on vacation with Hayward's family in Michigan, in an "apocalypse-themed" arena—post offices with collapsed roofs, bullet-riddled shacks, half-sunken sandbag walls. He'd paid for the rented gun, the paintballs, the CO_2, the time in the arena. And within minutes of simply trying to get his bearings and decide which way to run, some bearded, mullet-topped, paintball lifer had rolled out from under a pipe and stitched a yellow swath across Barkley's midsection.

"That's it?" he remembered crying. "I'm out?"

He was out. It was like every other sport he'd dabbled in—getting pulverized by a future Navy SEAL in a Thanksgiving Day football match, having his jump shots blocked by barking, gargantuan high schoolers in the seventh grade, finishing behind Charlie in nearly every contest since he'd been a baby. But no more, Barkley decided. He was in this

game to win. And he was going to be patient, and wait his turn, and as-
sassinate Mark Harrington.

With Harrington five feet away, Barkley rose from behind the log.
He pressed the stock against his shoulder, aimed, and slipped on a slimy
twig—the shot went over Harrington's head. The moron turned, firing
blindly. To Barkley's left, on the hill that overlooked the ravine, there
were three quick chirps, and Harrington's exposed face exploded in green
paint. He dropped into the wet leaves immediately, shouting, tearing his
mask off—

"Fuck!" Harrington screamed. "Shot me in the fucking ear!"

Barkley saw movement up high, seventy feet away—and ran. Charlie. Paintballs splattered the log to his left, the birch trees to his right.
He dove into rounded mounds of leaves, rolled, got up and kept running, laughing at the exhilarating absurdity of it. Behind him, he heard
the rapid clicking of Charlie firing on full automatic—the sound of someone nastily shuffling a deck of cards.

It's a clear day over southwestern Kabul, and the sky is propane blue, a
single white airship cloud passing over the broken city. Charlie sits on
the hood of a silver 1993 Toyota Corolla that's missing all four tires and
both rear axles. Broken glass is scattered around the car like a moat. The
highway, jagged and potholed from the recent attack, leads into the city
amid helter-skelter telephone wires that dangle like cut vines.

"Charlie, hey, Charlie," Bruiser says.

Charlie feels the cigarette dangling from his lips. It's not lit and tastes
like ink. The hot breeze blows. He closes his eyes. He thinks: Campo
dead for two months. And then he thinks: three more kills and I'm up
to ten.

"Brunson, you think we'll see any action today?"

"Yeah."

"How 'bout that shot yesterday? By me? By your old pal Bruiser?"

"Fair," Charlie says. "Fair."

"Hundred yards, moving target, half concealed, one shot. Up your
rating, ass clown."

Charlie thinks back to how he felt two months ago, after Campo, even. He still thought about movies, restaurants, vacations. Beyond the highway, the Kabul skyline is ramshackle—he imagines it as a Chicago suburb after decades of neglect, hotels and financial centers crumbling, mottled dwellings scurrying like roaches up the gray-backed mountains.

"Campo should be here to see this shithole," Charlie says.

"Yeah."

"You know he'd have stats on population, indigenous plant life, fucking cuisine—all of it."

"You're the foodie," Bruiser says. "I expected to hear about Afghani cuisine from your ass."

"*Was* a big foodie. It all seems like posturing now," Charlie says. "When I get back, it's burgers on the grill—that's all I need. You should have seen what I used to order. Rack of venison, medium rare, rosemary crust, raspberry demi-glace. Deconstructed rabbit pot pie. Who does that?"

"Don't know, but it sounds damn good."

"Nah. I'm simplifying. Burger, rare, bloody. All I need is that Tillamook cheddar. You had Tillamook cheddar?"

"I've had American cheese."

"It's from Oregon. They got all these kinds of cheese, but the most famous is the cheddar, and you know how good it is? It wins gold medals in fucking Wisconsin."

"Cheesehead nation," Bruiser says.

"All they do is eat cheddar and watch football. And Tillamook swoops in and crushes the competition."

"Out in Oregon, huh?"

"Oregon. Good golfing up there, too. A lot of it right on the cliffs. You been to Oregon?"

"I've been to Cleveland."

"Well, I'm revising my plan. When we're out, we all fly to Oregon. We get some burgers with Tillamook cheddar, we play golf on the cliffs, get drunk, smoke cigars. Got a problem with that?"

"No problem, Brunson."

Charlie can almost feel the salt spray leaping off the rocks on that Oregon coast. They've got fine wine out there, too, scattered all across the Willamette Valley, but he doesn't want to talk about wine, just like he doesn't want to talk about nice food and art films. Not here. All of those old opinions are on ice, trapped behind steel doors and locked cellars. In his mind's eye, he sees the man he killed, murdered. Shot dead against the rocks. He is a murderer. Had he ever thought, as a soccer-playing child, pulling off muddy cleats and drinking Capri Sun, the smell of summer grass all around, that this could happen? That it could happen to him? Yet here he is.

In the far distance, driving at sixty miles per hour, is a maroon Toyota Corolla, rusted orange along the sides. Bruiser waves at the car to slow down. Two of the other men do the same.

"Another Corolla?" Bruiser says, spitting.

"Ninety percent of the cars in Kabul are Corollas," Charlie says. "It's fucked-up, weird shit like that. Who knows why?"

"Campo tell you that?"

"Who else?"

"This car's not slowing down, either."

The warm breeze picks up again. The airship cloud has moved from the city to the highway. The Corolla keeps on barreling ahead.

"I need identification!" Bruiser shouts, motioning for the Toyota to pull over. "Slow! Hey, slow!"

Charlie runs his index finger along the barrel of the M4.

In the forest, Barkley ran. His face mask was fogging up, and he wanted to find Ginny and Hayward, but saw that he'd gone out of one ravine and into another, this one deeper, with wetter leaves. It looked like there was water ahead. He wondered if his brother would come after him. Hunt him. Like in that short story "The Most Dangerous Game," where General Zaroff waited on an island to play cat and mouse with shipwrecked soldiers. In Barkley's mind, the story was never as shocking as it was supposed to be. A man decided to hunt humans for fun . . . strange, yes, under the pretenses of a polite society. But humans had been hunting each other since the beginning of time. His brother had joined the war, knowing full well it involved hunting other humans. So what was paintball but simply a way to have your cake and eat it, too? Moving forward, he pushed aside more wet leaves and suddenly found himself up to his ankles in muck. Behind him, he heard an exchange of paintball fire—

pop pop pop pop, flit flit flit flit—the second octave coming from Charlie. In the end, there was a scream, a curse, and the sound of his brother laughing merrily.

Inviting Charlie—smart? Stupid? He'd asked him about it last Saturday, just before Halloween, when Hayward called and said he'd be in town again, and why didn't they go to the forest preserve and gather everyone up for an epic battle? And so, knowing that Charlie was probably still in the suburbs, glum and gloomy after that trip to Budapest, Barkley extended the invitation.

"You want to play?" he'd asked over the phone. "Hayward's idea. You'll get to see Hayward again. And Ginny will be there."

"Ginny's not bad," Charlie said, through a haze of static.

"That's correct. My girlfriend is not bad."

And then, with everyone meeting by the picnic tables outside of the forest preserve, Charlie had shown up with something colossal in his hands—"paintball gun" didn't do it justice. And his older brother was grinning.

"That gun looks pretty, um, serious," Barkley said.

Charlie held up the contraption. "Tippmann X7. Cyclone feed with a tac cap hopper. E grip, apex barrel, Trijicon ACOG sight, tri-mount sight-riser, tac light, picatinny covers, M4 stock and mag."

"He's going to kill us all," Hayward said.

It was last man standing they were playing, the demarcations clearly marked. Barkley, Ginny, Hayward (sporting a homemade paintball derringer that flipped from forearm to hand), Mark Harrington, three other friends who'd been B-Team football members, and Charlie, who'd already taken out Harrington.

Barkley heard a branch snap and swung his gun to the left, aiming through the endless rows of matchstick trees beyond the water. Two wine-red birds fluttered out past the branches and broke away, winding in urgent spirals, disappearing into the sky.

Charlie watched his brother run, fall, and roll his way out of the ravine and over the hill. There was a slapstick bent to his younger brother's movements, a kind of vaudeville show with heart. He felt himself

holding back laughter again. Charlie pulled out a map of the forest preserve, tracing a finger across their general location. Barkley was headed
for a series of interlocking ponds—none of them more than six feet
deep, but enough to create a bottleneck. Charlie could flank him and
snipe across the water, or loop around and catch him up close on the
other side. Or he could show his sibling some mercy, and let the kid
walk. At least for a while.

Fuck it. He'd let the B-Teamer have some adventures on his own. It
only made sense to get him last, anyway. The map went back into his
pocket, and he felt his knuckles graze the key chain.

Feeling the key chain was touching flames—as if he'd pocketed the
still-burning embers of some undying enemy campfire. And why shouldn't
it burn? As long as it burned, he was paying his toll.

The Corolla approaches at upwards of sixty miles an hour, heading toward the army checkpoint, into Kabul. From where he stands, Charlie
can see nothing behind the wheel—a shape, maybe. A shadow. A man.
The windshield is smeared with dust and sand and dirt. He flicks the
safety off the M4. It's happened before, these runaway cars. Most of the
civilians slow down, read the signs, submit to the demands of the army.
But runaway cars exist, sometimes bum-rushing, sometimes helmed by
those suicidal fuckers, those human Molotov cocktail hajjis, giving their
lives to blow a couple of soldiers into a funnel cloud of flames and car
parts and severed limbs.

"Motherfucker ain't slowing down," Bruiser says.

The Corolla is two hundred yards away, maybe less. Any closer and
Charlie and the other soldiers will be near the blast radius. He knows
the Taliban protocol—once the soldiers open fire, detonate—any dam-
age at all is good damage. But he thinks this one will want to get closer.
Besides the squad of fifteen soldiers, they have three MRAPs, and the
Taliban love nothing more than to take out army vehicles. He senses
Campo's words, Campo's thoughts and assessments, becoming his own.
What would Campo do? He'd take them out.

"Slow the fuck down, now!" Bruiser yells while Charlie raises the M4.

One hundred and twenty yards. He can make out the chicken scratch license plate, the religious bumper sticker. He weighs the options. Flustered civilians meaning no harm, 30 percent. Taliban supporter ready to die and meet his virgins, 60 percent. Random fuck-up, 10. Happened before, bearded, glassy-eyed motherfuckers stoned or crazy or even blind in one and a half eyes, charging a checkpoint, not knowing sand from snow. But in the Stan, you always play the odds. And the odds, right now, say take them out.

"Slow!" Bruiser screams. He waves his gun in the air. He fires a warning shot into the dirt, then another near the car's engine block. The Corolla barrels ahead.

"Call it," Charlie says.

"Wait, hold up."

"Call it."

"I think he's slowing down. Shit!"

"Now or never, Bruise."

One hundred yards. Charlie's got the stock against his right shoulder now, and through the Aimpoint he can see the shadowed mass behind the wheel and what might be canisters in the backseat. Finger to trigger. Semiauto, no, he feels himself switching to burst, let's light this fucker up. Blow the doors off the rusted shit bird.

He thinks of Campo, as he always does. Campo hanging from the olive tree, Campo's face after they shot it off—and the fact of the matter is that all of them did this to Campo, not one man. They're all the same, one dogma is all the dogmas, one insurgent the whole flock, they are a hive-minded, fucked-up, too-stupid-to-ever-change breed of evil bastards and Charlie is tired of waiting, he's tired of patience, he's tired of giving an IED-packed Toyota Corolla even one more yard in which to intrude on the space of the good and the mighty and the right.

"He's slowing!" Bruiser shouts. "He's slowing!"

"Too late," Charlie says, and actually feels the twinge of vengeance as he pulls the trigger, like a guitar chord being power-strummed. And then the trigger is down and the M4 is chattering in his hands, *pop-pop-pop, pop-pop-pop*, the windshield of the Corolla caving, imploding like a glittering piñata, the car wobbling, blood spattering the ceiling, and the driver's jaw jerking backward, like he's been sucker-punched. But the car is still coming and Charlie hears the rest of the soldiers opening up, blazes coming from all those barrels, holes puckering and denting the sides of the car, and Bruiser saying *aw, hell,* and now Charlie, through the Aimpoint, targeting those fucking containers in the backseats, if he can get them, maybe the car detonates because it's sixty yards away and any closer and they're toast.

"No!" Bruiser shouts.

Charlie thinks Bruiser is yelling about the proximity, and now his magazine is empty and the car is forty yards away and it's slowing, but Charlie is backing up, slamming in another magazine, lighting up the Corolla one more time. Finally the figure behind the wheel slumps forward and the car veers off the road and into the sand. The tires are shredded, metal ruptured, glass dissolved. A single hubcap spins as the car comes to rest. Dust and sand rise above it.

"No," Bruiser says again, and there is real grief in his voice, real hurt.

"Close." Charlie breathes. "You all right?"

"Oh, fuck me. Fuck all this to shit," Bruiser says, throwing his gun to the ground.

"We're good, man," Charlie says. "We got him."

"We got him? We *got* him? Look at what we got. Just look."

And only now does Charlie see the tiny arm hanging from the backseat window. Only now, and that guitar strum in his chest reverberates, changes, merges with the tinnitus that shrieks inside his ears. In the sky, the airship cloud has passed the highway, it's moving on, nothing above but that dome of deep, unrelenting blue.

Barkley received a gift. He was between two long ponds in the second ravine, completely and utterly trapped, and then, voilà.

Even while playing, he couldn't help but think of all the bad news, bad news floating around his family like dense mosquito clouds. His father— a secret he'd kept for over a month, and for what? There had been only brief check-ins, his father telling him nothing, telling him *chemo* but not saying where, and all the while Barkley imagining him getting smaller, losing more weight, his body that ever-deflating balloon. And his brother. Out here, sure. This was his comfort zone. But was old Charlie ever coming back? When should he tell the new Charlie about what was happening with Dad? Ginny said a family meeting was in order, couldn't believe the way things seemed to be crumbling and fissuring among four people who'd lived together for so long, each stranded on a solitary archipelago. You're the one, Ginny kept telling him. You're the one who can fix it.

What was the good news? Well, he had good news, didn't he? His mother did, she was moving forward for the first time in years, though he didn't know where. But her expression, it was like a cavewoman thawed from ice, exploring the new world for the first time. The awe in which she looked at things, the *purpose*. He'd stopped by after teaching the other day and saw her shooting baskets in the driveway with a befuddled Charlie; he drove up, and through the windshield saw his mother swishing a three-pointer that snapped the net right back, like a slap to the face of anyone who would stop her. He sat there in the car and watched her brush her hands off and thought, *This is the mother I heard rumors about, the one I never saw, except maybe when I was little.* When he got inside, she had cookbooks out, and was making something new, she was adamant about it— this was a *new* dish, there was pear and goat cheese and who knew what else but she was making it, wearing bright, pastel colors, all of this to the point where Barkley wasn't sure if she was duping him or not.

And on his end? He was doing well, too, wasn't he? He was. He was getting the hang of teaching. There was the legendarily awful department chair—Dobbs had continued to warn him about Margaret Carey— but beyond her withered, Scrooge demeanor, he'd felt zero blowback. The woman adored him. And he, Barkley, truly loved teaching, couldn't believe that he woke up every day excited. Excited for work. Did *anyone* else feel that way? Even Elise Rossi was good; after their moment in his office she had crossed from her side of the trench to his. She told him things now, dropped by after class, after school with a few of her cronies, told him who was dating whom and what embarrassing thing her parents had done and so on. She didn't quite flock to him, but he felt her on his side, he felt the blue laser beam stare hitting him differently, almost protecting. And it was so much of a seemingly good thing that now his entire life felt precarious—never before had so many things been so good. He was top-heavy with these everyday riches, these little things and big things that added up to a foreign, alien emotion that seemed to be embedded inside him, fighting against the angst that came before. He was happy. When had he felt this way? He stood there in the forest between the two ponds and those tall, white birch trees, and the piles of yellow leaves that rested like fallen aurochs or mastodons—these piles were huge, they really were—he stood among all these things and somehow he was dry and felt good and was happy. And how did happiness feel?

Like being a marked man.

Like he was walking around balancing an enormous golden sphere on his head, a seal training itself to accept the good life. And on top of everything else was his girlfriend. All of his life was top-heavy now, too many good things, and aside from feeling that alien emotion of steady joy, Barkley would wake up in the middle of the night fretting, Ginny by his side with her red hair trailing like a stream, and he'd think, over and over again, *how do I keep all of this?*

Another paintball exchange blasted unseen across the bend, and Barkley decided that he was probably screwed, stuck between these two bodies of water, he was definitely screwed, and this would be the metaphor for the end of happy Barkley. To Barkley, everything was a sign. Hole in the sidewalk, sign. Shooting star, cliché, but sign. Parking space when he needed it, sign, the universe on his team. Signs all around. And if he was shot now, trapped like this, well, probably another sign. He began to run, to trot, he had to make it to the other side of the water and veer left, and he was lighter now, he'd lost six whole pounds eating those stupid neon-green salads in the Eastwick cafeteria. The water went on for another thirty yards or so on both sides—were these actually ponds? Was there a compromise between a pond and a lake? He was screwed, trapped, he literally *felt* how much of a sitting duck he was. And then he saw that across the pond, Hayward was creeping along, staring at something in the opposite direction, no more than twenty feet away.

Gift-wrapped. Unbelievable. Barkley knelt on one knee, positioned the gun, lined up the barrel, felt that mental chasm that usually occurred, where the regular Barkley would have hesitated, but he simply thought, *fuck it.* He closed one eye and pulled the trigger, and green paintballs fired outward, wicked fast. Hayward heard but couldn't pinpoint the direction, and suddenly he was yelping and falling backward and green paint was splashing in the air.

"Gotcha!" Barkley cried. "He gone. You gone. Ra's al Ghul returns!"

"You little prick," Hayward mumbled, sitting up.

Barkley did a little dance. "I think I'm feeling it. I'm drinking my own Kool-Aid."

"Uh-huh. Barkley Kool-Aid smells like desperation and luck. And by the way, pretty sure your brother's taken everyone else out. Dude is like if Conan and a Navy SEAL had a kid, and then trained that kid from birth to play sociopathic paintball. Question: will he skin us and eat us afterward, or does it end with a straight-up guillotine?"

"Pretty sure we're all screwed," Barkley said.

Poor Ginny, Charlie thought, dropping down from the tree. She gave him a pouty face, tossing her hair back, gesturing to the swoosh of paint splotches across her chest and abdomen. And this look from his younger brother's girlfriend, this brief, playful glance that betrayed nothing but friendliness, brought him back to memories of his old self in Chicago, before he'd pulled the pin on his life. He hadn't wanted that existence, to be sure, but Ginny's look reminded him of all those times he'd gone from bar to bar, club to club, watching the girls swoon for him in the flashing lights, and he'd thought, *I'm just like Dad, but nicer. Better.* And yet, even though his father was the truest, purest form of asshole, Henry Brunson had never done any of the things that Charlie Brunson did. No, Henry Brunson only spurned his family. Charlie Brunson—and here the information squeezed out as if from under the crack of a tightly locked door—Charlie Brunson killed *children.* When the words echoed in his mind he wanted to keel forward and vomit. If he walked around with the key chain and thought about Campo and the rest of Alpha Team and all the other fucked-up shit, he wouldn't feel that slithering dagger of knowledge, the knowledge of what he'd done, at least not in those clear, uncompromising words. But even after closing door after door after door, it always came out, from underneath the cracks.

"You okay?" Ginny asked, walking up to him. She was wearing all-black, even her gun looked like oil, and gestured to it. "I thought my ninja black stealth unitard would help me win, Chas."

"That red hair is like a flare gun," he grunted, but managed to smile. "Okay, so who's left?"

"My brother, maybe Hayward."

In the far distance, by the second ravine, they heard Hayward scream and curse, followed by Barkley hooting and hollering.

"Okay, so just the little bro," Charlie said. He checked the ammo on his paintball gun. "The little guy never ceases to amaze."

Ginny punched him in the arm. "Be gentle. That's the boyfriend, okay?"

"I'm going to hit him in the jugular. You don't need to hear him talk, do you?"

"Ugh, how is he supposed to have a chance? You need a handicap. Use a slingshot."

"Don't think so, freckles. Brother Bear is going down."

"Barkley!" Ginny shouted. "Run! Look out! Get your ass to high ground!"

Charlie laughed at that, too. He could laugh at all of it. He could smile and nod and no one would really know what the key chain had done to him, how it was a ticket to watch that movie outside of Kabul all day, every day. Double feature. Triple feature. Constant loop.

Back at FOB Wright, Campo had said to him, he'd said—*You know how I survived two tours in Iraq? You know how I've stayed alive this far? Assume you're already smoked. They already got you. You're in a ditch somewhere. I know the army tells you that, but you gotta feel it. The ironic thing is, if you're already a dead man, there's almost nothing you can't accomplish. All that fear washes away like pig shit.* But now, Charlie thought, it didn't make sense to think like that. He was in the cyclical suburbs of safety and strip malls. It didn't make sense, but it was still in his mind. He was dead, he wanted to be dead, but he'd passed the timeline where it was supposed to happen and now here he was, inexplicably alive. And the thing was, it made him miserable, besieged, but still totally unafraid, and his younger brother was out there, and you'd better believe he was going to get him.

Barkley made it past the twin pond-lakes, green-gray water lapping against piles of smooth stones. Then he went to higher ground, scuffled through some leaves, and sat against a thick birch tree to reload his paintball gun. Charlie was out there. He had that damn sniper-scoped bazooka and superior training, and hell, Barkley had *zero* training. The only physically aggressive class he'd ever taken was karate as a nine-year-old, where he began and ended as a white belt—walking away with the knowledge of how to throw a dorky-looking punch. And he knew his older brother was going to make him feel it, really hit him hard.

Hayward spread his arms wide. "He's out there, can you feel it? He's coming for you."

"Uh-huh."

"Twenty-Second Man versus twenty kills."

"You're a bastard. And why don't you give me some space? Run interference or something?"

Hayward still had that long, angular head and close-cropped black hair. He was skinny but less gangly than before, and Barkley imagined him in Brooklyn, wearing skinny jeans and thick-framed glasses, drinking Belgian Trappist ales from hipster-approved goblets. He'd found his look. And Barkley saw that he had to find his own, and if he did, if he found a style that was actually *him*, maybe it would help him hold on to the good feeling he seemed to be fretfully balancing like a circus performer.

"I'm going over to that log to watch the show," Hayward said.

"Watch away."

"You got a plan?"

Barkley looked over the leaf-strewn ridge where he assumed his brother was lurking. He was tired of losing to Charlie. And he wanted his brother to acknowledge—to be forced to acknowledge—that things were different now.

"Hey, Earth to Barkley. You got a plan?"

"No plan. I mean, what's Charlie's weakness? He's precise, trained to kill, he's got strategy, he's smart, angry—" Suddenly, Barkley knew how he could beat Charlie.

Hayward stared at him. "Yeah, and? Angry . . . and?"

"I think that's all I need." He stood, heart thumping. "It's a small thing to go on, I realize, but I think that's enough to take the cocky bastard out. Charlie is the angriest person I know."

The Corolla sits there with that single spinning hubcap as the dust rises and slides, rises and slides. Charlie realizes he's been holding his breath. No one moves.

"Fuck me," Bruiser says. He is squatting down, looking at the open highway. "I don't believe it. I just don't fucking believe it."

"He charged us," Charlie says, but feels a sinking, draining feeling, a sensation he will later describe as his soul slipping away from his body.

"I said to hold your fucking fire, didn't I? Didn't I say to hold your fire?"

The tinnitus kicks up harder, steel I-beams struck with a thousand crowbars. Charlie approaches the car. The Corolla is ten feet off the highway, partially on its side, littered with bullet holes like rusted sores. He steps closer, sand on his boots and the cracked highway pavement. The rest of the men stay back. At ten feet away, he can see the driver slumped forward, a man, midforties, missing part of his face. Dressed like a civilian. But so what, they're all dressed like civilians, all the hajjis wear the sandals and beards, all of them dress like they mean no harm, and that's how they get you.

More disconcerting—the arm hanging out of the rear passenger window. What Charlie hopes as he approaches the rear door is that it belongs to a prop, a plastic toy, more Taliban subterfuge to sneak past soldiers and blow shit up. Yes, Charlie thinks, it's the only thing that makes sense. A prop.

But, of course, there's blood on her hand, and it's that detail—not the blood, but the fact that he knows it's a *her*, that causes Charlie to seize up, sucking air, almost dropping to his knees.

"I told you to hold your fucking fire!" Bruiser is screaming behind him.

Inside the car are the girl and her mother. The mother is dead, mercifully turned away—he can't look at her. But the unmoving girl, with her bronzed, oval face and charcoal eyes, is looking right at him. Nine, maybe ten years old. She looks fine, normal, a little wooden, maybe, minus the eyes that return his stare like an abyss. Her clothes, though, all of them, appear to be drenched with Kool-Aid. She's gone. Far gone. Charlie manages to tear his gaze away from her eyes. In the girl's right hand is a key chain. Minnie Mouse, a tiny cartoon caricature, is painted on the side. And instinctively, Charlie takes it. Pockets it. Feels the heat, the heft, the weight, immediately.

From that night forward, he builds a wall. Many walls, rows of them, all working to protect him from the siege of emotions. But it's the thinking he can't stop. Small ideas sown into truths. Aside from his assassination of three innocent civilians, and the ethical destruction it promised, were further associations, rushing forth like brutal tributaries. Maybe that girl would have grown up to do something special—really special. To cure a disease or bring peace to Afghanistan or go to school at Cambridge or Harvard or Stanford. And Charlie has ended that trajectory, has truncated her sacred path so completely that he can only surmise the things she would have done, could have done. And then he considers that one day she would have met a man who would have been impossibly happy to have her, who would have embraced her and clutched her to his chest and protected her, and now that man, in the future, has no wife. And they, as a couple, have no kids, and now two beautiful children, maybe three, don't exist because of him. *Can't* exist because of him. And in the future is a lonely man who will always feel an absence, a crater, who keeps looking but cannot find because of what Charlie has taken away with his anger and his rage and his big, black gun and his unthinking hail of death. Charlie can't imagine anything but this alternate future where the girl and her family are still alive. He has wiped them out. He is singularly responsible. Whole timelines disintegrated. And most crushing is that this is one incident out of how many—thousands? Millions? Charlie finds himself forever connected, forever responsible, this one timeline of millions, this web of innocent lives irrevocably stricken from the record.

He thinks it would have been better if her face had not been spared, if his bullets had rendered her unidentifiable, because then there would be nothing human to tie her to, then he won't think he sees her every day on the sidewalk, in the street, the playground, the park. The face he remembers is a doll's face, browned features stuck in amber, with the blank, unseeing eyes of the abyss. There is also the knowledge that if he had gotten smoked, shot down like Campo promised, the Corolla and the girl would have passed unharmed. And yet she is gone, and he remains.

Charlie moved on his stomach, working his elbows and knees, and sifted through wet foliage to the crest of the second ravine. He set up shop between two birch trees three feet apart, on his stomach, looking through the scope. In the ravine, the twin ponds stretched out, a mess of slippery waterways and random stones. No Barkley. Too quiet. He considered, uncomfortably, the idea of his younger brother getting the drop on him, but then calmed himself with the knowledge that Barkley's approach would be bumbling and leaf-shaking, like Tarzan on roller skates.

The laughter threatened to rumble in his throat again. Why did this feel so good? Being here in the woods, surrounded by trees and ponds, all things raw. But that wasn't all of it. All this crawling around and exchanging fire: a time machine. He could remember how he felt before that Corolla had charged his squad on the highway, he could remember the intricate levels of emotion that ran through his body like prairie dog tunnels, so many notes and routes, many of which, even when he was scared shitless, felt good. And he, too, before all of that went down, had been good. Strong soldier. Terrific shot. Friend of many. And imbued with that feeling of doing something right, even when the statistics of what they did seemed inconsequential.

His phone buzzed. A text message from Barkley—*Just wanted to let you know. I really care about you, bro.*

Charlie's stomach gurgled. He typed back furiously. *Stop that shit. I'm hunting your ass down.*

But Charlie, I think it's important that I let you know how thankful I am that you're my brother.

B-Team. Shut the fuck up, stop being a wet blanket, and play the damn game.

I love you, bro.

Charlie knew he was being played, and all the same, he hadn't seen it coming. He'd said precisely zero emotive comments to his family since returning, and this was like being stabbed with a warm butter knife. He felt his focus slip and then reel back as his phone buzzed again. He looked through the scope. Nothing. Then—there—movement. He concentrated. Was that Hayward or Barkley, just right of the easternmost pond? His phone buzzed a third time, then a fourth.

"Motherfucking B-Team!" Charlie screamed. He flipped open his phone, trying to turn it off, but the messages spilled forward.

Dear Chas, I miss playing Stratego with you. Remember when I took your Marshall with my Spy? We should hang out more.

Chas, I wrote a zombie story. I'd really like to share it with you. Love, Barkley.
I. Love. You. Bro.
These paintballs are actually love bullets.

Finally, Charlie yanked the battery out and the screen went dark. "Holy shit," he breathed. "Worse than the fucking Taliban."

And at that moment of cellular assassination, Barkley rolled out from under a tree, thirty yards to his nine o'clock, and opened fire. It was a piss-poor roll, Charlie thought. His younger brother still wasn't lithe, even though it looked like he was losing weight, and he wasn't very agile or coordinated, and there really wasn't a reason at all to roll. Charlie considered all this as if a second brain were watching from above, he considered it as he pushed himself into the air and swung his legs underneath his torso, bringing up the Tippmann X7 to return fire, and he considered it as Barkley's bright green paintballs thudded into his chest and arms and face mask. The impacts were harsh and needlelike, and he felt himself falling backward, foot catching a submerged root, blue sky swinging into view. He crashed against the wet leaves and dirt and heard Barkley's cheers along with the sounds of the birds and the wind ringing in his ears. Above him, in the tree, a squirrel—the same squirrel?—bounced across a high branch.

Charlie didn't move. He let himself sink back into the damp leaves around him. He lay there and felt the sting of the paintballs across his chest and shoulders, the bump forming on the back of his head, and looked up at the sky that was the same as it had always been. He considered, hearing the footsteps of Barkley and his friends approaching, that this is how it would feel if he had died, if the bullets were only too real. He'd be lying here, looking upward and hearing the sound of the approaching enemy, closing in, condensing around him. He'd keep his eyes on the sky. This was how it would feel. His vision would get misty, fingers of fog crossing his mind. There would be a lifting and at the same time a sense of dissolve, of hundreds of working pieces pulling apart, scattered like bolts and screws and rivets in the air. Here Charlie existed, now Charlie scattered, metaphysical dust. That big blue sky sucking what remained like a vacuum, all of him gone, all of him lifting and pulling apart, and below, his enemies circling the shell that was left.

Charlie finally felt himself laughing. It was like helium inside his chest, soap bubbles, champagne. He saw Barkley's face looking down at him, then Ginny's, then Hayward's. Didn't matter. It was all so simple, the realization, the freeing, gravity-defying, soul-lifting thing—so simple, yet he said it aloud as the knowledge passed through him. His own death, his own passing, even if it happened right now, *it wouldn't do any good*. If this was him getting shot, the end of his times, no, it didn't serve any purpose, it didn't atone and set straight, it was just more passing, more dissolving, more matter into blue sky. And he felt himself laughing with the knowledge, the sweet, pure knowledge that he didn't need to die.

"Charlie? You all right?"

"I think he hit his head."

Charlie cleared his throat. "You little bastard," he said, and started laughing again.

"I'm going to lift you up," Barkley said. "You big douche bag." He extended his hand.

Above him, the squirrel jumped from branch to branch, then diagonally, across one tree and into another. Charlie closed his eyes and took a breath. It was quiet out here. No sounds from America, no voice in his head, not a car to be heard.

MISS HENLEY
RETURNS

Christmas in Downers was a suburban Christmas. Lavender drifts swung up against the sides of houses, children puffed as if run on coal, icicles shattered like crystal vases. All around Julie's street, the decorations went up. The elderly Mr. and Mrs. Fox had the bulbous, colored lights, the size of glowing prunes, strung out across needled bushes. The O'Connors went for all-blue, turning their snow a luminous fluorescent. And the D'Agostinos, hosts of the epic summer block party, brought out the heavy artillery: flashing, animatronic elves, wooden reindeer pawing legs toward flight, candy canes like sentinels, and a great plastic Santa, glowing with cartoon mirth. Julie eschewed all of these options, deeming them easy, bizarre, or gaudy. She went for class. White lights strung along the eaves and the posts that flanked the door, a pristine front yard, and, as always, a majestic Fraser fir unfolding its branches in the front window. Only the Fraser was allowed colored lights, but they had to be small and softly winking, the tree giving off the scent of earthy pine. Its branches were adorned with stately glass ornaments, wood-carved bakeries, avant-garde angels, antique toyshops. It took days to put it all together. But these decorations—and her garden—had been the sole outlets of her creativity for years. And even though she was discovering new ways to be herself again, there was nothing wrong with staying true to what had worked before.

Some of the ornaments were from five years ago, ten years, thirty. With each object lifted from the storage box she remembered life at that moment—the friends who'd drifted or remained, the ever-evolving husband she'd struggled to keep entertained. The frosted glass snowflake from Marshall Field's? 1989. She was thirty-five, Charlie nearly six, Barkley two. Henry driving the Audi 5000 and screeching up the driveway, kicking open the back door, walking in singing, whistling, clapping his knees for the kids to come running. She—and she hated to admit the cliché of it—was at the stove. Making chicken Parmesan or beef bourguignonne for the family, burrowing her true desires into pockets she never knew she had. But Henry. It amazed her to remember that this version of her husband had existed: the youthful adult, middle-aged yet joyful, proud of a marriage that was young at heart. He kissed her when he came in, grabbed her ass when the kids weren't looking, mumbled any one of their countless jokes with his lips against her ear. And she'd had a jump in her step, too. Even with dance gone it seemed as if this could be temporary—she always had more time. And there was so much else to do, what with each of her children a vortex of energy, demanding worlds of attention on their own.

While the Fraser stood tall in the front window, Julie proceeded to load the adjacent fireplace with logs. Even if they didn't have a fire, she liked the wood in there, expectant. She hung three stockings on the brass hooks above the hearth—the first time she'd not done four—and sure, there was a sting, but she moved right through it, let it pass like a ghostly wasp. Emotions, she thought—it wasn't until lately that she'd started seeing humor in them, and the gravity with which other people experienced their spectrum. She placed a miniature horse and sleigh, dusted white with artificial snow, covered with a glass dome, atop the mantel. Emotions slugged left and right, frothed like rapids, flattened out and then leaped forth again. And the startling thing was looking back and realizing that they never stopped; from the moment she'd been born, she'd trailed her own river of constant, ever-changing emotion. And the key, what had freed her, was realizing that just because she rode the river didn't mean she *was* the river.

With Barkley planning to return home for all of Christmas break, it was nice to imagine the house full again—her youngest had declared that not spending the week that led up to the big day in his childhood home, with all the decorations, was simply wrong. Words like this were magic to the ears. She imagined it was like a painter being told that her depiction of something—a thatched cottage, an icy plain, vineyards under moonlight—had meant a great deal to a dear friend who had viewed it, thus validating the years it had taken putting brush to canvas, creating a vision out of nothing. Yet even with three-fourths of the original family together, she wondered about Henry. No contact, not a peep, just those monthly stipends showing up in her checking account, arriving automatically and without comment. When she'd asked the kids if either of them had heard from their father, Charlie had gruffly said no, not since being flown home from Eastern Europe, and Barkley had said *not really,* and followed that with a bout of fidgeting, like he'd suffered a sugar rush while wearing a straitjacket. *Anything of interest to share?* she'd asked, and Barkley had said, again, *not really,* and then got up and gone to the gym. And then Julie had gone out to prepare for her first dance class and the eleven over-forty female students who had enrolled. The conversation had never been finished, and Henry was still out there, a silent anomaly among the festive array of glowing decorations.

Well, she would hear from him soon enough, she thought, either by voice or by signature. The divorce papers had been sent out, crafted with a good deal of demand and urgency by her new lawyer, Raymond Askins, a bulldog of a man who was always chomping on a wad of Juicy Fruit and asking people if they'd heard the goddamn good word. When Julie had asked what the good word was, Askins had thrown his head back and guffawed and said *this here is a funny one* to his bombshell of a secretary. But when they got down to brass tacks, Raymond Askins revealed his clout, and promised to deliver her a divorce quicker than an inside fastball, faster than Jimmy John's. *We're gonna get this guy,* he told her, and Julie said that would be great, and then Askins had leaned over his polished wooden desk, placed a stick of Juicy Fruit in her palm, and said, *now you know what the good word is, don't you, Miss Henley?*

She hadn't heard her maiden name uttered aloud in decades, and that had certainly floored her, but all the way home, and all the days since, she'd been saying *Miss Henley* to herself and grinning like a madwoman.

PAPERWEIGHT

Barkley cleared his throat, feeling lighter on his feet, but as usual—hungry. Always hungry. Ten pounds lost, pants hanging off hip bones like loose hinges on a double-wide door. Outside the windows, a white mess of blizzard was coming down. Inside, the twenty-nine drooping heads in the class stared at Barkley, the snow, or the smudged tiles on the floor. Barkley tried to focus, but he couldn't stop eyeballing the cardboard cut-outs of elves and Christmas trees and halos that the student council committee had plastered to every spare bulletin board and drywall slab in the school. Maybe he was used to the streamlined, secular attitude of his public school upbringing, but there was almost something force-fed about all the Christmastime propaganda. The merriment was everywhere, suffocating, each holiday emblem stapled roughly and routinely and without even a grazing eye for interior design. Only his desk was untouched—a cedar rectangle of antique compartments and swollen drawers, each space stuffed with more and more essays, unit plans, and off-center, photocopied handouts. Mounted on the desk were a late 1990s Dell computer, two containers of ballpoint pens, and a black stapler, forever out of ammunition.

Barkley waited, pacing as the class completed their three-minute in-dependent reading response.

"Sixty seconds," he called out.

He gazed down at his feet, clad in black Banana Republic leather loafers—bought after his second Eastwick paycheck. The shoes seemed a little too nice, a little too mainstream, but the real problem was his feet. He'd noticed them three days ago, marveling that he'd never seen it before. They suddenly appeared to be shrunken and tiny, almost offen-sive to his senses. Bent and precarious, these shriveled, bipedal means of awkward transport confounded him every time he glanced at the floor. Bizarrely, this thought was a new one. He'd woken up in Chicago, seen them peeking out from under his sheets, and thought: just too damn small.

"Finish up whatever you've been writing," Barkley said, glancing at the smooth contours of his desk.

There was truly nothing there. At first, he'd been unsure of how to personalize the desk. Was he really supposed to? And what did *personalize* mean? To reveal the real Barkley, perhaps. Yet, if he brought in his ceramic hobbit figurine and the pterodactyl paperweight and the *Back to the Future* hand-painted model DeLorean, it would only cause his stu-dents to drop the nerd guillotine upon him. So that left traditional nonsense like miniature Chicago team pennants or a couple of framed photographs of his family, standing among the hair-ruffling winds of Lake Michigan. Boring. But better than nothing? In the end, he couldn't de-cide, and simply left his desk clean and bare as a sand trap. But he did keep the pterodactyl paperweight in the second desk drawer from the bottom, just in case he changed his mind.

In front of him, the class gradually began to lay their pens and pen-cils down—soldiers all too willing to surrender their arms.

"We done? Yes? Good. Let's get started then. Get right into it. What is Tim O'Brien saying here, guys? I want you to think of this specifically in terms of each person's individual cargo. Why would their personal belongings matter? Why not talk memories? Or give flashbacks? Why use actual objects?"

Barkley waited two seconds, three, then stood still by the wooden podium for a full, unwinding ten—an eternity. Todd Brennan looked vacant. The radiator underneath the windows popped. Shuman had what appeared to be a dozen paper clips assembled into some kind of hook.

"Put that away, Shuman."

"But it's for science class."

"No, it's not. Did you read the story?"

Shuman held up the paper clip hook. "For you, Mr. Brunson. The first gift of Christmas."

The class chuckled, and Barkley fumed, snatching the device and tossing it behind his desk. On the walls, the posters for Thoreau, Hawthorne, and Poe seemed weather-beaten—the corners coming undone.

"Listen up. Who read *The Things They Carried?* Anyone?"

The radiator popped three times, metallic clanks making Barkley think of his father, trapped in some kind of full-body CAT scan. Elise, sitting in the back, was texting, half discreetly. Not even worth it, Barkley thought. Forty-eight more hours and they'd all escape. And then, a sharp, deflating memory of his old self, as the bumbling student teacher, struck him in the temple like a barroom dart. He straightened up and raised his voice.

"Who read?" he asked again. "You guys shouldn't be afraid to admit that you've done the work and read a good story. Come on, it's the Vietnam War. I'm not assigning you *bad* stories."

"I read," Shuman said. "It actually was pretty good." Gradually, Gilroy, Tolliver, and Jennifer Alston followed suit and raised their hands.

"I did skim," Elise said. "I mean, I really did look at it."

"Fine. Now pay attention, class. I know it's two days before winter break, and I feel it, too, but we're going to have a discussion here. We're going to finish strong. Let's go. Shuman, I'm starting with you. Listening?"

"Yes, sir."

"Everyone else in here listening?"

The class mumbled their assent.

"All right. So every character in this story is in grave danger. Their lives can be taken away at any moment. It's the Vietnam War. It's the jungle, with sickness, traps, enemy bullets and mortars, little food, little water. Life is cheap. One minute alive, one minute dead. Imagine that, guys. Walking through a dense, humid, green wall of jungle, knowing that at any moment, a bullet could have your name on it. Okay? Got it, Shuman?"

"Got it."

"Now, *why* does it matter what these soldiers are carrying? Why does it matter more here, than it would if they were back in America, walking into the Gap or Jamba Juice or Caribou Coffee? When they're so close to death, why do we need to know what's in their pockets? Shuman, what have you got?"

"Well, um, I don't know. Because it's all they have?"

"Okay," Barkley said. "I hear you. That's a start. What do you mean it's all they have?"

"Um . . . like, they could die any minute, right?"

"Right."

"So, if you know you're going to die any minute, you're not going to carry, like, money or stupid stuff. You don't need credit cards. I mean, it's the jungle."

Barkley saw the eyes of the class on him now. "Guys, you hear what Shuman is saying? If you know you're going to die at any minute, certain things don't matter, do they? You wouldn't need to carry certain items, like money and credit cards. What else?"

"Eyeliner," Maggie Tolliver chirped, from the back of the class.

"Good, right, makeup is out the window. Who needs it? Appearance isn't that important. What else?"

"Car keys?" Todd Brennan said.

"Sure, keys, stuff like that. Typical things you use for everyday civilian life. There's a lot you wouldn't need. Now, what does O'Brien say these men are actually carrying? Give me an example from the text."

"I don't get this," Todd Brennan said.

Wolverine raised his hand. "I've got this, Mr. B."

"Go," Barkley said, feeling the current of the room change.

"So, okay, it's, like, what you actually care about, or what is a necessity, these dudes are carrying. I forget what page, but like, they say a couple things that the soldier really gets worked up about, like a picture of his girlfriend, and his favorite radio, and then some kind of emotion, like fear. Or something. I don't know. But in the book it keeps getting listed like that. It's the important stuff, and then it's the emotional stuff.

Whereas here in Downers Grove, there might be a whole extra layer of random items—iPhones and whatnot that keep us from seeing the real things we're carrying. And then, Mr. Brunson, beyond those layers is like, *life*, man . . . *life* beyond the layers, the ties which bind. You know, Plato, Aristotle—"

Barkley gave him the thumbs-up. "Okay, I'll stop you there. But the thing is, you're right. Before you went overboard you were absolutely right. Think about the contrast of—"

There was a rap at the door. Barkley saw Margaret Carey's head peering through the window. She waved him forward.

"Okay, class, good work. I'm going to step outside, you all just, um, catch up on your reading, all right?"

"This is still too much symbolism, even if it makes sense," Elise said, groaning.

"No, this story is pretty decent," Shuman said. "You guys just aren't paying attention. Right, Mr. B? See how I just stood up for the story?"

Barkley strode into the hallway and closed the door behind him, facing Margaret Carey, whose presence evoked the smell of mothballs and rubbing alcohol. Her floppy brown hair, thick glasses, yet another maroon dress—she looked the same as always, but with strange shadows under her eyes. Lack of sleep? Hard to tell.

Margaret Carey had been as kind as a cartoon grandmother during the first months of classes, bustling into his classroom to offer help, fussing over the smallest concerns, and relaying gossip about the other English teachers. But as Barkley became more and more confident in the classroom, Carey had smiled at him less and less. And even her gossip became more malicious. It was like a friend who first revealed her pottery collection, before opening the curtains on all the guns. For instance, the story from a week ago, about the recently pregnant Ellen Hennessy, who'd told Carey she could no longer run Yearbook due to her maternity leave. *I don't know,* Carey had said to him, *she just might be putting herself in a precarious position, if she prefers continued employment. Baby or no baby.*

Barkley had walked away from that particular encounter with his thoughts doing lazy shark circles in his brain. *Baby or no baby.* Each time he convinced himself that Margaret Carey hadn't just confided the idea of firing a pregnant teacher, another dorsal fin popped up, the bubbles breaking the surface, and he heard the loopy growl of her voice: *Baby or no baby.*

But he had to be okay. Safe, even. Just last week, another parent had called in to offer positive words—this time Shuman's mother. She'd dialed Danny Peters and said, *I don't know what Mr. Brunson is doing, but my son is actually reading. We don't even have to argue with him anymore.* Barkley had been filled with pride for days, imbued with that unique glow that came from producing an evolution—however small, however obviously fragile—in another person. Getting Shuman to read. It was an event so tiny, so tenuous, that Barkley felt like he was holding a feeble mockingbird in cupped hands. If he banged into a wall, or oversold a lesson, or pushed for too many pages, the bird would screech and flap away, changing back to what it had been. But so far, he had done it, and Shuman came in every day nodding and discussing, and Barkley gave his sarcasm a pass.

"*Barkley,*" Carey said, throwing a noose around his reverie. "I'm talking to you."

Barkley centered himself and nodded. "Yes, I'm sorry. Just thinking about the lesson. Some great short stories we've been discussing lately."

She stared at him. The blue-and-yellow hallways were quiet as tombs.

"So, what can I help you with, Margaret?"

"I still haven't given you my formal observation report," Carey said, tartly. "It's due before break begins."

"Really? I mean, you've been so helpful when you've sat in on class, and I thought those counted as—"

"Those were *informal* observations. I told you that. Of course, you remember that there's a rubric. And I think you recall my suggestion against using so much PowerPoint. *I* prefer writing on the board. And at this time, I have to say, I haven't seen any changes."

Barkley's mind swam, and he dove back in with the sharks. He taught with PowerPoint occasionally, mainly because his undergraduate teaching program had constantly stressed the use of technology in the classroom. It was a buzzword during applications and interviews. *What are your philosophies of education, Mr. Brunson?* And the buzzwords shot out like salvos from a battleship. Differentiating instruction! Using technology! Managing 504 plans correctly! Et cetera. But in the time warp that was the Catholic—Catlick?—school system, modern buzzwords didn't seem applicable. It was like a medieval community, all bell towers and castle ramparts and well water, witnessing the passing of a UFO. Carey, the most old-school of any teacher he'd met, tended to distrust unidentified futuristic teaching styles more than most.

"I've really tried to balance it out," Barkley said. "It's difficult. I can write completely on the board, but sometimes it helps to give the kids visual aids."

Carey glared at him, dark eyes magnified. "Don't misinterpret what I'm saying, Barkley. I simply asked for a *decrease* in PowerPoint, and it's something I haven't seen."

Barkley ran a slideshow of past lessons. Short stories—"Crazy Sunday," "The Killers," "Cathedral," "A & P." Had he actually been using PowerPoint with great frequency? Did it matter? His brow felt damp. No, it didn't matter; what mattered was agreeing with the woman. He would tear the intestines from the ceiling projector's belly if it meant Carey wasn't on his back, hounding him like he was poor Ellen Hennessy.

"Absolutely, Margaret, you're right. I think you will definitely see progress this time around. I'm sorry about that. It will be fixed."

"It's important to put the children first, Barkley."

Barkley felt himself recoil. And then, the pressing question: why was she having this conversation now, while he had a class going on?

"Yes, yes, I agree completely," he said, clenching his fists.

"And this still leaves the issue of your missing teaching observation, to be done by me."

"Well, good thing we caught it! I guess any time in the next two days. We're discussing *The Things They Carried* right now. It's really, really fruitful for classroom discussion, and very timely, and—"

"Do you know why we're in this position, Barkley? Why we haven't completed the observation yet?"

At the end of the hallway, Barkley caught the eye of Mike Dobbs, who was carrying a stack of photocopied instructions on frog dissection. Dobbs saw Carey and mock-gagged. Then he put his hand into a makeshift gun, raised it to his temple, and pulled the trigger, exaggerating the headshot. Thank God for Dobbs, Barkley thought.

"*Barkley*," Carey hissed.

"Yes, yes, I'm trying to remember the reason. I'm not sure. I thought you sent an e-mail, or maybe spoke with me in person, and said we had to get this done."

"It was e-mail. And I asked you to give me a date to come in. You never responded. It was crucial that you respond, and this was not accomplished."

"*Wait*," Barkley said. "Wait. I talked to you about this a couple weeks ago, one-on-one. I said you could come in anytime this week or last week. We talked about the short story unit."

"I don't remember that," Carey said softly.

Barkley looked back at the end of the hallway, but Dobbs was gone. Carey adjusted her glasses. Barkley felt his back against the classroom door.

"We spoke about it in your office," Barkley said.

"I don't remember that, and in terms of the e-mail, there was no reply. No reply, Barkley, tells me you're not putting the children first."

Barkley felt as if the hallway had been doused with freezing winter air. Something was happening. It wasn't gradual, it wasn't a slow evolution, it was happening *right now* and he couldn't figure out what it was. He remembered back when he'd been getting his teaching degree, his instructor Ted Vera had warned the class to *always* respond to e-mails. It was crucial. Even if conversation was easier, even if a response didn't seem necessary, always follow with the electronic response. Cover your bases, Vera had said. And Barkley had always wondered, until now, what exactly he had meant.

"You're right," Barkley said, feeling his throat catch. "You're right. I should have responded. I thought we talked about it in person, but I can see how an e-mail would have made everything clearer."

Carey peered into his classroom. "You should probably return and get your class in order. They appear discontented."

Barkley nodded, mumbled, and unclenched his hands so they could go around the doorknob. Then he thought, maybe, it could be smart to—

"One thing, Margaret. Some good news, actually. Danny Peters let me know that the Shuman family called in to say some good things about the class. They said Shuman was actually reading on his own, you know, autonomously, and completing all the assignments without having to be nagged. They seemed really happy. So, I just wanted to relay that—because that seems like good news, right? Something positive. He's come a long way, and I'm . . . I'm . . . um . . . Margaret?"

Margaret Carey turned and walked away, heels clacking like gunshots.

Barkley blinked. He realized his teeth were biting down on his lower lip. Carey continued down the color-smeared hallway, head down, barreling past the Christmas decorations like an ancient but incensed reindeer. Barkley tasted bile in the back of his throat. He'd had parents calling in to say what a good job he was doing—Mrs. Shuman had been the fourth that he knew of. Dobbs said he was doing great. But none of that explained what had happened. And as Barkley felt yet another awful memory of student teaching hit him in the temple, he realized he didn't feel deflated—he felt angry. A white-hot rage, a burning egg deep inside his chest, ready to hatch and spew fire.

For the rest of the day, he taught furiously, prodigiously. He wove eloquent, winding monologues about the nature of war and what human beings carry and the thought that maybe, just maybe, there was always a war going on, both before and after the cannons fired. He threw ideas like birdseed upon the class, he was a whirling dervish of feverish, nearly feral ideas. He split the classes into warring factions and made them discuss aggressively, he clamored for an anonymous poll on the abstractions people lug inside them, he had the students plot out graphs and pie charts of their own carried items, measuring importance, size, and frequency. He paced, listened, raged, took notes, and diagrammed on the board as if he were plotting an amphibious landing in Europe. By fifth period, he felt the sweat leaking through the pores of his undershirt, collecting on his neck, armpits, crotch, knee pits. Good. Keep it coming. By eighth, it felt like a Bic razor had been run along the inside of his throat. Each word of encouragement was scratchy and coarse. His feet, his tiny feet, those wobbly excuses for structural support and mobilization, sent pulse beacons of hurt from his heels to his brain. He forgot about them.

He hurled his bag underneath his desk at the end of the day. No, he thought, it wasn't fair, he always put the children first, what an insult, like being slapped with a glove by your own mother, except Margaret

Carey wasn't his mother, she was an imposter, a wild, senile Doberman who would have been long retired if this were a public school, but somehow, here, she was allowed to run free. And now she was on the loose, setting her lasers on him just like she had with Ellen Hennessy, but guess what, guess *what*? He wasn't lying down. He was going to out-teach the entire school. Sure, maybe there were some legends in here, and he wasn't in this to topple hallowed monuments, but he was going to erect his own, he was going to lesson plan until he was bloody, unplug his PlayStation 3—beer he would allow, yes, beer was fine—but he would decimate all other distractions, he would crush, pulverize, incinerate, and liquefy any prejudices this woman had and in the process get these kids so jacked on reading, so skilled at composition, it was a veritable literary army he would create, storm troopers with the minds of poets, muscle-bound GIs with lethal training in Fitzgerald, Updike, Hemingway, and Carver.

When he caught himself thinking about Faulkner, and his first encounter with Ginny at the bookstore, he allowed himself a grim, teeth-grinding chuckle, staring out at the continuous parade of blinding snow. No, he would not release his anger, his pride, his frustration, he would not laugh, he was going to bottle this feeling—age it in bourbon barrels, lay it down in a dark cellar. Get it strong. Good. He was glad she'd insulted him. It was excellent. He'd been pissed on for too many years by Charlie and his disapproving father and by the faces of girls who, instead of judging or ridiculing, didn't even register him on their radar. But now he had the girlfriend and he had the teaching job and he was going to drive his stake into the sand. Not only was he not going anywhere, he was going to win. And all of Eastwick would be forced to admit it.

Before he left, Barkley reached into the second drawer from the bottom in his desk and pulled out the pterodactyl paperweight. It was about four pounds, five inches tall, with detail even a paleontologist would love—sharply defined bone and wing structure, waxy yellow skin, beak open to reveal rows of glinting silver teeth. At the bottom, its clawed feet had snagged a wriggling, slippery-scaled, prehistoric fish. Below the fish was the dense metal square that served as the weight. He'd gotten the pterodactyl at a county fair up in coastal Michigan, where his family had vacationed for years. All he remembered of the fair was fluttering county flags and a woman with a graying beehive of hair, watching him as he spotted the dinosaur. As a ten-year-old child, he'd clutched it to his chest, displayed it by his bed like an athletic trophy, and written stories just so the pterodactyl could weigh the pages down. And here, now, his old friend was back. Barkley raised it in the air.

"Cheers, Margaret Carey," he said, even though it was only him and the paperweight and the snow against the windows. "Cheers," he repeated, feeling that white-hot rage in his throat, and brought the pterodactyl down like a gavel.

TOXINS

Henry held the divorce papers while he peered out the window of his penthouse, at the twilight sprawl of Lake Michigan, filled with chunky slabs of ice and distant blinking lights. Overhead, twin illuminated dots marked the passing of a 747, moving over the penthouse with a guttural hum.

Jets, Henry thought, feeling another wave of chemo-induced weariness. He sat down on his black leather couch. Charlie's first word had been *jet*. Barkley's had been *bottle*, and his own had been *mine*, but Charlie? His first word had been *jet*. And from that moment on, Henry knew his firstborn was destined for greatness. Henry loved telling the story. Some kids had first words like *ma* or *pa* or *hungry* or *potty*, some kids babbled and spit out gibberish that slurred together in a kind of slot machine of randomness until they said something that resembled a word, but Charlie's had been real. He'd pointed a chubby pink finger at the silver plane streaking across the sky and said, quite clearly, quite musically, *jet*. Still, it didn't stop other parents from inventing their own realities.

"Jessica just said *antique!*" Mike McCormick had gushed some twenty-seven years ago, leaning against the red fence that separated their back-yards. Henry had walked away chuckling. Sure she did. *Antique.* And her second word would be *polymer* and her third, *vestigial,* and so on. He'd gone into the house and Julie was bouncing Charlie on her knee in the kitchen and Henry could see in the way his son's soft brown eyes looked around the room and made solemn eye contact that the boy was intelligent, even-keeled, and without a doubt going to make it. A go-getter. This was his baby. Damn straight, *jet.*

In those days, Henry found suburban life a joy. Truly. He loved the city but had grown tired of its musty passageways, of the soot and traffic and the endless honking of the buses, of the knife-chill during winter and the horrible parking on slush-covered streets, not to mention the towering, honeycombed apartments that every day seemed to fill with more and more people who were not from Chicago, who knew nothing about Chicago, who complained about Chicago and didn't know its rhythms. More and more he saw tourists stomping toward the gray behemoth that was the Sears Tower and flocking to Navy Pier's rotating Ferris wheel and hustling with bulging bags down Michigan Avenue. And truly, regardless of the tourists, there were only so many art fairs and foggy Bears games and drunken sailboat excursions Henry could attend until it was too much, until he no longer *had* to be in the city, until something more was needed. Julie was that something. She was beautiful then, petite but warming, a new wife who for all her daintiness had an aura he seemed to fall into. When he was around her, all of his steely financial prerogatives and constant calculations dissolved, and he found himself almost childlike with wonder that a woman could have this effect on him, could keep him under her spell. Henry liked the person he became when he was with her—gone was the alpha male intensity he knew could take him over, gone was the careless sexual appetite, gone were all those little bad things that seemed to live in him like termites. With Julie, those bad things were fumigated, given knockout gas, and he was . . . something better. A good person, yes. He read books. He enjoyed long walks far away from the city, in the suburbs with the trees and the houses and the schools. And he was *funny.* Julie said he was. With her, he remembered the way he'd been as a boy in Michigan, looking out at a backyard that dissolved into woodlands and thinking, *look at all that can happen.* What a childhood he'd had in those woods, scooping minnows and frogs out of the creek, sifting through woodpiles for dinosaur skeletons, playing neighborhood football with Dad (all–Big Ten tailback at Michigan State in 1939), and always feeling the joy of adventure. But then, after Dad got sick and passed away while Henry was ice fishing with his friends, the first of the termites was born. And when Mom remarried that shit dog Kevin Alferman, that man who was nothing like Dad and had none of the wondrous attitude of adventure Dad possessed, Henry had felt the termites burrow deeper, multiply, and give birth to his new prerogative. If a guy like Kevin Alferman could have his mother, and if a champion like Dad could die young, without allowing Henry to say good-bye, before Henry was *ready* for him to say good-bye, then this meant certain things about the world. There was no more time for adventure. The frogs and minnows could have their creek. The dinosaur skeletons underneath flattened leaves and woodpiles could lie in their tombs. Good things didn't happen to the right people. So it was with this mind-set that the new Henry was born—Henry guessed he was thirteen or so when it became definite. It had served him well. He'd made influential friends, broken the hearts of the most beautiful girls, been intramural baseball champion at Northwestern for all four years, even though the competition sucked. But when Julie was around, when he'd finally found her, he felt himself taken back to the way he used to be. He remembered all those woodpiles and creeks, and the feeling of adventure.

Before college ended, there was a crisis. Henry had woken up in his purple-bannered Evanston apartment and had a vision of what he'd be like on his own, without Julie, in the metropolis that was Chicago. In this future vision he had lost himself completely, and the vision was so clear and so visceral that he panicked, had recurring nightmares of himself as a soulless abuser of other people's good intentions, and told Julie how much he feared this person, how much he feared those termites reawakening, how much he couldn't be with anyone else, not ever. Henry had reasoned with himself, convinced himself that if he married Julie, kept her near him and wore her like a talisman, he'd be fine. The part of him that was broken, cursed, would never see the light of day.

"What could possibly go wrong?" Julie had said, her brown hair curling over the side of her face, her legs slung over the side of the bed.

He remembered her bed. A king-size mattress, which in college was beyond rare. She'd saved up money working at the Evanston park district and had draped the bed in silky red sheets that made Henry's twin mattress and black comforter seem like the contents of a prison cell. When Julie got pregnant in 1977, when they were two years out of college, he'd proposed on the spot. It had to happen, because with her, he was *better*.

Henry put the divorce papers down. In the end, that first pregnancy had resulted in a miscarriage and was the first indication that the magic between them wasn't infinite. They tried again and again, by that time Julie so far away from a career in dance that he felt both guilty and special, knowing he was the one who had become bigger than her dream. Finally, at twenty-nine, she'd had Charlie. But by that day, even when his son was born, Henry already knew—deep down, he knew—that his separation from the family was only a matter of time.

When he sank into his bed to sleep, the sound of his boyhood fan came calling to him again. A low hum at first, then the accelerating whir of the blades, and then that constant drone of wind and sound. He'd loved that fan. That sound of perpetual motion and movement, undying. As a boy, he'd burrowed under the covers, easily finding sleep, the fan reassuring him—*I am constant. I am continuous. Close your eyes. Go to sleep.*

The next morning, Henry went to Arlington Heights for his bimonthly, eight-hour session of chemo treatment, waiting for that snaking tube to attach like a python to the port in his chest. The whole business was a war of attrition. Mentally, he was putting up fortifications about consequences and endgames and dreams of the future—simply not thinking about them seemed to do wonders—but the brutality of the chemo schedule, the one week on, one week off, was crushing him. By the time he was finally feeling good again, clearheaded and energetic enough to get out in the world, he was back in this prison cell, getting more toxins siphoned into his bloodstream. And the cycle began all over again. Tomorrow, he knew, he would take the portal chemo-gizmo home and wear it for forty-eight more hours, and when *that* was over? Who knew? It was a miracle he wasn't poisoned to death. This shit could fell an African rhino, kill Rasputin, et cetera to infinity. But at this point, his competitive juices had kicked in, and that above all other things—more than the fear of consequences and death, more than losing family and friends and spirit—the competition, was keeping him going.

Chelsea, the young woman of pink phone number notoriety, had slipped rather quickly from his life. He'd gotten used to their sometimes-weekly sleepovers, to her bizarre need to clutch his hand, to her early morning disappearances. Week after week following his diagnosis, he'd wondered when she would finally catch the drift. After the failed procedure, he tried to hide the port they'd inserted just below his collarbone by always wearing a T-shirt (he'd kept his hair, so sleight of hand seemed feasible). And then the true bane of chemo reared its head: not only did he have serious problems getting it up, he had problems even *wanting* to. The first time, Chelsea had laughed it off. The second time, Henry had shrugged and admitted the truth. Then, instead of waiting to hear her verdict, he'd blown up, summoned the energy to scream and rage, told her to get the fuck out, hang out with people her own age, and leave him in fucking peace. He didn't wait for a response, simply walked to the door and held it open until she left.

When it was over, he felt emptied. Not sad. Not even neutral. Emptied.

Since it was the first of the month, Henry also had an appointment with the oncologist, Dr. Fredrickson—a regular asshole. The man was full of clipped, staccato speech and angular features that betrayed not even a shot glass of sympathy. Henry imagined his face as one that third-world dictators would carve into statues to scare peasants into submission. No sympathy from Dr. Fredrickson, no compassion—just that leathery skin and hawk nose and those reflective glasses. The bastard was tan in January, which meant he was probably one of those awful snowbirds who "wintered" in Florida during the frigid months. Henry could imagine him out there among the stucco strip malls and drooping palm trees, driving a beet-red convertible, bronzed arm around a Botox-zapped wife, playing hours upon hours of very bad golf.

When Henry walked into Fredrickson's gray-walled office that

Monday (with more awful framed certificates), he closed the door behind him, hard.

"Mr. Brunson," Fredrickson said, looking startled.

Henry grunted. "We need to talk. We really need to game plan, here."

"Oh? What's wrong?"

Henry fell heavily into the seat across from the desk. "First of all, this medication is heinous. My muscles, Dr. Fredrickson—they're sinking away like my body's made of quicksand, and believe me, this is *unacceptable*. I'm fifty-seven, not eighty. We have to come up with a new plan of action. We need to start brainstorming, immediately."

Fredrickson pushed his glasses to the bridge of his nose. "Mr. Brunson, the 5-FU is the best course of action at this point, especially with your desire to remain aggressive—it combats the cancer in ways that the gemcitabine simply can't. If this doesn't work—"

Henry leaned forward. "If this doesn't *work*? You've already told me that I'm on some sort of a countdown. Here we are in January, and you've told me to be keeping an eye on April. *April*? It's like I'm waiting for an asteroid to hit. It's obvious that it's not working!"

And then, with his voice raised, Henry suddenly felt tired and dizzy, as if lukewarm dishwater had been poured into his brain. He leaned back in the chair and went quiet, closing his eyes. *Count*, he thought. Fight back. Count off the seconds in your head, let the dizziness pass, your strength will come back. A brief image of Julie came into his mind, a memory of time spent and time lost, but he shut the door on it. He heard the doctor clearing his throat.

"I remember that last visit, we had a conversation about expectations," Fredrickson said, crossing one leg over the other, in what Henry thought was a show of regal diplomacy. The guy was a prick. He'd put money down that he could not only beat the man in golf, but annihilate him, wipe his leathery ass up and down the Michigan fairways. In the old days, fresh out of Northwestern, he'd come back to Michigan regularly and hit all the links in Harbor Country, birdie, par, birdie, par, shooting sixty-eights and scorching three-hundred-yard drives as if they were nothing. And thinking about that, about the golf of his youth, he was able to close his eyes, and remember the green of the fairways and the wind off the lake, that slow walk from hole to hole, the heavy bag on his shoulders and warmth on his back.

"Mr. Brunson, do you remember our conversation on expectations?"

"Of course I do. This isn't a kindergarten class, Doctor."

"*Exactly*. That is exactly my point. You are an adult and I respect you, and I respect that you would like an accurate timetable by which to get things in order and spend time with those you care about. I know it seems like I'm being harsh and not cushioning the truth, but the truth is the best thing I can give you. There are doctors out there who will tell you wild stories—Paul Bunyan tales of survival—and Mr. Brunson, believing in those tales is the greatest danger there is. What ends up occurring is that these doctors foster almost superhuman beliefs in life expectancy, and the patient and his or her surrounding family do not respond accordingly. Instead of spending time together, they relax. Instead of coming together, they slip apart. And when tragedy strikes, everyone is wounded, regretful, saying *I thought you told me such and such*, and so on. And no, I'm not an authority on sociology or family psychology—this is strictly my observation as a practicing oncologist for over twenty years. But these doctors who quote three years of survival or more to stage four patients are doing those patients a disservice. The FOLFIRINOX is in place to give you the longest possible life span—beating back the cancer, trying to control and push back that prairie fire. We discussed quality of life versus really fighting back, going tooth and nail, even if that meant discomfort, and this is what you wanted. And to be honest, toxicity from the FOLFIRINOX is a concern, but so are effects from unchecked cancer. I think you're making the right move. And I'd like to say that you've handled it admirably."

"I'm not dying in April," Henry said, flatly. "That's not how it happens. I don't go out whimpering, you understand? You're talking to me like there's only one option."

"Mr. Brunson, let's talk about how you are feeling. Are you still going to work?"

Henry grunted.

"The reason I ask is the need to understand your stressors. While working provides goals and a clear sense of purpose—all of which are good things—it can also take a toll. Physically and mentally. Are you still going in, Mr. Brunson?"

"A couple times each week. For the health insurance." And to keep those pricks in line, Henry thought wearily. Dorfman and the rest. Blue Cross Blue Shield and Merrill Lynch were still in the rickety grip of his control, but it wasn't easy. The hyenas were truly circling now, just as he'd feared last summer, and he knew the biggest worry was that he'd begun questioning the meaning of it all. Why did he even care if Dorfman got his accounts? He surely *would* get them within the year, and maybe sooner, the way Fredrickson was talking. So why did it matter? They knew he was sick, so why couldn't he just give them up?

But, as if a shotgun slug were permanently lodged inside his gut, he knew that some force wouldn't let him. Something made of harder things than tendon or ligament or muscle or even cancer demanded that it did matter, and that he act accordingly. Henry Brunson did not cave, could not cave, would not cave. The absurdity of it all, the lack of inherent meaning, was something for the philosophers, something for the unemployed dreamers who spent their time staring at the clouds.

"And how are you feeling overall, Mr. Brunson?"

In Fredrickson's office, there was a tiny window looking out onto the parking lot, and Henry watched, surprised, as a pink ice cream truck glided up and stopped by a row of houses across the street, just inside his field of vision. Strange—he'd never seen one in winter before. Two neighborhood boys ran up and paid for their cones. It looked like they were laughing. Henry, infuriatingly, couldn't hear the truck's music. It was all occurring like some distant, silent movie, seen through a telescope. The kids looked to be eleven or twelve.

"Mr. Brunson?"

"I'm losing weight, all right? I'm losing weight and muscle, I'm keeping the fat, I'm dizzy half the time, I've got . . . problems with my intestines, or something. I'm going to the bathroom all the time. All the food runs right through me."

"I understand. We'll up your prescription on those anti-diarrheals. And my records show that last month you weighed in at a hundred ninety-two and today you dipped just below a hundred eighty-eight. Which, honestly, is not a terribly surprising shift. You've lost twenty pounds since your diagnosis in August, which I think is to be expected."

"Can you open that window?"

Fredrickson craned his head back. "Is it hot in here?"

"No. Just need some fresh air."

Fredrickson shrugged and nodded and stood up. He cranked the window, and just under the winter breeze, Henry heard the notes of the ice cream truck, twangs and chirps like something from a music box. His doctor didn't seem to notice.

"What else?" Fredrickson asked.

Henry sighed, and held up his arms. The skin was sallow and sagging, hanging loose from his bones like skin-colored molasses. "You see this? I'm losing everything. All that work—it's disappearing. I can barely see my biceps anymore. My energy is shit. I get dizzy all the time. I take naps in the middle of the day, even though I'm pounding energy drinks—"

"You shouldn't be doing that," Fredrickson said.

"If the end is inevitable, then I can be doing whatever I want. But I'll have you know, it's not the way I go."

"I fully understand the desire to be mentally strong during this time, and I've got to tell you, I respect it."

Henry looked outside for the ice cream truck but saw that it was gone—and it was winter, wasn't it? Snow covered the yards and curbs. It was likely, he decided, that the truck had never been there. Yes, of course that was it. As Henry left the office, he watched Fredrickson stand up and close the window.

Seven hours of chemo later, Henry was shut away in a private corner unit with beige walls, playing chess on his laptop, trying to corner the computerized queen with long-range attacks from his rook and bishop. The door opened and Barkley stepped in. It was post-Eastwick, a school night, and he looked well dressed but haggard, the color in his face drained like an empty punch bowl.

"Everything all right?" Henry asked.

"Fine," Barkley said. "How are you?"

Henry grunted. "Let's get out of here."

Soon enough, his younger son had helped him pack up his things, thrown away the bags of Doritos and cans of Diet Pepsi he'd consumed during the session, and packaged his laptop into its case. Barkley walked with him to the parking garage, the whole time Henry feeling like an arthritic old bag with vertigo—the entire experience was making him crazy. Barkley loaded everything in the Ford Taurus, and within minutes they were outside of Arlington Heights and on their way back into the city on the Kennedy.

"So how are you really feeling?" Barkley asked, loosening his tie while his left hand stayed on the wheel.

"Tired and depleted. But alive. This chemo is like trying to digest napalm, I'm telling you, kid."

Barkley looked at him. "Are you still losing weight?"

"A couple pounds."

"And how is the other stuff? The dietary stuff? Digestion and whatnot?"

Henry waved his hand. "Not important."

"*Dad*. All of it's important. And when are you going to tell the rest of the family? This needs to happen, like, now. I can't keep holding on to this. I'm seriously thinking about it all the time."

"You're not telling anyone," Henry said. He looked out the window as they passed the exits for O'Hare and Cumberland, the darkened highway flickering with intermittent light. Beyond the road, he could see glowing blue signs above darkened corporate buildings. He wondered what Barkley was really thinking about all of this—if he understood why the secrecy was so important.

"Dad, I'm not going to keep doing this, I'll tell you right now. It's not even morally ambiguous anymore—it's wrong. People are seriously going to be hurt. And if you told everyone, you could have someone driving with you to the treatment, staying with you there, instead of taking a cab from the Gold Coast to Arlington Heights, like a maniac. I mean, you're not in the CIA or anything—you *can* tell people. Does Al or Glenn know about this?"

"No. What about your mother? What have you told her?"

"Nothing. She's busy, anyhow."

Henry, his mind somewhere in a sprawl of toxic water, latched onto a sandbar, and pulled himself up. "What do you mean, she's busy?"

Barkley shrugged.

"Busy how?"

"I don't know, she's always out doing stuff. I think she's gone into some sort of dance instructor gig. Every morning she practices all these exercises, you know, the ones where the girl bends down, knees out?"

"Plié," Henry said, trying to decide just how precisely the tables had been turned. He'd left her, and for many justified reasons, and now Julie was busy and healthy and likely even happy, while he was in a penthouse prison cell, wasting away. He was paying for her livelihood, and she was trying to *divorce* him—divorcing the person who had asked for the separation in the first place. The entire escapade was backward, wrong, brutally unfair.

"She might even be dancing downtown," Barkley said. "Not sure if it's near you, though."

"And what else?"

"What do you mean, what else?"

"Is she seeing anyone?"

Barkley went quiet.

"Is she dating some lunatic or . . . or . . ." And then Henry felt his mind fall back with a splash of dizziness. He went quiet and waited for Barkley to respond.

"I don't know anything about that. But if I did, I'd be a moron for trying to talk about it. Don't you agree?"

Henry chuckled gruffly. "It would be pretty stupid, I guess. Getting the old man riled up. Though I guess it's her right to do what she wants. I did start all of this, didn't I?"

Barkley looked at the road ahead. "Yeah, Dad, you definitely did. But it's your right to do that, too. Nobody can stop anybody else. I've given up thinking about it."

"You have to understand that it was always going to be this way. You know that, don't you?"

"Sure, Dad. Sure."

When they pulled up to his building, Barkley sat silent, hands on the steering wheel, eyes ahead. His mind was elsewhere, Henry thought—

par for the course with his younger son. Yet Henry felt his own mind prone to wandering these days, frequently without permission.

"What's really on your mind, Barkley?"

"Well, school, obviously. Stuff at school."

"Beyond the damn job. Just what the hell are you always thinking about?"

Barkley turned to him, then stared back out the windshield. "Different things, Dad. But—in this case, I don't know. Some things Mom said about you, I guess. A couple years ago, when you started acting strange. I've been thinking about it again, is all."

"Oh yeah? And what did Mom say?"

"Dad . . ."

"I'm not going to get upset. What exactly did she say?"

Barkley sighed. "That whatever is going on with you—whatever you've been dealing with all these years—it started when you were a kid. With your parents. With your stepdad."

Henry felt an odd shiver, as if a splinter had entered the back of his skull.

"Is it true, Dad?"

"I don't know."

"Do you ever think about it?"

"I never think about it." But Henry knew that was a lie—he'd thought about it just this morning. Not his style. Yet he had an odd feeling of water pooling into the car, filling it up like a fish tank.

"I have to go," Henry said. He opened the car door and stood—found himself panting, out of breath. He had to find higher ground. When he closed the door behind him, Barkley honked once and drove away.

Henry trudged through the softly glowing lobby, nodded at Kurt, and made his way to the elevators. They were all stainless steel, the ride up to the top giving a smooth *whoosh* before dinging brightly. Back in his penthouse, waiting for him on the luxurious sprawl of granite countertops, lit up by radiant track lighting, were Julie's divorce papers. Of course, now everything made sense. Of course.

Above him, the penthouse rumbled, and Henry watched the blinking lights of another 747 making its way across the lake. He thought of Charlie again. He thought of Julie. He thought of airplanes and trajectories and flight paths. His sons were supposed to follow his lead, weren't they? Yet Barkley—and Charlie especially—had fought to divert themselves from every pathway their father paved. They all resisted his decisions, resented him, and the problem didn't start there. No, Henry thought, sighing as he watched the fading plane. Maybe Julie was right. It began with his father.

He sat down slowly on the couch—tried to steady his mind, to think through the morass of chemicals. Julie's words weren't new. From the beginning, she said that the shitstorm inside him began with his dad, and he'd always told her he was over it. Termites or not, he was a better person because of it. And part of getting over those ancient wounds meant forgetting them, meant casting them over the sides of his ship and sailing forward, ever onward, to bigger and better things. He eyed the divorce papers again. Felt the dizziness seep into every crevice of his brain. Felt the slow spiral, the inner drain pour, the strange way his life was turning. Maybe Julie was right all along.

Back in Michigan, as a child, Henry had idolized his old man. He remembered the feeling of pride when they drove into town, walked into stores, sailed on the lake. It was only in the weeks after the funeral, lying there during winter nights with his blanket pulled up to his neck, in that vast crater of sudden and absolute loneliness, that Henry had begun to resent him. His father had died young. He had not said good-bye. He had not visited him in dreams or visions or churches or any of the other places Henry had heard of loved ones visiting—he was, quite simply, quite irrefutably, *gone*. Bullshit. Henry remembered punching his pillow late into each night and saying the words, over and over again, *bullshit, bullshit, bullshit,* until spit and salt were dribbling down his chin. He was twelve years old and just beginning to understand his anger. And he was furious not simply over the way his father died, but how he had lived. He'd been a nice man—some said a great man. He'd played with him in those woodpiles and creeks, taught him to throw the pigskin like Unitas and play Texas hold 'em like his uncle. But there were also those irrefutable facts, weightier now that he was gone. For instance: after college at MSU, his father had settled in rural Michigan, even though he dreamed of New York. He stayed with his wife, even though she pined for that ever-loving son of a bitch she married after. He worked in sales, even though his real love was advertising, and he'd had the creative mind for it—deconstructing commercials about Schlitz and Alka-Seltzer and Sugar Smacks right in front of them, from the confines of their sagging couch. Yet the old man had never made a move. He never took what he wanted. Bullshit. All Henry saw, lying in that Michigan bed as snow blurred glass, was that his father hadn't had the goddamn balls to go get it. He'd taken only what was given, only what was *there*, and then he had died. He had died in Michigan, in the winter, away from the city and the life he'd dreamed of, in the arms of a woman who was all too ready to move on.

And so Henry had woken in that winter, felt the termites move inside him, and spurned the path of his father. He set out to find a new way, a better way. Life was finite, life was short, life was a light switch flicked by idle hands and fickle minds, on and off, on and off, anywhere, anytime. He would go out and take what he wanted. And he would learn how, if necessary, to cut ties—even with family. His mother married Kevin Alferman a mere eight months after his father's passing, shocking Henry from his cycle of afterschool fistfights and tears. Soon enough a stranger was in the house, an infiltrating bastard who didn't belong, an alien presence who showed no reverence for his father and no respect for his father's son. His stepfather. It disgusted Henry to remember. Beady eyes behind Coke-bottle glasses, a ragged wardrobe of plaid sport coats, and that asinine 1,000 DAYS SOBER pin he wore on Sundays, even when Henry could smell the alcohol. So Henry started building walls. He trained himself to forget each day as it passed. Six years later, when Henry left for college at Northwestern, he learned to cut ties for the first time. He dropped his mother and Kevin Alferman like he was dropping off broken furniture at the corner curb—not even worthy of a garage sale. Those two could have each other, rattling around in his father's house, already unhappy and drinking and finding new methods of disrespect. So he cut them off, stepped onto that Evanston campus for the first time, and was finally reborn.

Henry stared out his windows, at the black swath of lake that trailed into nothing. Almost forty years later, his entire family claimed that he couldn't commit, but it was precisely the opposite—he was fully committed, committed to the end. Since his first year in college, he'd crafted his own philosophy: that in spite of everything, in spite of the total im-permanence of this absurd existence, each person should go out and get everything he could. That meant family, sure. But it also meant money, and women, and experiences, and most important—some honest-to-God fucking autonomy. With a life so laughably finite and tenuous, so prone to death and departure, the only feasible option was to get the most that was possible, and accrue the financial security to allow one's family to get the most that they could, too. Being true to this methodology did not mean staying with a wife who no longer made him happy, especially when her power as a talisman, as someone who made those truths go away, faltered. She'd helped him forget for a while, sure. She'd made him better than he really was. But then the miscarriage, the monotony, the slow slide into late middle age. There was only one driver's seat, and it was his, and he would be damn sure to steer clear of the path of his father. This was the road Henry had paved for both children but Charlie especially; this was the bridge he'd painstakingly constructed, the bridge that took him away from the wrongs he'd discovered in Michigan. And the message he had for his sons? To get as much as possible out of life, to yank all that was offered from Earth, take it for yourself, and get what you wanted before your name was called. And if you didn't go get those things, if you didn't make that push, you'd have only your empty hands as company.

Strangely, though, infuriatingly, Henry's hands felt empty *now*.

The issue was legacy. Charlie had looked at the bridge Henry had built, and he'd taken a wrecking ball to it. Left a lucrative job. Threw away his girlfriend and his college degree. Enlisted in the fucking army. Henry couldn't fathom these decisions—he'd chosen war, he'd chosen to risk nonexistence, and for what? Because he didn't like what his father had done. He'd burned his father's bridge, and Henry, looking back, saw the bridge to his own father was burned as well. There was no path laid out, no continuity, no exchange of batons. He was on an island, without past or future, only a method, a philosophy to keep him warm. To ad-mit he was wrong would be to step off the island entirely. And if he did that—what was he? What was left? Julie said he'd acted petulantly with their children, had ruined everything they made together, and that what was once a good family had changed into something else. But he couldn't apologize. He couldn't be wrong. There had to be another way—another move left.

He paced around the living room, along the perimeters of the bay windows, and circled the divorce papers like a hawk unsure of its prey. He sat on the sofa to steady the dizziness. He stood up. Paced. Sat down. He was weak, he understood, but not tired. Not yet ready for bed. And so that left the papers. He pulled out his cell phone. There was only one logical course of action. Only one thing for him, Henry Brunson, to do. A way to remain himself, while fixing what was broken. He stood up and dialed Julie's number, holding on to the counter while another wave of dizziness crashed in.

Four rings, voice mail. A new voice mail, with strange sounds mixing into the background—the clank of what sounded like the El moving across neighborhood tracks. The message beeped and Henry put the phone to his ear.

"Julie, it's Henry. I've got news for you. Very important news." He took a breath. He nodded to himself. "I'm coming home."

CHURCH OF
BOXING

It began two months back, at the beginning of January, when Charlie got a call from Barkley to meet him at church. He immediately groaned, firmly entrenched in the leather folds of the living room couch, mowing through a film noir triathlon of *The Maltese Falcon*, *Sunset Boulevard*, and *Double Indemnity*. This coming from the aftereffects of watching *Transformers 2* on Netflix, and stumbling around afterward like a child who'd been force-fed sugar until his eyes bled. But his mood, which he'd been monitoring for months, was solid. Docile, even. And the most telling sign was that gradually, piece by piece, scene by scene, he found himself enjoying movies again.

He'd also begun what he thought was a slightly assertive cleanup process. He called up Bobby Leeds to talk about his disappearance abroad. He applied for some jobs at local gyms and weight lifting facilities. He almost contacted Veterans Affairs, but felt better about the idea of talking to Al, and so they'd had another meeting. He even drove downtown to visit Barkley, and there had been a night out during which he hadn't drunk too much or even felt like he needed to.

A few days back he'd finally reached out to the army buddies who'd come home—not Bruiser, but JB and Locklear and a couple of the others who were in the general midwestern area. JB, after losing the leg, had come down from Amherst, Wisconsin, where he'd settled into a job working for Central Waters Brewery with two of his cousins. Locklear had trekked cross-country, driving across white and wind-swept cornfields from Des Moines, Iowa. Both of them wanted to hang in Chicago, a midwestern Oz from their corn-fed perspectives, and so Charlie obliged. He gave them a tour of his old stomping grounds in Wicker Park, drinking and drinking more as that lakefront winter wind howled. They moved from Blue Line to Piece, pounding microbrews and thin-crust pizza, before finally crashing at the dive bar contours of Beachwood Inn, whose worn interior felt like the inside of an old baseball glove. They drank more beer and reminisced, the whole time Charlie waiting for some sort of judgment, some comment about what had gone down on that highway and how Charlie had to answer for it, had to pay. But soon enough it was clear that there was no judgment, and later JB had put a hand on his shoulder and said, *we're proud of you, man,* and Charlie had stared back, ready to throw a punch if his buddy was fucking with him. *No dude,* he'd said, *I'm serious. What you've been through, and how you've stayed strong, it's amazing. We all think so. We know how hard that hit you, and everyone knows it was a simple mistake. A snap judgment. Any of us could have done it, and you've got to know we have your back.*

Two days later, Charlie still tried to remember every syllable of that speech JB had given him—he wanted to own a music box that would infinitely play his friend's words into his ear. But the encouragement had been given amid copious alcohol consumption and clattering pint glasses and a jukebox twanging with Led Zeppelin's "Moby Dick." He'd only retained the drunken vapors of JB's speech, and so he'd tried to write the speech down. In the meantime, the old movies were always good medicine. He was thinking seriously about calling up Bobby and restarting *Cue Mark Reviews,* when Barkley called, babbling about this meeting at a church.

"Are you serious, dude? I'm trying to finish a movie. Can't we meet, like, I don't know, at the house that's five minutes away from you? The house you grew up in? Do I really need to go on a religious pilgrimage?"

"It's not a religious thing. We just need to talk."

"So come here, man. I'm ready to talk, let's do this. I'm all ears."

"No," Barkley said, through a crunch of static. "We can't. Mom can't hear anything about this."

"Okay, so Ballydoyle."

"Bars are a bad idea. I can meet you at the park. You want to meet at the park?"

"Two dudes sitting on a bench, feeding pigeons, touching pinkie fingers? Don't you have a girlfriend for that sort of thing?"

"Right, so just come to this church—it's not religious, we just need to talk. Sound good? There's going to be that Wednesday night service, so don't freak out, just sit in the back."

When Charlie arrived, wearing jeans and a Chicago Bears sweatshirt, he felt a sense of complication. It was a long, rectangular room, with Technicolor stained glass and a bronzed organ sporting rows of meticulously cleaned pipes. Yet looking at the stained glass made him think of the murals on all those Afghani jingle trucks, and the organ pipes looked like a truckload of RPGs, and then Charlie reminded himself that he was thinking clichéd, ex-soldierly thoughts again, going the Christopher Walken route, and he sat down in the pew and shut up.

"Charlie? Charlie Brunson? Julie's oldest son, am I correct?"

An old woman, covered in wrinkles and shocking white hair, was looking down at him. Her face triggered a vague familiarity, but he shrugged off trying to guess who it was. His old mind might have raced to procure a timely recognition of identity, but one of the benefits to having served was that civilians, thinking a soldier might be damaged, didn't take offense at the steady ignorance of social expectations.

"It's me," Charlie said, nodding. "And forgive me, I'm forgetting your name."

"Mrs. Potter, from down the street? We moved across town when you were in middle school."

"Oh, that's right. I remember now. You always had that 'Helping Hands' sign in the window. And the tree house in the backyard, from the previous owners, with the nailed-in ladder."

"Guilty. And speaking of guilty, I haven't seen you here for a few years now." She sat down next to him. Her pouf of white hair looked like an electroshocked Maltese.

"Well," Charlie said, "you know how it goes. Attendance declines after confirmation . . ." and he let the words trail, seeing if she would smile knowingly, or glower like the hard-bitten churchgoer he remembered—nearly Third Reich in her staunch, regimented attendance. If he remembered anything about Mrs. Potter, it was the way in which her eyes had glowered when they'd run under her elm tree during freeze tag, or gone into her daffodil patch to retrieve a fallen Super Soaker 300. And from the way the corners of her mouth made a little downward jab, Charlie knew he'd misfired.

"So you've stopped attending, Charlie?"

"I'm on hiatus."

"The sermons have been *excellent*," she said. "Pastor Rick, he really brought the humor out, and we were upset about his leaving, the whole congregation discussed it at length. But Pastor Wallace, the man is a true believer."

"I'll bet he is. He looks serious."

Indeed he did, mounting the podium with a look of stern urgency, his robe the color of dry-cleaned doves. His face, though clearly in its sixties, still looked pink and babyish, almost innocent, and the wrinkles gave him the look of an infant in a windstorm.

"Where's the rest of your family?" Mrs. Potter asked, placing both hands gingerly atop her exploded hairdo.

"Oh, busy I think. Different directions, responsibilities."

"Church is changing," she huffed. "The meaning of a service, what's implied, what we're meant to *do* with it."

"Well, I'm where I want to be," he said. "Life-wise. I'm doing what I can."

"And you've served your country, is the latest I've heard. The neighborhood is very proud of your service. You should know that. Spreading God's word in those terrible regions of the world, destroying ignorance among the savages."

"Spreading God's word," Charlie repeated.

She touched his arm. "What you did over there—everything you did—is for the greater good. Defeating ignorance with righteousness."

Charlie debated summoning the energy for an argument, but then he heard footsteps, and saw Barkley's unmistakable form ambling up toward the pew.

"And look at this, here comes the little brother," Charlie said.

"Oh, Barkley, I hardly recognized you," Mrs. Potter said.

Barkley nodded, smiling grimly. "Hello, Mrs. Potter, it's great to see you again. I'm just going to talk to Charlie privately for a second here." He slid into the pew to Charlie's right, looking steely eyed and gaunt, while Mrs. Potter huffed slightly before scooting to the other end of the pew.

"You look weird," Charlie said. "Why do you look possessed?"

"I'm *focused.*"

"B-Team, the only thing I've ever seen you focused on is dragons fighting zombies. And are you eating, dude? You look like you've taken a Somalian vacation or something."

"You know," Barkley said, "zombies against dragons is actually a pretty good idea. I don't think that's been done. And just think—they could be zombie *knights!* Wait, wait—zombie knights *on fire!*"

"Uh-huh. On zombie horses, too, I'm assuming. And you still look emaciated, man."

"I've lost fifteen pounds. That's a positive. And like I said, I'm *focused.*"

"What the hell are you so focused on? Teaching Chaucer?" Charlie assumed it was Ginny—she was fun, but Charlie wondered how many hoops his little brother had to jump through to keep her happy.

"School," Barkley said. "I'm focused on school. And I've got American Lit, not Brit Lit. I've only got about fifteen or twenty minutes and then I've got to get back to the city to lesson plan."

"*Lesson plan?*"

Barkley stared straight ahead. "I'm taking it to another level. No one over there is pushing me around."

"Who the hell is pushing you around? Want me to snap their collarbones?"

"It's not like that."

"You're scaring me, B-Team. Look at you. You look like an unfed cyborg. It's like that time I came back from football, and what was that girl's name—Jessie—she'd denied you for homecoming the same night I caught that touchdown bomb against Glenbard? You remember that? And you were just sitting in the living room, practically comatose, reading the annotated version of *The Hobbit*."

Barkley looked up, smiling. "You actually remember my annotated *Hobbit*? With all the pictures and footnotes?"

"Just because I remember it doesn't mean I *liked* it. But yeah, I remember. It had the green-and-blue cover or something."

Barkley leaned back and sighed. "That book was like therapy in high school. God, I love books with footnotes. It's like reading a novel, and then finding out the novel has tunnels inside it you can crawl through, which lead to more tunnels, which take you even further away from all the bullshit you're really dealing with. You know, aside from the famous scenes with Smaug, I used to always reread the first paragraph. In the end I tried to memorize it."

"Still got it?"

"Of course I've still got it."

"So recite it, you chump."

"I'm not even embarrassed, if that's what you're looking for."

"So show this esteemed institution what you've got, B-Team."

He cleared his throat. "'In a hole in the ground there lived a hobbit. Not a nasty, dirty, wet hole, filled with the ends of worms and an oozy smell, nor yet a dry, bare, sandy hole, with nothing in it to sit down on or to eat: it was a hobbit hole, and that means comfort.' Boom! Word-for-word, and yet another Barkley accomplishment."

"You've accomplished laying a dork bomb inside a church. Congrats." But Charlie was grinning, at ease. "So what's the news?"

Barkley sighed, and his smile flatlined. "It's about Dad, okay? And it's serious. He told me not to tell, but—I don't know, I just assumed this would be figured out somehow. That he would do the right thing, or cave in, or whatever. But nothing has been figured out. He didn't even see us during Christmas. And I've got too much going on right now to not tell anybody. I seriously don't know about telling Mom. She's doing good, you know?"

"I don't need to hear about what Dad is doing, either, man. We all know what he's doing. He's never going to own up to it, so just let him be."

"He's sick, Charlie."

"Sick in the head? You're telling me."

Barkley groaned. "No, I mean he's physically sick. He's dying, Charlie. He's terminally ill."

Charlie opened his mouth to speak, but found he barely had enough torque in his lungs to breathe. He clenched his hands and closed his eyes and felt something in his chest, some tether he wasn't sure was good or bad, snap cleanly in two, like a bungee cord severed during free fall. He looked up at the stained-glass windows. There was a depiction of a man handing a tiny container to a woman, and above it some sort of light.

"What did you just say?" Charlie finally hissed. Information like that about his father—it shouldn't feel good, of course, but it certainly shouldn't affect him so brutally, not like this. Yet he was already imagining himself in a bar fight, smashing faces into mirrors, tossing hapless drunks into regimented lines of whiskey bottles.

"He's sick," Barkley said again. "It's stage four. He literally, like, made me promise not to tell anyone. There's been chemo. I didn't know what to do, Charlie. It's insane. I mean, I'm trying to respect the guy, but this is just crazy. People need to know."

Charlie felt a thick emotion, viscous and oily, clogging his ability to think. "This is such bullshit. Such complete and utter bullshit. I can't believe it."

"I know, man. I'm sorry. I wanted to tell you guys right away, but after a while, I didn't want to say anything to anyone. I mean, you and Mom seem like you're doing good, and I saw that you guys got pissed when he left those voice mails about coming home, and this would only have made things worse."

"I appreciate that," Charlie said, nodding stiffly. "I see what you did. I see that. But I've got to get out of here, dude, before I start throwing punches."

"Okay. Do you want to call Dad? Both of us?"

"Hell no. He's been hiding this shit? What is wrong with that man?"

"I mean, maybe he's trying to protect us. Maybe he has good intentions. I don't know. I just drive him back from chemo—that's pretty much the only time he'll see me. We could go visit him downtown or something, though."

"That means he uses his sickness to bring us back to him, as opposed to using words, like a normal person. It's not *fair*. He's not answering for *anything*."

"I know."

"*Damn* it!"

From the other end of the pew, Mrs. Potter looked at them quizzically. Charlie stood up.

"I've got to get out of here, Barkley. I'm not mad at you, we're good. You kept a promise as long as you could. It was a tough spot. But I've got to get out of here before I hit something."

Charlie drove home from the church with his fingers feeling like loose wires spraying sparks. He could hardly grab the steering wheel. All this time mad at his father, his father mad at him, and the old man secretly dying, wasting away in some tower in Chicago, and for *what*? The idiocy of it all made Charlie want to kill someone—to bash heads against wooden bar tops, to strike a face until it turned to putty, to curb stomp some bastard until teeth scattered like dice. He went home and punched three succinct holes in his bedroom wall, then grabbed the phone number his mother had given him, the one for Jack Schoenwetter, the old man boxer who was probably senile anyway. He dialed immediately.

"Yeah?" a voice answered. There was the sound of a motor, or maybe a purring cat, in the background.

Charlie hung up.

The next day, he called again, around noon, and when Jack Schoenwetter picked up, Charlie heard the rhythmic drumming of gloves smacking bags, the slapping of plastic jump ropes against stone floor, and the creaking of a canvas boxing ring, weighted by fighters.

"That's some fantastic reception you have," Charlie said. "You must have about forty boxers over there, slugging the shit out of each other."

"And just who in the hell is this?" Schoenwetter said.

"I'm Charlie. You're dating my mother. And I'm hoping you can train me to beat some meatheads to a pulp, due to the fact that I'm a very angry young man."

Three days later, Charlie had his first appointment at Hamlin Park, an eight-acre Chicago Park District sprawl in North Center, whose perimeter was filled with a remarkable number of double-wide strollers and early-thirty-something couples. Charlie drove up and saw the baseball fields, the outdoor pool, and the brick and mortar field house, which led to the pit that held the boxing gym. The pit was gray and mottled yellow—red bags hung like old meat on the far wall, a sagging canvas boxing ring opposed them, and there was a small amount of humid open space to practice punches in front of a mirror. It was perfect, Charlie thought. And at ten in the morning on a Sunday, the place was empty.

Charlie walked around silently, circling the equipment, imagining the release that would come from striking, from getting struck. Hell, after Budapest, it was already clear that he liked it. He hit one of the strung-up bags with his left hand, then again, then a third time. *Pop, pop, pop.* Reset. *Pop, pop, pop.* Reset.

"That jab is already quick enough," a voice said. "But you want that right hand up against your cheekbone. And you're not a southpaw, are you? Get that right leg behind you. You don't want to get your ass knocked over."

Charlie turned and saw him—strong jaw, a few dovetails of wrinkles and scar tissue, and kind blue eyes. Eyes that had possessed fierceness once, but had eventually been softened by something else. What kind of thing that could be, Charlie didn't know.

"Jack Schoenwetter," the bulky man said, stretching out his hand.

Charlie shook it. "Charlie. I'm Julie's oldest."

The locker room door opened, and two Latinos entered the gym and immediately went into the ring, wearing sparring helmets. A gaunt white man who had to be around six foot five followed them.

"You know, your mother and I are just friends," Schoenwetter said, bouncing from one foot to another.

"You're not dating?"

"Well, we're dating when she says we're dating."

Charlie laughed. "Honestly, as long as she's in a good mood, I think everybody's happy. By the way, I heard you were a Chicago fireman."

"Retired, of course. I'm over at Links Hall most of the time, which my wife used to run, but I'm here on Wednesdays and Sundays. Now, before we continue, you need to know that your mother just suggested training you to get in shape—she doesn't want you fighting."

Charlie heard a bell ring and watched the two Latinos circle each other in the ring, each wearing a different-colored tank top. The smaller one lunged forward and unleashed a series of jabs and crosses, followed by one lightning hook that made Charlie shiver. The taller one fell back.

"Well, Mr. Schoenwetter, let me talk to my mother. But my goal is to fight. I want to fight everybody you've got, and then I want to go to the tournaments."

Schoenwetter chuckled. "Well, you've got your mother's spirit, that's for sure. I guess I can ask her—"

"Look, I like how you're respecting her with this whole boxing thing. But right now, I want you to separate the two of us. I need to train, and then I need to fight. It's not want, it's *need*. You see, I've been doing some thinking, and I think I'd start feeling a lot better if I could start doing something physical. Maybe certain kinds of pain are good, I don't know. But I'm sure at some point, you felt the same way, too. I'll pay you, of course."

Schoenwetter looked at him for a moment longer. He had deep creases under his eyes, bird nests of pulpy flesh that had no doubt come from time in the ring. Finally, he nodded, and Charlie felt a surge of victory.

"I'm still going to talk to your mother," Schoenwetter said, "but let's go get you some gloves."

All through January and February, Charlie trained with Jack Schoenwetter. He learned all the punches, Schoenwetter sometimes telling him to keep his form and stop punching so hard. He didn't care. It felt good. When he came home, he drank recovery drinks and watched television and listened to his mother screech on the phone at his father. They were talking again, which was strange, and every time the conversations started Charlie turned up the volume, hoping to drown out the image of his father, secretly sick and wasting away. He'd actually given in and called him twice since finding out the news, but as usual—no response.

On the phone, Dad threatened to come home, and his mother threatened to leave the moment he did. Something about divorce papers. About time, Charlie thought. One of them would always hang up on the other, but it was clear a dark momentum was gathering—storm clouds emerging from the cellular ether. A change was going to happen, sooner rather than later.

Occasionally Jack would be over when his father called, and in those cases he would watch TV with Charlie—turned out the old fogy liked the black-and-white film noir classics, too, as well as anything boxing. They could watch any flick from the 1940s to about 1990—*Goodfellas* seemed to be the man's cutoff—and the boxing movie debates always came down to *Rocky* vs. *Raging Bull*. They'd sit there and each have a Goose Island 312 while his mother got rid of Dad, and then she would come into the family room, smiling sheepishly and groaning in the direction of the phone. And his mother was in such strong spirits—even though Charlie thought she should know what was going on, some force wouldn't allow him to speak of it. It was between the two of them, husband and wife. He just hoped his father wouldn't cause any more damage as he blazed down from the sky like a falling fighter jet.

Charlie trained through the end of February, getting back into the shape he'd been in during basic, slathered in sweat and coiled muscle. He hit the bags expertly, followed directions, worked hard, didn't punch too hard (usually), went running for at least two miles after each practice. Eventually, he sparred with the short Latino who had given his buddy such a ringer, and Charlie had come at the smaller man with body shots, crosses, and uppercuts, blocking some punches, forgetting to block others, before a right hook from his opponent sent tangerine fireworks across his vision.

"Watch for the goddamn right hook!" Schoenwetter yelled. "We've been over this!"

Charlie fought back from the stinging blow, throwing in body shots, jabs, and crosses, and eventually they'd ended in a draw. The bell rang and the Latino came over and tapped gloves with him.

"Good fight. I'm Oscar, by the way."

"Charlie."

"You gotta watch out for those blind spots, you hear? You've got some good punches, but the hook is coming at you undefended."

Charlie nodded, took a drink from the water bottle, and heard Schoenwetter saying it was time to call it a night. He stretched out his arms and his legs and breathed in the humid air of the gym. Every Wednesday and Sunday he practiced, attending with the same dedication that Mrs. Potter attended church, but with Schoenwetter as the preacher and Charlie the parishioner and punching the prayer. Good. It made more sense than anything else. And Oscar or whoever could hit him all they wanted—after all, he didn't mind being struck or even beat up—and in the end, he'd keep hitting back. He packed up his things, walked toward the exit.

"Hey Jack," Charlie said, bag on his shoulder, hand on the door.

"Yeah, kid?"

"Sign me up for that first fight, all right?"

"Charlie . . ."

"No. No more waiting, no more waffling because of my mom. A fight. A real fight. With that South Side lug your buddy was talking about."

"Huntington? Maybe another month or so of practice—"

"No, Jack. Set it up."

Schoenwetter looked at him, and Charlie looked right back.

"All of this practice, Jack? It means nothing without the fight. I'm in this to fight. *That's* the point of it all. Okay? I've been trained by the army and I've been trained by you. I'm ready. I'm good. I can take a punch. Now sign me up."

Schoenwetter shook his head and walked away, but Charlie knew by his body language that the answer was yes. Maybe he'd give him some scrubs to fight first, but he'd get his big match soon enough. And why not? It wasn't pay-per-view boxing, it wasn't televised, it was simply a square ring in Chicago with two men and one agenda. It was the last day of February, and he finally felt like there was something to hold on to.

He drove back to Downers Grove thinking of the Chain Bridge in Budapest, about pathways over water and how they carried weight. He thought of the stone lions that marked the entrance. The big white bulbs, the vast Danube, the dim-lit boats that seemed to fade into dusk. He pulled into the driveway and noticed that the hairs on his neck were standing on end.

Something was different. Charlie opened the back door and felt a strange sense of absence, but also a change in voltage that made him queasy. Kitchen was dark—a mess. When he strode into the living room, he stood stark still and felt his heart lurch. His father was sitting on the couch, big feet tossed up on the coffee table, alongside two empty Guinnesses and a Lou Malnati's pizza box sprung open like a messy wound.

Charlie dropped his gym bag on the floor.

"So," his father said. "You're boxing now. Have some pizza."

It took Charlie a moment to focus. "What's happening here? What is this?"

His father belched. "What is this? It's a deep dish. Sausage, pepperoni, giardiniera, basil, and garlic. Is that perfect or is that perfect?"

"No, what is this, as in you in this house. You don't talk to me, you don't call me—"

"I don't talk to *you*?" his father growled.

"You haven't even been—"

Henry thumped his fist on the coffee table. "Running away from your life, your job, your responsibilities. Not returning e-mails in fucking Afghanistan. And now accusing me, your own father, the one who threw you the life vest in Europe? Asking *me* why I've returned to my own home? Look at you! You don't talk to me, brat!"

"Brat," Charlie said, rolling the word over. He felt his hand ball up, begin knocking against his leg. And then he remembered that his father was sick.

"If you don't like what I say to you, kid, then don't earn the words."

Charlie grit his teeth, tried to calm himself. "Okay, Dad, you know what? We're going to give each other a mulligan here. Let's start over. Like I was saying, what are you doing here? And are you drunk?"

His father looked away and seemed to lose the blunt force of his anger. "It takes more than a couple beers to get your father drunk."

Charlie sat down on the old rocking chair by the fireplace, the farthest possible seat he could take. His old man was wearing a tattered gray sweatshirt proudly displaying *Gold's Gym, New Buffalo, MI*. He had the beginnings of a beard—silver and bark-colored stubble covered his cheeks and jutting chin. A third Guinness was clutched in his right hand.

"You still have your hair," Charlie said.

His father nodded, before taking an enormous pull from the Guinness. "So you know the score, then. Barkley told you?"

"Does it matter? Leave him out of it."

His father looked at the television screen.

"What's your weight at, Dad?"

"Who knows?"

"I know you know. You're obsessive-compulsive and a narcissist. I bet you know down to the hundredth of a pound."

"Don't push it," his father said, and there was an edge to his voice that made Charlie wary.

Unbelievable, he thought. He'd been to war and back, he'd boxed and fought and trained, he was in the best shape of his life, and he still felt queasy if his father got that tone. By the front door, he noticed, was a pile of broken glass.

"You remember this gym?" the old man asked, pointing at the sweat-shirt.

"New Buffalo? I think so. That's the gym that's built out of that train station, right?"

"Not a train station. A roundhouse. The Pere Marquette Roundhouse, if you know your history. Built in 1920."

"I just remember you insisting on working out every day at like, seven in the morning. Crazy Nazi regimen. That was your ritual, wasn't it? Leave the family early, pretend that you were on your own. Then again, how many times did you wake me up when it was still dark out and try to get me to come with? Like every time."

"And you never did come. I could never get you to follow suit with anything. I'd say, 'Wanna work out with your old man, kid?' And you'd say, 'Nope, let me sleep.' And I did, didn't I? I let you sleep as long as you wanted."

"Dad, I still worked out, just not at the ass-crack of dawn while we were on vacation. It was a *vacation*, remember? At what point did you forget how to have fun?"

His father said nothing, appeared to be lost in thought. Charlie remembered this stare from when they were all a family unit—Henry Brunson animated one moment, totally engaged, and then moments later, preoccupied—looking out at darkened windows, the ceiling, the dents in the kitchen wall, his big hand massaging his jaw.

"There was always something wrong, wasn't there, Dad?"

His father grunted and rolled his eyes. "We haven't gone up to Michigan in years, you know that?"

"You've been gone, Dad. Gone. No one understands it. No one knows what you're doing."

"We used to go up into Harbor Country almost every summer when you two were in school, renting those lake houses. Remember how there was always something wrong with the houses? Like the one that had cockroaches? And the other had biting flies?"

"The whole of Michigan had the biting flies that summer."

"I know, Charlie. I'm making a list—"

"They were ravenous. I remember that jogger who was covered—"

"And then there were the other houses, you remember? None of them were what they were cracked up to be. The one with no air-conditioning? And the one in the weird little town where everyone was a territorial beach hermit? Then there was that pristine house, when you were twelve or thirteen. You remember that, I'm sure. The white one, with the bay windows on the bluff—in Union Pier? That son of a bitch flooded on the third night."

"That house was actually pretty nice," Charlie said, remembering a row of skylights, a view of grass-speckled dunes leading into Lake Michigan, and, on the last night, finding a *Penthouse* magazine that one of the previous guests had left behind. "I'll admit it was nice. But seriously, remember the biting flies and that jogger?"

His father closed his eyes. "I remember how that drugstore in Union Pier had no bug spray left. They were plucked clean—only lotto tickets and ketchup. I bought all the tickets and made three dollars. Call it a push. And I remember how the damn flies would follow us out to the sand bar—biting our fucking scalps—I mean, they were goddamn flying black hyenas that year. But I don't remember any jogger. I've got no recollection of that at all."

"Dad, we were driving back from dinner or something, and it was still light out, and that overweight jogger was *covered* with biting flies. You looked at Mom and said, 'Bubble butt buffet,' and I got the joke, even though I wasn't supposed to. You don't remember that?"

"I've got nothing for you, kid. But then again, you can't remember whose house this is, and you ask your own father what he's doing in it. So I guess we're even."

"Dad, you're sitting there like you're looking for a fight."

"You're the one with the hand wraps, kid."

Charlie thought on that one for a moment.

"You like boxing, then?"

"Sure, Dad."

"I'm serious. You like it?"

Charlie sensed the tinnitus coming on, but then eased up and it faded back. "Yeah, Dad. I like it a lot. It's the blue-collar version of physical therapy."

The old man chuckled at that, and they lapsed into silence. The television was on mute. Charlie wanted to say a litany of things, about how his father being sick didn't take away what he had done, or how he had done it. It didn't take away from his total lack of ethics with their mother, his lack of acknowledgment of or appreciation for his son's service, his lack of explanation, maturity—Charlie felt too many words swirling through his skull, and realized that he couldn't say any of them. He felt a grudging sympathy, too, but found that emotion burying itself with the rest. For some reason, his father in the room, even sick, changed the way he was able to talk.

"Barkley says your service is over, and that you've been discharged," his father said. "But you're not telling anyone why. Not that I can complain about keeping secrets, mind you, but what happened over there?"

Charlie hesitated, but he realized that the subject of his discharge, like his guilt, had finally relaxed its grip. "It was an honorable RIF, Dad."

"RIF?"

"Reduction in Force," Charlie said, measuring his breathing. "But everyone wanted me to apply for something else. For another kind of discharge. I refused. I . . . I just couldn't do what they asked anymore. And when I refused enough times, some people who cared, who actually gave a shit, pushed for the RIF, just to get me out."

"They wanted a discharge for something else? Like what, PTSD?"

Charlie fixed his eyes on the television. "I don't know why I'm telling you any of this. I haven't told anyone else."

"I'm your father."

"Right."

"I am, Charlie. And so? I'm the history buff, remember? Was it PTSD? That's what they wanted the discharge for?"

Charlie pursed his lips. "It doesn't matter now, does it? It doesn't matter how fucked-up I was or am or whatever. I got an honorable RIF, not the other thing, and that's that. Facts are facts and I'm out of the army and back here in Downers Grove."

"And now you're boxing."

"That's right. And now I'm boxing."

They lapsed into silence again. Charlie understood, more clearly now, that the path he was on was certainly not perfect—but it was workable. In and out, he breathed. He could do this. He could speak and form thoughts and get through it, just like Al said.

"So," Charlie said, waiting for his father to meet his eyes. "Are you going to tell me what you're really doing here? And yes, I understand it's your house."

He finished the Guinness. "I'm moving back in."

"Excuse me?"

"You heard me, loud and clear."

"You're *home*? Like home-home?"

His father nodded, then shrugged. "But your mother's gone."

THE PEAK AND
THE PLANK

"Diversey Harbor is where it's at," Barkley said.

He watched as Ginny looked out at the rows of bobbing boats and softly lit wooden posts that illuminated the hulls of the vessels. Beyond the boats was more darkened harbor, and then a bridge blurred with passing headlights, and then, rising like a jagged billboard, the unobstructed Chicago skyline, standing bold against the approaching dusk.

"It *is* nice," she admitted. "It's fancy. No one knows about this?"

"I mean, people know," Barkley said. "They know the location and name. But I've never seen it crowded. You'll get some joggers that go by. You'll get couples that sit on the cement edges by the water and take pictures. But yeah, never seen it crowded. Best view in Chicago, too."

"But no lake. Don't you need to add the lake for best-view status?"

"Nah. You don't. I see what you're saying, but this is it, right here. Symmetry, breadth, color, depth. And it's *contained*. It's beauty in parameters, in a tidy little pocket."

Ginny nudged him. "You're convincing today."

"It's because I'm right."

The breeze picked up. She took his hand. It was warm out—the first warmth of April—and Ginny's hand was cool and dry. In his other palm he felt the perspiring edges of the wine bottle.

"Want to sit in the grass and open this?"

"Sure."

They walked over to a stretch of tree-lined grass, and Barkley dropped his backpack, unzipped it, and pulled a blue-and-white picnic blanket out. He spread out the edges and fished the silver opener from the backpack, along with a Tupperware container of Gouda cheese, red grapes, and Carr's whole wheat crackers. In front of them, the sky darkened, and the skyline shimmered into honeycombs of light.

"I'll open the wine," Ginny said. "You're going to botch it again."

"No, just give it to me. Here. You see?" There was a satisfying hollow *thunk* as he yanked the cork from the bottle.

"I can't wait for this little chard," she said. "Listed as a best buy by the vino powers that be. Eh, little guy?" She nudged him and cackled.

"Ugh, don't call me 'little guy.' That sounds, you know, small and stuff. And I wanted that Gingrich Hills wine—I feel like we settled. No settling!"

"Grgich Hills? That was a forty-dollar bottle. The Boschendal is thrifty *and* delicious."

"Oaky something-something, hints of something else, a touch of honeysuckle something, translation: get me a beer."

"Barkley, listen to you! Being a sourpuss in front of the best view in the city!"

He felt a twang of stress course through him. It was a Sunday, and it was a truly gorgeous April evening—sixty-two degrees, soft breeze, cloudless nighttime sky, buildings clear in the distance, even the lapping of the water and the boats knocking against the dock. But through it all, he could only picture Margaret Carey's wrinkled face and calculating eyes, could only hear the scratchy assault of her voice.

"It's work," he said, gritting his teeth, trying not to feel resigned.

"Is it that troll woman? Margaret Cunty?"

"Yes. She's, she's—it's seriously out of control. She doesn't *care* that I'm doing well. I mean, she has a problem with me, I get that. But why?"

Ginny sat down on the blanket and began pouring the chardonnay into plastic wineglasses. "It's like I said before, Barkley. Number one, you're fun in the classroom. That's anti–Catholic school from the start. When I was at IC, it was note taking and nothing else. Direct instruction, isn't that what they call it? And you probably like discussion, right?"

"I mean, it's natural to discuss. That's what we're taught to do these days. And it doesn't even matter. Her latest issue is classroom cleanliness. She searches for scraps of paper on my floor like an insane prospector."

"Ugh. Okay, well your teaching style is the first issue. And the other thing, Barkley, is the fact that your class *is* going so well. The woman can't stand to see it. The kids like your class, don't they? They like you, don't they?"

"I guess. I'd like to think they like me. That they like the class." Barkley remembered the version of himself that existed as a high schooler, the bumbling goof who couldn't find a place or purpose; but now, so many years later, he finally had. Everything felt right, except Margaret Carey.

Barkley felt Ginny's arm sling itself around his neck. She kissed him roughly on the cheek, the mouth, then buried her head into his neck. "She's crazy," his girlfriend murmured. "She's totally, completely, insanely nuts. You're too good for this school."

But Barkley knew that a part of him loved Eastwick, regardless of its contradictions and absurdities. There were crazy old people there, and no pensions, and no union or even a human resources department—no one to go to if a teacher was in trouble. But he loved the building, the ancient history of cobbled stones and medieval towers, the way religion was somehow embedded seamlessly, and, of course, the students. Sure, many were entitled and pretentious. But many more were hardworking and patient, driven and intelligent, creative and insightful, and all the time quietly humorous about the countless oddities of their school.

"This week," Barkley said, "is the last week to prove our teacher contracts should be renewed. We find out on Friday. They call us to the principal's office, like we're children, and they tell us. This one's coming back, this one's not. I feel like I'm walking into a Shirley Jackson story. Carey will probably have a box of rocks waiting on her desk. But it's that simple—by Friday I'll either be employed next year, or not."

"I know. Have some wine. Drink."

"Maybe I can invite Peters to observe one of my classes. You know, to get more support?"

"Sure. You should do that."

"You think I should invite someone other than Peters?"

Ginny paused and closed her eyes. "Seriously, Barkley? It's a beautiful night. I can't handle this self-obsessing much longer."

"Self-obsessing? It's my job I'm talking about. You understand it's my job, right? Something I care about? Involving my livelihood?"

"Yes, and we talk about it every day we hang out. We text about it. I'm pretty sure we Skyped about it when I was in Portland. And if you had an Instagram account I'm fairly certain you'd send symbolism-laden pictures of half-eaten Fuji apples and broken protractors and *Beowulf* 'Thinking Critically' sections followed by hash tag 'worried,' hash tag 'job,' or maybe hash tag 'need to talk about the same shit again so I can drive my girlfriend completely insane and make her bore her temple out with a power drill.' Seriously, Barkley, I can't talk about this every time we hang out."

"Wow. That's a little exaggerated, isn't it? I mean, new things keep happening over there. Are you joking or are you actually mad?"

"Do I have to be, like, mad-mad? Can I just be annoyed? Justifiably annoyed?"

"I mean, what do you want me to do, not talk about it?"

Ginny grabbed his shoulders and shook him. "*Yes.* Precisely. Don't talk about it. You can't do anything. You've done a wonderful job preparing and it's clear that you care and you like your job, but we can't do this into infinity. Unless you want me to go insane. Unless you want that woman to win—I mean, think about it. She wants to make you crazy. She probably wants you to make your girlfriend crazy. Remember at Black Duck, when we had some interesting conversations about, you know, the world and all the stuff outside of ourselves? Society and whatnot?"

"Yes . . ."

"Well, this is the opposite. Subjecting your girlfriend to obsessive-compulsive nattering while distracting her from beautiful evenings at harbors with unobstructed skylines moves you *backward* on the dating board game."

"But sometimes I need to vent."

"Lose a turn."

"I'm serious, Ginny."

"Move back four, lose a turn, exchange your 1920s car token for a French poodle."

"Ugh. It's all a joke to you, I get it."

"I'm about to go from justifiably annoyed to actually mad."

"Seriously?"

Ginny threw up her hands and went silent.

Barkley watched the boats and let the silence expand into minutes—then set his gaze on the beads of perspiration on the wine bottle, dropping like tiny elevators toward the bottom. "Okay," he said, finally. "I get it. I'm being stupid. I'll fall on my sword."

She was silent.

"I'm sorry."

"You don't even know what you're apologizing for."

"For being annoying."

"Barkley, let me ask you this: how often do I complain about my shit?"

"I don't know. Not often. But whatever—your job is cool, and your family is totally normal. You want to trade with mine for a year?"

"*My* family is normal? My dad went up to a cabin in Wisconsin this weekend, and has been sending my brother and me picture texts of him trying to lasso a deer with a garden hose. He's a lunatic. My brother is constantly getting caught smoking weed by my mom. My mom is obsessed with studying weird pagan religions from tribes around the world, because she believes voodoo might be real. And so on. Everybody's family is weird. At least your mom has turned into a badass."

"I'm still wrapping my head around the parental switcheroo."

"So whose family is normal again?"

Barkley held out his hands. "Okay. I acquiesce. I admit it. I've been an annoying, obsessive-compulsive maniac, and it needs to stop. If I don't stop, Margaret Carey wins. And you get annoyed. I apologize. Let's change the subject, okay? What do you want to talk about?"

Ginny allowed a small smile. "He learns, ladies and gentlemen. And I don't know, what about Charlie? I do enjoy that SOB. He's boxing regularly now, right?"

Barkley nodded. "He's got a big fight coming up on Friday, not like televised or anything, but big for him. Against some dude named Hunting-something, who supposedly fractured a guy's cheekbone last time he fought. Pretty crazy, huh?"

"Very. You should go see it."

Barkley looked at the boats again. "Yeah, me and some friends are going. And then add in the fact that he's hanging out at home, living with my dad—equally insane. I can hardly imagine it. Anyway, what about your concert this weekend? Looking forward to it? I'll try to come right after Charlie's fight."

She lay back against the grass. "Eh. We just got a new rhythm guitarist—girl thinks she should be soloing more. I might challenge her midconcert to settle the debate. She thinks we can't tell that she's not *really* soloing, but give me a break. All she does is bend notes and memorize little patterns, and during the solos she gets this shocked look on her face, like a constipated cow. You know, with the wide eyes and clenched jaw? Like this? I think it's supposed to be her badass face."

Barkley winced. "Ah, don't *you* make the face. It's frightening. So you're taking it to her, then? Guitar duel?"

"Well, yeah. All in good fun, though. But I'm going to win. In case you're wondering."

"God, see that's what I need. I wish I had a skill like that."

"Teaching, Barkley!"

"No, no, I mean where I take something in my hands, and produce something awesome. An actual skill."

"Like whittling? You want to whittle me a turtledove? We'll get you a nice little knife and some balsa wood, and all night you can craft little trinkets for me. My boyfriend, Barkley the Whittler!"

He kicked his leg out at her. "Whittle me a refill, woman."

"Oh, 'woman' now, huh? Seriously, though. If not teaching, how about writing? Last time we were with your mom, she was going on and on about your stories. And you said my uncle ended up giving you a what—a B plus in the creative writing class?"

"More like a B minus. And every single story I wrote just got owned."

"Well, he says you've got some talent," Ginny said.

"I honestly don't even know what to write about. The goblins and knights are feeling a little long in the tooth these days. And if I go realistic, I don't know where to start. Besides, books are the world's biggest long shot. Everything feels like a long shot right now."

"What's that mean?"

"I just have this feeling, you know? That the floor on everything is about to drop out. Like us, right here, is the peak. The calm before the avalanche."

Ginny ran her fingers across his back. Behind him, past the trees, he could hear the soft *whacks* of the golfers in the city driving range, lobbing tiny white spheres at distant targets. Ginny's hand encircled his own. She squeezed once, twice, three times. He closed his eyes and thought, *even if it all goes to hell, even if everything falls apart, I'm still lucky. I've still got her.*

"Drink," Ginny said, and he did.

The next day, Barkley's eyes snapped open at four in the morning, and he lay very calm and still, waiting until the sky threw sunlight like egg yolk upon his ceiling. Ginny was next to him, still sleeping, a tangle of red hair and Slipknot-toting baggy T-shirt. Her new job as a guitar instructor seemed light-years ahead of his own career: she didn't wake up until nine, played music all day, and still had concerts with her band a couple of times a month. Her weekends were filled with restaurants, beer gardens, visits to the Green Dolphin and Kingston Mines, and occasional trips to Big Ten schools to play at bars. Every three weeks or so, she'd even go back to help out Mr. Doring at Myopic Books. Not a bad deal, Barkley thought—and no Margaret Carey in sight.

Soon enough he was up and pacing, a jumble of loose nerves, tiptoeing around the studio drunkenly, knocking into cupboards and couch edges. Four days to make someone over there see him as an instructional necessity. What could he do that he hadn't already done? He thumped into the coffee table, scattering coasters in the darkness.

"Ah, take a sedative," Ginny mumbled. "Sleep."

"Sorry, sorry—go back to bed."

"I can't, you sound like a blind, obese Wookiee out there."

"Okay, okay—I'll just get there early." He pocketed his keys, fastened his tie, and ran out into the early morning.

Approaching Eastwick in the Taurus, Barkley already felt hungry. His potbelly was almost entirely gone, sucked away into some calorie-decimated void, and the angular features that looked back at him in the mirror were constantly shocking. Through the windshield, tree limbs everywhere seemed on the cusp of blooming, dangling new buds like chocolates wrapped in red foil. Birds had finally returned to the Midwest; honks and chirps were everywhere. And all Barkley hoped was that it wasn't one of those pseudoironic things, where the spring unfolding revealed an awful surprise.

Inside, Eastwick's hallways were filled with an expectant hush. Spring break was the second week in April, and many of the kids had a contradictory look of disassociation and hyperactivity, as if they'd chased a handful of Vicodin with a gallon of Red Bull. The teachers themselves looked either bleary-eyed with worry or quietly sedate, depending on their status with renewals. Everything, Barkley felt, was a series of contradictions.

He spent first period teaching on tension-fueled autopilot, pacing and orating around his desk, which was now filled with trinkets that jubilantly celebrated his personality. On the front lines: the pterodactyl paperweight, hand-painted model DeLorean, and chipped ceramic hobbit figurine, as well as a printed-out map from *Lord of the Rings* (tacked to the wall), a plastic General Krang of *Ninja Turtles* fame, a Scottie Pippen bobblehead, a Willie Gault bobblehead, a leather-bound copy of *Dune*, and two coffee mugs, one with Chunk from *The Goonies* plastered to the front, the other with Wilson from *Home Improvement* peeking over a picket fence. His desk was no longer the bare and disappointing sand trap from earlier in the year; now he looked at it as his cheering section, his rah-rah-Barkley peanut gallery, his oddball mother ship of bizarre psychological support.

In the faculty bathroom after third period, Barkley stared at himself in the mirror. He felt trim and unrecognizable. Was he the same person? It wasn't just his waistline and cheekbones—with the help of Ginny, all of his clothes were nice now, more than respectable. He had a full closet of brand-new button-downs and matching ties, smooth rows of dress pants, black and brown shoes that gleamed the way his father's had, when he was at the top of his game.

The bell rang. Where the hell was Margaret Carey? he thought, absentmindedly checking his phone for messages about his father. Nothing. He usually found his ever-vigilant department chair before second period, watching him from the hallway, bursting into his classroom to "drop off books" or send volleys of poison dart comments that had him fuming for hours. Whatever. Barkley pocketed his phone, opened the bathroom door, and found himself deposited in the middle of a swarming passing period. A group of senior athletes paraded by, clapping and thumping into each other, while band students swung the other way, lugging instruments like tombstones, and there went the kids from his seventh-period class, each trailing bits of conversation, like airplanes with half-written messages.

Locker slam—"such a bitch"—locker slam.

Locker punch, fist bump, random hoot—"and he didn't even ask me, just hung out with her, said they were bored—"

"My ass—"

"Anybody could write like Salinger—" Barkley found himself turning his head around for that one, who would possibly think that—

"Mr. Brunson is, like, *hot* now—"

Barkley felt himself pinwheeling, coughing explosively, trying to find the culprit of that final comment, all the while thinking, in awe, that no one, not even Ginny, had ever described him as *hot*. He felt the perverse thrill of stepping into someone else's life, sticking a toe into the land of oversexualized jocks who experienced these sentiments with absurd regularity. His heart felt like a pounded keyboard. Who had said it? A large, overweight kid, probably a freshman, was walking past a group of sophomores—no. Two girls were walking east down the hallway, the shorter one—that was Maggie Tolliver. Yes, it was Tolliver who had said it, weird enough in its own right, and she was walking next to . . . Elise Rossi. Elise the taller one, the slender blonde, the one all the junior boys shamelessly hit on, thinking she could take it. And she could. And yet, Tolliver had said those words, *Mr. Brunson is, like, hot now*, and Elise had been the recipient. Barkley's stomach felt like fried circuits and acid rain. Had Elise said nothing? Had she laughed? Had she *nodded*? And thinking of her nodding made him remember that moment they'd shared in his office, when he'd first heard about his father, when her breath in that darkness was so close he'd felt it on his neck.

He shook himself. What the hell was he thinking about? He had four days to prove himself and he was analyzing ridiculous between-period gossip. He ran up the stairs, back to his classroom. Fourth period was a planning period for him, and he'd have the classroom to himself, and—

On his desk was a bright yellow Post-it note, waving like a planted flag. He grabbed it, already feeling his stomach turn. It read:

> *Barkley:*
> *Please try to keep a clean and orderly classroom.*
> *The custodians have it tough enough. I found these*
> *under the desks of your students, and I wouldn't*
> *want this issue to come up in your final review.*
> *Margaret*

Beside the Post-it were three small pieces of crumpled paper, each about the size of a half-dollar. Barkley felt himself begin to hyperventilate. To find all three of them would have required some effort. His fingernails dug into his palms. He threw his body back into his swivel chair, and let it roll until it hit the dry eraser board.

Barkley sat at his desk a moment longer. He stared at the pterodactyl paperweight, then at the Post-it from Margaret Carey. The silver teeth on the prehistoric bird didn't look as sharp as they had in December. They appeared worn down—rounded, graying nubs that could only help a child in a battle against action figures.

At the end of the day, Barkley slung his bag over his shoulder, a stiff feeling building up like drywall in his gut. He nodded at the students as he passed through the central atrium, then walked out of Eastwick and into the parking lot. The temperature had dropped since the day before at Diversey Harbor, and he felt the April chill and dampness hitting his face in gusts.

Looking up, Barkley admired the twin red-bricked drum towers that stood twenty feet above the roof of the school, one more ancient than the other and caked with moss and ivy. It looked natural enough, but

Barkley knew the landscaping crew was asked to maintain this aesthetic—a symbolic representation of the ancient ways and the new. A flock of crows circled and banked from high above. Between the drum towers stood the two-sided, ivory-faced clock tower, still working after its construction in 1949, but always six minutes fast. The rickety giant stood a full forty-seven feet above the third-floor roof, and cast a shadow across the limestone chapel that jutted out from the back end of the school. This was something Barkley always loved—the changing facets of the building, the way one age-morphed and shed its skin into the next, from the limestone and wrought iron of the 1889 construction to burgundy bricks of the 1940s to the glass domes of the 2008 library atrium and entranceway. Eastwick was half crumbling, half modern; half perfect, half medieval. And Barkley was obsessed with the exploration of its intricate bowels—walking the crooked hallways, wandering into classrooms coiled with exposed pipes, and disappearing into the basement to look at athletic shrines almost three-quarters of a century old. The most intriguing were fencing and sport fishing and polo, the latter of which came when Eastwick's property was sprawling, encompassing hundreds of acres, multiple stone churches, an off-site library, and two polo fields, plus almost five dozen stables for the horses. None of it existed anymore, and Downers Grove was now a dense and modernized suburban town, but that history was part of the intrigue. In Eastwick's basement, inside room 056, he and Dobbs had opened a locked door with a variety of cloak-and-dagger safety pins and found an enormous, dust-clogged billiards table, made of ruby felt and imported from England. In room 017, they'd found thirty sets of rawhide-bound snowshoes and matching coonskin caps—presumably, Barkley thought, for the teachers to get to and from school in the old days of winter blizzards and dirt roads. As always, the not knowing made it even more intriguing. But now, with that drywall feeling stiffening in his gut, all that mystery seemed like it might never be solved. And the thought of not coming back made the unknown bowels of Eastwick seem less like enticement, more like punishment.

"How you doing, kid?"

Barkley turned. Mike Dobbs was leaning heavily against the worn bricks of Eastwick's west wall, just ten feet away from him. His eyes were oddly pinched, and he took deep drags of a cigarette that hung out of his mouth like a broken arm.

"I thought you only liked cigars," Barkley said.

"Generally, true. Yes. But cigars are for celebrations. And firing machine guns."

"And this is neither?"

"That's right, kid. This is neither." He rested a hand on his paunch and took another drag. Smoke came over his face in wormy streams, the way it might exit vents in a burning building. Above them, crows circled and squawked.

Dobbs nodded. "Like vultures, aren't they? You ever wonder why people don't shoot more crows? I mean, who is going to miss a crow? What member of PETA is really going to get worked up?" He sighed, leaned his head back against the bricks.

"What's happening, Mike?"

"That is certainly the question. What *is* happening, exactly?"

"Well?"

"You know what I did before I came here? I never told you. I owned a restaurant. I started out as a chef—see, it's all chemistry in the end. And I had this idea of running a place that only made chili. Or like, eight kinds of chili, plus corn bread, plus apple pie, *and that's it*. No more, just that. Hearty comfort food, made well. So I opened up shop, and figured it would do average in the summer, make a killing fall through winter."

"And did it?"

Dobbs nodded. "Hell, yes. See, my masterpiece? The bison chili. You had to taste it to believe it. But I also had the Asian chili, the double-jalapeño chili, the four-cheese chili, the lamb and feta chili, the list goes on. I had the building guys put in a fireplace. A little stone hearth. Candles with orange bubble glass on every table. Smoking allowed. You could see these neon beer signs shining through the fog in the smoking section—I'm telling you, it was beautiful. It was right over on Ashland and Grace. Got my meat from the Paulina Market."

"Sounds amazing."

"It was. God, I loved that place. And then you know what happened? It started small. I had an employee that was stealing from me. Just yanking money from the register. So I fired her. Then she sued. That meant lawyer expenses, that meant distractions. A couple good restaurants opened across from me and like that, like *that*, everything changed. I'd missed something, hadn't been prepared. Been too distracted to update the Web site. Soon enough we were operating at a loss, and then—over. Done. Close up shop. And during those first two and a half years, I never knew how good I had it. You just get sideswiped when you act like that."

"Right, I hear you."

"So this time around," Dobbs said, gesturing to Eastwick's walls, "when I switched to teaching, I decided to be prepared. Because the thing I learned about the restaurant business, the thing I realized, is that sometimes the things you love, don't love you back."

Barkley, thinking of the things he loved, thought of Ginny, and thought of Eastwick.

Dobbs lit a second cigarette. "And it's not to say that I love this school. I *like* this school. Sometimes I *tolerate* this school. But I do enjoy it, and I'm always prepared for the worst, most ridiculous scenario."

"Mike. You're acting, like, apocalyptic here."

"Well," Dobbs said, "what's happening is that I'm gone. Poof! Gone."

"*What?* Mike, come on, man! You're not serious, right? You've been teaching here for years."

"Correction: I've been teaching here for three years. And instructors are the school's personal ragdolls. They can do whatever they like with you, pull off your arms and legs, bury you in the backyard, feed you to the black Lab across the street. *Especially* if it's a private school. Unions get a lot of shit, but without a union—no power at all. And Eastwick has four, maybe five people who come together, do each other favors, and pull the strings."

"Margaret Carey?"

"Hell, yes, Margaret Carey. She's been teaching here for forty-six years, department chair for twenty. Oh, hi there, Jenny."

Barkley turned and saw one of Eastwick's seniors walk by and wave brightly at Dobbs. A few more students walked past, and Dobbs held the cigarette at his side, then put it back to his mouth after they were gone.

"So," Barkley said. "Carey did you in?"

"No, no. My problem's not with Carey. *Your* problem is with Carey. Don't say I didn't warn you there, buddy."

Barkley settled back against the bricks, lined up with Dobbs. He imagined a firing squad aiming at them from across the parking lot, and tried to shake himself from the feeling that a bull's-eye was on his chest.

"I just don't know how to deal with her. I've tried, Mike. She just keeps coming after me."

Dobbs shook his head, then blew a wobbly smoke ring up toward the sky. "It's not on you. I mean, maybe an experienced teacher of twenty years could have gone toe-to-toe with her, at least for a while. But still, without tenure, and without a union, Carey always wins. You bow down to her, or you lose."

"But if she's not after you, then what happened?"

"Well, I've tried hard to buddy up to those powers that be. I talk to Peters, and I steer clear of Carey. But you've still got the other cronies—the other assistant principal, the old man at the top, and the athletic director. What I hadn't prepared for is Father Burnham."

"The president? The Dominican priest?"

He nodded. "Turns out the man has a nephew who wants to teach chemistry. Funny that *I* teach AP chemistry and biology. Funny that, like you, the kids both do well and like my class. Shouldn't be a problem, right? After all, there are two other teachers who dabble in chem."

"So?"

"So you have to understand, other favors have been done already. Tony Staccato, who teaches regular chem—the athletic director put him there a couple years ago, and that was as a favor to Saint Ignatius, who took in the AD's daughter as a geometry teacher. So the athletic director can't remove Staccato without getting Saint Ignatius riled up, and possibly costing his own daughter the job. Then you've got Brenda Upton, who sucks, who is literally an idiot and can't explain what baking soda and vinegar do if I showed her a picture of a volcano—she is the oldest niece of Bill Derby. That's right, the twelve-time state-championship-winning water polo coach, Bill Derby. Pissing off Bill Derby is like putting in a formal request for the gallows. You see what happens? How it works? I don't know anybody, so I'm gone."

Barkley watched the crows, which were now lined up on the telephone wires adjacent to the school. They were oddly still, their dark beaks pointed in his direction.

"What now?" Barkley asked. "And I'm sorry, that is one of the shittiest things I've ever heard."

"Who knows? I'll be fine. I've succeeded as a chef, as a salesman, as a teacher, at least for a while. Not sure if I'll teach elsewhere, or go back to the restaurant business. Who knows?"

"That's good. That's good you've got a backup plan, I guess."

Dobbs took a final drag on the cigarette. "And truthfully, even if we're both screwed, would you actually *want* to teach here?"

Barkley sighed. "I don't know what it is about this place, but I would. It's just—it's so messed up, and I know it. But it's unique, isn't it? And the kids are great. And the old building—I don't know."

"Remember what I told you," Dobbs said. "You're a romantic, so you need to remember. About what happens with the things you love."

One of the buses honked, and the crows scattered, rising into the air and flapping, their dark figures holes against the blue tarp of sky.

For Barkley, the rest of the week sped by with cruel efficiency. Groggy morning, first period, fifth period, ninth period, end of school day, two hours with Ginny, bedtime, smear of dreams, morning. And begin again. Barkley could feel the beating heart of Friday's decision waiting for him. It rumbled against the floors of Eastwick and throbbed against the walls, and there was nothing he could do, no decisive action he could take— if anything, the week felt like a mudslide of twisted inevitability. The kids finished up *For Whom the Bell Tolls* and began brainstorming for their literary analysis papers. Dobbs was checked out, grumbling as he went from class to class. The students seemed blissfully unaware of the approaching carnage. By Wednesday, certain teachers already knew they were leaving. The assistant librarian—gone. A pile of books by an empty desk. Cutting back costs, they said. Barkley walked by the weight room and saw the strength and conditioning coach packing up his gear and looking sadly at an elliptical machine. The new history teacher, a portly girl fresh out of Illinois State's teaching program, was sitting in the teachers' cafeteria with red eyes and a white molehill of used Kleenex. Eastwick's purging had begun, and the powers that be were pulling the levers and dropping the trapdoors.

But still, no word on his fate. Even Margaret Carey seemed strangely noncombative, a silent eel swishing through the hallways. And there were always the concerns outside of Eastwick, concerns that didn't just distract him, but also lowered him into a near fugue state where the cadence of every voice, the pulse of every thought and feeling, vibrated at the same octave and thus became a singular drone, like a sea of crickets or a fleet of planes departing from home.

On Wednesday, two days before the fight, Charlie called Barkley, asking him for backup with his father, and his kid brother swung by after a day of teaching classes.

The first thing he noticed was the mess. Outside, the house was the same blue-and-white construction it had always been. Inside, a little different. It wasn't absurd, it wasn't like a frat house, and it was clear that one or both of them were at least trying, but still—stained cereal bowls stacked in the sink, a mess of hardcover history books spilled across the family room floor, and pizza boxes fanned out like giant playing cards in the garage. Mom was definitely gone. She'd told all of them she was at a hotel (undisclosed) and looking for an apartment. *Will call soon with more information*, her text message to her sons had said.

His father, now growing a scattershot beard, met him at the door. He was wearing another gray sweatshirt, no doubt to hide the gaunt figure. Below that: baggy Diesel jeans, with the belt fastened to the last notch, and brand-new Reef sandals. Something told him that his father still hadn't given up—not yet. But it was his eyes that were truly different, blue-green orbs focused inward, on some unknown internal plane.

"There he is," his father said, with weariness. "There's the kid. Come on in, see what we've done with the place."

"I'm seeing, I'm seeing," Barkley said, but instead he moved forward and gave his father a hug. The old man flinched in surprise, then recalibrated with a couple of hearty slaps on the back.

Charlie appeared in the kitchen, looming like a chiseled Italian sculpture. "Little brother, things have changed, huh? See how I'm a beast now? The big match is on Friday—you're going, right?"

"Definitely. And that's the same day I find out if I'm teaching next year."

"Yeah, but you've got it in the bag, don't you? Got it handled?"

"One would think," Barkley said. "How are you feeling, Dad?"

His father was already seated at the kitchen table, popping open a box of Giordano's deep-dish sausage pizza. "Tired. Cold. Dizzy. Like my hands and feet have frostbite. Constipated. Tired. Dizzy. Am I repeating myself? Like shit, basically."

"I get him all these protein drinks," Charlie said. "And history books. Any hardcover nonfiction bestseller, I scoop up at the Barnes and Noble. And he reads them."

"There it is," his father said. "Once people start talking like you're not in the room, you know you're fucked."

"I'm just updating him," Charlie said.

"Go ahead and update me a Guinness."

"Aren't you not supposed to be drinking?" Barkley asked.

Charlie pulled him aside, deep into the family room. The television was on, *Check, Please!* reviewing a new Moroccan restaurant in Chicago. Barkley eyed the history books—was that one about Patton?

"Earth to Barkley," Charlie said. "There's another thing you should know. Dad is drinking beer, smoking cigars, and I'm pretty sure he hasn't gotten chemo in a couple weeks."

"Well, he's supposed to get it every two weeks. Are you going to take him?"

"I can't, like, tie him up and drag him there, man. He tells me no, that he'll go himself. He doesn't say anything about his schedule. Some days he's gone, some days he doesn't leave the couch. Some days he sleeps and eats nothing, some he drinks and orders food like a college freshman. Although his appetite has definitely declined. He still doesn't communicate."

"How's he been, otherwise?"

Charlie shrugged. "Has he achieved a series of spiritual paradigm shifts and transcendent truths? No. Not that I can see. But he's civil enough. If he's still grudging me for serving my country and bailing on his job, he's not showing it. In fact, he even asked to hear a couple stories."

"So you two are getting along, then."

Charlie laughed. "What you have are two people who probably need a lot—and by a lot I mean a fucking industrial-size quantity—of therapy. And these two people are tolerating each other, occasionally getting along, and occasionally getting angry. It's not like a sitcom with a laugh track, if that's what you're thinking. It's not *Cheers* in Downers Grove."

"I definitely wasn't thinking that," Barkley said. "But it's better than nothing, right? I guess we just find ways to spend time with him. It wasn't always like this, you know. I mean, we used to think he was king of the world. At least I did. I'm still not sure how all of it changed so quickly."

"We both thought he was king of the world, it's true. But the change? The minute he lost interest in this family—that's when it happened. Suddenly you're looking at everything in a different light, trying to rewind your past and inspect every granule for inconsistencies."

"Maybe we're not supposed to do that."

Charlie looked at him. "Little brother, you've always been the perceptive one. The thinker, the reader. Hell, even the writer. And you're telling me it's strange to look back at your own past? To try to examine if, during your entire childhood, your father slowly dragged your mother away from everything she cared about? And if your father always wanted out? Wanted out from day one?"

"That's not true," Barkley said, and he felt the truth of it. He knew about how his father felt, not from any conversation, but intuitively— he knew his father loved them, had always cared for them, but he also knew his father was one of those people who was always checking the horizon. What boats were coming in? Which ones were leaving? What was out there, on the high seas? Not everyone was anchored in place, not everyone experienced total happiness from living life on the ground.

"How do you know what's true and not?"

"I just know, all right? Trust me. He cares about us. This whole thing has been about him. The way he sees things. He's just restless, you know? It has nothing to do with us."

Charlie looked at the entrance to the kitchen, where their father was waiting. Barkley felt his older brother wanting to say something, but there was some kind of hitch, some kind of spiked speed bump in their communication.

"I just don't want to see this to the end," Charlie said, finally. "It's going to be a train wreck. Can't you feel that, at least? Can't you see how awful this is going to be?"

"I think we're going to be surprised," Barkley said. "He is Henry Brunson, after all. You think he's just going to sit here and take it?"

"So far, it's only been Guinness and deep-dish pizza."

"There will be more," Barkley said. "Come on, let's go talk to the old man. Grill him on history or something."

They walked back into the kitchen. Their father was cutting apart a slice of pizza, swollen with sausage and peppers and garlic, head leaned back against the kitchen wall.

"That's what I'm talking about. Spice of life. Good thing I've still got a small amount of appetite left."

"Like when Al came here, right, Dad?" Barkley asked. "This is what you two would always order."

"Except the moron always wanted light beer. Great guy, terrible taste in beer."

They sat down at the table. Their father cut slices of pizza and passed them around on paper plates. Barkley considered that, nearly a year ago, this was the same table that Charlie had thrown up on. But now, he truly looked better. He looked better for sure.

"What do you want to talk about?" the old man asked, sprinkling red pepper flakes across his pizza. "School? You want to talk school?"

"Anything but that," Barkley said. "How about history? I'd be down for a dynamite history lesson."

Charlie put a foot up on the vacant chair. "Yeah, I could hear something cool about history. What have you got?"

"What have I got? Come on, guys. You're talking to a double major in history and business, here. You're talking to a sensei. What do you want to hear about?"

"War," Barkley and Charlie both intoned.

"War, huh?" He scratched his beard. "I mean, I can go back to ancient Rome and Greece. I can give you Julius Caesar. I can give you Alexander. He was tutored by Aristotle, did you know that?"

"What about the Korean War?" Barkley asked.

Charlie frowned at him. "Of all the wars . . ."

"No, seriously, no one ever talks about the Korean War, but it happened like what—five years or something after World War II. And it's like totally under wraps. I mean, there were tank battles, weren't there? Didn't all kinds of shenanigans go down in the Korean War? Something about a damn or a reservoir?"

"The Chosin Reservoir," his father finished. "The Frozen Chosin."

"Yes," Barkley said. "Talk about that. Tell that story."

"I've got no problem with that. Can one of you two grab me another beer?"

Charlie grunted and snagged one from the fridge, snapped the cap off, and poured his father a motor oil–dark Guinness into one of the old mugs that were lying around. He put it down in front of him, and his father nodded. He reached toward an ashtray and picked up a partially smoked cigar, put it between his teeth, and flicked on his lighter, rotating until the entire end glowed red and leaked smoke.

"The Chosin Reservoir," his father said. "Have some pizza. It's a long story."

Thursday at Eastwick was a montage of tepid class work, inane faculty discussions, and rudimentary brain activity. Barkley walked through the day in a daze, thinking only, *Friday, Friday, Friday.* He would have a job, or he wouldn't. He'd be back at Eastwick, or he wouldn't. It was difficult to wrap his head around. Even though he wouldn't be teaching the same students, there was that expectation of seeing them next year, of seeing them in the hallways, of writing recommendations, of commiserating and congratulating. And to be gone from the school, to even contemplate not walking the hallways and not seeing the students he'd spent a year getting to know—it was more than a threat of losing a job, it was a threat of dismemberment, of organ transplant, of deportation. How could he know who he was, if he was ripped away from the place where he had found himself?

At the end of school, he sat at his desk, shuffling through essay outlines on *For Whom the Bell Tolls.* Soon enough, it was 5:00 P.M. Outside, a light rain was falling. It looked to Barkley like a thousand silver threads.

"Mr. um. Mr. Bruns—I just can't say it. Mr. Barkles?"

He knew who it was. He listened to the rain against the windows. "Elise," he said, without looking up, flipping over to another outline. He heard her close the door behind her.

"Hi."

"Hi, there. I'm just, uh, going over these outlines, trying to keep my head straight. For tomorrow."

"Tomorrow?"

He flipped another page, looked at another outline. This one belonged to Jennifer Alston, written in compact yet gorgeous script, and it was absolutely brilliant. The detail—even footnotes. He loved footnotes. "This outline is amazing," he said.

"What happens tomorrow?"

"Oh, well, we get our contract renewals tomorrow. Or nonrenewals. Some people have been finding out early."

"Obviously you're going to be fine," she said, and Barkley, even preoccupied, felt a sense of warmth from her side of the room. At the bottom of the outline, Alston had written, *Hemingway's iceberg theory comes full force,* and Barkley felt himself both elated and unnerved. The rain fell harder, began rippling against the windowpanes.

"Mr. Brunson?"

"Wow, you actually said it."

"Can you please look at me?"

"Yes, I'm just trying to grade these, um—"

Five slender fingers, with deep purple nail polish, moved over Jennifer Alston's impeccably written outline. Barkley looked up, and saw that tears were streaming down Elise's lightly freckled cheeks.

"Oh my God, Elise—"

"It's nothing, I just didn't know who else to go to. I just found out, I just, it's so stupid—"

And suddenly she fell forward and Barkley caught her, and at first her arms were at his sides, but then they were around him, squeezing tight, and her tear-smeared face was buried in his neck, and then Barkley, helpless, unknowing, felt his arms go around her in response, and he inhaled that scent of tangerines that seemed to follow her everywhere, and she didn't have a chair, no, she had practically fallen on top of him, and Barkley, very distantly, felt her lips graze the underside of his Adam's apple, her hand go to the back of his head.

He pushed back. Jesus, he thought. Get her back. "Let's find you a chair, Elise."

"Mr. Brunson, I'm sorry—"

"No, no, nothing to be sorry about, I'm glad you thought of talking to me. Here, pull up a chair."

Her mascara was smeared, and she tried to wipe it away with the backs of her wrists. Barkley stood up and yanked a chair away from the first row of desks. It thumped and growled as he pulled it up next to his own seat. She sat down heavily, both hands up against her eyes, and Barkley again felt the urge he'd experienced outside his office, to protect her, to wrap her up in comfort, to make some sort of contact.

"What happened?" Barkley asked.

She rubbed her eyes and inhaled jaggedly. "God, I hate this," she said.

"Talk. It's okay. Just talk about it."

"It's my—it's my fucking family, all right? I know you don't want me to swear but that's what's happening. They just suck. My family absolutely sucks. And everyone else in this goddamn place is like, *happy.* Wearing fucking sweater vests by a fireplace. Throwing Frisbees to goddamn golden retrievers."

Barkley chuckled. "I know you're hurting, but that's a fabulous description for some of the kids here."

"I don't care. I don't care about the *description,* Mr. Brunson."

"I know. I'm sorry."

Was he just supposed to let her sit there and cry? He reached over and touched her shoulder. He could feel the warmth of her skin underneath the fabric. "It's going to be okay, Elise. Just talk to me. It's fine. Just talk."

"So, my mom left my dad. *Again.* But this time they don't have enough money to keep doing the house payments, because they've been fucking around with lawyers for like three years straight. So now we're going to lose the house. Like, we're actually going to lose the house I grew up in. And now they're fighting over which of them gets which kid. Turns out my dad wants my little sister. He actually said this—he wants my little sister to go with him. That's his choice. And the fucking shittiest thing of all, the worst fucking thing in the world, is that I'm the one who wanted to be with my dad. And he doesn't even . . . he doesn't even *want* me. He said it. He said he doesn't even *want* me. Jesus Christ, I just hate this so much. I hate it so much."

She was really crying now, crying through balled fists pressed so tightly against her eyes that Barkley thought she was going to hurt herself. He squeezed her shoulder, felt pathetic, felt like an asshole who didn't care enough, who was too politically correct to help—

"I'm so sorry, Elise. If I was your father, you'd better believe I'd want you around all the time. You are, like, amazing. I would want you around all the time. You're absolutely fabulous."

This only made her cry harder. And then she was falling forward, toward him, and the only thing he could do was take her into his arms and let her cry, let her cry while he held her against him, while that silver rain struck the windows with force. He swiveled on his chair, knocking the essay outlines from the desk and scattering them to the floor.

"It's going to be okay," he told her, ignoring the papers. "It's going to be fine."

"I just don't understand," Elise said. "It's like no one out here understands what it's like to have a family like this. To have parents like this."

"I understand, Elise. I understand completely." And then it hit him, as he was holding her against his chest, feeling her tears that felt organic to his own insides. This was their connection, these were the tendons that gave them their spark. It was a communion of suffering, of familial bewilderment, of a pain not born of violence but by the inexplicable choices made by those who were supposed to be wise, supposed to be in charge.

"Elise, I know this sounds ridiculous right now, but take it from me— it's only going to make you stronger. And smarter. And better. It sounds crazy, I know. And it truly, truly sucks, I know this, too."

Both of her arms were around him. Barkley thought, with a particular feeling of lightness, that this was what it felt like to truly help a person, to help her beyond education and instruction, to make a difference where before there would have been absence. He patted her on the back, moved his hand in a circular motion—was there a right way to do it?

"I wish we went to high school together," Elise finally said, breathing into his shirt.

Barkley laughed. "I was a dork in high school. You would have brushed right past me."

"I wouldn't."

"That is so beyond debatable, Elise."

She pulled back and looked at him. "I don't care what you were like in high school. You're cool now, aren't you?" She sniffed. "I say yes."

He was cool now? The thought was hilarious, ridiculous, yet from Elise it made him buoyant.

"Are you okay?" Barkley asked.

Both of her hands were still around him. She lowered her forehead to his chest and then raised it again. "No, I'm not okay. But I can take it, you know?"

"I know."

"Thank you for speaking with me. Barkles. Thank you, Barkles."

"See? You're getting your sass back, already."

Outside, thunder finally boomed, and the rain fell harder.

"Okay," she said.

"Okay," he responded. "I'm glad you talked with me."

"I'm glad you were here, pretending to grade."

"I *was* grading, you genius."

She laughed, then leaned forward to give him a final hug. "Thank you," she whispered.

But before Barkley could answer, he felt something like icicles pierce his veins. Looking at him through the window of the classroom door, face only inches from the glass, was Margaret Carey.

ALICE COOPER
IN THE AFTERNOON

At Links Hall, Julie's favorite time was just after four in the afternoon. The sun was away from the easternmost windows of the studio, and soft, almost greenish light poured through the glass beyond the branches of the trees, making the gleaming wood of the studio glow.

And before her, right now, was her Intermediate Modern Forty Plus class, the eleven female students gathered into two lines, doing warm-ups.

"Begin in parallel, ladies," she called out. "Plié on one, stretch on two. Plié on three, good, stretch on four. Plié on five, stretch on six. Push the floor away and rise onto the balls of your feet, seven and eight, we call this relevé up, then slowly lower your heels to the floor, nine and ten, keep your legs straight, we call this relevé down. Now again in first position, heels together, toes apart. Second position, wider stance. Good. Fifth position, change your feet and give me a left fifth. Excellent."

They were adequate, Julie thought. Only three of them had danced beyond high school, and only one had some real talent, talent that Julie herself had once commanded, when she'd been Northwestern's—what could she call it—silver goose? Second best? But the women enjoyed the exercises. All of them seemed to, except maybe Cynthia, the bank teller who was too stiff and emotionally unyielding, wound up tight like a compact clock. She complained too much, and moved like someone with petrified ligaments. If I can get her to find herself in here, Julie thought, then I'm really doing my job.

The rest of the women were fine, and the work was good, and being in the studio felt like a daily baptism, a washing away of the nagging swarms of other developments.

The goal was for them to find the joy of moving again. Moving across the floor. Moving through space. To do that, she had to start at the very seed of dance: first and foremost, achieving body awareness in the kinesthetic sense, an awareness of a person's location and *physical* being in relation to other people and objects. She made them think about directions, locations. She put them into three lines—four, four, and three, at opposite sides of the room. They learned (or relearned) how to walk on a beat. Forward two, three, four; backward two, three, four.

Links Hall had no mirrors. Without mirrors, the dancers couldn't get lost in the distraction of their reflections, and they had to feel themselves, that internal empty space, from inside the body. She had them move to their breath, to everyone else's breathing. Inhale for this, exhale for that. They moved in lines around the room, the lead person changing the tempo, the others trying to react. Walking, jogging, swinging movements, circular movements, skipping. Locomotive movements. She had them reach and contract to the recorded beat of a conga drum. The drumming constantly evolved and recalibrated, and the dancers, the movers who were becoming aware of themselves and their space, had to react. The conga thumped hollowly, emptiness and space. Now it sped up. More accents, more dynamics on the first beat, then quiet rapping, then explosion, and Julie watched as they reacted, stumbling at first, then swaying, then laughing, then some of them actually getting the hang of it.

Next, she had them build to something with images. Reacting not just to sound, but also to the abstract visual. Circular, linear. Deep. Melting wax. Explosive firecracker. She watched as they wound into orbs, went low, melted like butter, shot up and rained sparks. The conga throbbed.

She put in a *Buddha-Bar VI* CD, giving verbal directions, keeping them moving, down to a low level, all the way to the ground.

"Find a way to come out of the ground!" she called. "Now make a round shape. Stand up, listen to the music. Every eight beats I want the leader to make a different movement. For the first eight beats, poke your arms out into space, then spin any way you want to spin. Start. Faster than a walk, a trot. And go."

They all wore leotards and tights or comfortable loose clothing. T-shirts, tank tops. They had to be able to stretch. Julie herself wore a black leotard with green stretch pants.

The constant movement, seeing it in her dancers, made her feet feel both mobile and rooted. Her stomach glowed. She watched their shadows on the floor.

"Diamond improv!" she called out.

They stood in three diamond formations, knowing the drill. Everyone faced the same direction. The leader of each diamond chose the movement. One diamond leader began moving like she was underwater, and the rest of the pod followed, all of them loosey-goosey, except Cynthia. The leader stretched one arm out, then the other, then drew the rest of the pod down on the ground.

"Turn to face the north wall! Leader switch!"

Now the northern point of each diamond pod was in control. They ran around the room. Laughter fluttered like bird wings. She had them switch directions again, the whole technique was called passing leadership. All the while keeping that sense of place with cardinal directions. The reason she ended with the diamond improv was that all of the students felt like dancers afterward. It was therapeutic, communal balancing, no one left out. All the while, Julie called out to them, saying slow down, don't speed up, change your level, middle range, high, low, explore new shapes.

The end of class came like a gust of wind, and the studio emptied. It was only she and her shadow and that forest-green afternoon light shining on the wood. She sat down on a metal folding chair and breathed in three seconds, deep belly breathing, held three seconds, exhaled three seconds. She repeated. The darkness against her eyelids felt layered, deep, endless. Full and empty, in three seconds, full and empty, hold three seconds, full and empty, out three seconds. She opened her eyes. It was only she and the room.

Her new home was the Inn at Lincoln Park, just off Clark and Diversey, and she'd chosen it for a few reasons. One, the area was exploding with restaurants and blooming greenery, and Lake Michigan was so close she could smell it on the harbor wind. She could window-shop along Clark and Broadway, stopping by Akira, Hanig's Footwear, Nine West. She could snag warm mugs of Turkish coffee at Senem's Coffee & Tea House, impeccable lattes at Saugatuck Coffee Co. Black Cat espresso from the chic baristas at Intelligentsia. Two of her friends still lived on the North Side, one in a Fullerton brownstone and another in an Old Town high-rise, and they met at neighborhood spots like the D.O.C. Wine Bar and Home Bistro—ahi tuna salads, wine flights, truffle fries. Jack took her to see *Million Dollar Quartet*. At the library, she rediscovered the Russian literature she'd loved at Northwestern, delving back into Chekhov, Bulgakov, and Pushkin.

The other reason—and she really thought this was fun—was that Barkley's studio apartment was right across the street. She knew what most postcollege children would think of this: instant horror. Maybe even sci-fi horror: *Return of the Moms*. But Barkley knew she was busy, and she knew Barkley was busy. And besides, it was only temporary, until she found a real apartment. But at least for now, it was important to be physically near one of her children, and why not her youngest? She'd been taking care of Charlie, and now Henry had taken up that duty, so why not? Or who knew—maybe Charlie was taking care of Henry. Charlie was an inkblot—the progress he was making was up to the interpretation of the viewer, the shapes of his transformation unknowable, and always subject to further evaluation. But Barkley—his progress was clear, visible, and to her, at least, inspiring. In the midst of all this shit, her younger son had made it.

Thinking of Henry, and the day he arrived in Downers Grove, still made her shake. It had happened so quickly. More than a month of threatening to come home, Julie threatening to leave, threatening more action from her lawyer, shouting at him to *just sign the divorce papers and be done*

with it. But he wouldn't. He wanted to come home. He sounded different, too. She asked him what was wrong, and he said—*You'll see.* What
did that mean? *You'll see. I'm coming home.* And so on, until their fighting
segued into an abyss of dial tone. Then, on the last day of February,
two hours after she returned from Links, she saw Henry's Mercedes
idling in front of the house.

She'd prepared for everything, in the event this scenario came to pass.
Each biting word, every lacerating sentence, and especially the final ham-
mer—her speech, her hurricane of moral force that would fold Henry
up like an envelope, postmark him for Siberia or the Yukon or deep space,
with coordinates that only and ever spelled unmitigated regret. And
after the karmic retribution was complete, Henry would finally experience
that rarest of male events: total and complete surrender. This speech was
something she had planned for weeks, perfecting it while power walking through the neighborhood, while sweating through exercise videos,
while tentatively resting her head against the rise and fall of Jack's chest
in the fuzzy hours of the night. Each word she chose was a hand grenade, every stressed syllable a machete, and she'd connected them all
and she'd waited, waited, waited. And then, through the living room
window, she saw his car outside her door.

What she hadn't prepared for was her own reaction, swift and violent and against her will. Her subconscious was still deep and unswim-
mable in many areas, and she knew that, but the sight of his returning
vehicle—a sight she'd rejoiced over for not just years but *decades* (Henry
home, Henry her suave and successful warrior, the best of all the men,
the man every girl had wanted and she had got, coming home, choosing her as a daily ritual, and reaffirming in his return her completion and
her worth and the life she led and chose to lead)—this simple sight of
his car triggered in her a chain reaction that combined each of those
thousand memories into a single moment that defined everything. She
saw herself at thirty in the kitchen and at forty in the family room and
at fifty down in the basement, looking up, hearing the rumble of his car
and knowing it was this sound and only this sound that made it all right,
that put the stamp on *her* envelope, that gave her the A-OK for all the
living she had missed.

What happened upon the sight of his car was this: her new self, Julie the dance instructor, the woman in the studio, the free and easy one, understood her own mortality. She had built a papier-mâché house on rotting property, and at first it seemed like Henry was that network of termites that would bring it down (much as he'd always feared), but then she saw and felt that it wasn't him, it was something inside her, something that was reaching in and pulling on her larynx and her lungs and her kidneys and her heart, tugging at her, grasping—it wasn't him, she understood, it was something inside of her, some fucked-up broken thing with hands like wire cutters. But that still wasn't all of it, and when she saw his form inside the Mercedes twitch and kill the gas she realized that inside each person was a second person, a second self, a dark grasping thing of weakness and surprising strength and she understood that her new self hadn't beaten this thing that had once run her life but had merely subdued it—placed it in a cage until it wanted out. It wanted— she wanted—her old life back. Henry back. Henry home. Henry that was like a tidal wave that the other girls had wanted and then resented but still never understood—Henry her husband, Henry her soul mate, Henry this man who was more than all other men and she dared you to say different, she dared you to name another man like this and don't pick a fucking actor or an idea because none of that was real but Henry was real and he was here, he was back, and with him back she wouldn't need the pills and she wouldn't need dance or Jack or anything but him and that was how it had always been, from the moment she'd first laid eyes on him.

She considered, feeling a humiliating need, letting him back in. She couldn't quite forgive him, but she could let him in, couldn't she? Couldn't she have him back, despite what he'd done? Maybe he was sorry. Different, even. And couldn't she feel that presence in this house like she always wanted to? They were married. They should be together. Every thought was a block of tumbling cement that hurt and felt good and she wanted to give in. Let him in. She could have it all again and part of her knew it was worth it—it was worth all of it, wasn't it?

Staring at the car, she found that her words were gone. Her speech in a paper shredder. That hand clamping her throat would not allow resistance. Henry was home—it was what she'd been waiting for, what she wanted, a return to the time before.

She would let him in. She would see that he was sorry. It would all come back together.

And then she remembered the quarry.

The image of that hole in the ground, that hole in the ground that had been like a mirror and an answer and an end to the darkness—that image was all she needed. Her time with Henry, her years upon years with him, had led her there, to that pit that had been their reflection, their marriage that was nothing more than a giant drop and probably even deeper. A marriage where, less than a year ago, only the sensation of falling had felt right.

Quite suddenly, Julie felt as if someone had tripled the voltage to the room. That thing, that second self inside her, seemed to shriek with pain, as if the bars of its cage were electrified. She turned up the voltage another notch. Her hands shook. What the hell was she thinking? What was this weakness, this sick fucking weakness? This was her life, right now, no one else's, and it was her time, her decision, and it was *her* goddamn space.

She found herself filled with a shrieking rage, hot coals directly behind her eyes, lasers coming out of her fingers. *Keep him out*—this was the only thought—*keep him out*. She took a ceramic plate from inside the kitchen cabinet, held it on the bottom as if it were a fresh pie, and smashed it against the wall. She screamed and took coffee mugs and hurled them at the door, real fastball pitches blitzed with the same torque she'd possessed as a girl. The coffee mugs shattered and split like concrete falling from decrepit buildings. She kept throwing. Plates exploded. A purple vase shattered. Through the window, she saw the Mercedes door open. *No.* Not here, not now, it wasn't fair, she'd finally found her space and here he was, breaking back into what he'd deserted, flooding back in to stifle her, to choke her, to drag her back.

"Fuck you!" she yelled, and hurled their favorite china dinner plate, the one with the wine grapes intertwined with legs of lamb. It blew up against the door as if she'd fired a shotgun. She threw champagne flutes as the form of her husband ambled toward the door. She threw the decanter, she threw the beer mug from Germany, she threw the 1997 Chess Champion pint glass. Everything exploded, and she kept throwing, each item in the cabinet a piece of artillery, a fireworks show of glass and china and ceramic shrapnel.

"No!" she screamed. "Get away from this house, Henry! Get away!"

The door unlocked and opened slightly, then heavily, scattering the mess of broken things that were strewn across the entrance mat.

"Julie?" a voice said, impossibly tinny, impossibly distant.

"Get out of here!" she raged. She threw a stemless wineglass above the doorframe, and Henry ducked as it shattered. "Get out!" She was practically frothing, rabid.

"Just hold on a second, Julie! Now, just hold on."

"I swear I'm going to spike you right in the face with one of these beer mugs. These fucking stupid beer mugs of yours, get out of this house! Get out of here! You left, now get out!"

He stepped into the light, over the mess and into the house. And then she saw. He was wearing a navy-blue Chicago Bears hoodie, and it was too baggy, there was too much empty space in there to account for the Henry Brunson she'd married, and then, truly then, she knew. He was not just sick, as his hoarse voice on the phone had made her suspect—he was terminal.

"Jesus," she said. She pushed aside the beer mug. Looked up at the ceiling and back at him. "Jesus."

"I'm home," he said, finally. "This is my house and I'm not staying out of it any longer."

His jeans were too baggy. His arms, even with the cushioning of the sweatshirt, were string beans. This wasn't the man who'd told her he could put a baseball into orbit, who wielded a bat like a battle-ax.

"What's wrong with you?" she asked, finally. Her knees wobbled. "What is the exact diagnosis?"

Henry sighed, looking around the house. "The usual. The most clichéd situation you could think of. Stage four, of course."

"Why didn't you tell me?"

He shook his head. "Because this isn't the way it was supposed to be. It wasn't supposed to go down like this. And anyway, now I'm home."

She took a jagged breath. "What do you think this changes, exactly?"

"Come on, Julie. We need to come together, here."

"Answer the question, Henry."

"Remember how you used to call me Hank?"

"Close your goddamn mouth, you cheating, disgusting, *deserting* son of a bitch! You piece of shit!" She picked up the beer mug and hurled it at him anyway, but Henry, drawing from some depleted, auxiliary resource of still-retained athleticism, reached up and plucked it out of the air. He tossed it behind him and grinned.

"Still got it," he said.

If she had a bomb, she thought, a bomb right here in this house, she would have detonated it.

"Julie, let's just talk. Be civil."

"You can't be here, Henry. You being here is wrong. Us being in the same room is wrong. I see that you're sick, and it's making me shake, and I'm still not processing it, but it doesn't change anything, do you understand me? Do you hear me, Henry? It doesn't change what you've done. Not any of it!"

He held up one of his hands, his face the very measure of boardroom control. "Just calm down, all right? Now, what I need you to do—"

And something about his delivery, about him instructing her like a peon, like an employee, made her see a deep red, made her mind disappear into a dark ocean of smashing charcoal waves. Suddenly she was in her room, ramming clothes into a carry-on bag, telling him if he came upstairs she'd kill him, she would fucking kill him with her bare hands. He was downstairs yelling that this *did* change everything, that family and marriage was what mattered, and hearing him say this was like turning on a power drill in her heart, making the walls of her new self crack and almost cave. She burst out, screaming profanities, all of her elegance and artistry stripped down to a raging animal, protecting itself from the one and only threat.

She brushed past him, not seeing the living room, not seeing the kitchen. Into the garage. Opened the door to the Honda, hurled in her bag, got behind the wheel. Jabbed the garage door opener, watched as it lurched open and let in daylight. She had to get the hell out of here *right now.*

In the rearview mirror she saw Henry. He was walking toward the car waving his arms, but she slammed down the automatic locks, turned the key, heard the motor bellow, put the car into drive.

"Get out of here," she whispered to herself, before stomping on the gas.

The garage around her dissolved into sunlight. There were the trees, there was the edge of Downers Grove, there were the strip malls, there was the quarry into which she'd almost thrown herself. There went Elmhurst, there went the exit to the Eisenhower, and there, in the distance, was Chicago. Immediately upon seeing it, Julie knew exactly where she was going.

On the way back from Links Hall, Julie blasted "School's Out" by Alice Cooper, laughing out loud at the looks from the yuppies and the DePaul college students. It was truly a ridiculous song, a symphony of tongue-in-cheek power chords that had been parodied and mimicked from the moment it came out, and now—even more so. But so what? The wind was swirling through her windows, spring dancing like flakes of mint across her nose. She was . . . say it again—finally happy. She was driving south on Clark toward Lincoln Park, past the wedding cake pillars of the Landmark Theatre, where Jack wanted to see the new Sundance films, past the backdoor beer gardens of Duke of Perth and La Crêperie, beyond the swollen crab legs of Half Shell and just short of the flashing mustard yellow sign of the Wieners Circle. She took an illegal left onto Diversey and went east.

Nothing could stop her now. She pulled into the compact parking lot of the Inn at Lincoln Park, feeling as if inside her belly was a melon of steady joy. This would be her second night here (after over a month at the Hilton), tucked into powder-blue sheets with cranked windows pouring in a sprawling cacophony of city sounds. The laughter of the drunks, the monotone of the businessmen, the shriek of fire engines, the squeaks and sighs of CTA buses. After leaving the silence of deadly still Downers Grove, listening to it all was therapy. Everything out here was intoxicating. Lakefront neighborhoods twisted together like entangled fingers, each sprawl packed with glowing bistros and clattering bars, each urban corridor flanked by vast stretches of parks and algae-rimmed ponds. Beyond it all, of course, one of the Great Lakes of the Midwest. Water you couldn't even see beyond. And all of this area—literally, this whole entire area—filled with twenty- and thirty-something individuals who didn't know how good they had it.

She stepped out of the Honda, grinning to herself, glad that the memory of Henry's return was getting easier to digest. She swung her keys in a flashing arc, and then stopped. There, his back against the faded brick wall of the hotel, was her son. Gray pants, brown shirt, silver tie. His hands were against his face, and when he saw her, he slid down to the ground pitifully, as if he'd been cuffed and robbed.

"Barkley."

"Oh. Hey, Mom."

"What are you doing?"

"Nothing. Just sitting on the ground, here."

"Talk to me, honey. What's going on? Are you hurt? Are you injured?"

Even with his hands smeared against his face, Barkley laughed. "No, Mom, I'm not hurt. I'm just totally, totally screwed."

"Oh, no. It's not Ginny, is it? I really thought you two were going strong."

"We are. We are going strong. It's school. It's my job. I just—I guess I messed up, I don't know. I thought I accounted for everything. *Everything.* I don't know what I would have done differently, Mom, I really don't. I was obsessive-compulsive about every facet—but I didn't account for random events, for things I couldn't control. Who knows, maybe I'm really *not* supposed to work there. Because it's over. It's flat-out over."

Julie bent down and put both hands on Barkley's shoulders. "What's over? What's happened?"

Barkley lowered his hands from his eyes, which were red and wet. The sight of them made Julie want to slap someone, made her want to hurl that fine china at the face of whoever had done this to her son.

"Talk to me, Barkley. What's happened?"

"My job, Mom. The only job I've ever cared about. It's going to be gone. It's like, *gone* already."

"Contract renewals?" she ventured. "It can't be contract renewals. You've done so well."

Barkley wasn't looking at her, and he wasn't looking at the surrounding parking lot or the city street. She could see him replaying something in his head, over and over again, the way she used to do.

"What happened?" she asked again.

"They brought me in. The principal sat me down and said that despite some serious opposition to the decision, he had planned on renewing my contract." Barkley took a breath. "But then he told me that due to recent information, they would have to reconsider the offer, and it would not be possible to offer me a contract renewal at this time."

"You're kidding me. What information?"

Barkley waved his hand. "He said I can try to appeal the decision, but those types of things usually don't go well. Would I want to do that? I said yes. So now I have a new meeting scheduled on Monday morning, before classes start. And that's not even the worst part. He said that because these are unusual circumstances, he's going to allow my department chair to have the final call."

"Uh-oh," Julie said. "You've told me about her."

"Right. It's almost like I should lie down and take it, but it's just so unbelievable. It really hasn't hit yet. Mom, I've taught *so well* this year. I've put everything I have into it. And sure, Margaret Carey was always going to try to get me for PowerPoint, for classroom cleanliness, for anything else she could find. But to lose my job due to a random event, at a time when I was trying to do the right thing . . . I don't know what to do, Mom."

"Speaking of that—what exactly did you actually do?"

"Nothing."

"Well, what are they saying you did?" Julie watched her son, thinking that his doing anything beyond being absentmindedly forgetful was truly impossible. She'd known him for too long, seen the way he cradled his favorite books, the way he practically leaked sentimentality over the smallest nuances of their life in Downers Grove.

"Nothing, Mom. I've done nothing. I had a student run into my classroom crying on Thursday after school, and she kinda fell on top of me, you know—like, hugged me—and I tried to make her feel better. I don't know, I put my arms around her, which might have looked bad or inappropriate, but what am I supposed to do with a girl who is sobbing, saying she doesn't know who else to go to? I tried to make her feel better. I can see how they're going to get me on this, how they're going to try to twist everything around, and yet—how would any human being act differently? If you care about your students? How would anyone act differently when confronted by a sobbing child?"

"A sobbing teenager," Julie offered.

"Great. You're on their side."

"Not at all, Barkley. It sounds like you probably helped this girl out. But you need to start focusing on how they're looking at it, and argue your side of it. Especially if your department chair is in charge. You still might have a way out, if you consider their opinion and offer rebuttals. And you have to know that they're going to be talking about the situation with you, alone in a room with a teenager. Making physical contact."

"Ah!" Barkley screamed. "*Physical* contact? I was consoling a girl who's been in my class all year. And she was crying about her family."

"Is this girl attractive?"

"What does that matter?"

"It matters because people are judgmental. Is this a cute girl?"

"*Mom.*"

"Okay," she said, holding up her hands. "Devil's advocate, here. You might not notice these things, and that's great. But if this girl lined up against a bunch of average citizens, would she be considered pretty? A plain Jane? Bloated and disgusting? Gorgeous?"

"I don't know. It doesn't matter."

"Barkley, you need to know. And it does matter. You need to start acknowledging the situation, as they might see it."

"Okay, so she'd be considered attractive, yes. I know the high school kids think so. But that doesn't mean anything! It has nothing to do with me comforting her or not."

"Of course not. And they really don't have anything on you. Like you said, this will be about how they twist what they saw, and how you respond to it."

"How *she* twists what she saw. It all comes down to Margaret Carey."

"I'm sorry, Barkley." Julie looked at him, pursing her lips. "But you know what? No matter what happens, you're going to be fine. Look at you. Look at where you are."

"On the ground in a parking lot?"

"No. Look at how far you've come. You've done a fabulous job. You have a girlfriend your family adores. You've finally gotten in shape. Either way, you've already won. You've made it."

"But I want Eastwick," Barkley said. "I want the job. I've earned it."

"Sometimes you get what you want, sometimes not. It's not over yet. And would you really want to stay at a place that treats you like this? Don't you think you deserve better?"

"That's what Ginny says."

"Well let me second her opinion. These people are not teacher-friendly, Barkley. And either way, it's going to be all right in the end. I can already tell. Are you going to watch your brother fight tonight?"

"Yes. What about you?"

Julie imagined a school of fists, swooping and striking her son, forcing him into danger yet again. "I can't watch him doing that. I'm already angry with Jack for allowing this to happen, but Charlie really wants it. And at this point, anything Charlie wants is a positive. And anyway, I have a dear friend who's coming downtown to meet me."

"Oh. Another new guy?"

"Don't be silly. Melanie, from college? She's been very influential over the past year."

"Okay, Mom. Sounds good, I guess. I'm still not wrapping my head around anything." He shakily got back on his feet. "Should I call you about how the match goes?"

"Send me text updates," she told him. "And Barkley?"

"Yeah, Mom?"

"One other thing. I know you knew about your father's condition, well before I found out."

"Oh," Barkley said. "He told you?"

Julie sighed. She looked up at the windows that opened into her hotel room. "No, he didn't tell me. But I know. And I see why you did it. I see what you were trying to do."

"He made me promise to keep it to myself," Barkley said. "Over and over again. *Don't tell your mother,* that's pretty much what I always heard. But it's more than that. You were doing so well. And he's been, like, poison to you. I just couldn't say the words. If I said the words, and you got upset and stopped what you were doing, it would have been like I was the one who cast the spell on you. I don't know what I would have done with myself."

"Well, I appreciate that," Julie said. "I really do. But I'm better than that. I don't need to be protected from anything."

"What about when things get bad?"

"With your father?"

"With everything. What about when everything gets bad?"

She ran her fingers through her younger son's hair. "We'll be ready for it. That's what will happen."

That evening, while having dinner with Melanie at Coast and feeling a little beyond the reach of the sushi restaurant's implicit hipness, Julie felt her phone buzz. Something told her not to look at it. All around them, young people lunged at ornate mountains of maki in the dim lights and Zen-like surroundings. Melanie, dressed in an immaculate blouse and matching skirt, spoke about Billy and her kids, about a new performance at the Hubbard Street Dance Theater, about how thrilled she was that Julie was back in the studio, living in the city.

"I'm just so relieved," Melanie said, brushing back a strand of hair. "I worried, after that day at the field. Even later. I thought it could go either way, I really did. Many women our age, from our generation—they come up for air after a divorce or a death, look around at the new world and what would be required for an independent life, in a culture that doesn't want to hear about them or their plight anymore, and they lose it. It's all too much, too busy, too complicated. Too many moving parts and not enough sympathy. They go right back under—*poof!* Institutionalized, as the sociologists say."

Julie nodded. "I hear you. I felt like that for a long time, even after we talked. But it was just so boring lying around, being afraid. That's really what got me. Being depressed is flat-out boring. Worse than violin."

"Truer words. And there's a man in your life, too, right?"

"Well, we'll see. He certainly wants it to be that way." She held up her hands. "No rush. No rush at all. But he's nice. A good person, as far as I can tell."

"You know who else was a nice person?"

"Jamie Dickson?"

Melanie leaned forward. "So, *so* nice."

"I was thinking," Julie said, "didn't he also have garlic breath?"

"Oh, for sure. Key fact: his mother was a dentist. These are the things we can't explain."

"I'm at a loss."

"But this new guy. He's a fireman, correct?"

"Correct. Retired." She felt her phone buzz again. There was an instinctive urge to push it out of her mind. The rest of them, the rest of her family, pulling at her with different ropes.

"I'm guessing he's more relaxed than the other men in your life. Even-keeled."

"Well, that is true. For the most part, at least." This last bit made her smile, because she'd sat in on a practice and seen how Jack was with Charlie—how he pushed him, got worked up, even shouted—all when he was in the ring. Something about this pleased her, this idea that all men needed an outlet for that strange energy, that lurking violence, and that Jack had found it and contained it. What's more, Jack could leave it all in the ring, and still come home whole.

"And how is the ex-husband?"

"Sick. It's difficult, of course, knowing that he's ill. But he demolished our relationship. There's nothing I can do, nothing I *should* do. We're finished. And it might be selfish, but I know if I see too much of him . . . who knows? He's not good for me. It's not like I think I'm weak, it's just—"

"Why get into a bathtub filled with poison?"

"Good way to put it," Julie said, smiling. Her earrings flashed and caught the candlelight. Their waiter, an angular Japanese man in his thirties, slid the fatty tuna and sea scallop nigiri across the table. At the other end of the room, a man with silver streaks in his hair, likely eating with his college-age children, smiled at her.

"Smells fresh," Melanie said. "I've been holding out on sushi, did you know that? The whole idea of an ocean fish in the middle of an enormous continent? I wasn't exactly buying it. But, okay. I'm chewing it . . . and I like it!"

"Stick with me, kid."

"No," Melanie said, "*you* stick with *me*."

Julie grinned. "Battle for dominance?"

"Of course. And by the way, there's a guy across the bar checking you out. Don't look. He's at your two o'clock, but don't look."

Julie's phone was ringing now, shocking her out of the pleasant trance. She let it go to voice mail. Bent down to pluck a fresh scallop off the plate. Her phone rang again.

"Unbelievable," Julie said. "Just let me check this."

She took it out of her purse. Jack. Why would it be Jack? The boxing match was still supposed to be going on. She flipped it open, held it to her ear.

"Jack? Is the fight over? What's wrong?"

"It's Charlie," the gravelly voice said.

"What do you mean, *it's Charlie?*"

And then he told her, without her really hearing, what had happened. Where to go and what to do. He talked and he urged and his voice, like so many of the others, became a drone that filled her ears. What was he asking? Did she need help? Did she want to be picked up from the restaurant and taken there?

"No," Julie said, looking across the table at Melanie.

"Julie—"

"No, Jack. No. I've got GPS. I'll get there myself." And when she was finally in her car with her hands on the wheel and the radio silent, she knew that it was true.

DUEL

"He's hurting," Schoenwetter said. "Rib cage. Left side. Body shots. Get it done, you hear me?"

Charlie tried to nod. Sweat came over his eyes in beaded curtains. Water struck his mouth from a bottle he couldn't see, but he knew Schoenwetter was holding it, from somewhere above.

"Get it done," Schoenwetter growled in his ear. "Body shots. Break those fucking ribs!"

Charlie's nose was chafed and stinging. He knew there was skin missing, breaking off and flaking like burned paper. Didn't matter. The cure for one ailment was the existence of many. Left knee popping without reason. Left cheekbone a disaster. A purple inkblot blooming where Huntington had hit him, but he wouldn't see it until later, through a dirty mirror. The bell rang.

Gravity changed and he was on his feet. Sweat in the left eye. Brush it off. Move the legs. The ring shifted. Huntington—slabs of steel-cut muscle, pecs like wrecking balls—was coming straight at him. A danger sign, when they stopped hesitating and walked at you like an angry, incredulous parent. His red shorts were too short—boy shorts, dork shorts, Charlie thought—and then Huntington's glove snapped up into his eyes.

Charlie's head whipped back, saw the ceiling. Time sped up. Huntington came at him with a combination, the gloves thudding, rumbling off his body like hail on the hood of a car. Charlie swung blindly, hit nothing, and Huntington backed off. He reset. Left jab, blocked. Left jab. Jab again. Everything grazing now, Huntington on him, more thudding, thinking of hail, and the bare skin of his back touching the ropes.

A right hook slammed in from the side and hung Christmas lights across Charlie's eyes. He fell backward, felt his ass graze the canvas floor, and stumbled back to his feet. Huntington strode forward, muscled chest heaving, gloves like padded bricks. Something in his black eyes, his insolence, maybe, his lack of focused respect, fired Charlie up, lit a match, and suddenly he felt lucid within the tight surroundings. *Break those fucking ribs.* Huntington was on him then, the big South Side fucker grunting with each shot, swinging at him heavily with his right—once, twice, three times. Charlie jabbed and ducked, then came in heavy with a two-three-two, gaining ground, forcing the bastard to put both gloves up. Charlie pushed him back with another right, took a partial shot to the lip, and slammed a glove into his ribs. Huntington gave a soft sigh, like a baby coughing up porridge. Charlie hit him again. And again. The big brute mumbled something, sagged back against the ropes. Charlie heard the assholes in the crowd shouting. His left knee popped, but he kept punching. Something inside Huntington crunched—his ribs? Had to be his ribs.

Earlier that week, Charlie had driven back to Downers Grove after another round of light practice for the fight—his third real match after winning the first two in March by easy decisions. And it was amazing how *tired* he got, even after a couple rounds, even if he was basically kicking ass. People didn't understand. Constant movement, arms shooting out like industrial pistons, again and again, not to mention blocking, feinting, shifting, taking hits—he didn't know if any sport was more exhausting in such a short amount of time. Full-court basketball was easy by comparison, up and down, up and down, simple cardio with layups. But in the ring, his arms quickly felt weighted as if by anchors, calves and thighs like they'd received an injection of molten steel. The body didn't want to move, the body wanted to lie down, and at a certain point it was up to the mind, willing it to move, to swing, to hit. If his fight in Budapest had been an awakening, these two skirmishes in March had been confirmations—he liked everything about them: the anxiety the night before, the adrenaline the morning of, and the pure balls-out rush inside the ring. It was a battle, the verdict unknown, and all those thoughts of past and future and guilt and the unknown melted away into the inescapable present. The ring was alive. It was awake. And stepping inside opened Charlie's eyes as well.

Yet, from a competitive standpoint, the first two fights Schoenwetter set up almost made him feel bad. Too easy. Wannabes with obvious weaknesses: skinny arms and a droopy chest for goofball number one, power muscles but no technique for turdbucket number two. Charlie had bobbed around easily, almost languidly jabbing, before coming in ferociously with those body shots, which Jack thought was his killer move, rapid-fire, lumberjack slugs to the trunk of each man. So—okay. He could fight. He understood that, and it gave him confidence. But this new opponent, Schoenwetter said, this Huntington kid, he had an edge in him, and regardless of Charlie's early promise, also had more fights under his belt. Don't fuck around, Schoenwetter grunted, all through practice, through sparring, through hitting the bag and jump rope and stretching.

"You hear me, kid? I'm telling you—don't fuck around."

"I heard you the first time," Charlie said, finally removing his hand wraps.

"And Charlie?"

"Yeah, Jack."

"Don't tell your mother I curse like a sailor in here, all right? She's not really acclimated to the whole jock talk type thing. Even though she was athletic growing up. Not that I'm not honest with her, you understand—she's just, you know, better than that sort of thing. I tried to keep it in line when she visited. And outside of the ring, I'm a perfect gentleman, mind you. You should know that, too. It's just that with her, and with us, you know . . ."

"It's a need-to-know basis?"

Schoenwetter gave a thumbs-up and grinned. "That's the phrase."

"Two totally different worlds."

"Now you're getting it."

"Yeah, Jack, don't worry about it. She's not even at the house any-more, remember? So not a lot of dialogue crosses between us, anyway."

They were alone in the gym. Humid as usual. One of the red bags slowly swaying from when he'd pounded it a few minutes ago. Schoen-wetter sat on a metal stool and looked up at him.

"How are you doing with all of it, Charlie?"

"With what?"

"The living situation. With your father. It's none of my business, of course. But we're working together here a lot now, and if you want to talk, or if you've got things you want to get off your chest, you should do it. You should feel that this is, you know, an open forum. Nothing leaves the gym, is what I'm saying."

"I've got nothing for you, Jack."

"Especially with a fight coming up. Anger can be an asset, sure. But feeling like you can't talk about things? Not good. Not good at all. You want to be spontaneous out there, moving and reacting. Changing tactics. Can't do it if you're bottled up."

Charlie sighed. "So it's all about the fight, then."

"Sorry?"

"You're only asking because of the match with Huntington. Same thing as correcting the form with my cross, or fixing my footwork, or whatever."

"Charlie—"

He raised his hand. "It's fine, Jack. It's fine. I've learned how to deal with it, and I'll box for you just fine. None of it will affect me. None of it."

Schoenwetter stood up. "Charlie, you little bastard, do me a favor and look at me."

Charlie, feeling strange pinpricks against the dam inside, finally looked. For a face like Jack's—strong jaw, solid mustache, that beat-up flesh around the eyes—it didn't seem possible that he'd have a habitual glint of kindness. But he did. Something had fixed him, at some point in his life. His work, his wife, something else, he didn't know.

Jack put a hand on his shoulder. "I don't have any children, Charlie. Not a one. Sharon and I—it just never happened for us. Now she's gone.

She's gone and I have no children or grandchildren and I never will. And that means something. And now, with your mother and with you . . . it changes things. You don't expect to get something like this later in life. Not at all. You think—I'm just going to ride the rest of this out. But then, your mother. And now you. So if you think this is about a couple local boxing matches that only a bunch of drunks and fanatics are watching, you've got the wrong idea. I'm not here to step on toes. But you're a good kid, Charlie, and I ask because I care."

Charlie tried to breathe. "Thanks, Jack."

"All right. So if you want to talk, then do it. Tell me how you're doing."

Charlie pulled out another metal stool and sat down.

"Okay. Sure, Jack. I can talk. My dad being home is . . . I don't know. Good, I guess. And strange. Does that make sense?"

"Sure."

"And I'm mad at him, but I've kind of forgiven him without really forgiving him, if you know what I mean. Like, he's still an asshole. He still left my mom and cheated on her like a madman. He still practically disowned me for joining the army. He still never really acts like a dad, or at least a regular person's idea of one. But he's my father, Jack. He's my dad. And maybe there's still time. Don't you think?"

Jack seemed to consider it. "I can't say anything about time, or how much is left, given my own experiences. Given Sharon. But room for change? Absolutely. If it can happen in the ring, it can happen out here."

"In real life, you mean?"

"That's right, kid. In real life."

They talked awhile longer, and then Charlie got in his car to drive home. He understood that talking to Jack, like Al, could make things better. A little, at least. A bit. But also—and a bizarre feeling seemed to descend upon his body and the car—he was forgetting something. His hands gripped the wheel. He was forgetting something important. Something big.

The tinnitus was back. The glare of the lights, and drunken shouts from the crowd. Faces he couldn't see but knew were out there, talking, yelling, texting, watching.

"You broke something," Schoenwetter said. "He's going down this round, right? This round!"

"I can't see straight," Charlie said. He felt his ass on the metal folding chair, saw again the blurred faces of the crowd. More water spilled on his lips. He spat it out, let it dribble down his chin.

"Get this prick," Schoenwetter said. "He's made of glass. Keep up those body shots, you hear me? Now go. Last round!"

Charlie's lip was split and stinging. He saw Huntington in the other corner, eyes closed in a grimace, barrel chest heaving. He was hurt. Something was broken.

The bell rang. Charlie rose and Huntington did the same. Schoenwetter in his ear again: "Watch out for that right hook. Give him some of that punishment back, Charlie. Break that fucker in half!"

They circled for a moment. Huntington didn't come at him right away—he was slower, lumbering, content to flank. When they were two feet apart, the big lug threw the first punch, and Charlie could tell it hurt him just to raise his arm. He sidestepped easily and, thinking of Campo, thinking of the girl, uppercut Huntington's rib cage with all his strength and anger. The big man dropped like a gym bag full of dumbbells. He was on his knees. Spitting on canvas. Charlie turned to look at the crowd—a decent-size gathering for this location. He looked back and Huntington whipped him with a right hook across the temple that made him see a flash of his father, sitting there with the beers and the pizza, his father not changing, even as it all went to shit. Charlie fell.

Driving home after talking to Jack, that week before the fight, Charlie had felt funny, as if he was forgetting something important—but what? There was a bizarre feeling that gravity had left the world around him. It didn't make sense. Jack's words had been kind, but he was still mad at his father, still not sure what would happen at home. He tried to hold the angst in. He kept driving. But, goddammit, the car felt . . . *light*. Airy. Very strange. Like he was driving the world's first inflatable vehicle, run on Flubber, headed for the moon. Christ, even the moon looked bizarre, big and yellow—a cartoon wheel of cheese. Van Morrison crooning his way through "Orangefield" on the radio. Just what the fuck was he feeling?

He pulled the car over and killed the gas. Looked at his battered knuckles, the chafing on his arms. Checked his grizzled face in the rear-view mirror. There was an edge—an edge that he depended on and needed. But it felt like someone had siphoned helium into the atmosphere. Was it Jack? His father? He didn't know. He sat in the car and found himself shifty, unable to stay still. He watched an old station wagon putter by—one of those outdated models with wooden paneling along the sides. Ugly car, hilariously ugly. He craned his head and looked out the window again. That big Gouda moon hanging in the sky. Van Morrison's voice rising toward it. What the hell was going on?

And then he seized up, almost tore the wheel off the car.

"The fucking key chain," he breathed.

Where had he left it? Where? He realized, with intense clarity, that it wasn't at home. He'd looked for it at home a week ago, no—two weeks. It hadn't been there and he'd thought, relaxing, *gym bag*. But he'd been through his gym bag today, looking for his headphones, and he knew there hadn't been even a whiff of the key chain in there, just dirty socks and hand wraps and the plastic jump rope, which meant not at home, not in the gym bag, so *where*? Pockets. He checked his pockets. Nothing but two dimes and an old Walgreens receipt. He could go home and sort through dirty laundry, but that didn't sound right either. He couldn't even remember the last time he'd taken the key chain with him, gone mobile with it. Paintball, maybe. November. But that still didn't explain how it could have moved, or when it would have disappeared.

He had, quite simply, forgotten about it. The thought would have been impossible even a few months ago. And during that period of time, he'd been so distracted with the boxing and the movies and the thoughts about his father and his friends and even Jack that he had somehow stopped obsessing. The last time he'd done the ritual, actually lit the candles? He couldn't remember. He must have carried the key chain somewhere, must have done it without thinking. Maybe when he went out with JB and Locklear. Maybe he'd left it at Beachwood Inn. That was months ago—no sane bartender would have held on to it.

Sitting there in the car, Charlie felt the hot rage begin to diffuse itself, almost against his will. His breathing became regular. His mind cleared. Maybe it was lost, maybe it wasn't. He looked out the window at the moon again. He couldn't gather how it had precisely happened, but somehow he was ready for this. He wasn't upset. He was—fine.

"About as cinematic as it gets, huh, Charlie?" he said out loud, chuckling to himself.

In his mind's eye, he'd always had an endgame for the key chain. Being the movie guy, how could he not? But for him, the drama of letting go was much more pure, much more immediate. It was a *scene*. And in this scene, he, the finally healed one, took the key chain on some sort of journey, maybe out to Lake Michigan. Yes. He rode a sailboat deep into the rolling waters, crossed into Lake Huron, anchored away just west of Mackinac Island. Pure nature out there, water and trees. Wind blowing. Sail rippling. He stood at the prow of the boat, held out his hand, and let the key chain drop. *That* was a scene. Or he hurled the key chain into a canyon or a bonfire or he did something that had at least a tiny shred of drama in it. Not that he needed drama, it's just that he'd imagined some degree of finality, of ceremony.

And yet, the ceremony he'd desired had taken care of itself. It had happened on its own time. He'd been busy boxing and living and doing, and he'd moved on, forgotten to have even a need for cinematics. The key chain was gone, he said to himself. His fight was ahead. His breathing was normal.

Charlie used the ropes, pulled up his body like he was hauling a chest from the depths of the ocean. He saw two and a half Huntingtons, and to his surprise they were still on one knee, eyeing him warily. His vision stayed blurry. He slipped a bit, gripped the rope tighter, and held himself up. The punch to his skull had been little more than a flailing haymaker, but Huntington had landed it, a reckless cruise missile that seemed to wobble his eye sockets. Charlie wiped sweat from his brow. There was a roar in the air, as if a perpetual, shrieking seashell were held against his ear. Soon enough, his tinnitus came back and buzzed with abandon.

Huntington finally rose to both feet, his left arm down by his ribs, protecting. Briefly, Charlie noticed the noise from the drunks in the crowd. They'd come with faint hopes of a good fight, and were getting a bloodbath. It didn't matter who won now.

Charlie had been better than most people, at least athletically, his entire life. Always he was the taller one, usually faster, forever the most mechanically sound. And his will to win, at least on those days when he still wanted to win, was second to none. This was the case here, too, but Huntington was trouble. He didn't seem to care that his sternum was floating with broken bone shards. He must have had his own moment of understanding at some point, his own disaster in a home or on a highway—he knew things, he'd had realizations, and he was as pissed off as Charlie about them.

Charlie came at him straightaway. There were still two and a half of him, but he could see the center, the nexus. Huntington was covering his ribs. Charlie swung at him and missed; the crowd roared in response. Huntington jabbed with his one good arm and connected, but the jab wasn't his strong suit. He struck out again and Charlie backed off, stumbling but not hurt. Huntington shouted something through his mouth guard, and Charlie came at him hard with a combination, and suddenly they were both on the ropes. He went for body shots, but Huntington was covering his ribs with everything he had. Two quick jabs in the mouth and Charlie had to back off again, his lip gushing blood. Huntington was cornered, an injured animal, still dangerous.

Charlie came right back, blocked a couple of crosses, and went straight for the ribs. This time, as Huntington went to block, Charlie threw a left hook that connected—beautiful, unimpeded—and snapped the brute's head back and forth like a bobblehead. A double jab and a right cross and Huntington was down again, flat on his back, black eyes reflecting the overhead lights. Charlie backed off and once more, Huntington rose to one knee. The bell rang.

Schoenwetter in his ear, shouting, white noise from all directions. Two and a half Huntingtons sitting on the other side of the ring, heads bobbing. Water hitting his lips and bouncing off. Charlie realized he was smiling.

He would keep on punching—that was the point, the purpose, his very own ebb and flow. His life and all the fighters', here under the harsh lights, on the canvas ring, two men striking out at each other, at the insanity of it all. Hitting, crushing, failing—yes, usually failing in the end—but striking out just the same. He felt giddy. More water entered his mouth. The ebb and flow, the rise and fall, the giving and receiving, was inside him. He felt the rhythm of it. The necessity and the truth. His arms ached. His head swam. Hit and be hit. Payback and punishment. Strike out and shout *fuck you*, and laugh as you hit the floor. In its own brutal universe, fighting was no different from a dance, an expression of resistance to all who refused to spectate.

His father was in the crowd. The knowledge fell over him like perspiration. As Charlie stood up, grinning again and facing Huntington, his ears started ringing, started humming, and like a switch everything went black. There was a sense of free fall, of something metal snapping underneath him, and of the crowd rising up and roaring, thundering like air support.

EXIT STRATEGY

From his seat near the back, Henry saw his son fall. He fell the way that Al had described soldiers in the jungle falling, after a bullet entered and exited their brains, hearts, necks, eyes. Straight down they all went, Al said, unceremoniously and without drama. One second up, one second down. And watching from his seat, Henry saw Charlie drop, like a distant round from some enemy machine gun, all the way back in Afghanistan, had finally caught up to him.

The blue canvas ring was illuminated. Charlie had fallen forward on his face, his right arm pinned underneath him, his right leg jumping slightly. The crowd was cheering, screaming. *Assholes*, Henry thought. If he'd had his strength he would have become a raging bull, picking up these drunken idiots and throwing them across the aisles, putting his boot against their temples, grinding them into the grimy floor. But he was tired. Always tired. Everything seemed like a replica of a replica, like something he had read in a book from grammar school, from a story his mother had whispered to him in his shadowed bedroom, amid the Jack London novels and the constantly droning fan. Even this scene—this boxing scene—it had happened before, hadn't it? Hadn't all of it happened before? He wondered about that theory, that the human spirit reincarnated back into itself upon death, that everyone relived the same life again and again, into infinity. He might have been diagnosed a thousand times, seen Charlie fall a million. Left Julie over and over, from the very beginning. Maybe everyone had been doing the same ballroom dance, across a floor made of glass and stars and space, unaware that each step they took was the same one they'd taken before. He despised this theory, hated the way in which it seemed to mock not just free will but the existence of randomness, of spontaneity in motion. Human beings were so predictable, the theory seemed to say, that even though they had choices, even though crossroads existed, they always took the same path, lifetime after lifetime after lifetime. He hated it, wanted to veer his mind away, but it grabbed at him, pulled him, possessed an undertow of strength he seemed to fall into, with every passing day. And it was true, now, in these days of tiredness and repetition, that even though he felt horror at watching Charlie's fall, even though he experienced the terrible thoughts of *what if he has brain trauma what if his neck is broken what if he can't speak what if*, it all seemed far away, delivered by telegram from a distant country, the letters faded, repeated, centuries old. How many times had he received this message? He was tired. So very, very tired.

He hadn't gotten chemo in a month, hadn't returned Fredrickson's calls, hadn't even considered driving to the oncology department to get that filth driven into him, that pesticide that was delivered with a smile. And making this choice felt like sweet release; he was on the way out and he had ended the grind that felt like Old World pugilism, like ancient torture delivered with futuristic tools. The dizziness had faded. The dietary concerns were gone. All of it was gone.

There were people around Charlie now. Some kind of doctor was down there, and they were turning him over. Huntington, that big lug, was still sitting in his metal chair, hunched over, hands protecting his ribs. Charlie's trainer, Jack Schoenwetter, who his son had admitted was dating Julie, had his hand on Charlie's forehead. He was speaking in hushed tones. It wasn't jealousy Henry felt upon seeing this. Instead, the gesture lifted a cloud of almost pungent sadness inside Henry—this small act, hand to brow, from father figure to potential son—this was what had escaped him his entire life. He'd always felt close to grasping it, to understanding the machinations, and he knew his children had waited expectantly. But he hadn't been able to do it, to place his hand on their brows, to say, without his voice breaking, that he loved them. He just couldn't do it. Or maybe that wasn't true. Maybe he had simply chosen not to. Loving his children was easy, an implicit and reflexive emotion requiring no skill, but showing that love, allowing it to animate itself in ways that were not clandestine, not hidden behind other gestures—he didn't know how. No, he thought. It was all right to be honest. He had chosen not to.

Charlie was still unconscious. They got a stretcher. Outside, in that Chicago night, he heard the sirens. They were coming, and they would take him away. He wanted to do something for his son. Easter had come and gone this past week and he had missed it, forgotten, been unsure if he *should* have done something. His son was grown up. Old. And yet, missing Easter, forgetting it completely, felt like another tally against him.

Jack, down there with Charlie, would be calling Julie, and Julie would be coming to the hospital. So would Barkley, who was sitting with some of his friends on the other side of the ring. And Julie wouldn't want him at the hospital, so he would go now, follow the ambulance . . . get there before anyone else did. And maybe, if he was lucky, he could swing by somewhere first—get Charlie a gift. Yes, some kind of gift would do perfectly.

The Easter basket was from Walgreens. Green Easter grass cushioning yellow plastic eggs and a chocolate rabbit that stared through the window of its cardboard casket. He'd asked the cashier and he'd said yes, they actually did have some leftovers—50 percent off, too, what a deal, *did he want two of them? Four?* Henry had simply glowered at the man and handed over a fistful of cash.

Henry stepped into the antiseptic air of the Northwestern Memorial Hospital, holding the basket, feeling okay. It was 10:30 P.M. and he was tired, eyelids wanting to fall back like metallic shutters. The mornings were always better; within those early minutes of sunshine and birdsong, he could almost forget what was happening. And he knew about the birds because Julie had known about the birds: the blue jays and black-capped chickadees, the downy woodpecker and northern cardinal, the cedar waxwings that came because of the hawthorn and holly she'd planted in the backyard. Her imprint was everywhere. Henry would wake up in the Downers Grove master bedroom, pictures of family all around, and not feel *that* tired—it could easily have been the lethargy from a long night out, a late dinner downtown, a party at a country club. He would walk downstairs and make coffee—even if he didn't drink it, the bubbling from the machine felt like promise, like purpose. Lemon meringue light would be coming in tender threads through the kitchen windows and the back door. Julie could have been anywhere: upstairs taking a shower (coming out smelling like lavender and lotion), or at the grocery store picking up chicken breast and cremini mushrooms and polenta, or taking a youthful Charlie and Barkley on a tree-lined walk to school. The whole house could have been any time in their life, any moment, any iteration of Julie and himself. She really could have been there, in the house—everything still alive.

The feeling didn't last forever, though. By one in the afternoon, the light through the windows changed, and it was clear that she wasn't coming back.

Henry took a right and then a left, winding through emergency room corridors, determined to do something differently. Walking through the reflective hallways, he realized he was here, but he was also everywhere, inside every time of his life. These walls and hallways reminded him of that winter in '88 when his uncle was recovering from a liver transplant, and he and his cousin David sat there and bitched about the white walls and the smell of rubbing alcohol and the curveless nurses who barely inspired a hard-on. They sat there bitching and smelling that antiseptic and tried to do anything they could, not to think about Uncle Phil, because once they started thinking they'd remember the canyons of misunderstandings that were laid out across the family, huge divides they couldn't cross even if Dad had still been alive. His father, he knew, had always harbored grudges against his younger brother. And when Dad had passed away, those bad feelings, instead of withering, had shot out across the family like shrapnel. Henry's idiotic stepfather had only exacerbated the tensions. But that was '88. Mike Singletary was still playing linebacker; the Bears were 12-4 and headed for the Fog Bowl against Buddy Ryan and the Eagles. A lifetime ago, before Joyce, even. And here he was in Northwestern Memorial in 2012, entering the curtained room, looking at the slumped form of his elder son. The rest of the family wasn't there yet; he'd told Barkley to hold Julie off, unless she wanted to see him. There was a fresh cast on Charlie's arm, bright white—the same white that lined the walls and made Henry feel like he was walking into an asylum, just with extra needles and shorter life expectancies. But his son was awake, cognizant, moving among the sheets.

"Dad," Charlie said.

He was lying back on the hospital bed, jaw clenched, eyes filled with pain—pain, yes, but was that also a bit of humor? His cheekbone was swollen black and blue. But it was his eyes, Henry thought, that were different: ever-changing chameleons of emotion and activity. In the time they had shared over the past month, Henry had noticed they transformed every day. Sometimes occupied and lively, sometimes morose, and sometimes utterly vacant—twin deserted motels. His son had been like that since coming back. They still ate dinner together and talked, and yet through it all Henry felt a building pressure that he was once again missing something, missing out on an opportunity, a second chance. He knew that Jack's hand on Charlie's head had something to do with that, but what could he do for a grown son who was no longer a child? Above Charlie's hospital bed, one of the daytime soaps Julie used to watch was on TV, showing a woman tearfully confessing some secret in a parlor.

"How you doing, kid?" Henry asked. Stay awake, he thought.

"Hurts," Charlie muttered. "Just a bad concussion, though—for a while there, they were worried. Thought I might be talking like Tarzan, re-learning how to draw stick figures."

Henry held the Easter basket out like a peace offering. "So bad luck and good luck. And here. I know Easter already went by, but I forgot to get you something. I brought you some goodies. Didn't package it myself, but, you know. Best I could do. Happy belated Easter."

"Thanks, Dad." Charlie smiled and then looked at the TV screen and the white walls.

"How'd you do it?" Henry asked, setting the basket on the counter next to the tiny sink. "You were winning the fight. Huntington was getting smacked around the room. You made him your pack mule—even broke two of his ribs, did you know that? That's what they're saying. Then I saw the fall. Assumed concussion, but look at that arm! What happened with that arm?"

"Fell on it after taking a hit. The guy had a hook like a wrecking ball. But it was delayed. I mean, he hit me two rounds back, and something in my brain shut off two rounds later. Like a light switch. I *was* winning, too."

"Your body broke it?"

Charlie sighed, grimaced. "I fell straight forward, even though I barely remember it. You probably saw it better than I did. I tried to put my hands out, but when I woke up it felt like someone pulled two Legos apart in my wrist."

"Wow," Henry said. "Ouch."

"Yeah. Sucks. But it's okay, though, you know? Being out there feels *good*. It sounds crazy, me here in the hospital bed, but it really does feel good. Like I said before, it's like physical therapy or something. I used to get that shooting baskets in the driveway. I'd clear my head by knocking down three-pointers and free throws—and now I get it throwing punches in the ring. And you know what? It's okay. I know it sounds messed up, but it works for me, Dad."

Henry once again felt that internal pressure, the feeling that he should be saying something, doing something. But what? He wasn't one of those emotive types; it wasn't like he wrote poetry—but then that wasn't true, either, was it? He'd written Julie a poem in college. It had started out funny, mentioning the incident in the food court their junior year, and the time by the reservoir with the raccoons. But later it turned serious, talking about the rise and fall of her body at night, and the way she looked around the falling snow, just outside the Deering Library. Had that actually been him? Had he actually written the words?

"Well . . . ," Henry said, and then trailed off. He should really say something to his son, and the pressure feeling was building, the dials spinning. But it just wasn't in him. No, it wasn't, and he needed an out. Anything. It was all too much, too strange, being forced to talk. Especially when there was nothing there to connect with anymore. His phone shook inside his pocket.

"Actually, Charlie," Henry said, feeling his phone buzz again. He raised his hand, almost daintily, as if something in the room might break. "I have to take a quick break."

Charlie looked away. Nurses outside the room monologued about blood pressure.

"It's Al," Henry said. "Remember Al? Great guy. You two talked, didn't you? I'm just going to take this, and then I'll be right back. Okay?"

"No, Dad. It's fine. Thanks for coming by."

"I'm just stepping out. I'm coming right back."

"Dad," Charlie said, turning toward him. "It's fine. I can tell you're uncomfortable. You don't like this type of thing. I'll see you back at the house, okay? Probably get out of here tomorrow afternoon. Maybe we can get Italian takeout."

"Sure, sure," Henry said, knowing he shouldn't leave, and yet there he was, walking out of the room, down the hallway and toward the elevators, feeling a guilty relief course through his veins, a bittersweet narcotic he'd accepted all his life.

Henry took the elevator down and watched the asses of the two nurses who stepped in after him. In an old life, the sight would have elated him. He could see the contours of their cheeks moving against the white fabric. The one on his left, with her hair all up in a rat's nest, barely had anything to work with. She was one of those purposely malnourished girls—papier-mâché skin covering fragile bird bones, lots of pointy an-gles, and probably only a Diet Coke and house salad consumed over the past forty-eight hours. Why did women try to emulate this look? As if a lack of vitamins and nourishment were sexy, even remotely arousing. The other nurse, the brunette on the right with the thick ponytail, was less emaciated. A little hefty, even, her ass protruding like the back of a compact pickup, but at least there was something to get his hands on. The old Henry, the Henry of confidence and strength, would have gone for it, dove right in; there was something about extra flesh that felt like real woman, and those bigger girls were frequently hornier than the rest. Henry wondered if he should say anything to her. Some of the best pickup lines came when they couldn't see your face; it added mystery, as if a masculine suitor were waiting in the atmosphere, ephemeral, just for them. The elevator passed floor five, and then four. He remembered then what he looked like—170 pounds of loose skin and sweatshirt and beard. A few months back, he might still have been shielding it behind a padded sports coat from Nordstrom's and matching alligator boots. But now, as always, it was jeans and a sweatshirt, this one from the Cubs almost–World Series appearance in 2003. He knew, with a sinking feeling that matched the elevator's plummet, that he wouldn't say anything to these nurses, that he would probably never speak that way to a woman again.

When he got to the parking lot, Henry cursed. Smacked his fist into his palm. What was he doing? Walking out on his son, who was in the hospital? He hadn't even taken Al's phone call. Around him, the April wind swirled. The gusts seemed to shake the parking lot. Tall lights illuminated the cars and pavement. This was something he could change, right here, right now. Yes. He could do it. He had never been a *bad* father, exactly; in fact, in the early years he had enjoyed playing sports with his children—sending them on patterns across the backyard, tossing the baseball and football maybe a little too hard—and telling them bedtime stories about everything from Genghis Khan to the Tet Offensive. He loved the vacations to historic locales like Gettysburg and Boston, teaching them about the world as it was. He loved laughing with them, lifting them up like chubby little airplanes. And then things had changed. It had happened quickly, too, like flipping a page and finding out your favorite character was actually somebody else.

The wind swirled and rattled again. He could change things now. Be better. Be better right now. He turned and walked back toward the hospital, thinking, his heart kicking strangely, that this was what it felt like to go against nature, to swim upstream, to do something for the better. He walked through the sliding doors and made his way to the elevators. There were no nurses inside, and he was thankful.

When he got back to Charlie's hospital room, he heard voices. And through a slight opening in the partition of the curtain, he saw everyone—Barkley, Julie, even Jack Schoenwetter, wearing a worn brown jacket. They were all gathered around Charlie's reclining figure. Talking to him. Comforting him. Jack had his hand on his older son's shoulder. Barkley was grinning at his mother; she had said something funny. Julie herself—she looked better than she had in years—short mahogany hair, shiny and well treated, a powder-blue cardigan, and black slacks that showed off her lithe, athletic figure. Two jade earrings dangled, but not too low. Classy. And then he saw that Jack had his other arm around Julie. Something inside him twinged; scaly hands gripped his organs like a tether of balloons. Jack had his arm around Julie. His wife—still his wife. But Julie was happy. And Jack had his other hand on Charlie. Charlie, very clearly, was receptive to this, *preferred* this, even. All of them inside that room together. A single, functioning unit.

Henry took a breath, allowed himself one last look at his family, and left the hospital for good.

In the rearview mirror, Henry said good-bye to Chicago. The buildings were glowing; ancient lights strung up across a jagged horizon. He marveled at how many times he had seen this sight, these skyscrapers that seemed like old friends. As the Mercedes merged onto the Kennedy, southeast into Indiana, he knew he would never see the buildings again.

The night moved around him. His car was oil, the sky was ink. He saw fewer buildings and more trees, great tall trees that already made him feel back home, in his wooded backyard. Ankle deep in the creek. Alone underneath the stars. Another life, that. But he was going home. The night expanded.

He passed the exits for Gary, for the Indiana Dunes State Park, for Michigan City, for New Buffalo. Highway lights grew less and less frequent, the blackness around him larger, stronger. Into Michigan, now. Trees and hills all around. He took an exit, and the Mercedes spilled onto Highway 1, heading north, flanking the vast expanse of lake, which now sprawled out to the west. Chicago was all the way on the other side, a distant blip, a pinprick of light on the horizon.

His original home was in St. Joseph, but he already knew he wasn't going that far. Too tired. Far, far too tired for any quest, for any quixotic expedition to his roots, for any feeble attempt at understanding *anything*. There was no road but the one he was driving on. Up ahead, he saw lights. A restaurant, a bar. Red wooden planks. Still open. Why not, Henry thought, pulling over into the gravel parking lot.

It was the Red Arrow Roadhouse on Highway 1, about ten miles north of New Buffalo—a place where he had eaten with his family many times, on many a summer vacation. He sat in a booth and nodded at the college-age waitress with wavy blond hair. He placed his order, lost track of time. It began to rain, and water splattered the windows while Henry drank his beer, Bell's Lager of the Lakes. Drinking was another no-no, of course, but at this point irrelevant: toxic pennies into a bottomless well. The stuffed animals around the restaurant—buck and moose heads, an auburn fox crawling over a rock, a wolverine in midspring—eyed him with communion, with understanding.

Later, he pulled into the White Rabbit Inn, a dark and leafy refuge from the highway. His room was simple: worn wood, a creaking bed with blue sheets, a single window looking out toward the trees. He lay in bed and opened his phone. Julie was probably with Jack. He closed the phone, then opened it again. Closed it.

There were things to do, he realized. Choices to make, decisions. He wasn't going back home. And he flat-out refused to hang himself—he'd seen pictures of people hung, and hated their crooked necks, their helplessness, the way they swayed without their feet even grazing the ground. It just looked . . . weak. And the fear he had of waiting for his neck to break or not break, of waiting for that hollow *snap* or *crack* and then going dizzy, tingling in his arms and toes, blood flooding into his cheeks, turning his face into a bruise, into rotten fruit, helpless, disgusting.

More definitive was a pistol. No, a revolver. It was the ultimate power move, the ultimate *fuck you* to an unfair world, a big-barreled Magnum blowing the world away, whitewashing it to oblivion. Henry Brunson, he thought, was worthy of a revolver. He'd lived a good life, made his mistakes but conquered more than most of the poor saps in the world, and a heavy revolver was his equal, his match. Hemingway had done it, shotgun to mouth, toe on trigger, *blam-bang-pow*, see you later, *sayonara*.

But two issues presented themselves. The mess left behind was ugly—grotesque, even. Bits of brain and skull across a hotel carpet, a human face turned to exploded watermelon. Not classy. Not worthy of Henry Brunson. It was too much a quick fix, too little concerned with others, with how they would view this final frame of his life, this epilogue of a broken man on a dirty floor. And besides, getting a revolver wasn't easy, not like it used to be. There was paperwork. Probably e-mails. Electronic forms and digital signatures. The world, as always, passing him by.

Everything else was too tiring to think about. Bathtubs and toasters. Cars in garages. Train tracks. Pills. He would not die in his sleep, that was for damn sure.

Fuck it. He opened his phone again and speed-dialed Julie, wondering if hospital walls would block her signal, prevent them from connecting. Outside his window, he saw the wind tossing the leaves in the trees.

"Henry," his wife's voice said, quietly, carefully.

He closed his eyes. He was running out of time. He simply needed to do one good thing, to say one thing right.

"Is Jack there?"

"Henry, is that really how you want to start this conversation?"

"No." He had something to say, maybe too many things, and they were all tangled up in cobwebs and ancient ego—he couldn't get them undone. "I messed up, didn't I, Julie?"

He heard her breathing on the other end of the phone.

"It was wrong, wasn't it? I mean it. It was the wrong thing to do. Listen to me. I was someone else, when I did those things. I was different—"

"No, you're the same. Being sick hasn't *changed* you, Henry. It's just made you more desperate."

"That's not true."

"It is."

"I don't want to fight."

"I'm not fighting with you, I'm simply telling you the truth."

This was the time when he would have hung up, torn the battery out, zapped her with a deep, suffocating swell of dial tone. It was the only power move he had left—to throw silence at her, angry absence, strength in a sudden disconnect. But it didn't do anything. Didn't solve anything. And it wasn't what he wanted.

"I'm sorry," he said. "All right? I'm saying the words. I'm saying the words to you, and I mean it. I never should have left. There was something wrong with me. *Is* something wrong with me. I don't know what it is. I should have talked to someone. Worked it out."

"You should have talked to *me*. You used to talk to me, you used to tell me about what was wrong—the termites, Henry. You used to talk about them. You used to describe them."

"Always hungry," Henry said, looking out the window. "Those termites. But it's no excuse." And as he said this, he felt a small, cool feeling, a feather-tipped lightness sift into his body. "It's no excuse," he said again. "Nothing makes what I did okay."

Julie was silent on the other line.

"I know it hurt," Henry said.

"Don't start with that. Don't go to me, to my feelings. I'm serious."

"Sorry."

"You've said that. You've said you're sorry." He heard her take a breath. "Okay, Henry. Okay. Thank you for saying you're sorry."

"It excuses nothing. I'm aware of this."

"I know. But it's good. It's good to hear."

In the darkness of the hotel room, the lightness came back to him, the feathery breeze that caressed his insides. He felt himself smile—a tight smile, but a smile nonetheless.

"Next time we do this," Henry said, "next time this happens, don't let me go. Don't let me leave. Okay, Julie?"

"It was for the best, dear. You were my greatest friend for a long time, but things are better now. They're better. I found my passion again. I moved on."

"No."

"It's okay. It's *okay*, Henry."

"It will be better next time. You'll still dance, you understand? You'll stick with dance, and I won't leave. And we will make it work. I loved that house. Our house in Downers Grove. All of those birds—I remembered the names of the birds, the other day. The black-capped chickadee, the northern cardinal. It will work, Julie. Next time we will make it work."

"Next time? You keep saying next time. What does that mean?"

"When we do it all over again. When everything repeats."

He heard his wife pause on the other line. "Where are you, Henry?"

"I'm out. I'm by the lake."

"By the water?"

"No, no. Near the water. But far away. Far away, my wife."

"Henry, you're acting very, very strange."

"No," he said, feeling the lightness still inside him, "I'm better, and I want you to know that next time it will be better."

"Okay. Okay, Henry. I believe you."

"We'll do it right."

"I know, I hear you. Henry, are you all right?"

"I'm fine. I'm alone."

"You're not alone." Her voice became urgent. "Henry, you *are not* alone. Just because we're not together, doesn't mean anything like that. You need to stop talking like that."

"Remember our wedding? At the Drake? The Gold Coast Room— all those pillars, the crystal chandeliers. Four hundred and thirty people at the reception. That place was shining, glistening. Marble floors throughout, Victorian drapes, Italian Renaissance—"

"I know, Henry, I know. It was beautiful."

"Those windows. Those enormous windows. And now . . . something else, I suppose. Something different."

"You know what you need to do?"

"What?"

"Something fun. You need to go have *fun*. Get out and do something exciting. Barkley would love to go with you somewhere, I know he would."

Henry remembered all the things his family used to do on the lake— coolers on the beach, tossing leathery footballs that trailed comet tails of sand. He remembered swimming out to touch toes against the mattress-soft sandbar, he remembered boating, tubing, riding in with waves that unraveled like liquid scrolls. Hell, he even remembered the biting flies. The flies and all those water sports. But he was too old for the water, wasn't he?

"Henry?"

"Yes. Yes, Julie. I'm going to go now. Tomorrow I'm going to do something fun. I'm going to take your advice."

"But, Henry—"

"It's a good idea. Fun is what I need. It's exactly what I need."

"Henry, wait—"

And he ended the call, right there. It was a dream, he knew, what he was trying to create, but the way it had ended, with Julie telling him to wait, with her wanting more from him . . . he could keep that feeling, that idea, even if it wasn't true. *Henry, wait*, she had said. He could bottle those words—he could bottle them and take them with him.

Henry closed his eyes, and the shadows crossed the room. He heard the distant drone again, the same sound that arrived each night, without fail. His mind drifted, and the hum of the old bedside fan washed over him, cleansed him, made him new.

The next morning, Henry drove to New Buffalo, whistling with the windows down. It was the first good talk he'd had with Julie in a year. Maybe more than a year. He'd actually apologized, and instead of feeling like he'd ditched his principles or lost himself completely, he felt as if a heavy backpack had finally been cut loose—thrown from his shoulders and back. It felt good, didn't it? The sour mood from the hospital had evaporated. He really *should* do something fun. It was sixty-five degrees, the sun was out, and the quaint, pastel-colored beach town of New Buffalo was spread out before him. There the Stray Dog Bar & Grill, there the ice cream shop with the strawberry shakes. There the harbor, clinking with swaying masts, there, in the distance, the beach. Big waves, it looked like. What he should do, he thought, what he should really do, was have some fun.

He parked the car on Whittaker, across from Casey's Bar and Grill, and walked to the Oselka Marina, wandering, admiring the big white yachts basking in the early spring warmth. The marina itself was only half full. Too early yet for the summer crowds. But still nice. Fresh, even. A grand opening. Lake Michigan swelled in the distance. From here, Chicago was impossible to see.

He purchased purple beach shorts at the Snug Harbor Mini Mart, along with two green energy drinks that he tossed down the hatch without a moment's forethought. Then he surveyed the picked-over T-shirt rack, and eventually chose one depicting a cartoon palm tree with an extra-large pair of coconuts.

"Looking to rent something, sir?"

Henry looked up. The energy drink bubbled in his veins like cola. He fought back the tiredness. The man behind the counter was wearing a denim baseball hat and had red sideburns melding into a thorny beard.

"Sure," Henry said. "Yes, let's rent something. How's the lake today?"

The man tilted his hand back and forth. "Waves are a little bigger than normal. Weather's going to be clear until about two, so you'll want to get there in the next hour or so to enjoy the day. Who else is renting?"

"What's that?"

"How many Jet Skis you need? Taking the wife, the kids, couple buddies? We've got more than a few you can take out there."

Henry hadn't thought about that. He'd pictured himself riding alone on a black Yamaha, cutting dovetail wakes across the water—yet from above he'd look like a lonely speck across frothy blue slate, and from the shore a distant creature without a tether. Friendless, childless, wifeless. Suddenly he was angry again. This wasn't how Henry Brunson acted, how he thought, how he *was*. One year ago today he was bursting into every club and restaurant in Chicago. He'd been six foot three, 215 pounds, his muscled chest like a gladiator breastplate. And the strength he used to have—astronomical. Bench press peaking at twenty reps of two twenty-five, no sweat, no creatine, no additive-whatevers, just a man on the cusp of sixty shattering the odds. On more relaxed evenings he sank back on his leather sofa with a city view that was top ten if not top five, looking out at lakefront to the east, Chicago skyline to the west. He'd have Glenn over, Al over, some of the college boys over, girls over, ancient ex-girlfriends over—sipping from his medium-size but robust wine collection and plucking Cuban torpedoes from a humidor even George Burns would have envied.

And where was he now? Wearing purple shorts and a slightly offensive T-shirt. Six foot three and a buck seventy, hunched over and on the lam from everyone he'd ever known. Now, being asked who else he was riding with, he'd actually gotten sensitive, bristled, turned a shade of grapefruit, worried what people would think.

"Just me," Henry said, looking hard at the man with the tangled beard. "Rent me the fastest one you've got. Rent it all day." And he slid his card across the table.

Henry *loved* the WaveRunner. This particular version, the VX1100, sleek and black like a stealth airplane, was safe *and* exciting. At fifty-eight years of age—fifty-eight years and still kicking—Henry rode half a mile off the coast to do wave jumps on his own, to feel himself lighten as he lifted into air. It was difficult to hold on, he thought, to not let his weakness overtake him. But he was still strong. Lake Michigan merged from green-tinted cloudiness to a deep black swell of expansiveness. The water felt colder, soaking his arms and legs and pattering against his life vest. The breeze blew against his face and the WaveRunner cut and bobbed through the water, spraying chilly droplets on his forehead and nose and lips, a twang of mineral on his tongue. The beach behind disappeared into a white strip of floss.

Water suddenly scoured his eyes, another motor roared, and Henry wheeled, veering the WaveRunner to the side. Through rubbery vision he watched a muscle-bound twenty-something blitz by on a yellow Sea-Doo and rocket into the distance, spraying frothy water as he passed. *Asshole*, Henry thought. *Jackass*. So irritating. He slowed down and let the idiot frat boy go far ahead of him, eventually careening off the wake of a speedboat and sending his Jet Ski high in the air. Of course there would be one of these types out here, roaring around him, ruining his solitary view. These types, he thought, swaggering around like he had done so many years ago, but with only a fraction of the intelligence. He felt a lurch of almost-afternoon lethargy, a steady weakness that seemed to drill itself to his bones and make him numb, but he cranked the handle, and the WaveRunner jolted forward, and with his craft bouncing and water soaking his arms and life vest, the lethargy and irritation were forgotten.

Henry didn't dare go for the jumps yet; he wanted to get close and make sure it was actually safe. It had to be; they had these babies for rent in the ritzy areas of Florida and they let them out to kids a quarter of his age—hell, Charlie said he'd done it half a dozen times on spring break trips. Henry got within a hundred feet of the speedboat, craning his body forward, almost losing balance with shaky arms on the rubber handlebars, watching as the young kid went up in the air off the rollers. The frat boy came down with the gracefulness of a pelican on the water, something about the hollowness of the craft and the aerodynamics, and so forth. This was technology, Henry thought. It crept up and you didn't know what was different until you started comparing it with the past. He looked down at his life vest and felt strange.

"You okay, Henry?"

He looked. Next to him, not really there, a vision really, was Julie. A young Julie, bouncing across the water with him, riding her own Wave-Runner. He was dreaming again—dreaming while the world spun on.

"Henry?"

"Yes. I'm here."

"You okay?"

"Why do you ask? You told me last night I should have fun, and now you're worried about me riding this little toy?"

Julie grinned. She had to be nineteen, maybe twenty years old. Her hair waved in the air like something underwater. "Just checking, old man. And snap together that life vest."

Henry looked down, saw the blur of orange flapping in the wind. It was a hindrance, really, a straitjacket—

Their WaveRunners hit a roller that bucked up the noses and sent a fresh spray of water and foam in the air. When they landed, Henry saw that the vest had partially slipped down his body, dangling on one of his forearms. He shrugged it off and felt the wind take it away.

"Henry!"

"It's okay." He laughed. "It's all in good fun."

Henry squeezed the right handle and twisted it up and the black stealth under him zoomed across the water, lightly bumping, leaving the vision of Julie behind. He looked back, saw nothing but water, water as far as he could see. Talking to himself, then. Whatever. He felt good, despite everything. He drove faster. His eyes teared up and his thoughts washed away with the breeze. The wind was getting wild, the sky turning gray on the horizon. Maybe he'd see a storm tonight after all, holed away in his little room at the White Rabbit Inn. He rode in silence, hearing only the whir of the motors, seeing the thickening green rollers that Lake Michigan hardly ever got but was getting now, because of this wind. The WaveRunner bounced again.

A storm. Stormy nights at those summer lake houses were usually enjoyable. Julie would bring out cards and they'd all play poker, and Henry would get enough booze in him to relax, quiet his insides, and feel a sense of peace. A storm would be nice—he remembered the way the heavy winds used to rattle the windowpanes when Barkley was a kid, and how Barkley would put his hands against the glass, fascinated, until he heard the thunder. Then he would scatter and run to bed, and Henry would pour himself a glass of red, a heavy cab, and listen to the storm by himself. Ahead, in the far distance, Henry saw a single white sailboat. He wanted to get a closer look at it, but the wind—it was still picking up. He went faster. He opened his eyes, looked out around him, really looked.

Straddling the saddle of the WaveRunner, Henry saw how the water angled out wide and just continued, and then something changed and he felt the way he'd felt outside the hospital, right after he'd been diagnosed. He sucked in freshwater spray and he felt the freezing emptiness inside him; he saw each glinting triangle of the vast and rolling lake spread out, extending to the sky. A white arrow of birds glided above his head. The sails of the distant sailboat rippled, the morning sun throbbed, and the moon was a fat nickel fading into blue sky, like a child's etching disappearing over time. Henry twisted the knob of the WaveRunner and the engine roared and the shoreline was behind him, far behind, but it was okay because the lake was all around, enveloping, exhilarating in its vast blue embrace.

For one moment, Henry lost all sense of sound. He saw his knuckles gripping the handlebars. He saw the lake moving—scooting underneath him—he saw every tiny swell, every line of froth, every rivulet of undercurrent. He saw the horizon like a circus tightrope, cutting the world in half. Everything, he realized, watching the blue world move silently around him, watching that feathery arrow of birds swing into a canyon of undulating sky—everything was in place. As intended. The nose of the WaveRunner bobbed, shot up spray that came down heavy. Everything was in place. Symmetry all around. And the thing about symmetry, he thought, was that maybe being aware of it meant you were part of it. For a brief second, Henry's stomach finally felt full.

The Sea-Doo came in over a swell just as Henry's hearing returned. It came in bouncing, shrieking at top speed, spray leaping over both sides like a hacksaw tearing open a wound. By the time Henry noticed it, everything was happening too fast. He knew it was the young man he'd seen earlier, and he saw the bullet-blur of his yellow Sea-Doo and calculated, somehow, in some primal, reflexive way, that there was no way to avoid collision. Unless he, very quickly—and Henry yanked the handlebars to the side, ferociously, like the Henry of old, and suddenly the WaveRunner swiveled wildly, Henry shouting now, roaring, his body lifting, falling out of orbit. Impact.

Henry—

Hears yelling, practically up against his ear, and sees a sudden snapshot of the young man's face and gold-flecked eyes, a quick frozen fear and then a wild smack of plastic on plastic and there's water in the air like a geyser and someone is mumbling while Henry is weightlessly, silently falling.

Henry sees nothing but white spray and turns in midair and suddenly the nose of his WaveRunner appears, sharp black, and jumps toward his face and strikes him. Stars swarm through his vision. There is blackness and a plunge of sheer cold and he hears motors above him like planes but knows he's underwater. A wave recedes and air opens up and one of his eyes is open, and he hears more shouting and sees blurred objects but another roller comes in and he's under again. He feels his head, numb and aching, slide against the upturned WaveRunner, drift under it, his nose a gaping hole with blinding hot needles. He chokes for breath but water snakes into his lungs like a cold tentacle, chilling him as he retches, and then the air opens up and someone has a fistful of his hair and is tugging, and someone is shouting something, it has to be the kid that hit him but it sounds to him like *Dad* and that's what he wants to hear. Henry opens the one eye that works and sees red rivulets all over his hands, coming from his nose and mouth, leaking down into the water, and then the hold on his hair slips and he drops into the cold depths like a stone.

The motors seem farther away, and Henry can't breathe now. The tentacle in his lungs is squeezing and he feels his feet kicking feebly at nothing, and briefly he thinks *sharks* but realizes that it's a lake and it doesn't matter, because he's still sinking, he hasn't stopped, and the cold tentacle tightens its grip in his chest, and he feels a queasy dizziness and a lifting away and a brief but startling image of Julie smiling. Too quickly, though, the figure vanishes and he's back with the lazy black bubbles, and he is grateful as he hears the sound of the WaveRunner above him, a sound so familiar he almost forgets where it's from. He hears splashing and an arm slings roughly around his neck, but he's thinking about the engines above, thinking as he fades, that they sound exactly as his fan did when he was a boy. The slippery arm is tugging him upward, trying to get him out but he can't see and everything is white even the water looks white and the cold tightness in his chest isn't cold anymore and a brief dream of his wife comes into the light again and then there is no vision but the whiteness and the bubbles and the lifting. All he can hear is the roar of the motors and he thinks that this is what he's heard all along, every night, not the fan but this, always these engines, always these engines.

DISTANCE

Barkley felt weary, rickety-legged like an old man, when he finally returned to Eastwick, bag in hand. Through the glass doors he went first, hearing the voices of his students echoing in the vaulted atrium, those students who were soon to be someone else's. It was the end of April, and his father's death and funeral had come and gone as his father himself had often appeared and disappeared—two quick gut punches and an exit through the back door. It was like his father in so many ways. Nothing had been said or accomplished, no last words on a hospital bed or in the Downers Grove kitchen with Guinness and deep-dish pizza. He had disappeared, blipped off the radar, hit the ground like a comet on the other side of the world.

Barkley walked into the mailroom and checked his slot in the honeycomb of teakwood (donated by the class of 1988, or so said the plaque). Nothing but junk mail, flimsy educational pamphlets, and advertisements for teacher magazines. No surprise, of course. One thing about his father, though—he'd gone out on his own terms. Yes, Barkley thought, he'd left the world as Henry Brunson, striking another Jet Ski like two atoms smashing together—and not stopping until he hit the bottom of the lake.

Still, his absence made the world seem out of tilt. No Dad. No Henry Brunson. How could a man like that really die, really leave, and do it off-screen? Yet he was gone. And as for Barkley—he had never said good-bye.

"Barkley, how you doing, my man?"

He looked up to see Mike Dobbs, who looked a bit disheveled, and smelled vaguely of whiskey and Tabasco sauce. He had stopped wearing ties to work and flaunted a maroon polo shirt with a gold emblem of something—maybe it was a cauldron—that Barkley didn't recognize. It was just the two of them in the almost criminally disorganized mailroom.

"I'm doing okay," Barkley said, remembering, as his mother had told him, to breathe. "Who knows? A little numb."

Dobbs clapped both hands on his shoulder. "It's going to be okay, buddy. People come together after this sort of thing—families, friends, even people you didn't know were your friends—you'd be surprised. But it's tough, I know. I'm really sorry, man."

"Thanks, Mike. But meanwhile, we have to be here, on death row."

"We'll both be out soon enough. This place isn't good enough for either of us."

"Right, right." Barkley sighed, unsure of what to say or emote, or how to put anything into words. "What's that symbol on your shirt? That golden pot thing?"

"Oh, this little number? Used to be the standard uniform for my chili restaurant. Nice design, right? I'm wearing it around Eastwick as a bit of an f-you to whoever cares to notice. Which is probably no one."

"So this means you might be going back to the restaurant business? Are you going to try again? Make the crazy chili with the feta and the lamb?"

Dobbs smiled. "You catch on quick. It's a major investment, and it would be brutal to lose it again, but yeah, I think I'm going to try. Teaching is almost more of a gamble—at least with the restaurant, I have some measure of control over my employment. And you're welcome to get on board, by the way. You could run copy, do the Web site, write beautiful

descriptive novellas about each menu item. You know—dropping Nabo-
kov nuggets, that sort of thing."

"Ha," Barkley said. "Actually, that doesn't sound that bad."

"Consider it, I'm serious. Let's both get out of here. Free food, *great*
food. Drinking big dark beers while on the job, stacks of the best corn
bread you've ever tasted."

"Wow," Barkley said. He felt a touch of warmth in his system, as if
he were finally thawing out after days in the snow.

"Anyway, how's your family doing?"

Barkley thought about it. "Actually, not terrible. Kind of rough for
the first few days. I mean, initially we were shocked, which I think would
be obvious. We expected him to pass away, just not that quickly and
not that way. My mom was really up and down for a bit. Now, though,
she seems better than anyone. It's strange, you know? In some ways it
might be better like this—he didn't have to trail away into nothing, into
a shell of himself. He went out at least doing something enjoyable. Maybe
that sounds strange."

"Doesn't sound strange at all. I lost my own father when I was about
thirty-two—a little older than you. He was sick, too. And when he slipped
away faster than expected, it was the right thing. Not everything needs
to be drawn out."

"To be honest, after you get over the shock, it becomes a kind of relief, in a really weird, sad way."

"Exactly right. Weird, sad relief. Not how I feel about this job though—
more like straight relief and a desire to drink copious amounts of alcohol. Where's the eject button, that's how *I* feel. And you picked a good
week to miss. Last one was rough. Two more teachers got the trapdoor—
Paul Flannery, that poor sap. He was boring, but so what? Isn't that what
Eastwick wants? Not a bad geometry teacher, either."

"So they're still cutting contracts?" Barkley asked. "God. It's surreal
to be back here. I'm getting that whole 'ghost haunting his former home'
vibe."

"Well, you've got at least one more surprise coming," Dobbs said. "Wait
till you see it."

And he walked out the door with a grin and left Barkley holding his
stack of junk mail. Surprise or no surprise, there was still one matter of

business he had to attend to. And finally, finally—he thought he was ready for it.

In her office, Margaret Carey was waiting for him. It was a tiny, cluttered place, with a small square window peeking out onto the Eastwick alleyway and parking lot. She kept both wrinkled hands folded across her desk.

"Sit," she said when Barkley walked in. He saw dust particles hanging as if in stasis across the beams of sunlight.

"Sounds good," he said. He felt weary, but oddly detached, looking at her. He dropped his bag beside the lint-laced blue chair that was waiting for him.

She was wearing a black dress with faded daffodils patterned across the fabric. Around her neck was a string of pearls, and behind her, on the windowsill, a row of tiny wooden canaries stood vigilant.

"I'm sorry for your loss, Barkley," Carey said, eyes magnified but unmoving behind the glasses. "We all are. We have prayed for your family's health."

"I appreciate that," Barkley said, and even though he was doing his best to hide his distaste for the woman, he felt his organs loosen slightly, the gears begin to move again. He *did* appreciate the idea that they had thought about his family. But had they? Had they actually even cared?

"Have you taken the appropriate time off work, Barkley?"

"I think so. I mean, the funeral, the service, everything is complete. There's nothing else I need to do, you know? Just move on, spend time with everyone, that whole thing."

"That's good to hear." She leaned forward. "And I suppose you can forgive my brevity as we turn to business? You know, despite what's happened with your family, we can't—and by we, I especially mean I—can't let it interfere with performance reviews and contract renewals. If we did, we'd never get anything done, and this building would have twice as many teachers as classrooms. You understand that, don't you, Barkley? The need to be objective in the workplace?"

"I'm actually glad you brought up the idea of objectivity, Margaret.

Because that's exactly why I've scheduled this meeting. And I wanted to—"

"By using the word *scheduled*, you're referring to my acceptance of your meeting *request*."

Barkley, staring at the wrinkled dough of Margaret Carey's twin sagging cheeks, and those magnified dark eyes that seemed ready to protect against foreign invasion, laughed out loud.

"Excuse me? You're extracting humor from this situation?"

Barkley wanted to scream, to shout about the pettiness, to yell that he'd just lost a family member and she was *still* acting petulant—but he held back. *Breathe in five seconds*, he heard his mother instructing.

"Nothing is funny," he said. "Truly nothing. I'd just like to get down to the reason for my meeting *request*."

"Barkley, this brings me to my first point in terms of contract renewals. There is an issue of attitude. Of following directions. Remember what I told you, Barkley, during your interview? About not treating each classroom like one of the thirteen colonies?"

"I remember," Barkley said. "And I thought I followed through with that."

"Thinking and doing, Barkley, are two very different things. And furthermore, this issue of attitude is something you've been blissfully unaware of during your tenure here. And attitude, as a seasoned teacher or administrator knows, greatly affects classroom culture, morale, and even our code of ethics and mission statement."

"Mission statement," Barkley repeated.

"It's in the handbook, Barkley. Have you read the handbook?"

He swallowed another laugh. What was the word for this? He didn't have time to pull the lever on an internal thesaurus, some slot machine of synonyms that would clarify what this woman was doing, but that would not help him here, not help him *at all*—

"Barkley, have you read the handbook chapters on classroom culture and the Eastwick Mission?"

"Well, I've perused the handbook over the course of the year, and I looked at the suggested areas intently during orientation. I can't quote passages for you, but I do know the general rundown. And I'm not sure how the mission statement relates to my attitude. Margaret, I've done nothing but work hard here. I've busted my butt for this school, and I think you're aware of it."

"Joking with the students, Barkley, trying to be their *friend*—that's not working hard."

Barkley felt himself shut down. All the monitors switched off, the plugs tore themselves from outlets, the red dials flipped to zero, the glowing keypads turned to black. It was clear, clearer now than it had ever been, that from his first day on the job, he'd never had a chance. The idea of a career here, of a life, of immersing himself in the hallowed hallways and becoming part of the success and the history—it had been a mirage from the start. Some petty game Margaret Carey was likely playing, if not with others, then solely with herself. Continually affirming the old way, even if it was all some play inside her head. He was simply one of the actors, entertaining her for a time but necessary for the slaughter at the end. How many new teachers, he wondered, had this woman booted out of here—simply to boot them out? A symbol of the old way triumphing over the new.

"Margaret," he said, carefully, "my goal this year has been to teach these frankly amazing students and give them the best educational experience possible. In order to do so, it's necessary to establish at least a cursory knowledge of who they are—to get to know them, to establish relationships. Teacher certification programs *tell us* to do this. We're not doing it to be their friends—we're doing it because education is better that way, more effective when it is benevolent and empathetic toward the students it professes to care about. And the kids are happier, seriously. And happy children will be more eager to learn, to follow instruction, to trust the instructor. I don't know how else I can make my genuine intentions and effort clear. I really, really worked hard at this job. I can show you the computer files of all my lesson plans. I can show you all the worksheets and handouts I created myself, and didn't download off Google. I can show you the parent e-mails professing how much their child is learning, and how much they enjoy the class. But I can't communicate with you, Margaret, if we're really that far apart—so far that you think my effort this year, my devotion to this job, has something to do with neurosis and ego and attitude and some sort of twisted need for friendship. If that's really what you've seen, then I don't know how to have this conversation with you. I really wanted to sit down here and go over the *logistical* reasons for your concerns. But what can we do, Margaret? I don't know what to do that I haven't already done."

Margaret Carey swiveled in her chair and looked through the narrow window, likely at the alley below. When she swiveled back her eyes were the same.

"Barkley, not even veteran teachers thinks they've learned everything they need to learn. And yet you're here, as a first-year instructor, telling me you've done everything."

"Did you hear what I said before that? About my passion for this job? My work ethic? My results?"

"You *have* shown diligence with getting the grades in on time," she said, "especially in the second semester. I acknowledge that. I acknowledged it to the administration."

Finally, Barkley thought, a bone. But it was a musty, gnawed-on, paltry bone that wouldn't have satisfied an emaciated Pomeranian.

"Okay," Barkley said. "I'm glad you noticed that. What about the students? The students are doing well, they're learning, their grades are up—"

"Barkley, have you ever considered that the students are doing well because your assessments aren't challenging them enough? That you're not challenging them and preparing them for senior year and college?"

"I can show you my assessments," Barkley said. "You can look at them right here, right now. I can show you the student essays that received the highest grades, and you can judge for yourself whether or not those papers are worthy."

Carey, for once, didn't have something to say. Her index finger began tapping atop her desk. Was that momentum? He pressed forward.

"I don't think, Margaret, that you can find a single real-world issue about why I shouldn't be teaching here."

She tilted her head back. "Contact with a female student."

For a moment, Barkley thought he would lose control. A great wave rose up inside him, and somehow, he allowed it to crash back down. His left ear buzzed.

"Margaret, that was a student who was suffering from a major family upheaval. Major."

"I suppose I could take your word for it," Carey said, "but then I need to be diligent about *my* job."

"Have you talked to Elise Rossi? Have you interviewed her about the situation?"

"Does it matter, Barkley?" She raised her voice. "You're on your way out. You played your hand, and you lost!"

"So that *is* what this is about, isn't it? The older teacher having the winning hand against the younger one?"

She looked away from him and said nothing.

"I think this meeting is over," Barkley said.

He stood and lifted his bag. Suddenly the laughter came back to him, and he tried to hold it back, to choke it down, but a few bubbles came up. Everything around him looked different. Carey, sitting there adamant and unbending in her daffodil-print dress, that index finger tapping, tapping, tapping.

"Thank you, Margaret," Barkley said. "Thank you very much."

She stared at him, narrowing her eyes.

"Thank you for showing me that this place—even though I had a great year—isn't for me. And it's too bad—because I really would have busted my ass for this school, you know that? Put everything I had into it for years. Even decades. But thank you for showing me that this is not the right place."

Margaret's hand curled into a fist. She reached over to her windowsill and picked up one of the wooden canaries, this one painted yellow with a light dusting of cinnamon on its forehead. She swiveled away from him, blocking his view. He wasn't sure if she was holding the thing, or trying to snap it, or simply finding a reason not to look at him. He waited a moment, and then walked away, closing the door behind him.

Barkley noticed the first sign in the hallways. When the kids saw him, they scurried, bolted into clusters, split apart like shifting amoebas. It was fifteen minutes before first period, and he noticed a blur of clipboards, at least ten students huddling around glowing phones, pods of children standing in formations he had never seen before. His mind felt like a strange computer, recognizing permutations in the expected data flow, a geometric shift in the current of the hallways.

Todd Brennan strode by him in the typical Eastwick attire, looking straight ahead.

"What's going on?" Barkley asked.

Brennan backpedaled. "Nothing, sir! Nice to see you back!"

"Okay . . . ," Barkley said, trailing off, watching the hallway swarm, a conglomeration of spinning ties and plaid skirts that were suddenly different, everything changed.

He walked into his first-period class, room 115, as he'd done many times before. All twenty-nine of the students sat there—not one missing. Wolverine, sporting a new buzz cut, was in his usual seat up front, twirling a tie depicting the Incredible Hulk punching a tiger shark.

"It's eight o'clock!" Wolverine bellowed.

The class erupted into screams and cheers. Jeremiah Gilroy, in the exact center of the class, threw a cloud of shredded pastel paper into the air, Elise Rossi and Maggie Tolliver sat and pounded their desks in the back, and Shuman's cheeks went red from repeatedly blowing on a kazoo.

"Success!"

"It's blowing up on my phone . . . we're crushing them!"

"Forty-two already went through!"

The class reared up and cheered again, collectively jubilant—now another student was trumpeting a kazoo on the opposite side of class. Was that Jennifer Alston, who hardly ever spoke?

Barkley sat down behind his desk, facing the class, looking out over his row of bobbleheads and fantasy figurines. Eventually the wild energy died down and they turned to look at him. Two students, faces obscured, high-fived in the back of class.

"All right," Barkley said. "What is this?"

"May I take it from here?" Wolverine asked, standing up.

Barkley stared at him, utterly bemused. "Sure, take it from here. What does that mean, exactly?"

"I have a PowerPoint." He held up a neon-green flash drive.

"You want to present something? Guys, I have to admit, I'm very, very confused here."

"Just watch the PowerPoint!" Elise Rossi shouted from the back.

"Please watch it!"

Margaret Carey would love to walk by and see this, he thought—not only using PowerPoint himself, but teaching it, creating little Power-Point disciples, preparing for a revolution.

"Is it cool to plug this into your computer and run the projector?" Wolverine asked.

"Um, sure. I mean, I do have a lesson for today. We're going to be reading Tobias Wolff."

Wolverine held up his hand. "We will all read the stories, just hold on. Can I plug this bad boy in? Very important. Timely, even."

"All right, sure. Go for it. I'm curious to see what's going on, here."

"Also, Mr. Brunson, you're going to want to take a seat . . . here, take my chair in the front. I'll work the projector. Shuman, get the lights, you gremlin."

Shuman growled, stood up, and the room abruptly plunged into darkness.

The projector, fixed into the ceiling, clicked on, and the wall in front of the class was bathed in blue light. Wolverine pulled down the projection screen and fiddled with the computer. The first slide appeared, turning the screen an emerald green. It read: "The Barkley Brunson Humanitarian Revenge Project."

The screen shifted to a picture of him writing out a literary diagram on the eraser board, probably from a month ago, judging from that tie he'd misplaced. The picture looked to have been taken with a cell phone.

"Okay," Wolverine said, stalking across the front of the classroom. "This is a picture of Mr. Brunson, code name Barkinator, strutting around class and being a beast. Any questions?"

"I like that silver tie," Maggie Tolliver said, from the back. "What happened to that tie, Mr. Barkles?"

"Lost it. Okay, Wolverine, where are we going with this?"

The slide clicked to a picture of Eastwick from across the street. "Now," Wolverine said, "while you were out, we heard down the grapevine that the *morons* running the school are actually stupid enough to not ask you to come back." The class unleashed a collective *boo* that enveloped the room like a foghorn.

Barkley laughed. "Wow, didn't know you guys were keyed in."

"Yep." The slide switched to a picture of an explosion. "When we found out, we were very, very angry. So angry that we wanted to fight back. So first—we decided to coordinate." Wolverine showed a slide of about fifteen or twenty students, crowded around a living room table that was saturated with computer printouts, coffee mugs, and a poster board labeled BATTLE PLAN in red marker. Barkley recognized Elise, Wolverine, Shuman, Maggie, John Byzantine from second period, Jennifer Alston, and more. He felt the beginning stages of awe.

"Mr. Brunson, the first thing we went after was backup." A new slide flicked on—a cell phone shot of countless student signatures—pages of them. "As of eight o'clock this morning, we have collected six hundred names on the 'Renew Mr. Brunson's Contract' petition. That's practically all of the juniors and seniors, plus a lot of our siblings who are freshmen and sophomores."

"Wow," Barkley said. His hands were shaking.

The slide flipped to reveal a screenshot of a Facebook page. Underneath the blue heading, he saw the title—"Save Mr. Brunson"—along with a photograph of a slightly heavier version of himself, cheering at the homecoming football game back in November, still wearing his shirt and tie.

"The Facebook page has over five hundred members," Wolverine said. "And counting. Also, we've created a Twitter account." The next slide showed his fake Twitter handle: @BrunsonsRevenge.

"Needless to say," Wolverine said, "you have a lot of followers. I made sure none of your tweets had f-bombs, as a kind of signing bonus."

"Unbelievable," Barkley said. "Can I stand up and thank all of you now?"

"Nope!" Wolverine shouted. A kazoo honked from the back of class. "Also inbound are the parent e-mails. We coordinated with our parents, so at eight in the morning today, a flurry of prewritten messages were fired out to the principal and the department chair. Elise and I both are getting bcc'd on the e-mails. Right now, they're probably sifting through the . . . what are we at now? Forty-something parent e-mails that go medieval on the Eastwick administration?"

"Nope," Elise said. "I'm at fifty-five. And counting."

Barkley imagined the explosion of unread e-mails sandblasting Margaret Carey's in-box. He laughed and shakily stood up, and the class cheered again. He flicked on the lights and Wolverine zapped off the PowerPoint, bowing for the class and receiving his own round of applause. Within moments, Barkley realized that they were all looking at him, waiting for him, and then he fully understood—all of them had really done this for *him*. But he didn't want it to be about that. He just wanted it to mean that he had actually, despite what Carey said again and again, done his job well. He wanted to know that his actions had been right and good, that his choices had worked, and that his effort had paid off. That in some way, he'd been a success.

"Wow," Barkley said to the class, which had now gone silent. "First of all . . . wow. Let me gather my thoughts, here."

He tried to steady his hands. Shuman blew the kazoo and the class roared again. He waited for them to quiet down.

"First of all, I am so completely honored that all of you went out of your way—on your own—and did this. I am ridiculously honored. After being out for a while with some family concerns, I can't think of a better welcome back to class. You guys need to give yourselves a round of applause. What a surprise that was. So thank you—thank you very much. It obviously means a lot to see all of you guys coming together, to see that you believe in me as a teacher, and this class as a collection of people, working together. It's really, really amazing. I am absurdly honored and I'm going to tell all of my friends and family members, every single one."

"Woo!" Elise shouted, and the rest of the class followed suit. Barkley held up a hand, and they quieted down.

"One thing, though. I am so glad you all showed this to me, and it really is insanely amazing, what you did. I'm serious. However, for me to feel—I don't know—*ethical* about this whole thing, and these efforts you guys are making, I need to stay totally out of it. I can't encourage you or give you ideas or even high-five you. I want everyone here to understand that. Am I blown away by what you guys just did? Absolutely. Will I tell everyone I know about my amazing students? Absolutely. But will I, from this moment on, be able to participate or urge any of you on? Absolutely not. I have to stay out of it and be completely ethical. Can you all understand that? Is that fair? Raise your hands if you think it's fair."

A flurry of hands shot toward the ceiling.

"All right. I'm a little overwhelmed right now—overwhelmed and amazed. So let's have you give yourselves another round of applause, and then try to move on to the lesson. Because I've got a really incredible story I want you to read."

Elise raised her hand.

"Yes, Elise, go ahead."

"Do you think this will work? Do you think any of this will make Eastwick change their mind?"

Barkley sighed, then smiled. "For me, guys, that's beside the point."

The last day of school was June sixth, and for the remainder of the year, Barkley felt an incredible shift corkscrewing through the building. For one thing, all administrators avoided him. If he walked down the hallway, they wallowed like shadows beside the lockers. If he entered a room, they went mute like unplugged PA systems. They didn't look at him, nod at him, smile at him, or acknowledge him. Margaret Carey must have been taking a different route through Eastwick, because he never seemed to catch even a whiff of her. In a sense, he thought, his enemies were vanquished. This was how it must have felt to be Henry Brunson on the corporate warpath, striding down corridors like he owned the world, silencing every room he entered.

By mid-May, it was as if Barkley were radioactive, like some sort of mutated English teacher had risen out of Chernobyl, forcing administration members into bunkers and bomb shelters. But the feeling of collective avoidance, rather than admonishing him, created a sense of clout. Wherever he went, they moved away. It showed flex, control over a previously restrictive environment. He doubted that the efforts of his students would change anything about his contract renewal, but their actions—petitions and e-mails and Facebook pages and tweets—had certainly forced his opposition into a crouched position. And it affirmed everything he had known about the job he'd done. In a certain context, it was the strangest feeling of all: he was on his way out, the powers that be didn't want him there, yet the feeling from the hallways was victory.

Near the end of May, Barkley graded fourth-quarter essays and prepared for final-exam week. He completed twenty-two online applications for teaching jobs across the city and suburbs of Chicago. He and Ginny met Charlie, his mother, and Jack for dinner, celebrating her closing on a condo in Lincoln Park. The Downers Grove house, she explained, was going to be sold. Charlie had started working at a city gym, rented an apartment in Logan Square, and returned to light practices for boxing.

Maggie Tolliver came into his class furious one Wednesday at the end of May, explaining that the dean had told her that their petition efforts *weren't going to change anything.* The class went into an uproar, but Barkley waved his hands and calmed them down. All good things come to an end, he told them. It was okay. He wasn't mad. He was over it. He had buried his father and would be leaving his school, and yet, instead of sadness, he felt a growing possibility that seemed to dance across each new day as June sixth loomed ever closer.

As it got warmer out, more and more nights were spent with Ginny and a bottle of wine at Diversey Harbor. On June fifth, to prepare for his final day at Eastwick, Ginny brought champagne and they spread out their blanket in the usual spot. Barkley lay on his back and looked up at the trees and out at the boats, listening to the sounds of the driving range behind them.

"What do you think about us?" Ginny asked.

Barkley smiled. When he opened his eyes Ginny was looking down at him, her hair spilling over, onto his face.

"I mean, good things," Barkley said.

"Psh. Do better."

"Ummm . . . really, really good things? Rabbits in the meadow. Unicorns surfing on rainbows. Fairy dust rattling around in mason jars. That sort of thing."

"Don't think you can get out of this by being weird."

"All right, all right," Barkley said. "I think we're great together. Fantastic, even. We have an amazing time."

Sailboats and yachts filled the harbor. The skyline glowed orange as the sun lowered, and the clouds faded into a darker blue.

"So," Ginny said, "things with us are great. Your family is doing pretty well, I think. Your mom bought that condo. Your brother is back to writing those movie review blogs. Did you read his latest post? Claiming that *Moonrise Kingdom* is more exciting than *The Avengers*?"

"That's just ridiculous. He's trying to be avant-garde."

"It's pretty convincing. And in the meantime, what are you going to do?"

"Work, I guess. Look for new teaching jobs."

"How about going on a trip?"

Barkley turned and looked at her. She was flat on her back now, cushioned by the blanket and the grass, looking up at the shadowed leaves lining the parkway.

"What kind of a trip?"

"I think the kind where we just drive."

"Just drive? You know, there was this time in college, when we were supposed to do that, drive straight to California, and everyone chickened out."

"I don't chicken out," Ginny said.

"Okay. So when would we do this drive?"

She turned onto her side as the buildings beyond them began to light up. "Tomorrow."

"After the last day of school? How?"

"Pack tonight. Take the train to work. I'll pick you up when you're finished."

"That easy, huh?"

She grinned at him. "That easy."

"And where would we go? Any ideas on that end?"

"I want to go east. Think of everything out east. Niagara Falls, New York, D.C., Boston, all of New England, Cape Cod—"

"Charleston," Barkley added. "And Savannah. The Outer Banks, Hilton Head, Atlantic City."

"Mmm, gambling. It would be fun to gamble with you."

"You said you played cards in college, right?"

"Oh, yeah. Put me at the poker table. It's like that Matt Damon movie, except a slight reduction of evil Russians. And you could spend some time writing on the trip. Right? I figure you've got something to write about now."

"Sure," Barkley said. "It's true. I guess there's a lot I could write about.

And you're serious about this? Tomorrow, after my last day of school, we drive east?"

"I'm totally, totally serious. Let's finish this champagne and get packing."

The next day, instead of passing moment to moment, seemed to unravel like a montage with missing reels. Barkley handed out Scantron answer sheets and proctored final exams. Pencils scratched softly across test packets. The clock went from ten o'clock to noon to two o'clock. In one hour, Barkley thought, he would never enter this school again—a place for which he held such complicated feelings, it felt like another member of his family.

When the tests were complete, he trudged up to the faculty workroom and ran the Scantron answer sheets through the machine, which buzzed and spit them out like grocery receipts. He went back to room 115 to plug in the final grades. Wolverine scored an 85 percent on his final, Elise an 88, Shuman a 95. Shuman, Barkley thought, shaking his head. The kid had really started to read.

At three o'clock, everything was complete. He packed the bobble-heads, the model DeLorean, the pterodactyl, the hobbit, and the coffee mugs in a duffel bag to take home. He dumped all of the student journal entries torn from notebooks, the stacks of worksheets comparing Cheever and Carver, and the extra finals study guides on "War References in American Literature" into the blue recycling bin by the door. He cleared off the desk until it was as smooth and bare as it had always been before. Every drawer was emptied. All supplies—paper clips, Post-its, tape, glue, tacks, and his stapler—were tossed into the duffel bag as well.

"I think that's everything," Barkley said to himself, surveying the empty room, the wide windows, and all those desks devoid of students. The emptiness of the place, the stillness—he felt like he was inside a lung that was ready to breathe out, out, out.

There was a knock at the door, followed by musical rapping. Wolverine, Shuman, and Elise stood peering into the window.

"Come on in," Barkley said, throwing the strap of the duffel bag over his shoulder.

The three of them strode in and surveyed the empty room with him.

"This is weird, Mr. B.," Shuman said. "I can't wrap my head around it. Totally emptied out. This is it, isn't it?"

"This is it," Barkley agreed.

They stood in silence, staring at the empty chairs, the bare desks, the windows that seemed to illuminate both absence and memory.

"There's going to be some random teacher speaking gibberish in here next year," Wolverine said. "He'll probably have suspenders and a monocle. That's just wrong. It doesn't make sense."

"It's all good," Barkley said, sighing. "I'm over it. And we had a great year."

"Sorry our revenge project didn't do anything," Elise said.

"Don't even go there," Barkley said. "What you guys did was unbelievable. I told everyone about you guys. Coolest students of all time. I'll never forget it, I'm serious."

"Would you mind signing our yearbooks?" Elise asked.

"Sure."

Barkley bent down and filled out as many jokes and words of encouragement as he could for the three of them. He stared at the cover: the Eastwick 2011–2012 Yearbook. A watercolor rendering of the school; red bricks and turrets smeared across a vibrant sky. His name was inside that book somewhere, and so was his picture. In a strange way, he would always be part of the school, part of that history that felt so elusive.

Shuman approached him first. He held out his hand, and Barkley shook it.

"Good luck, Mr. B."

"Good luck, Shuman. Keep working hard. Keep reading. I dare you— no, I *challenge* you—to read three books this summer just for fun. Real books. Novels."

"If I e-mailed you, would you shoot me back a reading list?"

"Sure thing."

"Cool. Thanks for making English not suck, Mr. B. Some of those short stories were pretty awesome. Tim O'Brien, man. What a beast."

"I hear you," Barkley said, shaking his hand one last time. "Good luck. Great having you in class."

Shuman nodded and went out the door, out into summer break and a life Barkley would never know.

Wolverine approached him next. "I've got something for you, Barki-nator."

"Oh yeah?"

He held out a long, white cardboard box.

"What's in here? Nunchakus?"

"Even better."

Barkley popped the top off the box and it clattered to the floor. "You've got to be kidding me," he said, laughing. He held up the Wolverine vs. Batman tie his student had worn on the very first day of the year.

"That's all for you, man," Wolverine said. "You've earned the right. I'm passing the torch."

"You sure about this? This is, like, a mystical relic and precious heirloom. I don't know that I can take it."

"Totally sure. You need to take it. You baptized me with my new name. And good luck, man, what a great year." He leaned forward to give Barkley a handshake, then moved an arm around and clapped him on the back. "Thanks for everything."

"Good luck, Wolverine. Keep up the good work. And don't terrorize your teacher next year."

"All right. And when I turn twenty-one, you're coming to my birthday party. We're going to knock a couple back. That's a fact." He walked backward, saluted, and made his way out the door.

Elise stood alone in the room with him, one leg positioned behind the other. She brushed her hair back and looked at him.

"I don't like this," she said.

"The leaving?"

"Yes, Barkles. The leaving."

"Well, it's sad, I know. I just don't know what to do about it. Everyone tried. You guys tried. I tried. We exhausted ourselves, and nothing's doing. It's like that saying, all good things—"

"Come to an end? That's bullshit. It's bullshit and you know it."

"Okay, maybe it is a little bit. But it's also true, logistically. All things do end. And then we move on to other things. And even if we don't like it, we go with it. We go with it because we have to, because we never know what's on the other side."

"Well, I'm tired of *going* with it. I'm tired of being tough."

"I know. Me, too."

"And I'm going to miss you, did you know that? Does that mean anything to you?"

Barkley looked at her—this student whom he'd felt a sense of communion with, *simpatico* or whatever it was called, this student who would now disappear from his life, with the rest of the school. He felt something caught in his chest, something both soft and sharp, whose lacerations were milky and bittersweet.

"Of course it means something to me," he said. "Of course, I'm going to miss you, too. I don't know what it will be like, coming into a classroom and not seeing you taunting me from the back of class. That's weird, right? I don't want to think about it."

"It sucks," she said.

They turned and faced the classroom again. Outside, a pickup truck drove by, then a bouncing U-Haul that was almost too big for the road.

"You know, you used to be kind of fat," Elise said.

"I know."

"A bit of a pudge."

"Okay, now you're rubbing it in."

She smiled, and Barkley felt the seconds counting down.

"So is this, like, the time where you tell me you'll never see me again?"

"No," Barkley said. "I would never say that to you."

"And this is good-bye, huh? The real deal?"

"Yes," Barkley said. "This is good-bye. Bring it in, Elise."

She moved forward and wrapped both arms around him. "Thank you for everything," she mumbled. "Thank you for being there."

"Thanks for being awesome."

"Okay then. Good-bye, Barkles."

"See you later, Elise."

And then she was gone, out the door, and there was truly nothing left for him in the vast, empty classroom and the winding halls of the school.

Outside, Ginny had the Ford Taurus parked out front, and honked madly when she saw him. Immediately, he felt better. He needed to drive away, to move from this place to another.

Ginny got out of the car, wearing jean shorts and a green tank top, and waved like she was signaling a freighter toward a bay.

"Hi," Barkley said, when he finally made it to her.

She popped the trunk and he tossed his duffel bag in. "Full tank of gas," Ginny said. "We're ready to go."

"Straight east?"

"Straight east."

"Wonder where we'll stop first."

"I have some ideas. Let's go. Let's get going right now."

He looked back at the school.

"Are you good?" she asked. "Are you okay?"

Barkley stared up at Eastwick's clock tower. He watched the black minute hand inch forward a notch. He remembered to breathe. "I think I'm okay," he said. "I'm feeling a lot of things right now, but I think I'm okay."

"Get in, buddy. I already picked us snacks. Sour Patch Kids. Swedish Fish. All kinds of drinks in the cooler. You better believe I brought Capri Suns."

"Wow," Barkley said, looking at the backseat. "You really outdid yourself. You're the best, you know that?" He opened the passenger door, sat down inside the car, felt the whoosh of air as he closed the door tight.

"Road trip!" Ginny shouted, bouncing behind the wheel. "We're traveling. Time to believe in something."

"Right," Barkley said. "Right. There's just enough to believe in."

Ginny squeezed his shoulder and honked the horn and they pulled away from Eastwick, pulled away from the old bricks and stony scabs, away from the mortar and the wrought iron and the pain and the feeling that something had been accomplished, they pulled away, and Barkley watched it in the rearview mirror, saw it go from a castle to a cottage to a tiny rock, and then to something only on his mind's horizon, forever in the distance, nudging like an elbow.

ACKNOWLEDGMENTS

The moment you hear the word *yes*, things change. So I'd like to thank my agent, Leigh Huffine, at Regal Literary—for saying yes, and for providing so much thoughtful advice, guidance, and support in making this book what it is. You made me feel at home when I had no idea what would come next.

I'd like to thank my editor, George Witte, at St. Martin's Press, for his constant enthusiasm, his deft hand in the editing process, and his sincere belief in this book. And thank you to all the intelligent, driven people at St. Martin's whose handprints are everywhere.

To my family, I'd first like to thank my father, who did not live to see the completion of this novel, but who was there, all the same. Dad, it's like you always said—I outkicked my coverage this time. It was our time together that helped make this happen.

I'd like to thank my immediate family—Mom, Paul, Lucie, Owen, Samantha, and Abigail—for dealing with my obsessive tendencies as I plunged again and again into a churning vat of Word documents, Web pages, biographies, photocopies, notebooks, and military histories, and for welcoming me back into the world when I came up for air (however briefly) and to say hello.

I'd like to thank the servicemen who helped me discern and digest the complexity of life as a soldier in Afghanistan—you provided details that weren't found in any book, and they resonated with me long after completing the work.

I'd like to thank Audrey Niffenegger, my mentor, adviser, and friend. Your help was invaluable, and I am constantly shocked by how much you know—about seemingly everything. Thank you so much.

I'd like to thank Austrian Bakery (now called Vienna Café) in Chicago, for serving me my usual—coffee and an egg croissant sandwich—every day, every month, and eventually every year, at my seat by the window, looking out onto Clark. When I think of this book, I think of that window, and my frequently misfiring laptop.

Last, I'd like to thank my wife and best friend, Kate. For everything, and for things so small and so large that only we know all of them, and for all the moments to come.